PUSHING
THE LIMITS

usa today bestselling author

BROOKE CUMBERLAND

Pushing the Limits
A Student-Teacher Romance

Cover designer: Qamber Designs
Cover photography: Lindee Robinson
Models: Megan & James
Editor: Heart Full of Reads
Proofer: Lawrence Editing

Content warning

Pushing the Limits is a stand-alone novel and recommended for ages 18+ for mature content. This book has mentions of sensitive topics: suicide, death of a sibling, mental health (anxiety and panic attacks), off-page self harm, and grief. This is a forbidden romance between a student and professor who are both legal and consenting adults. Please read with caution.

To women who empower other women.

"I'd rather lose myself in passion than lose my passion."

—Jacques Mayol

Prologue

Aspen

PAST

As I step through the doorway, I'm hit with the mixed aroma of mildew and floral. Narrowing my eyes, I try to adjust to the dim lighting. It's eerily quiet since the service isn't beginning for another hour.

My mother's been hysterical and cried in her room all night long. I heard her through the bedroom door but didn't go to her. I couldn't.

She blames me.

Mom hadn't said a word to me all morning, so I asked my older brother, Aaron, to take me early. I wanted to see Ariel before everyone else arrived. *See her one last time.*

I walk down the short hallway until I enter the room with Ariel's name on the display board. Chairs line up in rows as large flower arrangements surround the open casket. Soon, the space will be filled with family and friends coming to give their condolences.

Swallowing hard, I step in farther. Soft music plays overhead. It's supposed to be soothing, but nothing can soothe the ache burning in my chest.

Glancing at the walls, I notice the outdated paint, matching the faded, run-down beige carpeting. There's a table of vanilla-scented

1

candles. Nothing in this room represents Ariel except the collage board of pictures she had hanging in our room. She made it two summers ago and had been adding photos of her friends until she died. It's decorated with little designs and sayings and captures every part of her personality—outgoing, strong, and fun. I didn't lose a sister. I lost my best friend.

We grew up on farmland with only fields and pastures surrounding us. No neighbors or friends to play with meant we'd learned to entertain ourselves. I remember the day she got a new camera for Christmas and took pictures of everything. We'd giggle and snap some of each other, and then we'd torment Aaron and take his picture when his girlfriend was over. She'd taken about a hundred photos of our pets. I smile at the memories, but at the same time, I want to cry because there'll never be another picture of us. No sweet sixteen photos. No senior or graduation portraits.

The memories we made over the last fourteen years are all I have left.

When Pastor Jay asked us to bring in our favorite memories of her, I knew she'd want these. I examine them, even though I've looked at them daily for the past two years. Yet, today, they look different.

There's one of us standing in front of the middle school on our first day of seventh grade. We were assigned different homerooms and weren't happy about being apart. Another shows us with our dog, Fudge, the first day we rescued him from the shelter. We've only had him for six months, but she said she knew he was the perfect fit for our family.

After tracing the outlines of each one, I walk to her casket. I pleaded with Mom to let her wear her favorite purple dress, but she refused. She said it was an *occasion dress*, a.k.a., a *happy* occasion. Instead, she chose a dark, navy blue dress that Ariel loathed. My lips curl up, thinking how much she'd hate it. She hated wearing dresses, but now, she'd be so pissed. Part of me wants to laugh at the irony, and the other part wants to rip it off her and sneak the purple one on.

I glance at her face, curling my fingers tightly around the edge of her casket. She looks flawless, as if she's only asleep, but it still hasn't sunk in that she's gone even after seeing her like this.

Pushing the Limits

For the first time in days, I let myself cry. I cry harder than I ever have. I've held the tears in, trying to remain strong for Mom, but I can't do it anymore. I release all the pain I've kept inside and apologize to her repeatedly.

"I'm so sorry, Ari. God, I'm so, so sorry," I say, wiping my cheeks, then reach for her hand. "You hated that nickname." I chuckle lowly. "I'm going to miss you so much. I'm going to miss you sneaking in my bed and sleeping with me every time a storm hit. I'll miss staying up late on weekends, gossiping about Brady Carmichael and all the guys on the basketball team. Or the girls who think purple lipstick is in." A chuckle escapes me. "I'm even going to miss arguing with you over who gets to use the shower first. It was like our little tradition." My lips soften as I think about the happy memories. "Truthfully, I'm going to miss everything about you." I lean down and kiss the top of her forehead. "I love you."

I hear footsteps in the hall and take that as my cue to start heading out. Unfortunately, people will arrive soon, and I'm not sure I'm strong enough to deal with everyone. Half feel sorry for me, and the other half blame me.

I'm not sure which one is worse.

"Aspen…" I hear my dad's deep voice. I face him, his mouth set in a firm line. "Your mother wants to talk to you."

I swallow at his tense features but follow him out of the room. He barely speaks or looks in my direction. I'm a reminder of what happened, who he lost, and how our lives are forever changed.

He leads me to a small room on the other side of the hall where she's sitting with her nose buried in a handkerchief.

I stand in front of her and wait. I'm not sure what to say to my mom or anyone. I'm not sure there's anything I can say.

"I need to hear the story again," she chokes out. "I need to hear why my baby girl is dead."

Her head is low, refusing to look at me. I've told her and the police the story several times, but every day since the incident, she demands to hear it again and again.

"Mom…" My eyes fill with more tears. "I can't."

3

"Tell me!" She raises her voice and finally looks up, her face contorted in grief and disgust.

I do as she says. I repeat the story the same way I did the first dozen times. I explain what happened, no matter how much it hurts to talk about it.

"How could you let that happen?" she mumbles. "How could you be so careless? I don't understand!"

"Mom, it's not Aspen's fault," Aaron interrupts, stepping beside me.

"Mama, I'm sorry." I burst into a new wave of tears. I've apologized to her and Daddy over and over. But I know they'll never forgive me.

I'll never forgive myself.

Aaron wraps an arm around my shoulders and cradles me to his chest. My mom huffs in disapproval. I push against his chest, wiping the tears from my cheeks as I storm off.

I'll never forget the way her face morphed into fear as she fell to her death. The way her body lay on the ground, motionless. The way her voice begged for my help as she screamed on the way down.

I'll never forget it.

I don't tell Mom and Dad those things, however. The images already haunt me in my sleep. The sound of her screaming has woken me for the past two nights. Every time I attempt to fall asleep, her dead eyes appear in my mind. *It's no use.* There's barely a difference between existing and sleeping.

Life without her is pointless.

People start arriving, so Mom, Dad, Aaron, and I stand near her casket. I swallow my emotions down and refuse to cry. I shut down. I shut everything down. I let them hug me and say they are sorry for our loss. I allow them to cradle my head as they press me against their chests. I let them squeeze my hands as they tell me how much she will be missed. I let them do whatever they need to express their feelings.

But I don't cry.

I quietly thank them and look at my feet.

When the service ends, we gather at the cemetery to bury her. A large bouquet of white lilies rests on her closed casket. I pull one out for myself before they lower her to the ground. Mom and Dad do the same but ignore me. Dad wraps his arm around Mom's shoulders, holding her close as she cries.

I grip the obituary program tightly in my hand and stare at her picture displayed on the cover. Mom used her recent school photo this past year, although it wasn't her favorite. I don't know why. She looked stunning—a bright smile, sparkling green eyes, and flowing golden blond hair.

Underneath, it reads, *Loving Daughter and Sister. Gone too soon but never forgotten. 4-10-1995 to 4-10-2009.*

She died on our birthday.

I swallow as I take it all in. April tenth was our favorite day. We'd wake up early to Mom making us our favorite breakfast—the only day of the year she'd make it. Belgian waffles drizzled in melted cream cheese frosting and then slathered with homemade maple syrup. She'd use fresh blueberries—instead of frozen—on top. She called it our special birthday breakfast, and every year, we looked forward to it.

After eating, we'd rip our presents open from our parents and exchange the ones we made for each other. For the last few years, we'd talked Mom into letting us skip school for the day. She wouldn't even bother arguing with us, knowing she'd eventually cave anyway. So, when we got up on our birthday five days ago, we'd done everything the same.

We laughed all through breakfast, and afterward, Mom handed us each a card, and we ripped them open. We squealed when we saw the hundred-dollar bill tucked inside.

As we wrapped our arms around her, she lectured us, "Don't spend it all in one place, girls!" Finally, we begged her to take us to the mall so we could spend it on clothes and makeup.

"You'll have to wait until your father gets home," she said, piling the dishes into the sink. We ran upstairs and got dressed, then set our money down on the dresser before running outside. It was warm with a slight breeze in the air.

It was perfect.

I smile at the memory of our birthday traditions. It was something we've always shared—should have shared forever.

She'd always tease me about how she was older, granted it was only by three minutes, but now, the day would be pointless.

A painful reminder of what had happened.

Of what I lost.

Chapter One
Aspen

E ven after six years, I can still hear her voice in my head. Her giggles. Her silly jokes. The way she'd snort when hearing something funny.

I hear it all.

It used to disturb my sleep in the middle of the night. I'd wake up in cold sweat, heaving and panting as I painfully relived our childhood memories. I don't mind the dreams, anything to see or hear her voice again, but I could live without the anxiety attacks that come with them. They come without warning and wreak havoc on my entire life.

Losing my twin sister feels like a part of me is missing, as if my soul isn't complete without her.

Feeling the overwhelming survivor's guilt and wishing you were the one to die that day instead will get you an unhealthy dose of post-traumatic stress and more therapy than you can imagine. When standard treatment proved useless, the counselors decided to go another route.

Art therapy.

When you refuse to talk about your feelings to your therapist for eight months, you get placed into something that doesn't require talking. This was fine by me and ended up being a blessing in disguise. It helped me find my passion and pointed me toward a career in art history.

I think about Ari daily, especially in my studio, but she's always on my mind. We were identical twins, but sometimes, I think about what she'd look like now. Of course, we could still be a perfect match, but maybe she would've dyed her hair or shaved half of her head and streaked it purple. Maybe she would've needed glasses and braces, or she'd taken after my mom's rebellious side and gotten a tattoo on our eighteenth birthday.

Whatever she looked like, I know she would've been beautiful. Not only on the outside but the inside, too. Her soul was the most beautiful one I'd ever met.

"Are you going to order, ma'am?" An impatient voice interrupts my thoughts as I realize I'd dazed again. Kendall elbows me, grabbing my attention.

"Yes, sorry. I'll take an iced caramel latte, please. Grande."

She presses the buttons on her screen and tells me my total. I scan my phone and pay through my app.

"Your order will be ready at the handoff in a few moments," she says robotically as she hands me my receipt.

"Thanks."

Kendall follows me down as I wait for my drink on the other end. As she plays with her phone, I look out the window at the cars driving by. Berkeley is a chilly sixty-two degrees today, typical for this time of year. Being only a forty-five-minute train ride to San Francisco is one of the many perks of living here. Ari would've loved exploring the city and walking around Chinatown. She was always so adventurous.

Though I start to remember part of my dream about her last night, it's hard to know due to the sleeping pills I sometimes take before bed.

They knock me out until morning, but sometimes I can recall the dreams later. When I can, I replay them in my mind, scene by scene. They're a movie reel of our lives—memories of things we did, places we went—but other times, they turn dark. The motions aren't usually steady, however. We're generally in some slow-motion hell. I can never run fast enough or reach her quickly enough before I wake up or my mind goes black. Sometimes, I remember the conversations or events that occur in picture-perfect clarity, but other times, I worry it's my mind playing tricks on me.

The barista calls out my order, and I retrieve it. I thank her again before Kendall and I head out the door and begin sucking it down. We're meeting up with Zoe for breakfast down the road. Kendall and Zoe are roommates who live down the hall from me.

I first met them last summer when I moved into the building. I had lived on campus for two years before finally getting my own place. I've grown closer to Kendall since we attend the same school. It's a ten-minute walk from the university, but we carpool often when our class schedules match.

My phone rings as I open the door to my new used car—a green Kia Soul. My new baby.

I sigh and bite my cheek before accepting the call. "Hello, Mom."

"Hello, darling. How are you?" Her voice is tainted with fake politeness, always so smooth and sweet sounding. It's too early for this.

"I'm fine." I hop in the driver's seat and start the engine. "How about you? How's Dad?"

"We're good, thank you. Did I catch you at a bad time?"

"No, I'm getting into my car with Kendall. What's going on?"

"I wanted to confirm your arrangements for coming home to visit during spring break."

I frown, not wanting to have this conversation with my mother right now. Or ever. "Uh…that's like three months away." Spring break isn't until April and classes are starting tomorrow.

"I know. But since you're always *so* busy…" I can hear the annoyance in her condescending tone. "I figured I'd need to get on top of this beforehand. Set it in stone."

I exhale, rolling my eyes at her dramatics. "Sure, Mom. I'll do my best."

"Now, listen, Aspen…" Her tone is firm and deep as if I'm a child and she's sending me to my room. "We agreed to let you go all the way out to art school in California with the agreement you'd come

11

home once in a while. Even Aaron is driving in for a few days. He's bringing his girlfriend, Dana. It'd be nice if we could all be together."

I grit my teeth. *Not far enough, though.*

"I know." I agreed to nothing, but I let her think it anyway. I'm not going to let her guilt-trip me into coming home. The last place on Earth I want to be is with two parents who resent me. I left to escape the memories, escape the looks of sympathy on everyone's faces, and escape the constant reminder of how I ruined their lives. I could've moved to Mars, and it still wouldn't feel far enough.

Her tone changes but is no less condescending. "Good. We'll plan for it."

"Great," I reply flatly. We say our goodbyes and hang up.

"Everything okay?" Kendall asks, not taking her attention off her phone.

"Yeah. Just my mother crushing my caffeine high," I say, taking a long pull of my drink.

"You have a serious addiction." Kendall furrows her brows.

"Your point?" I counter.

"Waffle House serves coffee."

"Yes, but not good coffee." I smile, taking another sip.

"Ugh," she mumbles after a moment.

"What?" I face her, seeing the wrinkles crease in her forehead. "What is it?"

She groans. "Kellan."

"I thought things were going great?"

"They are!" she insists. "But when we went out last night, he got drunker than usual, and I thought maybe..."

She doesn't need to finish her sentence to tell me what's going on. Apparently, drunken Kellan isn't much better than sober Kellan.

"Still nothing below the belt?"

"Not even close. I thought maybe with a few drinks in him, he'd loosen up a bit and help ease his nerves. But he was all *I wanna make out with you. Your lips taste so good... blah blah blah.*"

"Maybe he had whiskey dick."

"Gah! Why won't he have sex with me? I'm a good lay!" she whines.

12

Her outburst makes me choke-laugh, the iced drink spewing right out of my nose.

"Jesus, Kendall." I wipe my chin. "Maybe you're going at it wrong."

"What do you mean?"

"Guys like the chase. If you're an easy target, it's not a challenge." The corner of her mouth wrinkles in disgust.

"Play hard to get," I explain.

She scoffs. "Why do guys always want to play stupid games? I'm your girlfriend...you've got me! Now, *do* me!" she shouts to the ceiling of my car.

"Rather, do that." I laugh and point at her pathetic plea. "That'll have him ripping your clothes off in a heartbeat."

She glares, and I smirk.

I park in front of the Waffle House and we walk inside, finding Zoe in one of the corner booths.

"Look who finally decided to show up," Zoe taunts in her thick, New Jersey accent as we shift into our chairs. She has her long, dark mane pulled up into a high bun, a few shorter pieces falling around her face.

Zoe moved to California three years ago when she turned eighteen to pursue a singing career. After one rejection after another, and eventually going broke, she moved up to Berkeley, found Kendall to live with, and worked at one of the bars downtown.

She says it's only until she figures out what she wants to do long term.

But I think fear is setting her back more than anything.

"Oh, please. We're thirty seconds late."

"I managed to get off, shower, dress, and arrive before the both of you. I deserve some kind of medal for that."

I snort. "You get the bill. There's your medal."

"Ooh...apparently someone had a bad Saturday night."

"It was fine." I narrow my eyes. "Kendall's the one stuck in make-out city," I tease, earning a glare in return.

The waitress arrives with glasses of water and we order our usual.

Sipping on my iced latte, I glare at Zoe's pleased smirk. "So, was this guy a keeper?" I inquire, referring to the guy she brought home last night.

She shrugs carelessly. "Maybe. But if we get married, I'm keeping my surname."

A wide smile spreads across Kendall's face and mine. "Why?" we ask.

She frowns. "Because he has a horrible last name." I raise my brows, silently motioning for her to tell us. "It's Litoris." She hangs her head in shame as we burst out cackling.

"I'm sorry," I say in between catching my breath. "But that can't be true."

"It is! I even Googled him."

"Dude, that's unfortunate," Kendall adds. "But if he ever runs for Senate, I'll be sure to vote for Mr. Litoris." That cracks us up even more as Zoe shakes her head and scowls.

"Laugh all you want," she groans. "But his tongue is *nothing* to laugh at."

"I bet not." I smile, biting down on my lower lip.

When the waitress arrives with our food, we start a new topic of conversation.

"So your mom wants you to come home for spring break this year. Are you going?" Kendall asks when we begin eating.

I keep my head down. "I don't want to."

"How pissed will she be if you don't go?" Zoe lifts a brow.

"Probably pissed enough to never talk to me again, which might be enough of a reason not to go in the first place." I smirk, knowing they'll understand. My parents and I never mended our relationship after Ari's death. Not moving or evolving. Once I graduated high school, I couldn't wait to move away.

"They have coffee here," Zoe says, eyeing my Starbucks cup and changing the subject. She knows I hate talking about my family.

"Gah! What is it with you two?" I grab it and pull the straw into my mouth before setting it down. "But they don't have it the way I like it."

"Filled with caramel and sugar?" Kendall muses.

Pushing the Limits

"I live on four hours or less of sleep every night. Caramel and sugar are the only things that keep me awake."

Kendall lets out an audible sigh. "I'd feel sorry for you, but the fact that you have more strange men doing the walk of shame every weekend than I have pairs of shoes, I don't feel sorry at all."

"Stop exaggerating," I retort as Zoe begins to laugh. "It's not *every* weekend. And sometimes they only get to third base."

"What's your definition of third base?" Zoe narrows her eyes.

"No penetration," I answer confidently.

She scoffs.

We continue talking and eating. If it weren't for these two, I'd be lost—more than I already feel. They're the closest thing I have to any kind of healthy relationship, even though they don't know me. They know what I show and tell them, but they see what I want them to see. Not the inside that's burning with unbearable pain and guilt. But they get more than I give anyone else, and sometimes I even find myself thinking of them like sisters—that is until the guilt eats at me.

Chapter Two
Morgan

I never expected to be in California after the way I left five years ago. I hadn't even come to visit my parents and thinking about it makes me feel like shit. However, six months ago, I said goodbye to Ohio and returned to my home state.

Not by choice.

Fortunately, I found a house to rent close to the California School of Liberal Arts, where I was able to get a teaching job. I had to leave Ohio without much notice, so when I secured a job, I had four months left until I began at CSLA. Between unpacking and prepping my semester syllabuses, those four months flew by. I did everything I could to ignore the ache in my chest at being in the same town as *her* —Jennifer—one of the reasons I left in the first place. Everything to ignore the pain and focus on something else—*anything* else.

Natalia is the other reason those months flew by. She's my demanding and sarcastic eleven-year-old niece, who's complained about my cooking every night since she moved in with me.

She's also taught me a lot in the time she's lived with me.

Eleven-year-old girls do not like when you walk them into the school building. They also don't like when you kneel to tie their shoe. They also may possibly scream when you walk into the bathroom—

16

forgetting that you do not live alone anymore—and they are only in a towel.

Oh, the things I've had to quickly learn to accommodate Natalia. But I love her. I wouldn't be here if I didn't.

And we're trying to figure it out—even though we're grieving.

My heart aches at the memory of getting the call six months ago. My mother was so hysterical that I could barely understand anything she was saying. Once they translated into actual words, the walls began to close in on me. I was in shock. I couldn't move. I couldn't speak. I couldn't breathe.

Six months later, and I still feel that way, except now I've learned to ignore it. The pain stings to the point of bitterness. Bitter that it happened. Bitter that I had to come back. Bitter that I have no idea how to raise a child.

Painting is my solace or *was* at least. I haven't been able to create a damn thing since then, which is fucking ironic since I'm an art professor. But what choice do I have? I need a job and it's the only thing I know. But if there's one thing I know about the power of art, it's that it pulls you out of whatever shit you're dealing with—or that's what I'm hoping for anyway.

"Knock, knock," I hear from my doorway. I quickly look up and notice it's Claire—*again*. She's been coming to my office every day for two weeks as I've been rapidly trying to prepare for my classes that are resuming soon. Since I'm coming in halfway through the year at the spring semester, I've been looking over students' portfolios to get ideas of their strong suits so I can coordinate my syllabus to their needs.

"Hi, Claire," I drawl out slowly, the annoyance in my tone going right over her head as she invites herself in. "What's up?"

She settles in the chair across from my desk. Her skin-tight pencil skirt nearly rips in two as she crosses her legs and arches her back, pushing her breasts firm against her thin blouse. She flips her blond hair, exposing the flesh of her neck. I shudder, wondering what's made this woman so insecure that she feels the need to throw herself at me.

"Since you've been working nonstop and have hardly taken a break to even eat lunch, I thought we could go out for drinks tonight." Her tongue runs along her lower lip before pulling it in between her teeth and biting it. "Celebrate your new job and the start of a fresh semester," she continues with an encouraging smile.

"As much as I'd *love* that…" She doesn't hear the condescending tone in my voice judging by the wide, girly smile that spreads across her face. "I'll have to take a rain check. I'm taking Natalia to a movie tonight before I get busy with work again." It's a lie, but she doesn't so much as flinch at another rejection. She's only asked me out a dozen times, and I've found a way to get out of each of them.

How her brain isn't connecting the dots to *I'm not interested* is beyond me. If she were any other woman at a bar or we shared the same mutual friends, I'd have no issues letting her know it was never going to happen. However, to avoid pissing my colleagues off before class even begins, I have to play nice.

Truthfully, if it weren't for a certain portfolio that's captivated my attention, I'd be doing all this prep work from home. But there's one specific student—Aspen Evans—who's grabbed my attention more than the rest. She has high honorable mentions, has excelled in her classes, and already has some letters of recommendation for graduate school. She passed into the accelerated art program with flying colors.

Studying her work over the past couple of weeks, I've grown to know her already. It sounds crazy, considering I have no idea who she is, but it's obvious by her work that she's a deeply emotional person. Her dark and dramatic pieces are consistent since her freshman year. Some are bright and bold abstract paintings, some are watercolor portraits, and some are pastel. Then there are some pencil-drawn and heavily shaded with sadness. She's creating from inner turmoil, and I can't help but be intrigued by the stories she's telling.

A part of me connects with them and aches for familiarity. The feeling of losing Ryan only months ago feels like bile in my throat and chokes all the air out of me. My eyes burn with tears I refuse to shed, considering the way things ended between us. It had been five years since I'd seen him, aside from his funeral, of course, but even though he died a hero, I fear I'll never have any real closure.

Not because of what he did, but *who* I let come between us.

Chapter Three
Aspen

After spending time with Kendall and Zoe, I come home and go straight to my studio. Several hours of staring at the same blank canvas, I brew myself a pot of coffee. It sits there on my easel, mocking me as I chastise myself.

I haven't felt this blocked in months. Everything I start, I end up tossing out or getting so frustrated I throw it across the room. I hate everything I make, and considering school is starting in less than twelve hours, the pressure to get my shit together is even stronger.

I've had the same song playing on repeat, which helps me stay focused. It helps me escape into a place where I can create the things in my mind. But five unsuccessful attempts later, I give up and sit in the middle of the floor—where I ultimately pass out.

The sound of knocking startles me out of my sleep. The achy feeling in my back and the sun beaming through the blinds indicate I've slept here all night. The knocking gets more persistent, so I lazily stand and walk toward the door. "Coming!" I shout.

When I whip it open, Kendall stands there with an amused expression.

"I hate you," I hiss.

She grins, eyeing me up and down with a raised brow. "You're covered in paint." I look down and see that she's right. "Fall asleep in the studio again?"

"Looks that way." I sigh.

"Well, rise and shine. We're leaving for school in forty-five minutes."

I groan and open the door wider for her to step in and wait while I shower. After a half-ass attempt at doing my hair and makeup, I quickly dress in jeans and my favorite heels and pack up all my supplies.

"Are you alright?" Her eyes narrow at my appearance.

"Ask me once I've had a couple cups of coffee." The half pot I sucked down the night before did nothing for my energy.

She leads me out the door and down the hallway.

"What's your first class?" I ask.

"I have a nine a.m. philosophy lecture."

"With Professor Hennington?"

"Yup." She sighs. "I plan to stay in the back and sleep."

"You get a B just for showing up."

"Then I'll go once a week and aim for a C." She grins as we walk through the parking lot toward her car.

We chat and plan to meet up for lunch as we drive to school. When she finds a parking spot, we head off in separate directions to our first classes.

The first day of school always goes like clockwork. A syllabus and a schedule of assignments are handed out, and I soon feel overwhelmed with five classes and working three to four shifts at the gallery each week. But when you leave home with hardly any money, you do what's necessary to survive.

Tuesday starts and ends just as uneventfully. I've been looking forward to my night class, Advanced Art, ever since I signed up for it last semester. I've had various classes throughout the years, but painting has always been my passion.

Kendall and I meet up for a quick bite to eat before I head to the Lakin Arts and Behavioral—LAB—building. I don't recognize the professor's name on my schedule, so I assume he or she is new this semester.

I walk into the classroom and notice all the chairs are arranged in a large half circle. Only a few other students have arrived and look like they're about to fall asleep already.

I choose a seat in the middle and start rummaging through my bag of supplies. I look up briefly as a guy sits next to me. He looks to be in his late twenties or perhaps early thirties. I sneak another glance and notice he has brown hair, nicely trimmed all around, but a tad longer on the top. He's wearing a dark blue V-neck sweater with only the collar of his white button-up showing underneath it.

His sleeves are rolled up to his elbows, accentuating his broad chest and muscular arms. I lower my gaze to his dark wash jeans and admire how well they fit as if they were custom-made for him. He looks casual but not overdone. I shift my body before he catches me staring at him.

He turns toward me as if he wants to say something, but before he can, Ellie, a girl I've had classes with previously, sits down on the other side of me. "Hey, Aspen! Back to the grind."

"Yup…another class, another semester closer to graduation!" I say happily.

"What's with the get-up? You going out after class?" Her eyes scan up and down my body.

"Uh, no."

Her brows rise. "You look like you're going on a manhunt while I'm here looking like a poor art student."

"You *are* a poor art student," I deadpan, ignoring her comments about my outfit.

"That's beside the point."

Pushing the Limits

I shrug. "I like wearing them. They make me feel good."
It's not the full truth.

Ari didn't like wearing dresses. She was all about the adventure and getting dirty, but I loved dressing up and wearing Mom's high heels. When she died, my mom and I struggled to find a common ground that connected us. I found any excuse to be out of the house to get a little bit of clarity.

Once I found my first babysitting job, I saved up enough money to buy my first pair of designer shoes. A whole summer of babysitting toddlers for one pair of heels.

My parents weren't pleased with me at all, but for the first time in years, I felt good about myself. I had earned something for myself, and they couldn't take that away from me. They'd already taken so much. It represented my independence, something I had fought so hard for—something I still fight for.

"Good news for you then, because I hear our professor is a hot piece of ass," she says with a mischievous smile.

I snort, shaking my head at her blunt words.

"What? It's like the university's way of apologizing for this god-awful class."

I hear a choke of laughter. The guy overheard everything.

"Jesus, Ellie…"

"Oh, come on…" She rolls her eyes and chuckles. "Wouldn't you agree with me?" She leans forward and directs the question to the guy on my other side. "A little eye candy never hurts, am I right?"

Directing my attention toward him, he responds, "Can't say it would." He smiles and shifts his gaze to mine. "However, I'd be more for the female eye candy proximity." He winks.

"The campus has plenty of that." She smiles and twirls her blond hair around a finger, batting her eyelashes like a love-struck schoolgirl, but his attention is on me.

"This class isn't going to be so bad," I defend. "If the professor has a nice, squeezable ass, then, yeah, it's a bonus. But most of us"—I scowl—"are here to *learn*."

She sits back in her chair. "But it sure as hell doesn't hurt." She smirks. "Either way, he'll be off-limits anyway, which is a damn tragedy. Hot guys shouldn't be teachers. It's a distraction."

I snort. "A distraction? You sound like a cat in heat."

I notice the other chairs have filled up, and my anxiety heightens. Professors are usually early, especially for night classes. But I don't see anyone in front of the class yet. If they're late, students take that as a pass and leave class early.

"Well, whatever gives me something to look at for the next four months. Night classes are brutal."

"Remind me to partner up with you on team projects," I taunt, exaggerating my tone as I smile at her scowl. "Unless you want to rescue me and be my partner?" I turn and ask the guy next to me who's already staring at me. Now that I'm intently looking, I notice his deep dimples and the brightest green eyes I've ever seen. One of his brows arches as he stares amusingly.

"As flattering as that is, I don't think that's a good idea." He flashes a knowing grin and stands up, walking straight toward the front of the classroom.

My heart sinks into my stomach as the realization hits me.

"Good evening, everyone," he begins, and I pray to vanish into thin air. "I'm Professor Hampton and this is Advanced Art 3. We'll be meeting every Tuesday and Thursday from six to eight for the next sixteen weeks. If you cannot commit to coming to every class, you should leave now. This class isn't an easy A, and if that's your hope, you're in the wrong room."

I swallow hard as he gives a side glance to Ellie and me.

"Oh, fuck my titties." Ellie leans over and whispers.

I sink lower into my seat and whisper, "What the hell happened?"

She looks over and grins. "Now that he knows we have a hard-on for him, maybe he'll give us As."

"Don't count on it," I mumble, covering my face with one hand. I sink as low as I can into my seat, hoping to make myself invisible, but then he announces we're going around the room to introduce ourselves.

I'm not sure this class could get any worse.

"Aspen Evans…" I hear him say as if he's reading from the

attendance list. I look up and he's looking at me and directing everyone else's eyes toward me, too. My cheeks heat at the unwanted attention.

I swallow and answer, "Yes?"

"Would you like to begin? Tell us a bit about yourself. Something interesting. Something embarrassing, perhaps." He crosses his arms over his chest, his feet parted shoulder-length. He looks amused with his lips curled up in a smart-ass smirk.

I want to die.

Literally die.

I clear my throat and stand. "Um, sure," I respond with a fake smile plastered on my face. "My name's Aspen. I'm a third-year student, double majoring in art history and studio arts. I started drawing and painting in high school. So, um…basically, I focus on art." I smile nervously. I want to kick myself in the shin for sounding so stupid.

"It's nice to have you in class, Aspen," Professor Hampton responds, flashing me a knowing grin. He then nods to Ellie, motioning for her to begin.

"Hi, y'all! I'm Ellie. I'm from Louisiana. I'm a theater major with a minor in art, hence having to take this god-awful night class." She laughs, getting a few of the other students to chuckle right along with her. "I'm only messing with you, Professor H." She winks before leaning back into the chair.

His shoulders cave in as he rubs his eye, hiding his amusement at Ellie's too honest response. I find it mildly entertaining, but I try to hold it in. I need this class to graduate and at least a 3.5 GPA to continue getting my scholarship. I wouldn't be surprised if he flunks me based on my first impression alone.

"Thanks, Ellie," he breathes out, motioning to the next student.

"I can't believe you said that," I whisper, leaning into her.

She shrugs unapologetically as the rest of the students continue their introductions. I try to sneak glances at Professor Hampton, but he isn't making it easy. He catches me every time I look up to see if he's looking at me.

Shit. I was so looking forward to this class, but now I can't even look my professor in the eye. Every time he turns his head toward me, my traitorous body shivers in return. I pull my lower lip in between my teeth to hide my smile, but then the nerves and tension take over my body.

Professor Hampton looks at me like he wants to do more than look at me.

Once introductions are over, he hands out the syllabus and supplies sheet. He instructs us to look over it closely.

It's fifteen pages.

"The next sixteen weeks are going to be fast-paced. You want to pass my class, you better make sure you pay attention and get your assignments completed on time. For the majority, this class is required for graduation. So I expect full participation."

"I'd like to participate in takin' off his pants..." Ellie whispers into my ear, making me choke on my own tongue as I try to hold in a laugh.

"Do you have a question, ladies?"

My eyes widen as I hear Professor Hampton's stern voice.

"Not an appropriate one..." Ellie giggles.

My cheeks heat.

I need to find a new place to sit.

"Perhaps we should separate into groups now," he responds, rubbing a hand along his jawline and shaking his head. Ellie's over-the-top teasing makes me flustered and as flushed as he looks.

Between the stress of a new class and the added attention from Ellie's outrageous comments, anxiety bubbles up inside me. My hands are shaky, and my chest feels tight. It always starts this way, and there's nothing I can do but ride it out.

Pushing the Limits

Professor Hampton is on the other side of the classroom grouping students, so I take the opportunity to slip out before he can stop me.

My heart is pounding in my chest, and I can barely catch my breath. I need to find a bathroom and fast before I have a complete anxiety attack in front of everyone.

As soon as I push the door open, I race to the sink and splash water on my face. I place my hands flat on the counter and slouch down, regaining my focus. I breathe slowly through my nose and exhale out through my mouth several times before the tightness in my chest starts to ease. Several moments later, my heart rate evens out and I'm over the worst.

I hear the door crack open and immediately jump upright. "Ms. Evans?"

Oh my God. It's Professor Hampton.

"Yes?"

"Are you alright?"

"Uh, yes. I needed a moment."

I hear the door open wider, and soon, his entire body is within view. "Are you feeling ill?"

I clear my throat and wipe my face. "No."

"You ran out like you were going to be sick. I wanted to make sure you were okay."

"Oh…no. Just your typical anxiety attack." I shrug it off with a pathetic laugh, but his soft eyes turn intense as he stares. "I'll be fine. I'm already feeling better," I lie with a fake smile, trying to make light of the situation.

He pauses a moment before responding, "Take your time. Come back when you're ready." I nod and watch as he walks out.

If I was embarrassed before I knew he was my professor, now I'm completely mortified. I hate when people see this side of me. It makes me look vulnerable, which makes them pity me. I don't like anyone knowing this secret of mine, but especially someone I want to impress with my art skills.

I collect myself and head into the classroom where students are chatting in their groups already. I stagger a moment, wondering which group I'm supposed to be in. Ellie looks pointedly at me and then shifts to Professor Hampton. Her lips spread into a wide grin, and my nostrils flare at her ridiculous assumption.

"Aspen…" His smooth voice catches my attention to the front, where he's leaning up against his desk. "You're in group two, over there." He nods in their direction and flashes me a concerned smile.

I walk over to a group with four other students. They give me the handout with a list of conversation questions.

"What are these for?" I ask softly.

"He wants us to get to know each other on a more *personal* level," one of the guys answers.

"He thinks it'll make us more comfortable to be creative during class," Lauren adds with a much better explanation. I grab the sheet and read over the questions. I hate this part of school. I don't understand why teachers always want us to share so much all the time. It's like they think we all need to be friends, but in doing so, it feels like I'm being forced to reveal things I never would under normal circumstances. It's like exposing layers of ourselves we aren't ready to give up yet—walls we intentionally keep up.

"Name your favorite memory," the same guy reads from the sheet. He answers right away. "My favorite memory is when my family flew to Florida from Ohio, and I swam in the ocean for the first time. I was thirteen and it was the best vacation we'd ever had."

Next to him, Lauren says, "Mine would be when I won an art contest in high school. I went all the way to state and won first place. I remember how proud my parents were and it was the first time they accepted that I was going to make it my career."

The other guy in our group tells us his, and then they watch me as they wait for my answer.

I swallow, trying to think of something. "Um…" I clear my throat, mentally preparing myself to share intimate details of my past. My birthday had always been my favorite day before the incident, but I haven't celebrated it in the last six years.

"That's okay, we can go to another one until you think of something," Lauren cuts into my thoughts. I smile in thanks, relieved I didn't have to give a response.

Pushing the Limits

We continue the rest of the questions. There are five in total, but with five people, it took us a half hour to get through. I answer the other four questions, as they were all basic, but no one mentions the first one I missed, so I don't bring it up.

Once all the groups are finished, Professor Hampton directs us to our seats.

"Before we begin the first assignment, I have a short exercise. I want you to draw or paint one of your answers from the questionnaire. Make it brief. It's only a draft. But do the best you can." He looks up at the clock on the wall and continues, "I'll give you about thirty minutes, and then we have to move on."

Students immediately leave their chairs to grab the easels and sort through their supplies. Soon, we're in our half circle, silently working. I prefer to work standing, so I move my chair out of my way and get into position.

The peace and quiet, only broken up by soft chatter, is comforting and reminds me of all the times in high school I'd work for hours in silence. My thoughts would stay focused on the paper, making me feel free to create whatever I wanted.

I do the one I never answered—my favorite memory.

Which also happens to be my *worst* memory.

I start the outline of the tree's trunk and then move upward to the branches, adding in shading and twig pieces. Since this is a brief assignment, I can't get too detailed. The trees didn't blossom yet in Illinois during April. Then I work on extending the branch Ariel and I always sat on or hung from. It was the thickest and sturdiest one. Thinking about it, I'm surprised it held us from all the climbing, hanging, and bouncing on it we did.

She loved challenging herself to climb higher and higher. She was always fearless. That was what I loved about her. She made me feel brave enough to take risks, to try new things. Now, I felt more scared than ever.

As I'm tilting my head, shading in the rest of the tree trunk, cold air blows past me. Goose bumps cover my skin, and a shiver runs through me. I feel his presence before I see or hear him. He's watching

29

my every move. It feels intimate, the way he's silently studying me. Slowly turning my head, I lower it to his feet.

"Don't stop," he says sincerely. "I enjoy watching you."

"Being watched makes me nervous," I admit.

"Just pretend I'm not here." I hear the humor in his tone, but I keep the smile from forming on my face.

"I don't think that's possible," I whisper softly. My body shivers, heat centering right in between my thighs at how close he is.

"That's a shame. You have a beautiful craft." My gaze moves up his body and lands on his eyes. He's watching me intently with a crooked smile.

"Thank you."

"I mean it. The way your focus glides over the paper as your hand moves is a perfect blend of focus and creativity. I can see the thoughts running through your head as your body takes the lead."

His words are so honest that I'm not even sure how to respond. My lips form a small, pleased smile. "Years of practice. I preferred to work alone for a long time," I explain without giving away too much.

"And now?" he prompts, his voice smooth and rough at the same time.

"Now, I'm still getting used to an audience. But it's getting easier and easier with each class I have."

"That's good to hear. I've seen some of your portfolios from your other classes. You have a lot of talent, Aspen." My body hums at the way his voice sounds when he says my name—deep, *hoarse*.

I swallow, trying to hide the anxiousness and fear that he's seen my older works. Art is personal to me and even though it's meant to be shared with the world, I tend to be over-critical of myself. Most of them are somber, intense pieces. Even the brighter colored ones have a darkness surrounding them.

"Thank you."

"You have a unique style. I'm looking forward to seeing what you make this semester."

Rubbing my tongue along my lower lip, I suck it between my teeth as I stare intently at him. "I'm looking forward to seeing what you teach this semester."

Pushing the Limits

His mouth curls up into a satisfying grin as he shoves his hands in his pockets and heads toward the next student.

Turning around, I continue working as my heart pounds rapidly in my chest. I associate drawing and art with many things, but most significantly, Ariel. Every time I get my head into a creative mindset, my heart goes with it.

Chapter Four
Morgan

I never should've sat next to her, but once I saw her, I couldn't help myself.

From the moment she walked in, I recognized her facial profile from the few self-portraits I studied in her portfolio. So detailed, so emotional.

I had only meant to introduce myself and get a few minutes alone with her to discuss her portfolio. However, that plan derailed as soon as her friend sat next to her.

The moment I hear the sweet hum of her laughter, I'm even more intrigued than before. For someone who draws such passionate pieces, I assumed she'd be covered in black clothing, wear heavy eyeliner, and be plastered with a permanent scowl on her face. But she's nothing like that at all.

She's the complete opposite.

Her laughter is infectious. Her golden blond hair lies in loose waves against her shoulders, and I can't help but notice how tight her purple shirt hugs her breasts and waistline. I lower my gaze and smirk at the leopard print fuck-me heels she's wearing with her dark skinny jeans.

Not what I imagined at all.

The moment I hear the girl next to her call me a hot piece of ass, I nearly choke on my tongue. She turns and we make eye contact, but it doesn't last for long before her friend continues with her inappropriate string of comments.

Aspen confesses that she's thrilled about class, and for some reason, it makes me weirdly giddy inside.

Fuck.

Scratch that last part. I haven't felt giddy in over five years, not since I've lived in this godforsaken state.

However, the tinge of panic doesn't go unnoticed as I notice Aspen's expression when I stand and walk to the front of the classroom. Her eyes widen as her cheeks flush pink. A small part of me feels guilty she's so embarrassed, but I find it freaking adorable. Ellie's whispering in her ear and Aspen looks like she's about to die.

"Aspen Evans…" I call out because I want an excuse to look at her again. And hear her voice.

That voice.

It's so small and smooth that I'm afraid she'd float up to the ceiling if her six-inch heels weren't weighing her down. I hadn't expected her to stand, but she does. I should tell her we don't have to be so formal in this class but smile in return when she flashes her white teeth.

When introductions are over, I hand out the syllabus and repeat my typical mantra. Look over the syllabus carefully. Don't skip my class. Don't be a lazy participant.

I make sure to look around at all the students so I don't get caught staring at her. Although that's where my gaze is directed since Ellie's once again whispering over to Aspen.

"Do you have a question, ladies?"

I don't appreciate students talking when I'm talking and make sure I'm firm so the rest of the class doesn't take advantage.

Ellie's quick-witted response takes me off guard, and I fight to hide the smile that wants to spread wide across my face.

I need a second to breathe, so I put the students in groups for their first exercise. I start numbering students off into groups of five, but when I come across Aspen's seat, she's gone. I look around and catch her as she's running out the door.

I finish grouping everyone and hand out the worksheet I want them to start on. I wait a few minutes to see if she returns, worried I've embarrassed her. When she doesn't return, I decide to go after her.

I'm not exactly sure what I expected to see when I found Aspen, but it wasn't this. I know an anxiety attack when I see one. I've experienced them myself, but she's a mess. It's unfair that a beautiful and talented woman suffers this way. From the outside, I never would've guessed she held this kind of pain.

I don't believe her in the least when she says she'll be fine. I want to comfort her, wrap my arms around her so she doesn't have to handle it alone. But I barely know her and it'd be inappropriate, given I'm her professor. I tell her to take her time and wait anxiously in the classroom for her to return.

When the groups finish and everyone is seated again, I discuss what I want them to do next. Although I was able to look at their portfolios beforehand, I want to see how well they each do with a shortly timed assignment. They all grab their supplies and sit in their seats except Aspen. She stands.

It's hard not to notice her as it is, but now I'm able to watch her while she works. She moves her hand so effortlessly as her focus follows every stroke her pencil is making. I walk around the classroom, silently watching, but I stop behind her as she begins to shade in her outline of a tree trunk. I can't tell which number from the questionnaire she's using, but the intensity of her focus tells me how important it is to her.

She grabs her putty rubber to lighten an area near a branch when she finally senses my presence behind her, but I tell her not to stop. I could watch her for hours. The simple act of watching her eyes and body captivates my attention to the point that I forget we aren't alone.

Students begin filing out at exactly eight o'clock. They have plenty of time left to work on their project before it's due, but that doesn't stop the wave of sadness that overcomes me as I watch Aspen pack up her supplies and leave. Her portfolio is so somber, but in person, she radiates light. She's friendly and gives off that carefree vibe on the surface, but when she's lost in her work, her persona changes into something completely different.

Pushing the Limits

I'm just not sure what that is yet.

I pick Natalia up from school every day in between my classes. She was able to continue attending the same school once she moved in with me, but it hasn't been an easy transition. She's been getting into trouble for her attitude, pushing girls in the locker room and even throwing food in the cafeteria.

They've been sympathetic given her situation, but she's still had to do detention multiple times. There's nothing I can say that'll help her feel better or give back what's been taken from her. There's nothing I can do that'll change it either. And that guts me.

"Hey, Short Stuff," I say as she hops into the passenger side. "What number?"

I ask her every day after school. It's a rating system from one to ten that I came up with so she'd talk about her day.

She tosses her bag into the back seat and scowls.

"If you're expecting me to read your mind, this could take a while."

Natalia huffs. "It was an eight…" Which means her day was going well. "Until Cooper Turner spat on me."

So much for that.

I pinch the bridge of my nose. *Oh, for fuck's sake.*

"What happened?" I angle my body toward her.

She hands me a piece of paper that was concealed in her palm. "Here."

I unfold it and quickly read over it.

"Natalia Hampton!" I purse my lips to avoid laughing. "You said *what?*"

"I said he had an itty-bitty penis and that must be why he's such an obnoxious airhead."

"*Why?*"

"Because he's compensating for having a small—"

"*Not that!* Why did you say that?"

"Well, it's not a lie." She shrugs.

"I don't think talking about those body parts in school is appropriate."

"Whatever."

"So now what? You have another week of detention?"

She shrugs again, but I take that as a yes. "I don't know why Mrs. Fields got so upset. He's the one who spat on *me!*"

"Before or after?"

She frowns and it's all the answer I need.

Tonight, she has her therapy appointment, so when I drive us to the building, I wait outside the room for forty-five minutes while Dr. Kingston tries to teach her ways of dealing with her feelings by using a healthier outlet. Six months of therapy later, and we're still trying to help her manage the way she acts out.

Not that I can blame her, though.

Once her session is over, we drive home, and I start browsing in the kitchen for something to make for dinner.

"Shit, I forgot to go grocery shopping," I mumble as I stare at the half-empty orange juice container and Chinese takeout boxes in the fridge.

"You shouldn't swear."

I slam the door shut, not realizing she was behind me. "You shouldn't creep up on people," I tease, spinning around to her sitting by the breakfast bar.

"Grandma says swearing is the devil's voice."

"You should ask Grandma what whiskey is then."

"I already did," she responds. "She says it's the Lord's blood."

I snort. "Grandma's a liar." I begin opening cupboards and digging through boxes of food.

"I know." She grins. "So what are you making? Or should I say…*burning*?"

36

Pushing the Limits

"For an eleven-year-old—"

"I'm almost twelve," she interrupts.

"Whatever. For an *almost* twelve-year-old, you have quite the smart mouth."

"I prefer *gifted*."

"I prefer it shut."

Her nostrils flare and then she sticks her tongue out.

I opt for pizza delivery instead of cooking until I get to the grocery store again. And even then, I'll probably grab frozen pizzas and boxes of mac 'n cheese.

Back in Ohio, there was this small family-owned deli and sushi bar that I always stopped at on my way home from work. But now that I have Natalia with me, I need to remind myself to hit the store.

Either that or I'm going to go broke from ordering seven days a week.

Chapter Five
Aspen

I arrive at my night class early Thursday, knowing the room will be empty beforehand. Although I can work in my apartment, there's something about the atmosphere and being in a room filled with other art that give me motivation. Once I grab an easel, I settle in with my headphones and begin.

I've had the same song on repeat for several days and every time I draw or paint, I'm able to tune everything out when I listen to it and think happy thoughts about her.

The lyrics inspire me to do an abstract of her face. I use the entire canvas to lightly outline her features—her heart-shaped face, protruding eyes, and the strong bridge of her nose.

When I finish, I lightly draw a line down the middle of her face to emphasize her different layers—happy on the outside and depressed on the inside.

I take a tube of red and squeeze it out onto the palette and then swirl a brush into it before outlining the lines and angles of the face.

I focus on one side at a time. Warm colors with light shading reflect her outside personality the best, so I add in some yellow with a blending brush over her cheeks and jawline. I use a bit of white to emphasize the lighter shading around her eye and the slant of her nose. Once I'm finished with that, I add some teal and use my fan brush to accent the cheekbones with the yellow underneath them to create a lighter illusion.

When I finish up the left side with my pointed round brush, I make the eye blue. After that's complete, I smooth everything with a flat brush and wait for it to dry. I stand back and study it for a moment before deciding I'm satisfied. It feels like her—happy and energetic—the teals and yellows of my past life.

I begin the other side with a base coat of purple and then layer a light shade of blue on top. This side of the face is meant to be dark and oppressed—her inner personality—so I add in the shading to exaggerate the features more.

I wait until it dries a bit before adding another layer of blue, this time a couple shades darker than before to accent the cheekbones. I run the angular flat bristles alongside the jawline and up near the ear, making the blue stand out more than the purple. Once I'm done with the blue, I blend in the white to outline the other side of the nose and eye.

The song continues repeating in my earbuds as I sing the lyrics aloud. I step back and look at the two sides as a whole.

Tilting my head, I check out the different angles before adding another layer of blue to the right side.

I quickly glance up at the clock and see I still have a good twenty-five minutes before I need to clean up and pretend I was never here. As I'm dipping a clean brush, I feel someone behind me.

A hand on my shoulder startles me, and I jerk around so quickly the brush between my fingers follows. A streak of blue wipes across Professor Hampton's face before I even realize it's happened.

"Oh my God!" My cheeks heat with embarrassment. I quickly yank my earbuds out. "I'm so sorry!" I lower my hand and examine the damage.

He smiles, and a small laugh escapes his throat as he blinks. "Guess I deserved that."

I frown. "It wasn't on purpose."

"Never sneak up on an artist," he confirms. "Sorry about that. I was trying *not* to startle you, but apparently, my plan failed."

"It's fine," I assure him. "I wasn't expecting anyone to come in yet."

"Yeah, I figured I'd come early and prepare." He smiles that crooked, drop-your-panties-and-beg-for-it smile, sending a rush of excitement through me. I've had some amazing professors in the past, but they've never made me feel as nervous to be around them as he does.

I can feel his breath against my bare arm, alerting me we're too close. After I set the brush down, I look away. When I start cleaning up my supplies, he grips my wrist.

"Wait."

I turn to look at him staring at the canvas. I swallow at the intensity of his voice. His hand stays wrapped around my wrist as he stares intently at it, almost as if he's examining every detail.

"You started this today?"

"Yeah, about an hour ago." I look at it. "It's a rough start. Something I did on a whim."

He releases me and smiles. "It's stunning. The contrast between the warm and cool colors catches your attention and draws you into the tones. It's almost like they are forcing you to feel the agony and heartache she's feeling from her struggles."

"Thank you." I lower my head to hide the blush creeping over my cheeks. When I need to get out of my own head, I start painting. Getting lost in whatever piece I'm working on helps me cope. It's the only non-medical thing that keeps my anxiety under control.

"I was trying to show her two contradicting personalities by putting them side by side," I explain.

"She's struggling with inner demons but doesn't reveal it on the outside?"

I nod. "There's a struggle with who she wants to be on the outside and what she feels on the inside."

He frowns. "Sounds intense, but I love it, Aspen. Would you mind if I kept it in the classroom to exhibit for a bit?"

"Um…" I hesitate. "Actually, it's personal."

"I won't tell anyone it's yours." He grins slyly, and I find myself having a hard time resisting those damn dimples.

"Okay, if anyone asks…" I prompt.

"I'll claim it's a student from the old college I used to teach at. Someone named…" He pauses briefly. "Regina Hopintale."

I bite my lip to keep from laughing but fail. "Thanks."

He smirks, showing off his dimples again—dimples like fresh strawberries covered in melted chocolate. They look so delicious and perfect that you can't deny the explosive flavor once it hits your tongue.

*Oh my God…*did I just compare my professor's dimples to chocolate-covered strawberries?

I need to get some fresh air. Or perhaps a second pair of panties.

He walks to the front of the classroom and sets his briefcase down on the desk. I clean up my area and put my supplies away before the first few students walk in.

"How's it goin'?" Ellie questions in that Southern twang of hers as soon as she sits in the chair next to mine.

"You're surprisingly early…" I suspiciously narrow my eyes.

"Not that early," she denies, her cheeks turning a soft red.

"Does this have anything to do with that guy over there eye-fucking you?" I noticed it during our first class. He stares at her every chance he gets.

"Who? Kyle Simmons?" She pretends not to notice him as she digs through her bag.

I playfully scowl at her. "I don't know his name! But it's apparent you do."

"We might've had a couple classes together last semester."

"And?" I prompt, knowing there's *so* much more to the story.

"And…" She lingers. "We might've hooked up at a party."

"So you came to class early to what? Have a staring contest?"

She wrinkles her nose. "No. I don't know. Once class starts, the easel will block my view."

"Go sit next to him. Wouldn't that solve your problem?"

"Oh, bless your heart, Aspen."

I furrow my brows, confused.

"He should come sit next to me. It'd be the gentlemanly thing to do." She crosses her legs and folds her hands in her lap.

"Ah…" I say when it finally clicks. "So what you actually want is to eye-fuck him and play hard to get until he takes the initiative to come talk to you?"

"Is that too much to ask?"

I laugh at her sharp-witted Southern accent. "You were ready to jump on the professor in a heartbeat, but Kyle needs to be a Southern gentleman and come to you?"

"That's exactly right," she answers.

I shake my head and smile at her.

Soon, class begins, and I watch Professor Hampton walk around the front of the room and discuss our assignment. I should be listening, but my mind wanders to the abstract I painted earlier. The one that portrays *her* inner demons…

It'd been raining all night long, and eventually, the storm woke me up. A flash of lightning temporarily blinded me as I squinted, trying to see if Ari was awake. Her bed was empty and the light in the hallway peeked under our bedroom door.

I threw the covers off and opened the door, deciding to tiptoe down the hallway to see where she had gone. "Ariel?" I whispered. I stood in front of the bathroom door that was closed, but I knew she had to be in there. "Ariel, you in here?" I knocked lightly.

Silence.

I slowly opened the door, hoping I wasn't interrupting her, but when I stepped in, my entire world stopped. "Oh my God, Ariel!" I ran to her where she lay on the cold bathroom floor, blood running down her hand and fingers. "Ariel, wake up!" I screamed, pulling her into my lap.

I grabbed a towel from the hook and wrapped it around her wrist. A razor blade lay next to her, covered in dried blood. Tears fell down my cheeks faster than I could wipe them off. I couldn't understand what was happening… Why had she done it?

Why hadn't I known she was hurting?

. . .

Pushing the Limits

The sound of chairs sliding on the floor knocks me out of my past nightmare. Everyone's hustling to grab their easels and spread out their supplies. I grab my project that we started last class after our memory exercise and drown in my thoughts as I keep my gaze down and to the canvas in front of me. Professor Hampton continues walking around, but I don't need to glance up to know he's studying me from the front of the room.

Before we're dismissed, he reminds us to keep an eye out for his email about our first blog assignment.

I have a feeling Professor Hampton is going to take up much more of my time than I suspected.

Chapter Six
Aspen

The sound of my alarm wakes me up and before I can even manage to open my eyes, I reach for my phone and tap on the screen until the noise stops. It's Saturday, and I have to be at work in less than an hour, but the heavy weight next to me reminds me that I'm not alone.

Jake, or maybe it was John, is a guy I met during happy hour, and when two drinks turned into four and six, I invited him to my place.

But I don't have time to casually escort him out and exchange numbers—not that I'd give him mine anyway. That's not how this works. I avoid any attachment, friendship, or even a fuck buddy. I don't feel that compassion toward relationships that most women do. I can't be open, discuss my feelings, or have 'talks' about my past. It's the exact reason I avoid it all in the first place. One-night stands and casual hookups are all I'm emotionally capable of giving.

I need to shower and leave before I'm late to work again. So I slide out of bed, grab my towel hanging on the back of the door, and walk to the bathroom.

He has exactly forty-two minutes to leave before I kick him out.

I wash my body and hair, trying to remember the events of last night.

Pushing the Limits

Kendall and Zoe met me at Happy Joe's for the two-for-one happy hour special.

It was only meant to be a quick, fun girls' night out, but it soon turned into a party of six when Kendall invited her boyfriend, Kellan.

Jake, or John, was there with a friend from work—some name I can't remember either—and I can only assume Zoe took him home after Kendall and I left.

As soon as I'm out of the shower, I dry off and go to my room to search for some clothes. What's-his-face is still lying face flat on my bed.

Fucking hell.

I open one of my drawers to grab some jeans and purposely slam it shut, hoping it'll startle him enough to wake up.

No such luck.

On to Plan B.

I walk over to the other side of the bed and start shaking his shoulder. "Wake up!" He barely flinches. I grab the covers and rip them off of him, only to realize he's completely naked.

I tilt my head and admire his firm ass for a quick second, but then shake my head away from the distraction. "You need to leave!" I say loud and insultingly slow.

He finally starts stirring and mumbles something but doesn't open his eyes.

"I'm going to pour a bucket of cold water on you if you don't get the hell out of my bed," I threaten. "You have three seconds."

"*Jesus,*" he mutters, slowly shifting around, searching for the covers with one hand.

"I have to get to work." I walk around my bed and look for a shirt in my closet. "Which means you have to leave." I spell it out for him.

"Where the hell do you work that you have to be up this damn early?" He finally sits up and starts grabbing his clothes that are scattered on the floor.

"I work at an art gallery."

"Sounds boring."

I pull my shirt on and grimace. "Out," I say firmly.

"*What?*"

45

As he pulls up his jeans, I glare at him. "You can get out *now*."

"I'm working on it. Geez. You weren't this bitchy last night."

My lips form a scowl, and I bend down to grab one of my heels and throw it directly at him.

"Ow! What the hell?"

"First, you diss where I work, which is one of my favorite places to be in the whole world. And second, you call me a bitch!"

I'm ready to throw the other heel at him, but he finally uses his two brain cells to leave.

"*Bye*, Jake," I call out.

"Bye, *Satan*," he shouts from the hallway, and I can't help bursting into laughter.

Sadly, this isn't the worst morning *after* I've had.

The door opens and then closes with a slam. A few seconds later, I hear it opening and closing again, this time much quieter.

"Do I even want to know what that was all about?" Kendall asks from the hallway. "He looked like a scared cat in a cold bath." She tiptoes to my room as if she's coming to get the dirt.

"He couldn't handle my classic morning wake-up call," I explain, brushing the knots out of my hair. "Amateur."

"Kellan woke me up in a way that made me never want to leave the bedroom." She flips her hair over her shoulder with a smirk.

"Well, Jake was nearly in a coma until I threatened him with cold water." I grab my makeup case and begin my routine, but in a fast-forward motion.

"Are you sure his name is Jake?" She furrows her brows. "I could've sworn it was James."

I shrug. "It wasn't worth remembering."

"Clearly."

"So, I take it your night ended without penetration. How about Zoe's?" I rummage through my makeup case and grab my eyeliner and mascara.

"From what I could hear last night, it went well. And then again, this morning. He's still there. I think they went in the shower together."

Pushing the Limits

I shake my head and grin, applying my eye makeup. "Those poor guys never saw us coming."

"Speak for yourself! I'm dating the guy I brought home."

I thread my fingers through my hair after unsuccessfully brushing the tangles out. Since there's no time to blow dry it, I pull it up into a messy bun and wrap a headband around my head. That's going to have to do for today.

"Alright, I'm ready. Let's go." I grab my purse off the vanity and follow her out. "Whose turn is it to drive?"

"Yours." She looks over her shoulder and smirks.

Kendall works with me at the Broadway Street Gallery. It's a chic and popular gallery where many students work and visit. It's across the street from the university, so when I first moved here my freshman year, I immediately applied for a job.

I was hired as a paid docent that gives tours to larger groups in hopes they'll make a purchase. Even if they don't, they often give a donation at the end. The gallery gets a commission from each sale, and then they give a portion of each year to school art programs in the area. It's one of the major reasons I applied to this gallery in the first place.

I love going through all the exhibits and watching people's expressions and answering questions about the pieces. Exhibits switch out every sixty to ninety days, so it's my job to stay updated.

My end goal is to be a curator so I can be the one to pick which artists and paintings a gallery displays, but that takes years of practice and more school. Until then, I plan to apply for a curator apprenticeship after graduation. Mr. Cross is the gallery curator, but he's due to retire within the next ten years or so. All the administrative tasks are starting to be more than he can handle.

I wave to Ms. Jones, the gallery director, as we walk past her office on the second floor. She's a widow in her mid-sixties who's been working here longer than I've been born. She's yapping on the phone in Spanish, so I can't be sure if she's scolding someone or not, but with the way her features tighten, I can only assume the worst. She's fluent in four languages, so she can communicate with a diverse group from around the world.

I think about all the things she's achieved in her life and look up to her so much as a role model. I can only hope to be as successful and driven as her one day.

Kendall and I walk into the employee lounge to lock up our things. She's a gallery attendant and sits at the information booth and welcomes everyone who enters. She answers phones and takes messages if someone isn't around. If it's not too busy, I'll sit with her until another tour arrives.

As I'm adding another layer of lip gloss, Shane from the security walks in.

"Good morning, Aspen." He smiles wide as his gaze roams up and down my body. I let him look without consequence, but it's as far as I'll ever go with him. Even though he has biceps bigger than my head and the bluest eyes I've ever seen, I don't mix pleasure with business. So that automatically means no sleeping with coworkers.

"And good morning to you, Shane." I flash him a sultry smile in return and layer it with a wink. I even suck in my lower lip and bite it, earning a throaty groan in return.

I'm not ashamed to say that I've thought about it. Shane would be sure to give me one hell of a night, but then what? We come to work as if nothing happened? What if he wanted more? What if he told everyone at the gallery that I was an easy lay?

To avoid all the what-ifs, I've made it a firm rule to only sleep with guys I have no intention of seeing ever again. With demanding art courses and a busy work schedule, the last thing I have time for is a clingy guy who thinks they own me.

"You are going to make that poor guy walk around all day with a boner," Kendall teases, shoving her purse and sweater in her locker.

"Well, it's not like anyone's died from blue balls before. I'm sure he'll take care of it."

"Yeah, with you in mind."

I shrug. "Whatever helps get the job done."

She slams her locker door shut. "Explain to me again why you can't fuck him out of your system?"

I nearly choke on her words as a few heads turn and glare at us.

Pushing the Limits

"Jesus, Kendall. Parade my sex life a little louder, will you? I don't think the teenagers in the mall across town heard you."

"Oh, it's not like your little eye-fucking affair with Shane is a secret. You two have been flirting for months."

"Yeah, so?"

"So get on with it already!"

I quickly shove my purse in my locker and grab my employee vest and lanyard nametag before locking it.

"Maybe you should worry about your own sex life." I wink, knowing she's nearly dry-humping the air for any friction at all. I quickly pull my arms through the navy blue vest and wrap the lanyard around my neck. "I'm heading out. See you at lunch."

I find the gallery manager, Christine, at her desk and sit my ass halfway on top of it. "Your main bitch is here. When's the first tour?"

"I'm getting sick of your damn early morning perkiness, Aspen." She frowns, slouching. "It's making the rest of us look bad," she mocks. She's a great leader and is almost always on top of her game, but she is *not* a morning person.

"You're such a hater."

"Yes, of mornings."

I laugh when she groans. "What you need is a good dose of dick. You'd learn to love mornings, too."

"Sorry that I don't participate in the same *extracurricular* activities as you, but I happen to enjoy being in relationships."

"Yeah, so did Katie Holmes. Look how that turned out."

"You're such a pessimist."

"I'm a realist," I correct, grabbing the tour schedule from a pile of papers. "Looks like my first tour is in fifteen minutes. I'm going to use the restroom and grab a quick drink." I jump off her desk.

As I walk toward the door, I call over my shoulder, "Go drink some coffee to lighten up those dark circles under your eyes."

"I hate you!" she bellows, and I chuckle at her dramatics.

Once I'm finished, I wait for my first group to arrive. Tour buses and schools make trips here regularly, so I've met a broad diversity of people. However, today's group is the spunkiest group of women I've ever met.

49

"What is your organization called again?" I ask as I lead them toward the first room.

"The Red Hat Society," one member explains.

"We also brought you a hat!" another member adds. She walks up and places a pink fedora on top of my head. "Since you're under fifty, you can't wear red," she explains. "You're a Pink Hatter."

"Wow...it's like Mean Girls for seniors," I tease, adjusting the hat to fit over my messy knot.

"Don't feel bad, darling. Pink suits you well." She winks, and I know their tour is going to give me a run for my money.

My first half of the morning with the Red Hat Society is filled with hilarious, animated stories and random fits of laughter. I try to stay focused and remain professional, but these women have kept me on my toes.

"Ladies, you have all been so wonderful!" I smile and feel like I'm saying goodbye to a part of my family. "I hope you come back!"

"You've been a hoot, Aspen!" Eva, the sassier one, I've come to realize, says. We exchange goodbyes and a few hugs before they take their red hats and purple scarves out the door.

I walk into Christine's office with a smile and plop down in one of the chairs. "Oh my God! That was the most fun I've had on a tour."

That grabs her attention. "I could hear them all the way in here! They did sound sweet on the phone, though, when they made their reservation."

"They were. Normally, strangers don't ask anything about me, but they were all *where did you grow up* and *are you married*. It was refreshing."

She tilts her head and gives me a questioning look. "Where *did* you grow up?"

I realize this is something I don't normally talk about with people. Even people I know. It's not something I like to bring up because it usually leads to other questions, which ultimately leads to me dodging them as much as I can.

"About two thousand miles to the east." I grin, not willing to give her a clear answer.

"I know you aren't married, but are you seeing someone?

Exclusively." She cracks a smile. "I don't even know if you have
siblings or what your favorite color is."

"That's because I don't feel the need to parade my life on social
media." I grimace. "And I don't talk about my personal life much."

"Why's that?"

"Because there's nothing to talk about," I lie. I shrug it off, hoping
she'll let it go. "Is my next tour soon or can I grab something to eat
quickly?"

"Oh!" She snaps her fingers in the air. "They canceled, but Ms.
Jones was looking for you."

"Alright. I'll go find her." I smile. "See ya later!" I call over my
shoulder as I begin to walk away.

My mind wanders as I imagine what Ms. Jones would want to see
me for. She's in charge of the upcoming gala this spring, which means
she's been super busy. I only talk to her if she's around.

My phone buzzes in my pocket as I start walking toward the stairs
up to her office. I reach for it and read over a couple of missed
messages. As I get closer to the staircase that leads up to Ms. Jones's
office and the employees' lounge, I notice a guy's silhouette standing
near the edge of the steps.

"Are you lost?" I ask, trying to grab his attention.

Stepping closer, he faces me while keeping his gaze locked on
mine. I try to get ahold of myself, but when his deep, intense green
eyes burn into mine, I remind myself to breathe.

"No," he answers with a sly smirk.

"Professor Hampton," I say in surprise. "Didn't realize it was
you."

"That's okay. And please, call me Morgan. We aren't in the
classroom, Aspen."

I swallow, and I swear he winks. "Oh, right. Can I help you with
anything?" I step forward and wonder if he's heading up the staircase,
too.

"I'm looking for my aunt. I think her office is up there." He nods
toward the steps.

"Oh, who's your aunt?" We head upstairs as I try to act unaffected
by his good looks and charm.

"Melinda Jones."

I nearly choke as I realize he's Ms. Jones's—*my boss's*—nephew.

"Oh, um…her office is upstairs to the left. I was headed there."

"I had no idea you worked here," he states as we climb the steps.

"Yeah, mostly on the weekends, but I fit in a couple shifts in between classes during the week when I can."

"How do you like it?"

"Oh, I love it. I work nearly every day in the summer."

"I bet you enjoy that." His lips part, and I trip on the step in front of me. "You okay?"

"Fine," I insist, quickly recovering by grabbing the railing. "Damn stairs came out of nowhere."

He snorts. "They do that sometimes."

I lower my head to hide the stupid grin on my face as we walk the short hallway to Ms. Jones's office. I knock on the door, and seconds later, she whips it open and squeals as she sees Morgan next to me. "Finally!" She wraps her arms around him as best as she can, but considering he's well over six feet tall with a solid chest and arms, she struggles with getting her arms around him.

I stand awkwardly as I watch them, wondering if I should even be standing in the middle of it all. I glance at them as they break apart, her smile wide. "I'm glad we can see each other more often now that you live back home."

"Me too."

Back home? I wonder where he's been and for how long, but I keep my mouth shut until Ms. Jones looks in my direction and finally acknowledges me. "Aspen! Great, you're here. This is my nephew, Morgan. Morgan, this is—"

"Aspen."

I glance at him as he cuts her off. He says my name way too smoothly.

"Oh, great! You've had a chance to meet." Her eyes light up again. "I have a phone conference in about two minutes, so, Aspen, be a dear and give Morgan the grand tour. I'd do it myself, but I can't get out of this godforsaken waste-of-my-time meeting."

"Oh, okay," I say breathlessly.

"She doesn't have to, Aunt Mel. I mean"—he glances at me—"I don't want to be a burden."

"Are you kidding?" She nearly gasps. "Aspen loves giving tours! And she's the best at it." She winks, and I wonder if she knows something I don't.

I haven't even told Kendall about him. She knows I have a night course this semester, but I haven't mentioned that I want to take the professor home and do *very* bad things to him. Bad and inappropriate things.

However, inappropriate went up about ten notches.

"Yeah, it's no problem. My group canceled, and I'm free for the next two hours." I smile at Ms. Jones, avoiding eye contact with Morgan because I don't want her to get suspicious.

"Sounds good." He turns toward me and grins. "Lead the way."

"Where would you like to start?" I ask as we walk down the staircase.

"Hmm…what's your favorite exhibit at the gallery?"

"That'd be the Fashion Faire." I smile. "I'm a sucker for historic fashion trends."

"I would've pegged you as more of a Paris Fashion Week guru," he says, lowering his gaze to my flats that I wear at work, but I know he noticed my heels in class.

"Well…a girl can love both," I say matter-of-factly, biting my lip to keep from smiling. "And I'm concerned that you even know about fashion week."

He flashes that deep-dimpled smile, and it takes all my willpower to look away and avoid the flutters that will surface if he continues looking at me like that.

I take him through the exhibit and point out my favorites. I can tell he's bored with my fashion vocabulary, so I breeze through them without making him suffer for long.

"Maybe we shouldn't have started there," I say, laughing.

"I'm starting to doubt your tour guide skills, Aspen."

I roll my eyes. "I haven't had any complaints."

"I bet not," he murmurs so low I almost don't hear him.

"You should see the local student exhibit since you haven't been here in a while. It's a collaboration of the high schools and colleges around here."

"Would love to."

We walk side by side down the hall as I lead him toward the exhibit on the other side of the gallery.

"So much has changed since I was here last." He looks around, noticing all the new features that have been added and remodeled in the last few years.

"Oh, yeah? How long has it been?"

His expression tenses as he faces me. "Five years."

"Wow…That's a long time to be away from home."

"Sometimes it feels like it's been a long time. Other times, it feels like it hasn't been long at all."

"I know exactly how that feels," I say. "I've avoided going home ever since I left."

His lips curl up, showing off those impressive dimples again. "Sounds like we've both been running from home."

I smile at the truth in his words, his voice so somber and hoarse. "I guess so."

We step into the student section of the gallery. His gaze bounces from wall to wall.

"Are those Ariel Rose Collections?" He tilts his head as he studies them.

"Yes." My heart skips a beat at the mention of her name. I called her Ari, but naming them the Ariel Rose Collection felt more like a tribute to her. "How'd you know?"

He stares at them, mesmerized, and takes a couple steps forward. "She has a distinctive style. Raw, dark, edgy. *Gothic*. The abstracts are so emotional, it's impossible not to be affected by them." He pauses a moment, collecting himself. "I would recognize her work anywhere."

I'm stunned into silence, feeling a little awkward at the fact that he knows her work. Rather, *my* work.

"She's a student?"

I hate that I have to lie. "Uh, she was. Couple years ago. You like that style?" I shouldn't ask questions, but I can't help myself. Even though it's the exact reason I use a pseudonym, I can't fight the feeling of excitement beating in my chest at him being a fan of my work—especially since he has no idea it's me.

"Yeah, I have a couple of her paintings I found at an online shop. I had no idea she was from around here, though." He rubs the back of his neck. I want to know what he's thinking, why he's so intrigued by her, how he heard about her, but I stop the questions before the words escape my throat.

"I like the different way she connects you to the pieces," I casually add.

"It's deep. But there's a sense of vulnerability to it, too. It's breathtaking."

My breath hitches, the corner of my eyes tearing up as I hear the passion and sincerity in his tone. The way he talks about the AR Collection is almost too much, but I hold myself together.

"Yeah, they're inspiring," I say, edging away and hoping he follows me to another part of the exhibit.

"From what I've seen so far, Aspen, you have a distinctive style."

I look at him, puzzled. My cheeks heat, and I hope to God he doesn't recognize the similarities. "You've hardly seen any of my work."

"Actually, I have."

I raise a brow, intrigued.

"I saw your portfolios before classes began. I wanted to know what kind of students I was getting, being that I was teaching at a new school. Not just anyone gets into the art program at CSLA. Once I got a glimpse of your work, I requested the entire portfolio."

My body halts in front of him, his intense stare making it impossible to think straight. "Why?"

"It's not every day, or even every year I get a student like you." His words take me by surprise. I blush, lowering my gaze to avoid his intense ones. I don't talk about my work with many people. It's deep and personal, and I prefer to keep it to myself.

"Like what?" I ask softly, unable to drop the subject. We slowly begin walking again, the gallery getting quieter and quieter as we walk to a more vacant area.

"You have similarities in each of your pieces. Almost like a trademark. You use bold and bright colors to accent a dark, painful image."

He's right, so I can't even argue with him. When I paint for the AR Collection, I do it completely raw and free. No expectations. No boundaries. No pressure. But when I do as me, I only cover the surface of my emotions. I don't show the extent of the pain or guilt I suffer with inside. I don't let anyone see that part of me, so I pour it into the AR collections.

"When I first saw you, I almost didn't believe the artist behind them and the girl in my classroom were the same person."

I notice we've gotten closer, almost touching.

My lips curl up, intrigued. "What do you mean?"

"Well, you walked into my classroom with your curve-hugging shirts, tight, dark skinny jeans, and leopard print fuck-me heels. It's not hard to miss, considering none of my other students have ever shown up to class dressed like that."

His eyes stay fixed on mine, so deep that it feels as if he's looking into my soul. I can feel how hot my body is, heating with every noticeable breath he takes.

I shrug, acting unaffected. "Perhaps I have a good fashion sense."

"Perhaps." He smirks. "Or perhaps it's a cover-up. You're guarding what's inside with an outside distraction."

My mouth tenses at how blunt and forward he's being. *I distract him?* I don't care how my body and heart react to him. I don't give that part of me to anyone. "You don't know anything about me."

His stare remains intense. "I might know more than you think."

Before I can ask what he means by that, Kendall interrupts us. "Oh, I didn't know we were giving one-on-one tours," she teases with a flirty tone. We quickly part from each other, putting much-needed space between us to relieve the evident tension that's there. "Not that I blame you." She gives him an obvious once-over and winks.

"Kendall," I say with a sharp edge in my tone and grit my teeth. "This is Morgan, Ms. Jones' nephew." I purse my lips, hoping she'll get the hint to stop undressing him with her eyes. "He's also my Advanced Art professor twice a week."

"Oh!" She stands up straighter as if that changes everything. "It's a pleasure to meet you." She extends her hand to shake his, and I fight back a smile at how formal she's acting.

He takes her hand in his and shakes it. "It's a pleasure to meet you, as well."

"Kendall lives down the hall from me and goes to CSLA, too," I explain. "And she works here." I nod awkwardly before adding, "Apparently, she can't get enough of me."

He smirks and then the three of us continue standing in uncomfortable silence.

"I better get going since there are only a few minutes of my break left." Kendall gives me a wide-eyed look that I know too well: *you better tell me everything later!* and then waves to Morgan. "Nice meeting you!" When she's out of view, I sigh.

"She seems nice," Morgan drawls.

I burst out laughing at his attempt to break the tension. "Yeah, she is. Obnoxious and loud at times, but she's a good friend."

He turns toward the wall. "Why isn't any of your work in here? I'm sure Aunt Mel would give you a prime spot."

I can hear the sincerity in his tone. I can't blame him, considering I work here and most people would jump at the opportunity, but I could never explain my real reason for keeping them to myself.

"I'm a little more reserved when it comes to showing off my work."

"It'd be great exposure and look great on grad school applications. Not to mention, your pieces are one-of-a-kind. I'm sure people would love them. You wouldn't have to tell people they're yours during your tours, but at least you'd get to see their expressions when they look."

I purse my lips, swallowing down the guilt and pain of keeping the secret of my sister's death. "Maybe. I'll think about it."

He smiles in return, content with my answer. It's a complete lie, but at least it'll keep him from asking more questions.

We continue the tour, looking through the rest of the exhibits. By the time we round back to where we started, I'm starving.

"Thank you." He faces me and almost blocks me in near the staircase.

"Sure."

"I mean it. You're a great guide. Entertaining even." A small rumble of laughter escapes his throat as we face each other chest to chest.

"I'm glad to have thoroughly entertained you then."

"So have you thought about it yet?" He lifts his brows and my heart beats faster.

"Thought about what?"

"Putting some of your work in the student section here?"

I bite the inside of my cheek, covering up the anxiety that's brewing inside. "You mean since you asked me thirty minutes ago?" A sly smile forms on my face at his eagerness.

"Yes. Figured it couldn't hurt to again." His flirty tone makes it hard to stay sincere, but I won't let that part of my life slip out.

"No, I don't think so. Not my thing."

It's not a complete lie. I don't have any intention of putting my pieces out there as *me*.

"That's a shame, Aspen." He drawls out my name, seducing me with his gorgeous green eyes, making it hard to remember he's off-limits.

Remember that *I'm* supposed to be off-limits.

"Like I said before, it'd be impressive for grad school applications."

"Oh, Aspen! Morgan!" We turn at the sound of Ms. Jones's voice. She grabs his arm and pulls him down, connecting her lips to his cheeks. "How was the tour?"

"It was great, Aunt Mel. Aspen knows her stuff." He looks at me and winks. "It's stunning."

"Oh, I knew you'd love it! I'm so happy you moved back!" she squeals. "Look, I was about to grab some lunch. Wanna join me?"

"Oh, um…sure." He glances in my direction.

"I have another tour, so I better get going." I take an awkward step, distancing myself.

"Thank you so much for taking him around."

"Anytime." I smile and walk away, feeling like I should change my panties before my next tour.

Chapter Seven
Aspen

I try to block thoughts of Professor Hampton out of my head, but after seeing him at the gallery, it's all I've been able to focus on. I end up walking into the wrong classroom for my Monday morning course and even lock myself out of my apartment. I called the landlord, but of course he didn't answer or return my calls. I decided to wait outside of Kendall and Zoe's apartment until one of them gets home since we exchanged spare keys months ago. But even sitting and waiting in the hallway for one of them to show, he consumes my thoughts completely.

I know nothing good can come from this fascination I have. This is the exact reason I keep my distance in the first place and get involved with guys who mean nothing to me, but he's making it *really* hard to stay away.

If my past has taught me anything, it's not to get attached. I don't talk about my past or why I prefer to live alone. Kendall's asked me a million times why I don't have a roommate or why I don't date exclusively. I give her or anyone else who wants to know a vague explanation—*I prefer to paint and work alone, and I don't need the distraction of a relationship.* It works most of the time, but Kendall has tried to dig for more. I brush it off and change the subject. Although I have told her bits and pieces of my past, including parts of Ariel, it's all she knows. No one besides me knows the whole story.

And if I've learned anything from this past week—guys are *definitely* a distraction.

Then today I got stuck staying later than usual for my shift at the gallery, and now I'm running so damn late for Professor Hampton's class. When I finally got off work, I ran home to grab my schoolbag and change clothes. However, I spent much more time than necessary trying to pick out an outfit.

After circling the parking lot, searching unsuccessfully for a spot, I give up and park on the street. I sigh and grab my bag as it starts sprinkling out. It's a longer walk, so I dig through my trunk for my umbrella, but it's not in there.

Great.

I look up and see the dark clouds moving in. I beg them not to rain yet. *Just wait*, I plead. I slam my trunk down and begin walking. I pull my sweater tighter against my chest and keep my head low.

I'm about halfway there when the skies unleash, drenching me in a matter of seconds. *Son of a bitch.* I try to walk faster, but it's no use. I'm completely soaked.

I grab the railing to the staircase that leads to the LAB building. As soon as I take the first step, my heel slips against the wet cement, and I'm mere milliseconds from face-planting.

An arm catches me from the side, wrapping around my waist and pulling me up before I can even comprehend someone is there. I notice the rain has stopped pouring over me, giving me the opportunity to stabilize myself. Once my feet are firmly on the ground, I inhale deeply, feeling relief.

Pushing the Limits

"Are you okay?"

My eyes widen as I hear Professor Hampton's voice next to me. I swallow and turn to face him. "Yes, thanks to you." I try to sound casual, but the nerves in my voice make it impossible to look unaffected by him.

"You almost gave yourself a shiner there." His lips curve into a sympathetic smile. "Let me walk with you." He releases his grip on me, and then I notice he's holding an umbrella over me.

"I swear I'm not always this jumpy and clumsy." I lean into him as we walk the rest of the steps, but he acts unaffected.

"You need to be closer," he says, throwing me off guard. Before I can respond, he pulls me tighter to his side. "The umbrella isn't wide enough," he answers my unspoken question. I nod in return and keep my head down as he leads us into the building. His body feels warm against mine, his scent overpowering my senses.

"Thank you," I say as soon as we're inside and out of the rain. He shakes the umbrella off before closing it. "Oh, shit," I gasp, taking a step closer to him and pressing my hand to his chest. "I got your suit jacket all wet." I panic and begin brushing the water off but stop when his hand covers mine.

"It's okay, Aspen. A little water won't kill me." His voice sounds sincere and rough at the same time. How does he do that?

We stand there, staring at each other, unmoving. My stomach is somersaulting at the way his hand feels against mine. The way he looks at me, I can't bring myself to break away.

The sound of the building door opening and closing breaks me out of my trance. Stepping back, I remove my hand from his chest. Professor Van Bergen stares suspiciously at us. She teaches art classes for freshmen and sophomores. I've had her as a teacher a few times as well. She's in her mid-thirties, but the scowl that's permanently etched on her face makes her look over fifty.

Professor Hampton clears his throat and shoves a hand in his pocket. "Claire," he greets, nodding in her direction with a forced smile.

My breathing speeds up as I notice the intense glare she's giving us. My mind starts spinning at what she must be assuming. My hand was on his chest, our bodies inches apart.

After Saturday's tour, I can't deny the chemistry between us. I know he feels it too, but that doesn't mean anything. He's my professor. It would risk everything, and that's why I must resist those irresistible dimples and charming smile. I usually have no problem keeping my emotions out of it, but he's managed to get inside my head just enough to make me second-guess exactly what's going on with my body and why it reacts to him this way.

"Morgan." She looks between us before adding, "Finally raining. The trees were starting to look like corpses."

"Yeah, we need it," he responds politely, but I can no longer see the two of them. My eyes lower to the ground as everything blurs and my heart hammers in my chest.

"Have a good night."

"You as well."

I hear the inner door open and the clacking of her heels as she walks down the hall.

"Are you alright?" Professor Hampton's voice captures my attention again. "You look pale."

I blink a few times before responding. "I need to sit." My knees feel weak, and I can feel the blood draining from my face.

"What's wrong?"

I sit on the wet floor, not even caring that the rain from our shoes brought water inside.

"Are you ill?" he repeats the same question he asked me in the bathroom that first night of class.

"No." I shake my head and bring my knees to my chest. "I'll be fine. I need a minute to calm down."

"Are you having an anxiety attack?" He kneels in front of me.

"Feels like it," I respond honestly. "I just need to get through it. It'll pass."

"Do you get these a lot?"

"Sometimes. It depends."

"What can I do?" He brushes a rough hand through his hair. "God, I feel so helpless."

"Count with me. Sometimes that helps."

He nods as I begin slowly counting, his husky voice a balm to my anxious mind. When we get to seven, his warm palm is on my shoulder, his hand slowly tracking down to my elbow before he repeats the motion as we count down to one.

I inhale through my nose and slowly exhale through my mouth once more, feeling the tension ebb away.

His gentle caress continues as his brows rise. "Better?"

I smile. "Yes, I think so." I'm still trying to focus on my breathing, but with his body so close to mine, I can hardly focus on anything except envisioning what his lips would feel like pressed against mine. "Thank you."

"You're welcome." He smiles. He reaches his hand out and waits until I place mine in it. "Do you know your triggers?" He pulls me up so we're standing again.

I want to ask why he cares so much, why he's taking such an interest, but I don't. That'd be rude, so I respond, "Yes, I have a list," I say softly. "I'm aware of them." My cheeks heat at the embarrassment of having another episode in front of him.

"Are they avoidable?" He opens the other door for me and waits until I pass through. "Is there a way to avoid the triggers?"

This heavy conversation is making my head spin, so I decide to lighten it up and get the thoughts out of my mind. "Why do you think I come to art class twice a week?" I turn and smile at him, but quickly face forward again. The last thing I need to do is run into a wall.

That'd be the icing on the freaking cake.

Halfway through class, I'm starting to feel normal again. Ellie and I chat quietly as we work on our assignments.

"Damn, Aspen. That's incredible," she exclaims, peeking over my easel. "I love how detailed you are. It's so…" she hesitates, searching for the right word.

I smile as she praises me, feeling good about myself before I hear a deep, familiar voice behind us. "Moving," Professor Hampton fills in.

"Yes!" Ellie agrees. "It's so moving. Absolutely." I keep my face down to hide the blush that's creeping up to my cheeks. Ellie smiles before grabbing her things to put away.

"Great work, Aspen." I still don't face him, hoping he can't see the goose bumps on my arms and neck.

"Thank you," I say softly.

"I'm starting to notice a theme," he continues, not backing away like I wish he would. I realize most of the students have left, leaving us alone once again. "This girl…she's in a lot of your pieces." I curse the fact that he's seen my other projects before. He places his hand against my lower back before he leans in and touches the drawing, rubbing the pad of his thumb along her jawline. "She has strong features."

"Yes," I confirm. Although we looked alike, we had differences. I have a brown birthmark under my eye and she didn't have one at all. I part my hair on the left side and she parted hers on the right. She had a mole on her jawline, and I have one on the right side of my neck, under my ear.

He steps away, removing his hand, but now we're shoulder to shoulder. "She's my sister." My heart aches the moment I tell him. I don't talk about her, and I'm surprised I admitted that to him.

"She's an important person in your life…" he prompts, turning his body toward me.

The genuine curiosity in his gaze makes me feel comfortable enough to continue telling him a bit more. "She was. She passed away six years ago," I explain.

"I'm so sorry." His features soften. "It's had a strong effect on you."

"You could say that."

"Keep it up. Whatever you're feeling is feeding your ability to create. I've never seen someone concentrate so fully before."

Was he watching me?

"I can see the way your eyes study the lines of your pencil and how it's like an extension of your hand. You're talented."

"That's nice of you to say, Professor Hampton. But I don't like to talk about her. I hope you understand."

"Of course." He flashes a sincere smile my way. "I wanted you to know, that's all."

"Thank you. I appreciate that."

64

Pushing the Limits

I hear his footsteps as he walks out of the classroom without another word. As I focus on the drawing, I think about her. I think about the empty darkness that lives inside me. I think about how different my life would be if she were still here. I think about how unfair it is that she isn't experiencing college with me. I think about how much I hate her for dying. I hate that she's not here with me. I hate that I hate her.

I hate everything.

On the surface, I'm a girl who uses art to express myself.

On the inside, I'm still lost and confused.

I'm drowning so deep in my thoughts that I don't even hear Professor Hampton walk in. "Are you still here?" His voice comes from behind me, sending a pulsating ache right in between my legs.

"It appears that way," I respond without looking in his direction. "The silence helps me think."

He steps next to me, looking at the painting. "What are you thinking?"

"That maybe I need more challenging assignments." I laugh, turning to face him.

"I agree." He smirks.

"I was *kidding*."

"I wasn't." He crosses his arms over his chest, showing off how tight his shirt looks against his biceps. "The most talented students usually need to be pushed out of their comfort zone the most."

I grab the drawing in one hand and the easel in the other. "I think, Professor Hampton, that's considered favoritism," I say over my shoulder as I put my things away.

"Technically, class is over. So I don't think that counts," he counters, his tone thick with amusement. I turn and see a wicked grin spread across his face.

"I think it *definitely* counts." I grab my bag, then stand in front of him. "Thank you for earlier."

"You already said that."

"I know." I blush. "But maybe we can pretend it never happened?"

He takes a step closer, adjusting the strap that was sliding off my shoulder. My breath hitches as his knuckles press against my bare arm. His eyes remain locked on mine as he responds, "What didn't happen?"

I smile in return, my gaze dropping to the floor before looking up at him. "Thanks."

"Have a great rest of your week, Aspen."

"You, too." I try to control my breathing as I walk out the door. I don't know what it is but being around Professor Hampton brings out emotions in me I haven't ever felt before. One minute my heart is beating so hard, I think it'll beat right out of my chest, and the next, I'm practically hyperventilating in front of him and gasping for air. It's as if he intentionally gets closer, making it nearly impossible to think straight. But when it's the two of us alone, it almost feels natural. A teacher and student who both enjoy art, who are attracted to the same types of pieces and enjoy discussing it. A teacher and student who can't stay away from each other in or outside of the classroom. A teacher and student who hardly know anything about each other, but with an attraction so intense it pulls them together.

A teacher and student who *cannot* become more than a teacher and student.

Chapter Eight
Morgan

As I take Natalia to her weekly therapy appointment, I drive past the church Jennifer and I used to attend. The church we made new friends in. The church we'd planned on saying our *vows* in.

I clench my teeth at the thought of how everything here reminds me of her, which of course, I fucking hate. I grew up here. I met her here. We'd planned on making a life here.

As far as I knew, we were happy. Besides art, she was my life. We met during our first semester of college at Berkeley, and right after graduation, I proposed. I continued on to graduate school, so we set the date for two years later.

A dog, a house, and a new job later, we had everything going for the next chapter in our lives. I couldn't wait, and then I saw her naked on top of Ryan, moaning and screaming out his name.

The image of them together is burned into my memory, and every time I think I can move on, fear and doubt raise their ugly heads.

My own brother betrayed me. My girlfriend of six years threw it away.

Once I was done yelling and punching holes in the wall, I'd learned they'd been having an affair on and off for the past year. My mind was completely blown away. My heart—*wrecked*.

For five years, I've tried to get her out of my head. I'd fuck women until I'd tire of them. Drink until thoughts of her vanished from my mind. Sleep until I was too numb to care.

But it was never enough. No, the memory of that day still haunts me…

"I swear, Morgan, it's not what you think." Her eyes are red and swollen, her voice squeaky and barely audible for the frantic crying she's been doing for the last hour.

"You must've lost all your damn brain cells from banging your head against the headboard as you were fucking another man if you think I'm buying any of your shit."

"Morgan, please! Give me the chance to explain!" She grabs ahold of my shirt as I begin to walk away.

"There's nothing to explain, Jen. It's over…get out." I jerk my arm out of her reach and stomp away.

"You can't kick me out of my own house! We can work this out. I promise it'll never happen again!"

I glance at her as fresh tears roll down her cheeks, but I have no sympathy for her. Nothing.

A bitter laugh rumbles up my throat as I hear her pathetic pleas. "Fine, I'll move out then. Fuck it. I'll move out now."

"No, don't! Let's talk this out. Please!"

I lean down so we're eye level, mere centimeters apart. "There's nothing to talk about. You fucked around on me weeks before our wedding! I'm never touching you again," I hiss.

The anger boils up inside me as I think about one of our last encounters. I packed a bag that night, left town, and didn't look back.

Until six months ago.

That phone call changed everything.

"Do I have to go tonight?" Natalia groans with a serious side of attitude, pulling me into the present.

"Are you still causing trouble in school?" I raise a brow in her direction.

She glares.

"That's what I thought."

"It's a waste of money." She crosses her arms. "I just sit there."

"Perhaps you could try talking then," I mock. "Plus, it's your money you're wasting."

I knew that'd grab her attention. She jerks her head in my direction. "How so?"

"Your dad's social security."

"What's that?"

"It's what the government pays when a child is left behind from a death. He also had a retirement fund and pension from the Berkeley PD that you'll get when you turn eighteen."

She stays silent, turns, and stares out the window. "What if I don't want it?"

My brows furrow. "What do you mean?"

"I don't want his money," she repeats.

She hasn't spoken much about Ryan up to this point, and I know her therapist hasn't been successful in getting much out of her, so I try to keep her going. "Why not?"

"Because I hate him."

"Natalia, you don't mean that."

"I do."

"Why would you hate your dad?"

She faces me and frowns. "Because he left me. First, my mother left and then he did. No one wants me."

I hear the sadness in her voice, which I can't even blame her for, but thinking her parents *chose* to leave her isn't something I can let her continue to believe.

"You shouldn't think that. You know they wouldn't have ever left you if they had the choice."

She answers with a nonchalant shrug.

"Your parents loved you so much, Natalia, *so much*. I know you're angry, but it only hurts because of how much you loved them."

Her face softens, and I notice her eyes watering. "It hurts too much to think about loving them. So I would rather be mad at them instead."

Surprisingly, I know exactly how she feels. It's a complicated feeling between grieving for someone you loved and grieving for a relationship you once had. The last time I spoke to Ryan, I was ready to smash his face into the pavement, but the biggest regret I have is not fixing our relationship before he passed away. Now it's too late, and I'll never have that closure. I'll forever have to live with the guilt of my last hateful words to him.

"Go to hell, Ryan. Go to hell and take Jennifer with you. You two deserve each other."

Remembering those last words to him pulls me into that moment —one I'll never forget. Ryan tried to get me to talk to him and tell me some bullshit about how it *just happened*, but I was too pissed off to hear any of his excuses. It was over between Jennifer and me, but I should've mended things with him. Should've looked past it because we were family—*brothers.*

I was more than surprised to hear that he granted me guardianship of Natalia in his will. I hadn't expected that at all.

"Natalia, I'm going to tell you something that I think you need to hear."

"Okay," she says softly.

"I'm mad at your dad, too. I'm mad that he died. I'm mad that you lost your parents so early. I'm mad that we didn't get to reunite before he passed away, though it brought me to you. So sometimes when I think about how angry I am, I think about the positive things instead."

"Like me?" Her eyelashes rise.

"Yes, like you." I flash a genuine smile at her. "Even if you hate my cooking."

"Well…you've been improving."

"Or you're adapting." I wink.

"I wouldn't go that far."

I chuckle at her honesty.

We arrive at the therapist's office, and for the first time in months, Natalia isn't pouting the entire time. Dr. Kingston said she answered some of her questions and even talked a little about her anger.

"I finally see some progress with Natalia. She's opened up a little, but I think she still has a long way to go. She may even backpedal a little before coming to terms with what's happened," Dr. Kingston reports after her session.

Pushing the Limits

"As I expect." From how Natalia's handling everything, I'd have to agree with Dr. Kingston.

She leans down in front of Natalia. "I'll see you next week."

"Splendid."

"Nat." I flash her a warning look.

She shows off a fake, toothy grin. "See you then!"

I walk her out and wrap my arm around her shoulders. I know she uses sarcasm and sassy remarks to hide what she's feeling, but I want her to know she can be real with me. Know she can count on me.

"Natalia, you can always talk to me if you feel you can't talk to Dr. Kingston. About anything."

She looks up through her eyelashes and nods. Her lips barely spread into a smile, but I know she understands.

"So should we grab some food, go home, and watch a movie?" I nudge her, lightening up her mood.

She looks up and smiles. "Sure. But I'm not watching *Gladiator* again."

I laugh at her scowl and agree. "You've got it, Shorty."

After devouring Chinese takeout and watching *Thirteen Going on Thirty*, Nat passes out on the couch next to me. I look over at her and reminisce about how she has her whole life ahead of her yet. She's been dealt some rough cards, but I think we'll eventually pull each other out of this anger phase—or at least I hope so. Any more school suspensions and she might get sent to an alternative school.

I carry her to bed and cover her up with the sheets. I know she keeps a ratty old stuffed bear under her pillow. She claims she's too big to sleep with stuffed animals, but she's had it since she was a baby.

I grab the bear and stick it underneath her arm before pulling the heavier comforter over her body. I brush my hand gently over her hair and kiss her on the forehead.

My life has sure changed a lot in the past year. Before I moved out here, I was living the bachelor life. No responsibilities besides going to work and paying bills, no one telling me what I could and couldn't do, no one holding me back.

But if truth be told, it was a lonely lifestyle. It wasn't all it was cracked up to be. Having no one to come home to, no one excited to see you after a long day, no one checking up on you to make sure everything's okay. Before I left, I lived for that. I loved being in a relationship and coming home to someone I loved.

But that's all changed. I'm not sure I'll ever feel like that again.

Chapter Nine
Aspen

I work at the gallery on Thursday morning. I'm at the information desk since Kendall is out sick and Ms. Jones and Christine have a conference meeting. It's completely mundane since I'm only allowed to answer the phone, but on the bright side, the gallery is gorgeous. I love walking around and looking at everything. They're all titled, but their meanings are up for interpretation.

There's a story in every piece and sometimes the artist is the only one who knows what it is. It's almost as if each one speaks their own language. You can appreciate the beauty of the words without knowing the meaning. That's what I love about it. What one painting means to me could mean something completely different to someone else.

I walk in front of a large abstract canvas titled, *Rain at Dawn*. It's interesting, but it doesn't give away much. You have to look at it, study the details to see what the artist is saying.

In this one, they focused on the raindrops the most. On one side, a puddle is forming, and on the other, a large raindrop is about to land on the black cement. You can see a house in the background, but it's shaded and almost blurred. There's a light on through the window, but you can't see inside. The trees are all bare, which means it's fall or winter. The sky is dark and gloomy except for one small part on the right side where the sun is starting to peek out.

It's beautiful. For me, it feels like peace and happiness. I love the sound of rain. Ariel and I would play in the rain every chance we could or until Mom would yell at us to get inside. When we were kids, we'd go fishing with our dad in the summer rain or shine. One morning, he woke us up before sunrise. It had been raining, so we sat out on the boat and watched the sun come up as the rain poured down over the water.

Those days were perfect.

The longer I stare at it, the more emotional I start to feel. My eyes water, and before I know it, small tears are falling down my cheeks.

God, I'm a mess. I never let myself cry.

I head out to grab a tissue and dry my face. As I'm walking out, Professor Hampton is by the information desk.

"Holy shit," I gasp. He turns toward me and smiles. He looks delicious in his form-fitting gray suit and pale white shirt underneath. His hair is styled in a way that makes me want to run my fingers through it and…*Oh my God*. My fingers twitch at the thought. I blink, forcing my mind to stop racing long enough to speak. "You have a habit of scaring the crap out of me."

"I'm sorry. I thought you'd hear me come in." He points above the door where a bell is hanging. Every time someone comes in or leaves, it rings.

"I was getting something," I lie, hoping he doesn't question my bloodshot eyes. "What are you doing here?"

"I'm looking for my aunt. Is she here today?"

"Actually, no. She and the curator had a meeting. Kendall's out with a cold, so I'm manning the door."

"I see."

"I can tell her you stopped by." I dig around for a pen and a piece of paper. "You can leave her a note."

He smiles and steps closer. "Sure."

"Here." He stands across from me when I hand them to him.

"Do you mind writing it? She won't be able to read it otherwise if I do."

"Oh, um, sure. What should it say?"

He clears his throat as if he has something important to say. I smile but keep my head down. "Dear Aunt Mel, I stopped by to discuss an important matter with you." I look up at him and he's grinning.

"Continue…"

"Your employee, Aspen Evans, has impeccable talent, and is refusing to show it off at the Spring Art Gala…"

I glare at him.

He notices I've stopped and nods at the pen. "Keep going."

"I'm not writing that."

"Alright. I'll call her then."

I sigh. "You're insufferable."

"Determined," he counters, smirking.

"Why's it so important to you?" I ask.

He keeps his gaze locked on mine. "I've been teaching for five years and have had many students on all different levels. Some have no business being in a college-level art class, and some have so much talent, it makes me wonder why I'm the one teaching them. You are the latter." He pauses, and I suck in my lower lip at his compliment. "You've completely blown me away."

I'm at a loss for words. I don't know how to respond. I don't know what to think. My entire body is on fire, and I can't keep my eyes off him.

I swallow and focus on finding my voice. "You're very passionate about art."

I want to slap myself for sounding so dense.

"I was." He shrugs. "I've taken some time off. I haven't even thought about it in months—that is until I saw what you're capable of doing. It's inspiring."

"How does an art professor take time off from painting?"

"Actually, it's easy," he says with a laugh. "I hand out the assignments, show a video here and there, and critique everyone else."

I chuckle at his honesty. "What made you stop?"

His chest rises and falls slowly as if he's debating his words. "I haven't been in the right state of mind. Everything would look awful and then I'd get even angrier with myself."

"I know a thing or two about being angry. That's how I got into drawing," I admit but immediately wish I could take it back. I don't want him asking questions that'll lead to Ariel's death. Questions I don't want to answer.

"I like to work when I'm in a happy state of mind, which hasn't been often."

I'm surprised by how honest he's being, and a bit confused as to why he is in the first place. "Have you tried?"

"Tried what?"

"To do it when you're angry?"

"No. I have no desire to," he states firmly.

I flash a weak smile. "Maybe you should try. You might surprise yourself."

Before he can respond, the phone rings and makes me jump. Neither of us moves as the phone continues to ring. His gaze is locked on mine. "Don't you have to get that?"

"Get what?" I blink, finally focusing. "Oh, right."

He grins. "You're O for two."

"Good thing door-watching and phone answering aren't my majors."

I turn to answer the phone.

It's Ms. Jones.

"Yes, everything's fine. No, I haven't burned it down yet. Yes, I'm watching the door." I turn and see Professor Hampton smiling wide. "As a matter of fact, there's someone here. So I better let you go. Yes, I'll put my friendly face on. Mmkay, bye-bye."

I hang up and point at him. "Don't even say it."

He's laughing. "Say what?"

I'm flustered and can't think straight. "Anything. Don't say *anything*."

He's still laughing. "Okay."

Pushing the Limits

I watch Professor Hampton as he effortlessly explains our next assignment. You'd never guess by how passionately he talks about art and how knowledgeable he is in the classroom that he'd be going through some inner turmoil himself. He has such a strong, confident aura, but when you get to know more about him outside of being a teacher, you realize he could be as damaged and broken as I am.

We're working on optical illusion 3D images tonight. I love painting with colors and telling a story, but sketching is a nice break in between pieces.

I've done 3D drawings before, but I've never done them outside of class to get practice. I've done simple objects, nothing too over-the-top, but now we're stepping it up a notch and adding an illusion factor.

"Think of your favorite character. Disney, anime, hero, whatever. As long as you add a backdrop. You may have to cut parts of the paper out to pull it off but get creative."

We each settle into our areas, and as everyone's pencils are already furiously moving, I stand anxiously and stare at the blank paper.

"What's wrong?" Ellie asks, noticing my puzzled expression.

"I can't figure out what to do…"

"Girl, I've been drawing for ten minutes, and I still don't know what I'm doing."

I cackle at her confession.

"Just wing it."

"You're so helpful. Thank you."

She grins. "I'll be here all night."

I smile as I think about the Disney movies Ari and I used to watch as kids. We'd always argue over which ones to watch first. She always wanted *The Little Mermaid*, so she could say she was Ariel, the mermaid, and I'd get stuck being Ursula. I preferred *The Lion King* and *101 Dalmatians*, anything with animals, but I probably won that battle once out of every four times.

Sometimes I didn't mind, though. We'd dress up in princess gowns and dance around the house while singing—or rather shouting—the lyrics we made up.

We were so carefree and happy in those days. It's bittersweet to think about. My chest tightens as I think about those memories. Although they're happy ones, I hate that they're all I have of her. I miss everything about her, even when she was bossing me around and making me be the villain as we watched Disney movies.

And just like that, I knew exactly what I want to do.

I tune everything out and hardly notice Professor Hampton walking around even when he's watching me. I create the water, making it look like it's *in* the paper and the rock is on *top* of the paper. Ellie leans over my shoulder and gasps.

"I love that!" She has no boundaries.

"Thanks. I haven't even done the mermaid yet."

"Doesn't matter. That fucking rocks."

I smile, looking up and seeing Professor Hampton standing next to us. "What is it?"

He tilts his head and furrows his brows.

"Wow, rude much?" I crack a smile. "Like I said"—I turn toward Ellie and scowl—"it's not done yet."

"It's not bad," he says, half-impressed.

"Not bad?" Ellie gasps. "Then, for the love of all that's holy, don't look at mine."

I laugh, avoiding eye contact with Professor Hampton. "It's the Little Mermaid," I explain. "I'm going to put her body on the rock up here and then cut the paper out around her so it looks like she's coming right at you."

He nods, staring intently at the piece. "Try going deeper with the water to exaggerate the rock's placement. Then widen the rocks surrounding the water so you can see the depth of it."

"Alright. Thanks." I flash a small smile.

A faint, amused grin appears on his face as he winks before walking over to another student.

Students begin packing up and heading out as soon as it's eight o'clock. I'm right in the middle of drawing the mermaid's tail and failing miserably at it.

"I've never seen anyone curse at a Disney character before," I hear from behind.

"You haven't known me long enough. I always verbally abuse my work before I finish."

"That's an interesting concept, however…" I hear his amusement. "Let's try this."

My heart jumps a beat when he presses his chest against my back. He grabs my right hand and wraps his around it with the pencil in between our fingers. The simple action sends a lightning bolt through my fingertips straight to my heart, and for a brief second, I swear I can feel it beating harder, louder, *faster*. I close my eyes, wondering if he feels the intense electricity between us, too.

"The scales on the tail should be angled this way. The illusion should make it look like her tail is wrapped around the rock. So essentially she's on top of the rock that's sitting on top of the paper." He moves our hands to show me where to shade on the scales. "Make sense?"

I can barely comprehend a word he's saying with him so close. My body hums when his muscles contract against my skin when he brushes the pencil over the paper.

Jesus. I need to breathe. I don't think I've exhaled since he started talking thirty seconds ago.

"Aspen?" he questions again.

I clear my throat, releasing a breath. "Um…" I blink, trying to think of something smart to say, but nothing is coming. My mind is literally blank.

"Here…" he offers, gripping my hand tighter, as his other hand wraps around my waist and squeezes my hip. My breath hitches as I work on calming down. "Ninety-degree angles, see? Then shade the tail in over here."

"Okay…" I choke out, gulping. My eyelids feel like they're taped against my skin as I try to comprehend how close we are. I inhale and can smell his scent. *Christ.* I need to focus. "I think I understand. Thank you."

Our bodies are still fused, our hands still touching. "You're welcome."

The room is so silent I can hear the vent above us blowing out air. His breath tickles my neck. I'm two seconds away from spinning around and slamming my lips against his. Especially since I can feel his distinct bulge against my lower back, confirming he's struggling with the same forbidden attraction as I am.

Moments later, reality crashes back into my mind, and I know making out with my hot art professor would be a bad—*but hot*—thing. The only reason I came out to California, besides needing to get away from home, was because I was offered a scholarship. My parents offered to pay for my entire education if I went to a college closer to home, but I wanted nothing to do with that idea. I didn't want their money or any ties to them at all. I don't know the exact rules of my scholarship, but I'm certain having an affair with your professor is grounds for losing it and possibly being expelled.

"Well, I'll continue this next class," I finally say, breaking the tension. "Thanks again for your help."

He releases my hand and steps away from me. "No problem. It's my job."

"Right." I turn and smile before grabbing the easel and drawing to store away.

He walks to his desk and collects his stuff as I pack up my supplies and start heading out. "Have a nice night, Professor Hampton."

He looks up, a flustered expression on his face. "You too, Aspen."

Chapter Ten
Morgan

As soon as my hand slides against her smooth skin, all rational thinking leaves my mind. I know I shouldn't be crossing the lines with a student, but with Aspen, I can't help myself.

How is it that a girl with so much talent, so much beauty, is filled with so much pain? I know she hasn't told me much, but it's enough to figure out. Her sister died years ago, leaving her feeling empty and bitter. She uses art and solitude to cope, to express her emotions and feelings, but she has this uniqueness about her. Every time I see her, she's glowing. Her smile, her laugh, her body language. It's as if she's strong on the outside but falling apart on the inside. I can tell because I've been doing the same for five years.

Five years too long.

I think about her all day Friday, and once Natalia goes to bed, I head downstairs to where I've packed away my supplies for the past six months. My paints, pastels, canvases, and brushes—they are all here, mocking me. I've avoided it all this time, unable to connect with anything other than anger.

I used to work on my art a lot in Ohio, relieved to have a fresh start. I used that optimistic feeling as a guide to create new inspirations. However, after Ryan's death, I hadn't been able to focus on anything at all. I only thought of him. Then I'd see his face in my mind and be disgusted with myself that I allowed so much time to pass before we could make amends. But now that time was useless. I waited too long, and I hated myself for it.

I get out the old easel I had tucked away. I set up my old brushes and tubes and stare at the blank canvas in front of me.

Blank canvas.

That's what being in California truly represents. That's what I need to stay focused on.

It's what Natalia and I should be focusing on.

I only hope it's good enough to help her move on—to help us move on. However, six months wasn't that long ago, and I know she'll be hurting and grieving for years, but it's something we need to work on together.

You should try it sometime…you might surprise yourself.

Aspen's words repeat in my head as I look at it. Taking a breath, I close my eyes and search for courage. Moments later, I open them to the same blank canvas and no desire to change it.

Frustrated, I throw the brushes down and walk out. I know Aspen's probably right. If I can get out of my cluttered mind and connect my frustration and anger to that creative side of myself—the part that takes control when the brush is in my hand as if it's another extension of myself—I could use it as the motivation, but it's not there.

I head upstairs and undress before getting into the shower. After the day I've had and the intense encounter with Aspen, I need a cold shower. I've never had someone affect me the way she does, especially a student. I've always been professional and kept my distance, but she's making it nearly impossible, even though I know I should be making more of an effort.

As I wash my body, thoughts surface of her in those leopard print fuck-me heels and tight, painted-on jeans, and I feel myself getting hard again.

Just as I remind myself that I need to be more careful around Aspen, I find myself lost in thoughts of her. My mind goes blank on what's right and wrong, and my body happily responds to the image of her.

Her voice, her lips, her soft skin.

Pushing the Limits

The visions haunt me while I work on thinking of anything else. Unable to erase the thoughts, I reach down and stroke my cock. I know it's wrong, and I shouldn't be fantasizing about her but fuck it. I haven't been able to stop thinking about Aspen since the moment we met. Hell, since the moment I started looking through her portfolio. The emotion she pours into her work and the way it captivates me is something I can't explain.

Resting a hand on the shower wall, my head falls, and I tighten my grip. Her soft giggle echoes in my head as I imagine her perfectly curved body. Groaning, I punish myself, gripping tighter. As my hips thrust wildly into my palm, I imagine Aspen's wet pussy instead of my rough palm. She'd beg for more as I thrust deeper with each solid movement. I wouldn't stop until she cried out my name, screaming in ecstasy as I released inside her. Pumping faster, my body tightens with the thought of her juices covering my cock.

I'd look down at her, pleased with how her body looks flush and sated. Those pert breasts would bounce every time I buried myself. Imagining my name falling from those cherry red lips again takes me over the edge, and I come powerfully, groaning her name.

Once my breathing gets under control, I turn on the warm water and slowly wash myself off again.

What the fuck am I going to do with this fascination? Better yet, how the hell do I convince her of what I know we both want?

Chapter Eleven
Aspen

Kendall and I make plans to meet up for lunch at a diner near campus. She's loud and bubbly as usual, but I still feel half asleep. After last night's class, I hadn't been able to sleep.

My mind was occupied elsewhere with a certain professor.

"So what do you think?" Kendall asks, breaking me out of my self-induced coma.

I blink. "Of?"

"Jesus, Aspen. What's gotten into you?" She brings a forkful of mashed potatoes up to her mouth and devours it.

"Nothing, sorry. I'm tired. What were you saying?"

"My cousin, Piper, is coming to visit from Arizona. Can she stay in your apartment since your couch pulls out?"

"Um…" I drawl out, grabbing my cup of coffee and taking a long sip. "Not sure that's a good idea."

"Oh…" She continues chewing. "Alright." I hear the disappointment in her tone as her lips turn down.

"Sorry, I don't do well with having a roommate."

"Didn't you have roommates your freshman year?"

"Yeah, and it was pure hell. I had a single bedroom, which was nice, but we had to share everything else. So that sucked."

"She'll only sleep there. I can tell her to hang out in my apartment during the day or whenever you're home if that'll help."

"Okay, maybe. I don't do well sharing my space. I get anxious, especially when it's someone I don't know well." I shrug, hoping she understands. "It's fine."

"No, I understand. Sorry, I forget how bad it can sometimes get." She flashes me a sympathetic smile, making me want to change the heavy topic as soon as possible.

Kendall's witnessed a few of my embarrassing episodes before. We were drinking at her place one night, and I ended up falling asleep on her bedroom floor. In the middle of the night, I had a night terror and woke up screaming and shaking. She was two seconds away from calling 911, but once I convinced her I wasn't having a seizure, she calmed down enough to let me explain.

"You going out this weekend?"

"Maybe. Is Zoe working?"

"Yeah, I think she has the dinner shifts Friday and Saturday, then we'll stick around to hang out afterward."

"Yeah, I'll probably head out for a bit. I have some studying to do tonight, though."

"It's only the second week of classes. How can you have homework to do already?" She grimaces.

"Because I don't want to get behind. Some of us"—I narrow my eyes at her—"are trying to get into graduate school."

"Graduate smaduate."

I shake my head at her and laugh. "I'll come out as long as you buy me a drink."

She smiles. "Don't I always?"

When we finish eating, we go to our afternoon classes. Once I'm home, I work on the blog assignments I have for Professor Hampton, and I quickly get them done. Then when that's finished, I have the urge to clean.

And by clean, I mean scrub every inch of my apartment until my fingers bleed.

I'm not always this neurotic. Cleaning helps clear my mind when I have too much going on to focus on painting. I go through episodes of manic behavior, but more often, it's depression that takes over.

I see my doctor regularly to consult about my medication and to make adjustments. After six years of suffering from depression, I was diagnosed with post-traumatic stress disorder, or PTSD. Recurring dreams of the event, flashbacks, anxiety, depression, and avoidance are all areas I suffer from. Not to mention the secondary trauma from my mother and the way she's blamed me all this time. But no matter how much I try to get my life together and move forward, a dream or flashback will suck me back in. It's a vicious cycle and it's hard to see any light at the end of the tunnel.

A loud beating at my door grabs my attention and when I whip the door open, Kendall is standing there with a tense look on her face.

"What's the matter?" I ask, dumbfounded.

"What the hell, Aspen? I've called you like four times, and I've been banging on your door for like five minutes."

"You have?"

"*Yes!* Why is your music so loud?" she shouts, covering her hands over her ears.

"It is?"

She lowers her hands. "What's wrong? Are you alright?"

"Yeah," I lie. "Fine. Just doing some cleaning." I hold up the towel from my left hand.

"Oh my God…" Her eyes widen as she pushes through and walks inside. "It smells like bleach and Pine-Sol had a love child and then threw up all over your apartment."

I scowl and shut the door. "I told you I was cleaning."

"No, you're getting high."

I burst out laughing. "I am not."

"Between the loud rap music and toxic bleach smell, the cops will be called in no time."

I hadn't even realized my music was on. I walk over and shut my stereo off and then open a window. "There. Better?"

"A little."

"Sorry. I lost myself for a bit." She walks toward me and gives me a sympathetic frown. "I'm fine," I repeat, hoping she'll drop it.

"I'll have Piper stay with another friend, okay?"

"This isn't about Piper. I said it was fine." I wave her off.

"Aspen, I may not have known you for long, but I know enough to see when you aren't *fine*."

I exhale. "I'm sorry. I don't know what's wrong."

"Obviously the anxiety of having a stranger stay here is too much, and I'm sorry I even asked. I should've known better."

I hate that she says that.

"It's not about Piper, okay? My mind is a clusterfuck right now."

She sits down and pats her hand on the couch. "Are you sure? Wanna talk about it?"

I sigh. "What? Are we going to have a slumber party and talk about our hopes and dreams?" I mock and sit next to her. "Because if that's the case, I'm going to need wine."

Wine in hand, we plop down on the couch and Kendall wastes no time asking me about what caused me to go crazy Merry Maid on my apartment.

Taking an exaggeratedly large gulp of wine, I consider my words carefully, knowing I can't tell her the truth about what is going on and hating that I have to evade her questions.

"Honestly, it's a bit of everything. My mom wanting me to come home for spring break, my hectic school and work schedule. I'm overwhelmed, and cleaning helps me regroup."

She takes a quick sip from her glass. "Yeah, that makes sense. I know the pressure can increase anxiety, too." She knows certain triggers can increase my anxiety.

I nod, thankful she doesn't pry further. "Enough about my crazy life. Tell me, how's Kellan?" I empty my glass. "Coming along yet?" I tease, waggling my eyebrows. "Or rather, *coming* at all?" Her cheeks heat, and I know I've successfully changed the subject.

"You're such an ass. You know that, right?"

"So that's a no?"

"That's an...*almost*."

I shake my head. "That's unacceptable, Kendall. Maybe he's not that *into* you?"

"He gets hard just fine, *thank you*. He doesn't want to screw it up by moving too fast. Even if my vagina is filling up with cobwebs."

"Cobweb pussy," I confirm. "I hear it's a brutal disease."

"So is *too much cock in the mouth* disease."

"But it's oh so worth it." I wink and she pretends to gag.

"Alright, screw this girly crap. Let's go hang with Jack and José."

"Deal."

We run to the liquor store and grab two large bottles that are sure to keep us company.

Chapter Twelve
Aspen

Everyone starts packing up after class Tuesday night, but I stay put. My mind is focused and centered, and I don't want to stop.

"You know you have another week to work on this, right?" I hear him directly behind me as I stand in front of my easel. But I don't face him.

"Yes."

"I can tell you're passionate about art."

I smile in return as he steps to my side. I can see him out of the corner of my eye. "You don't have to stay. I'll be done in a minute."

"It's fine. I've nowhere to be."

"Oh yeah?" I glance at him. "No wife or girlfriend to get home to?"

A pleased smirk spreads across his face. "That's a personal question."

Fear etches over my face and my fingers still. "You're right. I'm sorry."

"But..." he drawls out slowly. "Class is over."

Our gazes meet and he steps toward me.

"So, there's no rule against asking personal questions."

"You made that up."

He stifles a laugh.

"Even after hours, you're still my professor and I'm still your student."

He takes another step closer.

"I'll answer it if you answer one."

I act unaffected by his proximity, but inside I'm screaming as I continue moving the brush over the canvas.

"No, I don't have a wife or girlfriend waiting for me," I deadpan. His crooked smile encourages me to keep going. "Although, I am known to get *friendly* with my girlfriends after a few drinks."

He nearly chokes, making the tension slip away.

He's even closer now. The only barrier between us is the easel. But it's situated more to my right, so his body is in full view. He stares intently with his lips in a firm line.

"Husband or boyfriend?"

"Why would you want to know something like that?" The heat builds between my legs, my breath uneven and raspy as I realize we're nearly toe-to-toe.

"Because I want to know if I can kiss you or not." His voice is low and steady, confidence radiating off him as he towers over me, his hand resting on my arm.

My heart thuds against my chest as I come to terms with what he's said.

He wants to *kiss* me?

I don't know how to react. My head is spinning, and I think perhaps I heard him wrong.

"That's hardly appropriate, Professor Hampton."

"Why? Because you're my student or because you've been thinking about kissing me, too?"

My brush freezes mid-stroke. I swallow, trying to process his words.

He leans in close, bringing my attention to his face.

"Answer the question, Aspen."

"Which one?" I counter, feeling the rapid up and down movements of my chest.

Before he can respond, a soft knock grabs our attention behind us. Professor Van Bergen.

Pushing the Limits

I jerk at the same time Professor Hampton takes a step, removing his hand from my arm.

"Am I interrupting?" The distaste in her tone doesn't go unnoticed as she notices the space between Professor Hampton and me.

"Not at all," he replies smoothly, shoving his hands into his pockets. "What can I help you with?"

She steps closer. "I saw your lights were still on, so I wanted to make sure everything was alright." Silence lingers in the air, and I lower my head to avoid the awkwardness.

"Everything's fine."

My head tilts up to see that he's turned his attention to me.

"Aspen wanted some advice on her project."

"Oh, okay." She's not buying it for a second, and the fake smile on her face indicates her irritation. "I'll catch up with you later." She shifts her eyes to mine as she glares, almost as if she's giving me a silent warning to back off her territory.

We watch as she leaves, and then it's the two of us again. My shallow breaths echo as he continues to stare as if he's still waiting for my answer.

But I don't give it to him. I grab my bag and swing it over my shoulder. "I should go."

"You don't have to leave."

"It's fine. It's late and you probably have to lock up."

I grab the painting and put it on the rack to dry, then quickly wash my brushes before I take the easel and put it away. He continues standing in the same spot with an intense gaze.

"You can stay if you want." His voice is low before he clarifies, "To finish working."

I glance at him, trying to read his expression. I scrape my teeth along my lower lip and watch as he lingers on my mouth. I swallow and reply with a hint of hesitation, "Maybe next time."

Chapter Thirteen
Morgan

No matter how hard I try, I still can't get the girl with the feisty attitude, driven determination, and glossy cherry lips out of my goddamn head. It makes me want to cross all the lines to feed the intense urge building up inside me. I think about her mouth and how I want to press mine to hers to see if she'd kiss me back. Every time those bright green eyes look up, I envision her kneeling in front of me with her lips wrapped around my cock and she tastes what she does to me.

As soon as I'd release inside her perfect throat, I'd throw her on top of the bed and wrap those red heels around my shoulders as I sucked on her clit until she came screaming my name.

Yes, I've fantasized about plenty of scenarios that all end with Aspen Evans naked in my bed.

Except, I wouldn't be able to stop there.

But it's more than what she does.

I think about her paintings and how the world melts away from her as she focuses on the assignment with intense concentration. I think about how beautiful and intelligent she is. About how humble and shy she acts whenever I compliment her talent. I think about how moving and emotional her pieces are and what they truly represent. I think about how we've suffered losses of people we love and how differently we've handled it. She puts her feelings on paper and the emotions spill out perfectly. I've never met a student like her before. Her talent is far beyond her years of schooling. But then I think about her anxiety attacks and wonder what triggers them. For someone who looks so put together, she must be hiding a much darker secret inside.

As of late, I'm finding any excuse at all to see her.

I swing by the coffee house Thursday morning after my second class of the day. Instead of ordering my usual house blend coffee, I order two lattes.

I can't contain my smile when I walk into the art gallery and see Aspen at the information desk playing on her phone.

She looks up as soon as she hears the bell over the door.

"You're getting better at this job already." I set the cups of coffee down in front of her.

"You're going to need a punch card if you keep coming in here." She gives me a sideways glance that tells me she doesn't mind my visits.

"I came to force some caffeine on you. I don't need you falling asleep in my class again."

Her jaw drops. "I did not fall asleep!" She wraps her hand around the cup and takes a sip of the drink anyway.

"Don't think I can't see my students because you all have easels in front of you."

"I closed my eyes for twenty seconds," she deadpans.

"It was two and a half minutes."

"Most students would've filed a harassment claim with the amount of time you spend staring at me."

The corners of my lips curl up in pure amusement, but the excitement in her tone tells me she likes it when I stare at her. "The only way you can know how much I'm staring at you is if you're staring, too."

"I'm not. I don't," she clips.

"*Right.*" I bring the cup up to my mouth and watch as her gaze lingers on it. "Think you can come to class early? I have a project for you."

"Just me?"

"Yes."

"What do I have to do?" she asks suspiciously.

"Show up and you'll find out."

A playful grin spreads across her face, and I know she's thinking exactly what I'm thinking. "Alright, fine, but you should know I carry pepper spray in my bag at all times."

"Duly noted." I smirk and tap the bottom of my cup against the desktop before taking it away. "See you in class, Aspen." I wink, leaving her speechless as I walk out the door.

Just as I'm reading over blog posts, Claire knocks on the door, grabbing my attention. The moment I look up, she's again asking me to go out with her. She does this randomly and tries to seduce me with her body and words.

"I have to pick my niece up in a minute and drop her off at my parents' before my night class. But thanks for the invite." I give my best sincere tone and smile without coming off too rude. I don't know how many times I have to reject her invites before she gets the hint, but apparently, she's going to keep trying.

"Sure, no worries. Maybe another time." I hear the hopefulness in her tone and hate that I'll have to eventually crush her hopes if she thinks I'll ever go out on a date with her.

"Of course," I lie, but considering I need this job, I keep it as friendly as possible. I know how tight-knit these small schools can be. You piss off one professor, and suddenly, the dean is uninviting you to his annual summer BBQ.

I start packing up my things, hoping she gets the hint to leave. Once she finally does, I head out to my car and drive to my parents' house.

Pushing the Limits

As I arrive at the school and wait for Natalia to come out, I think about the last university I worked at out in Ohio. It wasn't much larger than CSLA, but still heavily focused on the arts. I knew all the professors by name and we often went out on the weekends. When I first moved to Columbus, I hadn't known anyone. Another professor, Trent Wiser, befriended me right away and introduced me to the majority of the other professors. It was nice having people I could connect with on a professional and personal level. It took some time, but after a while, it became home.

Since having to leave, I've been trying to get that feeling back. The feeling of being comfortable in your own surroundings. But as long as my past was here, mocking me every chance it could, I worried I'd never have it again.

The sound of the car door opening grabs my attention to Natalia getting into the passenger side. Her face etches in a frown, and I know before I ask, her day wasn't good.

"Hey, Short Stuff."

"Hi."

"What number?"

"Three."

"What happened?"

"Henry Ashby is a douche."

"No swearing." I remind her. "Did the teacher write a note for me?"

"No. I didn't tattle."

"What'd he do?"

"Nothing. Just drop it." She stares out the window.

I wish I understood girls.

"Natalia. Tell me what he did."

"He makes fun of me, okay? He calls me Fatty Natty and then tells his friends to call me that, too."

My jaw locks as my palm tightens around the steering wheel. "I'm calling your teacher."

She whips her head to face me. "No, I said drop it. I'll take care of him myself. He's such a little prick, I—"

"Natalia!" I scold. "I'm calling your teacher. End of discussion."

She rolls her eyes and looks away. "Whatever."

We're halfway to the house before I speak up again. "You're not fat, Natalia. You're beautiful."

She ignores my compliment, but I know she heard me.

"You look a lot like your mom," I say softly.

She finally shifts. "I do?"

I smile. "Yes. You have the same wild and crazy curls. And you have her sassy, take-no-shit attitude."

She flashes a weak smile, then lowers her head. "I wish I remembered her."

"I know, Shorty. I wish you did, too."

We arrive at my parents' house but stay put until Natalia's ready. I wait until she wipes away the tears she pretends don't exist.

"Okay. Let's go." She whips open the car door and gets out as if nothing happened.

I feel for her. As much as my situation sucks, hers sucks worse. She's lost both parents before the age of twelve. She's angry and bitter, and I wish I knew how to help her.

But I've been angry and bitter for five years, and I have no clue how to even help myself.

I hear the clicking of her heels before I see her. I look up and see her walking in with her bag hanging off her shoulder. She looks stunning in her black skinny jeans and a white top that hangs off her shoulder just enough to see the smooth skin underneath. I look down and smirk when I notice bright red heels.

Waiting for her to come to me, I stay behind my desk. I lean back in my chair and cross my arms over my chest.

Pushing the Limits

She tilts her head and rolls her eyes. "You're kinda bad at this teacher thing."

"I take offense to that."

"You should." She laughs. "Now you want to tell me why I've been sentenced to early class time?" I can see her mind spinning with the way she's fidgeting with her strap, but she's trying to put a straight face on.

It's fucking adorable how antsy and nervous she gets around me. Which makes me want to do it more to see how far I can push her.

"Grab a blank canvas, easel, and three oil paint colors."

She drops her bag on the floor and glares. "You're so bossy."

"It's part of my job."

She looks up at the clock on the wall. "Technically, it's not for another forty-five minutes."

I sit up in my chair and arch my brow until she budges.

"Fine."

I flash a victorious smile as she continues glaring.

It only takes her a minute to set up and then she's eagerly waiting.

"Make something happy."

Her brows furrow and she frowns. "What?"

"Happy. To feel delighted, pleased, or glad."

"I know what the definition of happy is." She shakes her head. "*Why?*"

"I want to see if you're capable."

"I am."

"Prove it," I insist.

She sighs. "Fine. But you can't watch me."

"That wasn't the deal."

"Deal? I'm here against my will."

"Don't be so dramatic."

"You're lucky I love art."

Smiling in return, I say just above a whisper, "I know."

I am definitely the lucky one here.

She bites her lip before looking away. She dips her brush and then strokes it against the canvas. Watching her gives me goose bumps. I could watch her paint for hours.

She glances over the top every few minutes or so. She doesn't say anything as she continues and checks to see if I'm still watching her. I can barely peel my eyes away when I check the clock to make sure we don't run out of time.

"Alright. Done." She sets the brush down and smiles.

I'm intrigued to see what she came up with in a matter of thirty minutes. I hadn't expected her to do a masterpiece, but I wanted to challenge her to explore a different part of her psyche.

"Ready?" she asks.

"Let's see it."

She spins the easel around and stands next to it as she waits for my reaction.

It's simple, but so perfectly fitting. "It's a vase of lilies," she explains softly, all teasing aside.

The vase is tinted in a light pink color. The green from the stems pops out, bright and full of life. The lilies are left white, but only half of them have bloomed all the way.

"It's stunning," I say honestly.

She shrugs. "Had I been given more time and supplies, I could've been more detailed."

"As true as that may be, that wasn't the assignment."

The corners of her mouth curl up. "So, do I pass?"

I round my desk to where she's standing. "Not quite."

She looks up, her brows furrowed.

"The meaning. What's the meaning behind a vase of lilies?"

Her head bows. "Nothing. It's just a vase of flowers."

"Aspen…" I say roughly, and she meets my eyes. "What's it mean?"

She inhales slowly and lowers her gaze to the floor. "It reminds me of my sister."

"The one who passed away?" I probe.

"Yes."

"She passed six years ago, right?"

"You remembered?" Her mood shifts immediately.

"Yes, of course. That must've been hard. Losing someone you loved so much at such a young age."

"It was." She inhales deeply. "It is."

"I'm sorry. I know how it feels to lose a sibling."

Her head pops up. "I'm sorry. It sucks." She gives me a sympathetic glance.

"Do you want to talk about it?"

She frowns. "I hate talking about it."

"Is that why you paint her so much?"

She sighs, releasing a relieved breath. "Yes. It's my way of coping. I don't think I'll ever get over it. I don't think I want to get over it because that means I'm accepting it, and no matter how much time passes, I don't want to accept it."

"That's the most honest answer I've ever heard." I want to wrap my arms around her and squeeze all her pain away. "I haven't accepted my brother's death, either."

"When did he pass away?"

I step back and hesitate before responding. "Six months ago."

Her eyes widen as her lips part. "Oh my God! I'm so sorry, Professor Hampton. Honestly, I'm such an ass."

"What? Why would you say that?"

"Because I've been crying over my dead sister for six years when your brother died only months ago."

"Everyone grieves differently and there's no timetable." I give her a sincere look. "You either heal and move on, or you learn how to hide it better as time wears on."

"I'm not that good at hiding it. If I didn't get to make art, I'd be a mess."

I take a step closer, much too close, closer than I should, but I can't help myself. I bring a hand to her cheek and rub the pad of my thumb softly over her smooth skin. "We can be a mess together if that helps."

My gaze's drawn to her mouth as she pulls her bottom lip between her teeth. I want to pin her up against the wall and kiss those lips until they bruise. Then I want those smooth, long legs wrapped tightly around me while she's wearing those bright red, incredible fuck-me heels. I want to feel her nails dig into my back as she moans in pleasure.

And I want her not to be my student so I can do those things to her.

She covers my hand with hers, and for a split moment, I'm afraid she's going to pull it off but doesn't. She pushes deeper into my hand and closes her eyes. "I miss her. Every day." She inhales slowly. "Every damn day I feel broken and that I'll never feel whole again."

I can hear the pain in her voice, and it nearly breaks me.

How can someone so beautiful and so gifted bear so much pain? She's an oddity in my eyes, and every part of her pain has obviously contributed to how she expresses it on paper.

"I'd like to say I don't understand, but I understand too well." She releases my hand and it falls to my side, feeling cold the moment it loses contact with hers.

"Were you two close?" she asks, and I hear the genuine interest in her voice, but my jaw ticks at the thought of how I have to answer that.

"Growing up, we were. But then we weren't for a long time." Saying it aloud hurts more than I had anticipated. She looks at me with sincerity, and for some reason, it makes me feel safe in telling her. "We hadn't talked in a long time."

"Five years?"

My brows furrow in question. "Yeah. How'd you know?"

She shrugs. "Lucky guess." She lets out a low, sweet chuckle. "Ms. Jones mentioned you hadn't been home in five years."

"Ah, yeah. I'd forgotten about that."

"So, what happened?" She clears her throat. "Sorry, I shouldn't ask that."

"No, it's fine." I'm quick to brush her concerns off. I take a deep breath and fight the emotions. "I found him in bed with my fiancée. He had lost his wife a few years prior to that and it changed him."

"Oh my God…" Her eyes widen in shock as a hand covers her face. "God, I'm sorry." Her hand drops and my gaze focuses on her mouth, so full and *off-limits*.

I purse my lips. If she only knew how sorry *I* am.

"I haven't forgiven myself for not returning before it was too late. I left and hadn't come home. I'll never get those years back." The words come much too easy, but her silky voice filled with agony and understanding makes it feel natural to talk to her.

"It's a double-edged sword, huh?" Her voice is soft with a tinge of agony. "Understanding the pain and living with the pain."

"I recognized it the moment I saw your portfolio."

She tilts her head but doesn't say anything. She sets down the canvas and goes to the drying rack where she left the portrait of her sister she'd done weeks ago.

"This one speaks to me the most." She brings it over.

"I can see a lot of you in it." I take a step so I'm standing next to her. I point a finger at the contrast of her painting. "The dark shading and light elements represent a battle. The battle of feeling happy and guilty that you want to be happy." Her expression's frozen. "You live through the pain every day, but it's dual. The pain of what happened to you and the pain of feeling guilty for wanting to move on."

She swallows. "Every day is a battle. And yet, no one wins."

"You never do when it's a battle against yourself," I say, stepping closer. "With internal battles, you either give in or end the battle altogether."

"What if you can't do either?"

"There's always a choice," I remind her.

"The choice to feel happy or let the pain consume you," she confirms. "I wish I could push out the pain and invite the happiness in without feeling guilty about it."

"Why can't you?"

She glances at it and then at me. "Because I'm reminded of her every time I look in the mirror."

"Do you think she'd want you to be happy?" I ask, knowing damn well what her answer will be.

"Yeah, of course. She was always so energetic and smiling. It was contagious. I wish I could stop missing her. Stop thinking about the what-ifs and if it had been me instead."

Without permission, I wrap my finger around a misplaced piece of her golden hair. She keeps her gaze locked on mine as I slowly tuck it behind her ear. I'm closer than before, and this time I don't back up.

The air between us is electric. There's no other way to explain it. The way her stare bleeds into me, the way her lips part when our eyes connect, and the way she looks at me when I'm the only one who knows how to speak her language—it's *electric*.

I wait for her to make a move—indicate that she wants what I want—but she's barely breathing.

Deciding I can't wait for her anymore and that the risk is worth it, I lean in, but before I can do anything, she breaks away at the sound of a door creaking.

"Professor Hamp—"

I lower my hand and turn toward the door to a student of mine.

"Kara…" I say to avoid an awkward silence. "What can I help you with?"

Aspen starts busying herself with her supplies while Kara continues walking in and begins talking again. "So sorry to… interrupt. I thought I'd catch you before your next class starts. I had a quick question about our latest assignment."

"Sure, what can I help you with?"

The way her arm brushes against mine doesn't go unnoticed, but neither does the fact that Aspen walks out without a second glance. I know she'll be back before class starts, but I have the urge to run after her even though I know I can't. Almost getting caught by a student is enough to make me realize I need to get my head straight.

But around her, I can't think at all.

Chapter Fourteen

Aspen

By Saturday, I need to clear my head of all thoughts of Professor Hampton.

I invite Kendall out to lunch with me, hoping for a much-needed distraction. I would've invited Zoe, but she was still in bed from her late Friday night shift.

However, if there's anyone who can drown out my own thoughts, it's Kendall.

"I've never asked. What made you pick California?" she says after our food arrives.

"I needed to get some sun," I say dryly, avoiding eye contact.

"Oh, speaking of sun, you should come with us paddle boarding this summer. My friend, Beef, is an instructor and is going to teach me. You'd have a total blast!" Her eyes light up as I fork a piece of chicken in my mouth.

"His name is Beef?" I inquire, furrowing my brows.

"Well, his last name is Beefer. I've always called him Beef because he's all *beefed* up."

I snort. "Nice."

"Don't be judgy."

"You two never hooked up? Does Kellan know you plan to paddle board with hot, beefy guys?"

She glares, and I laugh.

"I'm just asking," I say innocently.

"Don't even get me started."

"I'm starting to notice a pattern."

"If you must know, we have not. Not from a lack of trying, though. Before Kellan, I ended up dating a wide range of weirdos."

"Do tell." I grab my drink and take a quick sip.

"Beef is into fitness, which is fine. But I'm more in the *I'll only run if I'm being chased by a bear* category."

"So nothing in common?" I offer.

"No. We're better off as friends." She finishes chewing and takes a drink, her cheeks reddening.

"So what about these other guys you dated?"

"There was Lance. He was great…*at first*. From the outside anyway. Good-looking, full-time job, owned his own car and house. Then we met up for drinks and dinner."

"I'm afraid to even ask…"

She sighs and rolls her eyes before speaking in a high-pitched mock tone. "This restaurant—*brilliant!* This food—*brilliant!* The music—*brilliant!* My outfit—"

"Brilliant?"

"Oh my God! It was a fucking nightmare!" I can't stop the round of laughter that escapes my throat at her facial expressions. "And then when I asked about his job, he said *brilliant* thirteen times!" Her jaw drops. "Thirteen times! I counted!"

By now, we're hysterically laughing.

I manage to swallow my food down without choking, but not without effort. When the waitress checks on us, she responds, "Brilliant. The food was brilliant. The drinks were brilliant. *You* were brilliant."

I don't know how she manages to keep a straight face, but once the waitress purses her lips and responds with a cold, "Great, I'm glad to hear it," comment and not so casually leaves the bill on the table before walking away, we burst into a fit of giggles again.

"I don't think anyone will ever be able to top off Mr. Brilliant." I shake my head, reassured he has to be the worst of the worst.

Pushing the Limits

"Sad thing is…I'm sure some of the others could." She takes another drink although she shouldn't.

"Don't you do background checks on these guys? Urine samples?"

"I should," she agrees, but the frantic bobbing of her head lets me know it's the alcohol taking its course. "Or someone should. Oh! Like an agency! A pre-dating agency." She clears her throat and continues, *"We provide the work up so you can do the work down!"*

I cover my mouth. "That's the worst slogan I've ever heard."

"But admit it…you'd use it."

"It might scare them off."

She shrugs. "Then at least we'd know beforehand. No time wasted!"

"Speaking of wasted…" I murmur, but she waves me off. "Alright…so who else?"

"Oh! There was Quinn. I met him through a mutual friend from high school. So we start talking online, which leads to texting and *other things*, and when we finally plan to meet up, he tells me he doesn't drink! Like what are we, cavemen?"

I burst out laughing, and when I start to notice that other people are staring at us, I suggest it's time we get going.

I put some cash down on the table to cover the bill, plus her tip, before sliding out my chair and motioning her to do the same.

"I get being all religious and not drinking, or even being sober because you used to fancy the bottle a little too much, but he's never *ever* had alcohol even when he turned twenty-one."

We begin walking out to the car when I loop my arm inside hers, mostly to make sure she doesn't fall on her ass.

"How's that even possible?" I wrinkle my nose, getting into the driver's seat.

"I don't even know. That's like staying a virgin after you're married. It doesn't make any sense at all!"

We're about halfway to the apartment building when she brings up the one thing I had hoped she wouldn't ask.

"So, I know you're busy at school and work, but have any art nerds grabbed your attention long enough to stick around for more than a night?"

105

I giggle at her choice of words. I know I can't tell her, although I'm dying to tell someone I'm crushing hard for my professor—but I need to be careful. Even though I'm almost one hundred percent certain she wouldn't say anything, I can't risk it.

"Nope."

"C'mon…no one who's interested you for more than twelve hours?" She perks a brow, sporting a devilish grin.

"There's been an *interest*, but that's it. We just talk and flirt."

"And?" she prompts.

"And nothing. It's best if we stay friends."

"Well…friends can have fun, too."

I smile at her insinuation. "As much as I wouldn't mind some of that *fun*, it can't happen, either."

"Alright, Aspen. I'm starting to notice a theme."

"Which is?"

"You have a boring life."

"I beg to differ." I scoff. "Since we're on the topic of interests, when are you finally going to kick that non-grabby-hands boyfriend of yours to the curb?"

She exaggerates a gasp. "He is *plenty* grabby."

"Oh, has he reached the elbow finally?" I snort.

"I hate you!" she hisses with a laugh, throwing a pathetic punch. "We are way past the elbow!"

"Oh, good!" I glance in her direction. "So I can expect a graphic second base story coming soon?"

"Gah! I wonder if it's because he's small. Do you think that's why he's put off on going all the way?"

She leans her head back on the headrest and squeezes the bridge of her nose, sighing.

"There's only one way to find out, isn't there?"

"That's it…we're doing it. It's been three months, dammit. I'm gonna get naked and jump on top of him. There's no way a guy would push this"—she waves a hand down her body—"away."

"Agreed. I'd even let you get to a few bases before I pushed you off."

"You're such a bitch!" She chuckles.

Pushing the Limits

We arrive at the complex and head inside. I plan to nap before we head out for the night. "So you're meeting Zoe at the bar around ten?" she confirms before we each head into our apartments.

"Yup. Save me a seat." I wink before unlocking my door and stepping inside.

I wouldn't normally think twice about going out with the girls and finding a guy to take home, but since getting closer to Professor Hampton, it makes my stomach turn thinking about bringing anyone to my place. Although I have no claim over him, it doesn't stop the burning desire to wish I did. The way it feels to be around him isn't a feeling I've ever had before.

He makes me feel things I shouldn't.

Seeing Professor Hampton twice a week is messing with my head. The next week goes like the previous three weeks—work, school, noticeable throbbing between my legs, painting, daydreaming of what Professor Hampton's lips would feel like against mine.

How his naked body would look and feel...

The constant struggle of trying to stay focused around him while wondering what he'd look like naked and tangled in my sheets is distracting to the point where I almost left the house without a shirt on and about walked into a closed door when I finally realized it.

It's becoming a safety hazard.

Every time I'm concentrating on a project in class, I sense him watching me. Even when I'm not facing him, I feel his presence near me, and I wonder if I'm crazy for having these mixed feelings. I know he feels them too and that confuses me even more.

I've never wanted a guy to have those types of feelings for me. I know I can't return them. I know the emotional baggage I carry around is too much for anyone to be burdened with, so I keep it inside. I push it deeper and deeper, never exposing it for what it is —*fear and guilt*.

It started in high school after Ariel's funeral. I was allowed to take a week off before returning, but it might as well have been one day because no matter how long it was, it never would've been enough. Students stared at me, teachers pitied me, and my counselor, Ms. Newman, pulled me from classes that I wasn't participating in.

Although my parents were called several times about it, they were as mentally absent as I was. I'd isolated myself from everyone and everything. One day during study hall, Ms. Newman stood in front of me and told me to come with her. It wasn't a request. It was an order.

I followed her into the room where students were all quietly working on their projects. Mr. Bakersfield sat at his desk when Ms. Newman walked me in and introduced us. I was told to come to his room every day instead. Without questioning anything, I did as I was told. It didn't matter where I was anyway.

The first half of the semester, I just sat in his classroom. I didn't talk. I hardly listened. I didn't participate in any of the assignments. After a while, I'd pick up a pencil and start doodling. That led to drawing, which later led to painting. I began participating in class every day, silently working alone. One day, after class had already been dismissed, Mr. Bakersfield handed me a large blank canvas. He didn't say anything, just winked and walked away.

I stayed late and made the darkest image I've ever seen. I let my guard down and let everything inside of me out on that piece. I wasn't exactly sure what it even was, but it released something I'd been holding in.

I continued working on it for weeks, adding to it and trying to make sense of what it could be. It looked evil on one side, but on the other, it was bright and happy. By the time I finished, I knew.

The painting was me.

What I couldn't express verbally, I did through art. I was furious with the universe that she had died. I was angry and bitter, and I hated everyone for it.

But she represented happiness and laughter. Her memories would always be with me, and deep down, I knew that. I was battling with so much inside that I didn't know how to express myself with words. Art gave me that outlet. I stayed after school to use the supplies as Mr. Bakersfield cleaned up the rest of the room. He never barraged me with questions or asked how I was doing. He was just there.

I hadn't realized it at the time that my counselors put me in art classes due to my lack of interest in talking things out. It's what finally clicked for me and gave me what I hadn't realized I needed.

But then school wrapped up for the year and my outlet was gone. I was back to being bitter and angry. I wanted my paints again. One day, I grabbed the mail for my mother and noticed an envelope addressed to me. I flipped it over, looking for a return address, but there wasn't one.

I ripped it open to a folded piece of paper. When I unfolded it, I immediately knew who sent it.

Mr. Bakersfield.

It was a flyer for an art class at the local college. It was open to high school and college students. At the bottom in his handwriting were the words, *Make a masterpiece. Do her proud.*

I cried, relieved and happy that I'd be able to do that.

I spent the next three years focusing on it. I signed up for every high school art class and any available at the college. I started at the introductory level, but by the time I graduated high school, I was mastering techniques college seniors were still trying to nail.

So when it was time to start thinking about college and majors, it was a no-brainer for me.

Go to art school as far away from Illinois as possible.

Graduate and find a job.

Never stop painting.

Create something worth making—and I plan to do just that.

As I head to my Monday restorative art class, my earbuds pumping with Adele, Professor Van Bergen steps right out in front of me, scaring the earbuds right out of me.

Grabbing my iPhone to mute the music, I flash an annoyed glare and wait for this unfortunate meet and greet to pass.

"Oh, hi, Aspen." Her voice is sweet as sugar but laced with fake politeness. "I was just in Morgan's class…" She pauses and clears her throat. "*Professor* Hampton's classroom. He was showing me one of your pieces, and I have to say I'm impressed. He thinks you'll go far in your career."

Returning her fake smile with one of my own, I mimic her sweet, fake tone. "Thank you. Your opinion means *so* much to me." I place a hand over my heart, pretending to genuinely care about her opinion.

The undercurrent of my statement doesn't go unnoticed, and she stands taller, trying to assert her importance. It would be comical if she didn't have an infatuation with Morgan and my relationship— even if there is no relationship.

Clearing her throat and tilting her nose to the ceiling, she says, "As it should. Tell me, Aspen, are you still planning on going to graduate school?" She doesn't give me a chance to answer, railroading on. "Because it'd sure be a shame if anything got in the way of *such* a promising future." She mimics my gesture by pressing a hand over her heart.

My eyes narrow in on the conniving bitch. My mouth opens to respond, but I quickly close it. I've got a dozen inappropriate things I'd love to say, but I know my boundaries. She smiles in victory and pats my shoulder as she takes a step to walk around me. "Ta-ta, Aspen."

Ugh! I want to throw one of my high heels at her, but it's way too valuable to waste it on someone like her. Plus, I'm not sure I could get myself out of that jam. *"Sorry, Dean Fletcher. The shoe just slipped off my foot and flew into Professor Van Bergen's face."*

I curse under my breath and continue walking to my classroom. Hopefully, the universe will help me out and a meteor will fall to Earth and land right on top of her, sparing me the time and energy of having to plot something myself.

But in case the universe doesn't come through for me, I better start plotting.

Chapter Fifteen
Morgan

I remember waking up one morning in Ohio, and the ground was covered in fresh snow. Being born and raised in Southern California, it was a rarity to get snowstorms. On my way to work, I underestimated the conditions and slid my car right into a ditch. It flipped once and landed in the culvert, my head smacking against the window in the process and causing a slight concussion.

The cliché of how your life flashes before your eyes is exactly what I wasn't expecting. Ignoring the pain and relying on the anger to get through day to day, I hadn't expected to see my life with her flash through my mind the moment I thought I could possibly die.

As I lay in the hospital, I recalled those flashes, which brought up the reason why I left in the first place. I hated that I thought of her at that moment. I hated that she even crossed my mind. I hated that I gave her so many years of my life that ended up being wasted.

When my phone rings with her name flashing on my screen, all those painful feelings rush in and anger boils through my veins.

"Is there a reason you're calling?"

She clears her throat before responding. "I'm just checking up on you." She pauses, but I don't speak up. "I heard about Ryan." Her words are genuine, but hearing her voice again makes me want to punch a hole in the wall, which I've done several times before because of her.

"It was six months ago," I reply harshly.

"I didn't have your newest cell number. I ran into your mother last week and she gave it to me."

Of course she did.

"It wasn't hers to give out," I state firmly. She's the last person I wanted to hear from.

"Look, Morgan…" I hear her hesitant breath through the phone, and I'm quick to cut her off.

"Don't." I hang up and let out a frustrated breath. I don't want her pity. Or anyone's pity. But Jennifer—the person I was about to walk down the aisle with five years ago—I don't want anything from her at all.

"Morgan?" I hear Natalia call out from the hallway.

"In here, Short Stuff." I brush a hand over my face to wipe the firm lines off my face. The last thing I want is for her to worry about me when I'm always worrying about her. "Whatcha need?"

Shrugging, she sits on a chair. "There's a dance tomorrow night."

"Oh?" I lift my brows. "What kind of dance?"

"It's stupid." She lowers her eyes.

"Natalia, what kind of dance?" I repeat.

"Valentine's Day dance."

"You don't want to go?"

"No, it's stupid."

I notice the little wrinkles around her lips, and I know there's more to the story.

"Didn't someone ask you to go with them?" I question, wondering if eleven-year-olds still think boys have cooties or not. She stays silent, not moving or making a sound, and I know I've nailed the issue. "I take that as a no," I say softly, hoping she'll feel comfortable enough to talk to me about this. I know she's grown up without a mom for half her life, so I assume she and Ryan were close and talked about everything. "Are you sure you don't want to go and hang out with your friends?"

She finally looks up with a scowl. "No. I said it's stupid, okay?"

She stands up and marches out of my office, and I'm left with my jaw on the floor, wondering what the hell just happened. She's the one who came looking for me in the first place and mentioned the dance. Did that mean she wanted to talk about it? Why else would she bring it up then?

I'm stumped as I think about her words. I have no clue what I'm supposed to do. Of course she wants to go, but the boy she wants to go with hasn't asked her yet?

Ah, fuck if I know.

I turn my laptop off and walk out to find her. She's in the living room flipping through channels, staring at the TV as if her life depends on it. I know she hears me walk in, but she doesn't acknowledge it.

I grab my keys off the counter and shout, "Come on. Let's go."

She finally looks up, dumbfounded. "Where?"

"To the store. You need a dress, don't you?"

Her face drops. "Do you have wax in your ears? I said I wasn't going." She turns away again. I don't know if this is where I should be handing her a pint of Ben & Jerry's or something, but I'm not about to let Natalia mope around all night when I know she wants to go.

I walk toward her, grab the remote out of her hand, and switch the TV off.

"Hey!" she screeches, but I ignore it. I grab her by the arms, lift her up, and toss her over my shoulder. "What are you doing?" she screams, kicking her legs and hitting me with her pathetic little fists. "Put me down!"

"What? What was that? I can't hear you over all the wax in my ears!" I walk out to the car and throw her in the passenger seat. "Buckle up." I grin at her before slamming the door, and she flashes me a death glare.

I get in the driver's side and start the engine. I have no idea where to buy a dress for a girl, so I quickly call up my mother.

"Hello, darling," she answers.

I'm in a hurry, so I bypass all the ritual greetings. "Where do I go to buy a dress for Natalia?"

"Oh! What's the occasion?"

"A school dance. Where do I go?"

"I'd go to Petunia's on Stanley and Rivers. Does she need her hair done?"

I turn and glance at her. Her hair is up in one of those messy knots. "Yes."

Two grueling hours later, I'm home with a half-satisfied eleven-year-old and an appointment to get her hair done tomorrow afternoon. She's pretending to be annoyed by my persistence, but I notice the corners of her mouth tilting up from the smile she's trying to hide.

As I'm tucking her in for the night, I kiss her forehead and say good night. She mumbles a response and before I head out, she calls out my name.

"Yes?" I turn and ask.

I can't see her eyes because she's buried herself in the blankets, but she mumbles a response. "Thank you."

The corner of my lips tilts up as I stare at the back of her head. "Anytime, Short Stuff."

The more I think about her, the more I think I'm going crazy.

I left California for this reason.

To get away. To never get hurt again. To avoid putting myself out there and feeling vulnerable around someone again.

But she makes me want to risk it. Not only my heart but everything that I'd jeopardize as well.

Instead, I worry about hurting her. Aspen Evans could be the woman to bring me back to life or the woman to destroy me. The real question is, would she ever consider letting someone like me in? My past has held me captive in a lot of ways, but besides that, I'm raising an eleven-year-old child. Aspen's so much younger than I am, with a whole world of possibilities in front of her. Would she even take the chance?

Better yet, could I even let her, knowing that I'd possibly be holding her back?

The self-doubt eats at me as I think it all through, but the more I think about it, the more I'm certain I've lost my mind.

Besides that, I have Natalia and the fact that she is going to her first school dance tonight. I don't know how to feel about that, honestly. I'm freaking out. Add one more thing to the pile of things I'm not sure I'm doing right when it comes to raising her. At least my mom could help get her ready, which speaking of…

"Come on, let me see!" I call out again, groaning at how long they've been. Natalia's been in her room for hours with my mom. She got her hair and nails done this afternoon, so I can't imagine what's taking so long.

"Just one more minute!" my mom calls out.

I can't hold in my sigh, but it's not in frustration, it's from the ache in my chest. This moment of seeing Natalia dressed up and ready for her first dance is something that Ryan should've been able to experience with her. He'd be so proud of his little girl but probably ready to threaten any little boys who tried to dance with his baby.

Today hits home that her dad won't be around for these important milestones. I worry that all these special events in her life will be tainted with sadness because he isn't here. When I came back, I made the decision to dedicate my entire life to making sure Nat was taken care of and help her heal so she can thrive, but moments like this break my heart.

I grab a beer from the fridge, and by the time I slam the door shut, she's walking toward me. Natalia's glowing in a sparkling blue gown with her hair up in curls and light makeup. Her smile is so wide, nearly touching her eyes.

"Wow…" I smile. "You look beautiful, Shorty."

She blushes, and I know she's going to have an amazing time.

"Thanks." She smiles wide again. "And thank you for doing this." She brushes her hand casually along her dress. "Even if I think this whole dance thing is stupid." She purses her lips but tilts one side up in a crooked smile.

"Even if it's stupid, at least you'll look good doing it."

She laughs and wraps her hands around me. "Thank you, Uncle Morgan."

"You're welcome, Natalia." I wrap my arms around her and kiss the top of her head. "We should get going."

"Pictures!" my mother interrupts. "I need some pictures first."

Natalia releases her arms and groans. "You get one."

My mother manages to get seven, and when she's satisfied, we head out.

"Are you meeting some of your friends?"

She stares out the window. "Amelia will be there."

"Oh, good."

"She has a date, though."

I blink. *Since when do eleven-year-olds date?*

"Meh, you're too young to date anyway. Boys should still have cooties at your age."

She turns toward me and grins. "Oh, they do. Girls don't mind anymore."

"Hmm…you could always ask a guy to dance with you."

She snorts and rolls her eyes. "Yeah, like that's going to happen."

I reach over and pull her hand into mine. "It will, Shorty. Maybe not tonight. Maybe not anytime soon. But someday. You're going to have guys waiting in line to dance with you."

"If that's true, you better tighten the deadbolts."

"No worries. I'll leave my rifle out in plain view."

"You don't have a rifle."

"I could."

"But you don't."

"Fine. I'll get one."

"You're ridiculous." She laughs.

I pull up to the school and watch as students fly out of cars all over the parking lot. They're all dressed up, much more than I ever did at their age, but times have changed.

"Have fun, okay?"

"Sure thing."

"Call me if you want me to get you early. Alright?"

She opens the door and steps out. "Fine."

"Bye!" I call out as she slams the door.

And just like that, she walks away and joins the rest of the students flocking to the door.

Red, pink, and white decorations cover the doors and windows of the school. It looks like a scene from the eighties and all I can do is smile at the memories of my previous Valentine's Days.

Before Jen, I never even acknowledged the stupid day. After Jen, I drank until the memories were a blurry reminder. I'd go out with the guys, pick up a chick, and bring her home. Of course, she thought it meant we were going to be a couple and have a future, but I made sure to clear that up by morning that there wouldn't ever be a chance of that happening.

I settle in with a beer and a movie. Right when I kick off my shoes, my cell rings.

It's Natalia.

"Shorty. Everything okay?"

"Yes, I'm fine."

"Then what is it?"

"I-I just wanted to tell you thanks again." I hear the giddiness in her voice, and I can't stop the proud smile that forms on my face. "I'm happy you made me go."

A sense of pride overwhelms me. This whole time, I'd feared I was screwing this up. I have no idea what I'm doing most of the time, but this gives me a little validation that it's in the right direction.

"Anytime, Natalia. I'm glad, too."

"I'll call you soon, okay?"

"Sounds good. Have fun."

We hang up, and I gladly stay in all night waiting for her call.

Chapter Sixteen
Aspen

"This is the dumbest holiday of the year," Zoe groans, leaning an elbow on top of the bar.

"It's not even a holiday," I counter. "But I get your point." I take another sip of my beer as I sit across the bar from her. Zoe's working at the bar tonight, and Kendall went out with Kellan for Valentine's Day.

"Before I got to know you, I would've pegged you for a girl who goes gaga over Valentine's Day," she admits.

"Why's that?" I wrinkle my nose. "Because I brush my hair and wear lipstick? Or is it the heels?" I crack a sarcastic smile.

"It's the whole package."

I frown, leaning an elbow on the bar top. "Guys are too needy. I like focusing on my paintings and classes. It's hard for guys who aren't passionate about something to understand how time-consuming it can be. At first, they say they understand and then within a couple weeks, they complain about the lack of attention I give them or that I don't want to go out all the time. And then it's *see ya around*."

"That's an easy fix," she says. "Find a guy who's passionate about what you're into."

"Most guys are *passionate* about sex," I mock.

She glares with a smirk. "You know what I mean."

"It's not exactly that easy."

"Yes, it is. It's like when famous people marry famous people. They get the extreme work schedules, the traveling, the paparazzi, the tabloids."

"Yeah, and most of them end up in divorce!" I defend. "If you research famous people who stay married, you'll notice it's those who rose to fame together, or around the same time, and the ones who married a non-famous person. Or someone less famous than they are. Having two people with crazy, strict schedules and cameras in the face all the time wouldn't make them understand more—it'd make them twice as crazy."

"Well, you aren't famous, avoiding the cameras, and being pressured to look half your age."

"No, but being into something that someone else isn't doesn't work either."

"But don't you attend a college primarily based on the arts?" A wrinkle forms between her eyebrows, and I sigh.

"Yes."

"So...shouldn't it be like swarming with guys who are passionate about arts and all that stuff?"

"You'd think so. But then you have two people who are overly passionate about the same thing and then neither of you cares about spending time together."

"Wouldn't you spend time doing the same thing? Like when couples watch movies because they're into action movies, or when couples run or work out because they're into fitness?" She turns the dishwasher on before slicing the lemons. "I think you're making excuses."

I scowl. "I'm a realist, that's all."

"A pessimist is more like it."

A few customers start flagging her down, so I don't get the chance to respond. The before dinner rush begins, so I walk back to my booth. I sit alone as I watch the overly PDA couples make out.

I think about Professor Hampton and how we share the same passion. Putting the fact that he's my professor aside, I wonder if someone like him and someone like me could work out. I'm not exactly emotionally stable, but he makes me want to try. He makes me want something more.

"Dude, why are you sitting here alone?" I look up and see Kendall shifting into the seat across from me with a beer in hand.

"Because there are literally no single guys here tonight. It's all couples and desperate chicks."

"You're a desperate chick." Her words ooze with sarcasm and pity.

I glare at her and take a drink of my warm beer. "If I'm desperate, then those chicks have no standards at all." She snorts. "Why are you here, anyway?" I ask.

"Kellan got called into work."

My brows furrow. I know she's lying. "Oh yeah? Your car salesman boyfriend got called into work?"

"Y-yeah." She quickly grabs her beer and takes a swig. "They had someone call in sick last minute and they needed an extra car detailer."

"Hmm…" I'm not buying her shit for a second.

"Yup. So are we going to find you a hookup or what?"

"I doubt it."

"Oh, come on. The choices can't be that bad. Look! A group of guys walked in."

I check my phone and notice the time. "It's after midnight. They're in here looking for a drunk, easy lay."

She narrows her eyes, confused. "Isn't that exactly what you want?"

"Oh, well, yeah," I stumble, confused at my own words. "Of course."

I've never wanted more than just a fun few hours with a guy, but lately the thought of having more has been circling in my mind more and more.

"I'll grab us some more drinks and see if I can get a couple of them to follow me." She winks as she gets out of the booth, and I laugh at her implication.

It's not long before there's a crowd of drunk guys at our booth.

Kendall managed to hustle at least four of them, as well as buy our next round of drinks and shots.

Tim, or maybe it's Trent, has squeezed my knee at least a half a dozen times. Every few minutes, he grips my leg and slides it upward, and every time, I grab it and slide it away. Kendall shoots me a look that tells me she's wondering what the hell is wrong with me, but even I don't know, so I shrug and make an annoyed face.

My phone lights up with a text from her.

KENDALL

He's cute! Why are you acting like he's covered in mold?

I sigh in frustration because I don't know. Considering I've never thought twice about bringing a good-looking guy to my place, tonight feels different.

ASPEN

I think I'm going to head home. Not feeling it.

She shakes her head in disapproval.

KENDALL

You're staying! Come on. Give him a chance.

ASPEN

Since when do you encourage one-night stands?

KENDALL

Since I haven't seen you bring a guy home in weeks, which means you're sex-deprived! And you're like an angry octopus when you don't get laid.

I scowl and put down my phone.

Fine, I mouth to her and glare. She has a point, but that doesn't mean I'm taking Mr. Grabby-Hands home.

"So, Tim. What do you do for a living?" I try to make actual conversation.

Pushing the Limits

"I'm a club promoter," he slurs proudly.

Pretending to be interested, I ask, "What does that consist of?"

"I find little honeys like yourself and encourage you to visit one of the clubs I represent." He eyes me seductively and licks his lips.

I cringe at his suggestive tone. "And what does that entail? How do you encourage people?"

"I promise them a *real* good time." He winks, and I shudder—and not in a good way.

"So what happens when you neglect your promise and they leave unsatisfied?"

Kendall covers her mouth, trying to conceal her amusement, but he hears her anyway and shifts uncomfortably in his seat.

"Oh, sweetheart." He shifts closer. "You'd never leave unsatisfied." His thumb plucks my lower lip, his gaze on it like lasers.

"On that note, I'm going to go before I catch a disease." I grab my purse and push my way out of the booth. "Good luck with your promoting or whatever it is you do and with getting laid in real life."

I walk to the bar and say bye to Zoe before heading outside. I hear Kendall trying to catch up with me as I dig around for my keys.

"Aspen, wait!"

I can feel the adrenaline pumping through me, my heart beating rapidly as I speed walk to my car.

"Aspen, hang on!"

She's out of breath by the time she reaches me. I spin around and lean against the driver's side door as she stands in front of me.

"What?" I ask harshly.

"What's wrong? What the hell was that?"

Shrugging, my jaw tenses. "I'm sick of guys like that."

"Sorry. I didn't know."

"I didn't either."

"Talk to me. What are you thinking?"

My throat begins to burn as tears threaten to pour out. "I have no idea, Kendall. I don't wanna be that girl anymore. The one who lets strange men into her bed, the one who can't form or hold an emotional relationship, the one who pushes people away. I hate that girl."

She reaches for my hand and grips it in hers. "Aspen…I don't know what to say."

A tear slides down my cheek as I close my eyes. "I have feelings for someone, and it scares me half to death."

"Who?"

"It's not important. There's no scenario in this world that allows us to be together."

"What do you mean? Why not?"

"He's almost ten years older than me." Eight to be exact.

"So? Age is just a number."

I snort at her cliché response.

"He's also a professor at the university."

"Okay?"

"He's *my* professor," I clarify.

"By professor, do you mean Ms. Jones's smoking hot nephew?" Her brows waggle.

I groan. "Am I that predictable?"

"No. I saw the way you acted around him."

I sigh. "I can't stop thinking about him. And I know nothing can ever happen, but the way it feels when he's around is something I've never felt before and it's terrifying. I have anxiety attacks over it."

"It's completely normal to be scared and nervous around a guy you like, but I suspect even more so when it's someone you can't openly express your feelings to."

"On top of it, I don't even know if I could let someone like him in. Not all the way, at least."

"Why not?"

I shoot her a look. "You know why. I feel guilty even being alive, Kendall. How am I going to date and have a stable relationship?"

She gives me a sympathetic look and a smile. "You evolve."

I exhale. "I don't know. It's like I have no idea what I'm doing anymore. Weeks ago, sure, I'd gladly take Trent home and fuck him six ways to Sunday, but now I don't even have the desire to."

"His name is Tony," she deadpans.

"Whatever." I shrug. "I feel so lost."

"I know how that is."

Pushing the Limits

"What do you mean?"

She lowers her eyes. "Kellan broke up with me tonight."

"What?" I gasp. "Why didn't you tell me sooner?"

"I was embarrassed and trying not to think about it. I wasn't going to let him have the satisfaction of ruining my night."

"What happened?"

"He said I was pressuring him when he wasn't ready."

"Seriously?" I almost laugh. "You get turned down for sex, and I can't turn it away fast enough. We have some messed up lives."

"Yup," she agrees. "So let's go wallow with a bottle of wine and a box of chocolates."

I open the car door and hop in. "Deal."

I'm not sure how late Kendall and I stay up drinking and eating heart-shaped chocolate, but when I wake up the next morning, my body is covered in sweat. My breaths are coming in harsh pants while my heart pounds in my chest. Normally, waking up like this would be from a nightmare, but this time it's from dreaming about Professor Hampton—and not just any dream. My body is still humming from the way he had me moaning and crying out his name.

The feel of him between my legs was so real that I could feel the exquisite fullness of him moving deep inside me. He completely overwhelmed my senses as he worked my body as if that was what he was born to do. He devoured my pussy. His tongue teased my slick folds before wrapping his mouth around my clit and sucking it between his teeth. The roughness of his stubble rubbing against my thighs—the perfect counterpoint to the pleasure he was wringing from my body.

My pussy clenches at the memory of how he sucked my nipple, rolling the tender flesh between his teeth as if he knew how I'd liked it. Then he thrust hard and deep, moaning my name before he gave me a scorching hot kiss.

I squeeze my thighs together, feeling how swollen and wet I am at the memory of it all. He was eager, kissing and sucking down my neck, chest, and torso until he landed right where I begged him to be. I haven't even felt his mouth on mine yet, but I can feel my lips still tingling.

After spending weeks with Professor Hampton in class, it's not getting any easier to be around him, especially since the dreams have started. He continues watching me work in the classroom, and I continue to let him in. It's a slow process, but I take it one day at a time. The tension between us has apparently been more obvious than I thought because Ellie is starting to get suspicious—either that or she's giving me shit. It's hard to know for sure, but enough to make me concerned.

Today during class, Ellie flat out asks me if I'm getting "special treatment" from Professor Hampton *outside* of the classroom. My paintbrush nearly drops from my fingers as I choke on her words. I quickly recover with a nervous laugh. Although I know it's not funny, considering what special treatment I'd like to be getting, but I managed to play it off. What else could I do? Say, *not yet, Ellie, but I've ridden his tongue repeatedly in my dreams. And that man can sure lick me to an orgasm.* I'm proud I didn't choke on my tongue or die on the spot. Thank God Morgan was on the other side of the room because that would have been more than awkward.

When class is over, I stay behind to finish up a piece, and as usual, Professor Hampton finds a reason to stay behind and watch me.

He walks out with me and to fill in the silence, I talk about the gala at the gallery that's approaching. "I hear you've been roped into helping your aunt at the gallery this week," I say to Professor Hampton as we walk out of the classroom.

I've known about the Spring Gala since I started. It's a huge charity event that the gallery hosts to raise money for school art programs all over the city. It's usually one of the first courses to get dropped when a school has budget cuts, so to avoid financial stress, the gallery hosts an event to help ease the burden as much as possible.

Pushing the Limits

The gallery curator, Mr. Cross, had been in charge of these events for years, but for the past five years, Ms. Jones has taken over the majority of the planning as he gets closer to retirement. She always gets super stressed and overwhelmed with it, but ever since she's taken over, each year has been more successful than the previous one.

The gala allows buyers to purchase and bid in the silent auction. There's an extravagant display of food and alcohol. Everyone dresses in fancy dresses and tuxedos, making the whole thing a big deal.

"Yup. She's been calling my mom every day in a panic, so I was volunteered by default." I smile at his honest words.

As soon as we turn the corner, I practically run over Professor Van Bergen. She gasps, acting as if she didn't know we were coming. We weren't exactly quiet, so I don't believe she's the aggrieved party here.

"Oh, Morgan!" She squeezes his shoulder. "I didn't realize you were still here." She flashes a flirty smile at him, but her tone is so sickeningly sweet, I'm tempted to puke on her knockoff shoes.

"Yeah, I'm heading out now. Aspen was finishing up a piece and needed some help." His reply is polite, but I can see the annoyance on his face, which makes me selfishly giddy.

At least this time, it's not a lie. He was helping me—I couldn't get the texture I was trying for on my project and he was showing me a few unconventional techniques to get what I wanted. We won't mention the flirting and accidental touches that we know weren't accidental at all.

Professor Van Bergen perks up and looks at me with one of those forced smiles. "That's Aspen for you. So driven and talented." It's evident in her tone that Morgan spending extra time with me irritates her. She shoots daggers as she continues, "She's a shoe-in for any graduate program she chooses. If she stays on track, of course."

And with that, she has not only made herself look good in front of Morgan but also warned me off yet again. I'm distracted and when I finally tune into their conversation, Professor Van Bergen is asking Morgan out for drinks. Instead of waiting around to see what he says, thinking my heart can't stand it if he accepts, I quickly toss a goodbye over my shoulder and get out of there like the hounds of hell are chasing after me.

Chapter Seventeen
Morgan

I clear my Wednesday afternoon when Aunt Mel asks for my help at the gallery. I know Aspen will be working, and I know she's off-limits, but that doesn't stop me from thinking about her and wondering what her lips would taste like pressed against mine.

I think about that often.

Her bright smile, the way she tries to act unaffected around me, and the way her gaze burns into mine tell me she's thinking about it, too.

Christine is at the front desk and greets me as soon as I walk in. "Hey!" She sits up. "Ms. Jones had to take a quick phone call. She said to tell you to wait down here."

"Thanks."

I try to avoid looking around for her, but I catch myself listening for the clicking of her shoes as I walk to my favorite part of the gallery.

The student section is the most diverse. It's filled with paintings, drawings, abstracts, watercolor, black-and-white photographs, and even a couple of sculptures. It's a blend of everything you'd imagine when you think of the word *art*.

As I walk around, I examine the different techniques each artist uses. I stop in front of the three Ariel Rose Collections I first saw when

Aspen gave me the tour. I haven't seen on her site before, so I use the opportunity to look at them and brush my thumb over the texture of the strokes.

The three canvases are made to look like one large abstract when next to one other. Each section captures a piece of the larger picture, but the way she separated it tells a lot about the story itself—she wanted it presented that way for a reason.

"Haven't you ever heard of the phrase, *if you have time to lean, you have time to clean?*"

Aspen's taunting voice takes me by surprise. I hadn't even heard her walk in, but when I turn around, she's not there.

"Up here, Romeo."

I tilt my head and see her standing on a ladder in the next section. She's adjusting some of the spotlights that shine on the pieces below. The portable walls in between blocked my view of her when I first walked in, which means she's been able to watch me the whole time, and I hadn't even realized it.

"Ah…she speaks." I grin and walk closer to her as she stares down at me with a smirk. "Oh, speak again, bright angel! For thou art as glorious to this night, being o'er my head, as is a wingèd messenger of heaven."

She sucks in her lower lip and keeps her gaze fixated on me. "Ah…Shakespeare fan."

"Maybe." I shrug.

"What a cliché." She laughs, stepping down. Her golden blond hair is pulled up into a high ponytail, making it sway effortlessly in loose waves from side to side as she moves. She looks flawless as usual, wearing tight jeans and a curve-hugging shirt, but I notice her infamous heels I'm used to seeing her wear in class are missing.

"What is?" I inquire as she walks toward me barefoot.

She takes the final step, closing the gap between us. She's shorter without the heels, making the top of her head barely reach my shoulders. "Talented artist, not-bad-to-look-at professor, and Shakespeare know-it-all. It's an impressive résumé."

"I never claimed to be a know-it-all, but I'll accept the rest." My mouth spreads into a wicked grin, the scent of her perfume overpowering me and making me forget I shouldn't be this close to a student. But at this moment, I don't care what rules I'm breaking. I'm not backing away from her again.

"However, you've never even seen any of my paintings. So that's based on assumption."

"Perhaps, but I always go with my intuition."

"And what's your intuition telling you?" I lower my face to hers, focusing on the warmth of her lips.

A sly smirk spreads over her face, feeding the anticipation of kissing her.

"That you are way overdressed for this." She slaps a clipboard against my gray dress shirt, and when I look down, I notice it's Aunt Mel's gala to-do list. "I'm putting you to work, Professor." She winks.

Groaning, I follow her to the front section of the gallery. The walls are bare, waiting for pieces to be displayed. The gallery and the college work closely together, so this event is important for both. The gala raises money for the program and provides funding for students to come to the school.

"Since the focus is to get people to buy and bid in the silent auction, Aunt Mel wants the student pieces in the front to represent the school they'd be donating to. Normally, they're in the back…well, you've gotten the tour, so you know," she rambles. "Anyway, she wants them displayed by assignment."

"Alright…" I glance around the tables where they're waiting. "Do you—"

"The list is on your clipboard."

As I flip through a couple of sheets, I begin wondering how the hell I got myself into this situation in the first place. Aunt Mel and my mom were close growing up, so I spent a lot of summers with Aunt Mel and her then-husband, Henry. I have another aunt and uncle, but they live in Tennessee, so they usually fly in once a year for the holidays. So when Aunt Mel asked me to come help in between and after classes, I couldn't say no.

"Okay, Boss," I mock. She spins around and glares. "So, what's first?"

"You tell me." She nods toward the clipboard I'm still holding.

"Landscapes."

"Okay, that'd be from first and second-year students. They should be on that table over there." She points behind me. "Those can go over here." She walks in between the portable walls.

"Sounds good, Boss."

"Would you stop?" she snips. "We're out of the classroom, remember?"

"Which means what?" I challenge, begging her with my eyes to say it—say we're more than just a professor and student.

"That we're on equal ground." She walks toward me with confidence, but her gaze lowers with restraint. "We're two normal people setting up for an event."

I can't help the wave of disappointment, but I know she's right. Although she feels the same, I have to be careful about my approach. She battles with anxiety, but I hadn't considered her fear of getting close to people.

Though, I can't say I blame her. Without knowing her entire back story, I know I can relate from my past alone.

I just have to figure out how to crack her and get her to say what she's feeling.

Once I check the list again, I realize after landscapes, it's abstracts, and then portraits and pastels. We're each working on a different wall when Aunt Mel comes in to check on us. She's working with the curator and Christine on setting up. Tables, booklets, silent auction pieces. She looks stressed out and a bit over-caffeinated.

"How's it going in here? Doing okay? Need anything? Perhaps some water? Is the temperature okay for you guys?"

Aspen spins around slowly, wide-eyed and pursing her lips. "Everything is fine," she replies sincerely. "It's coming together."

"Good. Great. Okay then. Holler if you need me!" She waves quickly before nearly running out.

"I'm starting to see the resemblance." Aspen laughs.

"How so?"

"Highly energetic. A bit crazy." The corners of her mouth tilt in a taunting grin. "Obsessive."

"Perhaps that's just the nature of the Hampton genes."

"No, I'd say it's more nurture than nature."

"Oh. I didn't realize this turned into a psychoanalytic review."

"Professor Hampton…" she drawls out slowly, seducing me with her voice, "just because you're the teacher doesn't mean I can't teach you a thing or two."

I'm two seconds away from rounding the table in front of me and pushing her up against the wall, demanding that she *show me* when another visitor interrupts my thoughts.

"Oh my God, A! You'll never believe—"

I turn and meet Aspen's friend, Kendall, as she freezes mid-sentence when she notices me.

"Oh, hi, Morgan."

"Hi, Kendall."

"Sorry to interrupt, but Ms. Jones flew up the stairs screaming in *Spanish*." The corner of her lips tilts up in amusement. "Shane fucked something up in security. You should go save your boyfriend before Ms. Jones bursts from an aneurysm." She nudges her with her elbow.

My brows rise at the mention of the word *boyfriend*. I turn around and continue working to avoid looking interested in their conversation. The last thing I need is for her friend to get suspicious of my inappropriate feelings.

"Shane doesn't even speak Spanish," Aspen deadpans.

"I know. That's just how mad she is." Kendall giggles.

"It's so unhealthy how crazy she gets before these events." I hear Aspen setting things down on the table.

"She needs a valium," Kendall adds.

"I'll go see if I can do anything, although I doubt it. Ms. Jones can be stubborn."

"Stubborn?" Kendall laughs. "That's putting it lightly."

I hear the clacking of shoes as Kendall walks away, leaving Aspen and me alone again. "I can go talk to her if you'd like." I turn and face her. "See if I can help your boyfriend out."

An amused expression flashes over her face as she bounces her feet from left to right. "No, it's fine. I'm used to it. After three years, you learn to get out of Ms. Jones's way during times like these."

"Ah…high-stressed."

"Just a bit." She smiles. The awkward tension in the air is killing me, and so I suggest taking a break.

"Yeah, sure. I could use a drink anyway."

"Great, I'll meet you back in like ten minutes."

"Perfect." She smiles, but it's forced.

Walking away, I'm defeated and hopeless. I go upstairs and find Aunt Mel in her office. Her brows furrow and her body is tense.

"Everything okay?" I ask.

"Jesus, Morgan. You scared the living daylights out of me." She places a hand on her chest.

"Sorry. I didn't mean to sneak up on you. I heard you were having some issues and wanted to see if I could help."

"Oh, you sweet boy." Her mouth spreads into a genuine smile at the mention of the nickname she used to call me as a child. "It's nothing. One of my idiot security team ordered the wrong part, and now, I have to rush ship it here in time for the gala. Big event means more surveillance."

Once I walk inside her office, I stand in front of her desk. "If you need anything, let me know. I have my mom taking Natalia to her therapy tonight."

"Oh, how is she doing?"

"She's making some progress." I shrug, uncertain. "Baby steps."

She frowns. "That poor child. She's lucky she has you, Morgan." Her lips curl back up into a sweet, sympathetic smile. "You're good for her."

"No...I think she's the one who's good for me." I wink before walking out and heading down the hallway.

Three guys in security shirts are standing in the hallway, and I find myself eyeing them up, wondering which one of them is Shane. I know it's stupid to even compare, but I can't help wanting to know, considering I'd even asked her if she had a boyfriend and she'd told me no.

Perhaps she lied.

As I round the corner toward the staircase, I hear one of the guys yell out Shane's name. "You're in so much shit, dude." One laughs.

"Ms. Jones is going to skin your ass and hang it up on display." The other joins in.

I turn and hear his response. "Fuck you, guys. Ms. Jones should order her own shit then."

My jaw ticks at the sound of his disrespectful tone toward my aunt. I'm tempted to spin around and beat the guy's face in when I spot Kendall coming up the stairs. "Hey! Did you see where Aspen went?"

I brush a hand through my hair to calm my nerves. "Uh, no. She mentioned getting a drink or something."

"Oh, okay. Probably went to go straighten out Shane's ass then." She muses and my fists tighten. "If you see her before I do, tell her I'm leaving early."

"Sure, will do."

She walks past me.

My head is a mess, but I know I have to get my shit together. Aspen isn't mine, and technically, she's off-limits. Ever since the first tour, Aunt Mel hasn't stopped talking about her. About how she's like a daughter to her. How she's come from a rough past. How she's one of the hardest working employees she's had and how she feels protective over her well-being.

I exhale a frustrated breath as I walk toward the front of the gallery.

"Oh, hey!" Aspen calls out as soon as she sees me walk in. "I think we're almost done with organizing in here. We still need to reposition the lighting above."

"Sure," I mutter out a short response. "I'm surprised you're back already."

"Oh yeah. I grabbed a bottle of water from the vending machine. I'll eat when I get home. I have some studying to do anyway."

"I figured you'd be with your boyfriend," I blurt out, trying to make my voice sound as casual as possible. "You could've taken a longer break. I wouldn't have minded."

She tilts her head and frowns. "He's not my boyfriend." She shifts her gaze down to the table and grabs another piece. "Not even close."

"Really?" I raise my brows.

Pushing the Limits

"I don't have a boyfriend, remember?"

"I do but haven't figured out why not."

She flashes me a hesitant expression. "Because I don't." She shrugs, but there's more to it—much more.

I want to press for more, but given we're surrounded by gallery employees, and anyone could be listening in, I stay quiet.

But that doesn't stop me from thinking of every possible way to bring it up later.

Chapter Eighteen
Aspen

Working side by side with Professor Hampton has been intoxicating. I've felt a high most of the day. He gives me nervous butterflies anytime he's nearby. It's like a combination of a six-year-old just finding out she's going to Walt Disney World and going to an interview for your dream job.

It's a pile of mixed emotions, but there's also fear.

I don't date for that reason. I choose not to get too close to guys to keep from getting attached, but I haven't even kissed him, and I already feel attached.

"What made you choose CSLA?" he casually inquires as we fold the tables down.

"It was as far away from home as I could possibly get," I reply a bit too honestly. He tilts his head up and looks at me as if he's trying to read me. "I'm from Illinois originally. I didn't want to stick around after high school."

"That's understandable. I think kids your age like to get away for college."

Most kids? I brush it off and ask him the same. "What about you? Where'd you come from?"

"From here originally. Then I moved to Ohio for a job."

"And?" I probe as we move the tables off to the side.

Pushing the Limits

"And what?"

I suspect he's not telling me the whole story, although I can't blame him. It doesn't stop me from trying to get it out of him, however.

"And why are you back in California? Where'd you teach before that? Why'd you move? Give me something..."

"I got my heart broken and needed to get out of town. I taught part-time at Ohio University but had some things here I needed to take care of, so I found a job at CSLA."

"Add in a dog custody battle and you've got yourself a country song."

He snorts.

"What made you want to major in art history?"

"Wanted to incorporate something I'm passionate about into a future career," I say, reciting my usual generic response I give to anyone who mentions my major.

He stops what he's doing and stares. "That's the biggest piece of bullshit I've ever heard."

I glare at him. "It's not bullshit. It's the truth."

"You know how I know it is?"

I flash him a bemused expression. "Please tell."

"Your left eye twitches. That's a dead giveaway."

I'm immediately hyper-aware of my eyes, wondering if it actually twitches. "Maybe I have a twitching problem." I fold my arms over my chest. "I'm sensitive about it."

"Is that so?"

"It is," I say curtly.

"Then I apologize for my rudeness." I can tell he's mocking me, but I'm not about to give in to the fact that he caught me lying.

"Thank you." I can feel the tension in the air between us getting thicker and thicker. My thighs clench at the thought of his full mouth on mine—*kissing, licking, sucking.*

I blink the fantasy away.

He smirks, obviously not buying any of the shit I'm feeding him. However, I'm not about to go down memory lane with a guy I hardly know. A guy who's my *professor*, nonetheless.

"What did you major in?" I find myself asking to fill in the silence

137

as we walk out of the room. "Something in philosophy?" I guess, knowing most students majoring in philosophy end up in a completely different career.

The corner of his lip curls up in amusement. "Biology."

My brows rise. "How'd that happen?"

He glances over with an amused shrug. "I was making a political statement."

"Ah...defiance against your parents."

"Exactly."

"So, how'd that pan out for you?"

"Well, I dropped out in my third year."

I raise a brow, urging him to explain more.

"I told my parents I needed to take a gap year to *self-reflect*."

"Ah...self-reflection. The best excuse to take off from college."

"It was." He smiles. "I did a little of everything. I read and wrote for fun. Eventually, I branched out into drawing and painting. Then I tried learning the guitar."

"What made you stick with art?" I ask as we slow down to a halt, facing each other chest to chest.

"Ended up being the only thing I was good at."

I burst out in laughter.

"You think that's funny?" he challenges, closing the gap between us.

"No...I..." I place a hand over my face. "It's pathetic. Sad even."

He rubs his fingers along his square jawline, a wicked grin forming on his lips. "I'm going to let that one pass," he states. I focus on his hands and mouth, at the same time wondering how they'd feel on me...his lips soft and sweet, and his hands greedy and firm.

"It's probably not too late to reconsider putting one of your pieces in the student section."

I blink. "Huh?"

"For the gala. Are you scared?" He takes a step, and I walk side by side with him again.

"No."

"C'mon. Just one? It could be a gorilla even." He flashes a teasing grin.

"I don't paint gorillas."

"Dogs?"

"No."

"Sunsets?"

"Nope."

"Landscapes? Trees? Trees are a popular choice. You could do a full, green-leafed tree, or fall colors like reds and yellows, or even add a brook flowing nearby. Add in a sunset and you're golden."

I wish he'd stop talking. The moment he mentions trees, my body tightens, and I hold my breath.

"Or we could always make a bet. I win, you have to put something in, you win—" He pauses briefly. "Aspen?" He tilts his head and steps closer. "Are you okay? You aren't blinking."

"No, I just need a moment."

"What's wrong? You're pale."

"I'll be okay in a minute," I confirm.

"You're not okay. Are you having an anxiety attack?"

Yes. "No."

"Yes, you are. Sit."

I comply and sit on the chair he grabs for me. Closing my eyes, I focus on my breathing. Good air in, bad air out. I imagine my body relaxing, starting with my toes and working my way to my head. By the time I get to my hips, my heart rate has decreased, and my breaths are less labored. As I continue through the breathing technique, I know Morgan is going to have questions once I'm back to normal.

"Doing okay?" he asks, still kneeling in front of me. His hand brushes against my cheek, brushing a piece of my hair that fell out of my ponytail behind my ear. "You scared me there for a moment."

I nod, keeping my gaze low as my cheeks flush. "Yes, I think so."

"Can I get you anything? Water? Crackers? Soup?"

I meet his eyes. "I'm not sick. But thank you. I'll be fine."

He's got that look, the one I dread anytime someone sees me like this—weak and helpless—and I hate it.

"You should go home. I can finish…"

"It's my sister." I exhale.

"What?"

"She fell from a tree," I explain. "That's how she died. I watched her fall to her death."

"Oh my God, Aspen…" He gasps, his features dropping in a frown. "I'm so sorry."

"She's the reason I started in the first place. I needed an outlet, a way to express my emotions."

"She's your muse."

"Yes. I paint her to keep her alive. I know it sounds stupid—"

"Not at all."

"I'm afraid I'll forget her. That day after day, I'll forget what her voice sounded like. How her obnoxious dancing made me laugh until I cried. How her smile was contagious." A tear slides down my cheek, and I close my eyes to keep them in. "I feel so guilty."

"Aspen," he says softly. "Aspen, look at me," he demands, but I can't do it. I squeeze them tighter, hating that I'm sitting in front of my panty-melting hot professor, crying like a toddler. His fingers press under my chin, bringing my attention to him. "There you are." He smiles sweetly. "There's nothing you could've done."

"I can't believe that. I was up there with her. Her hand was in my hand, her eyes pleading for me to save her. I should've fought harder."

"If it was her destiny, you couldn't have," he says genuinely, but I hate the truth in his words.

"You believe in destiny?" More tears slip down my cheek, my throat burning with every beat in my chest.

He sucks on his lower lip for a moment before responding, "Yes. I do."

I whisper, "I'm not sure what I believe in anymore."

"It can't be easy losing someone so close to you, especially at a young age."

"She was my identical twin. Not *easy* doesn't even touch the surface."

"You hadn't told me that before."

I look up, his gaze filled with concern. "Like I said, I don't like to talk about her."

"You can always talk to me about her. Or even about how you're feeling."

"Why?"

"Why what?"

"Why would you want me to?"

"Because everyone needs someone to talk to, and I can relate in some respect. If you'd let me, I can be a great listener."

I'm surprised by his generosity, but I'm still reluctant to talk about it. "It's not that I don't *want* to talk about her. I have this fear that talking about it will mean I'm accepting it."

"Well, you can talk about it, or you can bottle it up inside yourself until you burst with resentment for not having anyone to talk about it with."

"Bottling it up has been working fine for the past six years," I retort. He glares, and I know I'm only fooling myself. "I…" I pause, trying to collect my thoughts and find the right words for what I want to say. "Do you think it's possible to feel like a part of you is constantly missing? Like…never feeling complete."

He nods but stays silent.

"It's like I'm only half a person and it's the half that doesn't know how to function emotionally."

"Considering she was your twin, I'd say it's possible. Twins share a bond that regular siblings don't." The truth in his words causes an ache deep in my chest. Sharing a bond doesn't sound strong enough for what I felt with her.

"Ever since the accident, my soul has been ripped out from underneath me. Not only is a part of me missing but also, it's the part that knew how to function emotionally and mentally. Most of the time, I find myself faking it."

"Your art isn't fake," he says earnestly. "It's real and deeply emotional. It tells a story that your mind is expressing visually since you can't vocally."

"Yeah." I smile, choking back a sob. "It feels like home when I paint. Comforting. It feels natural."

His fingers slowly rub against my jawline as he lifts my head up. Our gazes meet, and before I can take a breath, his mouth covers mine. His hand slides around my neck, pulling me closer and kissing me deeper. I lean into him as his warm lips nudge mine open, sliding his tongue in to claim mine. His other hand wraps effortlessly around my waist as he shifts his body between my legs. A deep moan releases from my throat as his chest presses firmly against mine. I can feel how chiseled and toned his body is as he squeezes my hip and closes the gap between us.

A soft whimper escapes as he gently pulls away. My chest heaves rapidly as he draws my lower lip between his teeth, lightly biting and groaning. My body goes into overdrive as I wrap my arms around him, soaking up every inch of his mouth. His hold on me tightens as our bodies mold in a heated kiss. It's better than I even imagined, and the soft groans coming from his throat tell me he feels the same.

My heart races in my chest, thumping hard against my ribs at what this man does to me. I've kissed plenty of guys before, but it's never felt like *this*.

Reality crashes back that we're at the gallery and someone could catch us at any time. I don't want to stop, but I know we'll be risking it if we don't.

"Um…" I say against his mouth. "Someone's going to—"

He smirks, my body shivering at the way his lips feel on mine. "Going to what?"

He softly kisses me, slower, almost *torturous*. "I've wondered what it'd be like to kiss you." His voice is smooth and genuine, my breathing speeding up at how hard my heart is pounding in my chest.

He releases me for one short moment before wrapping a hand around my throat and pulling me closer again, his eyes intense and greedy.

"And now that I've found out, I can't stop." He flashes one of his deep dimples.

"Do you normally go around kissing your students?" I tease, breaking away and seeing the hunger in his features.

"Only the ones I like." He winks, and a soft chuckle releases from my throat.

"Good to know."

He presses another soft kiss on my mouth before standing and holding his hand out for mine. I place it in his and stand so we're chest to chest.

"And for the record, I've never kissed a student of mine before." His finger rubs along my cheekbone, brushing the hair behind my ear.

I smile, loving the way his hand feels against my flushed skin. "I've never kissed one of my professors before. But then again, none of them ever looked like you either," I taunt, earning a pleased smile in return.

"Good to know."

The sound of easy chatter grabs our attention as it becomes apparent people are coming this way.

"I should go—"

"I'm going to—"

We say at the same time. I laugh at how nervous I am, how nervous he makes me when a moment ago, his body and lips were all over mine.

"We'll talk later, okay? I'm going to help Aunt Mel finish up." He places a soft kiss on my forehead before sliding his hand down my arm and giving my hand a quick squeeze.

I watch as he walks away, my mind spinning at what happened. I bring my fingers up to my mouth, swollen and warm, my body still humming at the way it felt to have him pressed against me.

Smoothing my hands down my shirt, I stand straighter before heading to the front of the gallery as if nothing had happened.

Chapter Nineteen
Morgan

K issing Aspen is something I've fantasized about for weeks. I know I shouldn't have, considering she's my student and the consequences could screw me, but the moment she opened up, I couldn't stop myself. She walks into my classroom, so strong and confident in her work, but there's so much she's covering up on the inside. The force that compels me to be near her is undeniable.

I hate that I had to leave her, but I don't intend on staying away for long.

Aunt Mel and I go through the rest of her to-do list for the event. Going over and over the same things I already know, but I humor her and listen anyway. I know talking about it aloud helps her mentally organize everything.

We go over the catering instructions, the wine list, the guest list, and the itinerary. She repeats herself so much, I start filling in her words for her.

"Morgan!" She scowls.

I chuckle. "You've told me the list three times, Aunt Mel. I got it." I kiss her cheek. "It's going to be amazing. Stop worrying."

"Alright. Fine." She sighs. "I'll be relieved when it's over. Let's say that."

"Yes, but all your hard work will pay off. I'm sure of it."

144

It's after seven before I finally get out of there. I know Natalia is going to be mad, but I'm hoping the sleepover she's planned for this weekend puts her in a good mood.

I arrive home with Natalia half asleep in the passenger seat. My mom said she'd been quiet all night and couldn't get anything out of her. So I plan to fix that.

"Wanna talk?" I ask as soon as I kill the engine.

"About what?"

"Whatever you want."

She furrows her brows. "Nothing comes to mind."

"Natalia, c'mon. How dense do you think I am?"

"Going by your Ralph Lauren slacks, button-up shirt, and slicked-back hair, I'd say it's a safe bet."

"You have way too much time on your hands if you know the brand names of my clothes."

"I have good fashion sense, so sue me." She grips the handle and lets herself out.

"What's wrong with my pants?" I chase behind her, but she ignores my question. "We can order pizza and binge on ice cream," I offer, unlocking the door. "But you have to talk."

I push open the front door and she steps in. "Fine. Let's talk about why you hated my father."

My breath hitches, and I swear I hear a pin drop the moment her words hit me. But I know she's not stupid. Of course she knows something was up between us, considering I never called or visited.

I wasn't planning to have this conversation for at least a few more years.

We settle in with a cheese pizza and a quart of chocolate ice cream on the couch. I know I can't tell her everything, but it's only fair she knows I didn't hate him. I was mad, sure, but I've always loved my brother.

"Okay, spill. I'm eating, aren't I?"

I narrow my eyes at her snarky tone. "I didn't hate him, Natalia. I shouldn't have gone so long without talking to him. I'll regret that for the rest of my life."

"Why'd you stop talking to him?" she asks, taking a bite.

I don't want anything I say to change how she feels for her dad, so I sugarcoat it the best I can. "We had a disagreement. I was mad and hurt for a long time and instead of mending our relationship, I let it stew."

"Are you still mad?"

"Yes. But not at him."

"Then who?"

"Myself. I'm mad about our last interaction. I'm mad I didn't come home before it was too late."

"Being mad is a lot of work," she admits.

"It is."

"Do you think God punishes people?"

Her question catches me off guard and it takes me a moment to grasp what she's asked. "I can't say for sure."

"Yeah, me neither."

"Do you think you're being punished?"

She shrugs and bows her head. "Sometimes. It's hard not to feel that way when you lose your parents before they even get to see you graduate middle school. I miss him so much."

I wrap my arm around her and pull her closer. "I do, too, Shorty. But I do know one thing…" She looks up with hopeful blue eyes. "He loved you so much. He'd want you to be happy."

"I feel guilty."

"For moving on?"

She nods.

"Yeah, I know that feeling, too."

"How do you get over it?"

I wish I knew the answer to that. "That's something we're going to have to figure out together."

She smiles and leans her head on my shoulder. I kiss the top of her head and let her lie there until she passes out. I carry her into bed and tuck her in as quietly as I can without waking her. I put the pizza and ice cream away and then finish cleaning up the rest of the living room.

I sit on the couch with a thud and stare up at the ceiling. Thoughts of Ryan and me come to my mind. Thoughts of how close we were, how much I looked up to him, how much we had in common.

Pushing the Limits

I should've known he'd had a thing for Jennifer, but I ignored all the signs. I didn't want to think that my own brother would go after someone I was dating and planning to marry. Even though I was enraged, I wish I would've given him a second chance. A second chance to explain, apologize, admit he loved her—anything.

I wish I had given our relationship a second chance before it was too late.

Though I try to hold in the tears like all the other times, this time, I let them fall. I let them fall so I can relieve the pain inside.

"Morgan?" I hear Nat's voice, and I quickly rub my hands over my face.

"Yes?" I stand and find her leaning on the doorframe.

She flashes a sweet smile and says, "He'd want you to be happy, too."

Natalia's words repeat over and over in my head all night long. I try to sleep, but it never comes. I think of all the things we used to do as kids, the way we'd mess with each other and spend every Saturday outside.

There was a time we were inseparable. That was all before Jen, of course. He went off to college before me, but once I met her, our time together became less and less. There were holidays and special occasions, but it wasn't nearly the same. We lost contact somewhere in between, and I have no one to blame but myself.

Natalia was born and a few years later, his wife, Lena, passed away. It was hard on all of us, but it destroyed him. Ryan was alive, but he was hardly living. It was obvious he was taking Lena's unexpected death hard.

She was driving to work one day when an elderly woman hit her straight on. Lena was killed instantly. I tried my hardest to get closer to him after that. Raising a child on his own and feeling lost, he began drinking. I'm not exactly sure when he started to fall for Jen, but I know I hadn't seen it coming. Although I should've, I was too invested in my own little world to see what was happening around me.

Natalia would stay with my parents a lot. I'd help by picking her up and taking her out to do fun things. She was only a toddler, so

147

we'd go to the pool or park, anything to keep her out of the house while Ryan drank himself to a near coma.

I tried to help, get him into counseling, but he refused. My mother cried daily, wanting to help and send him to rehab, but again, he refused.

Perhaps it was Jen's psychology background, but she managed to get him talking. She'd spend hours over there, trying to get him to express the pain he was feeling. I can't say I blame him for falling in love with her. She was easy to fall for, with her sweet Southern belle personality. I figured she was finally getting through to him, finally helping him sober up, but she was helping him fill a void that ended up ruining all our lives.

Chapter Twenty
Aspen

After Thursday's class with Professor Hampton, I'm more nervous than ever about the gala tonight. I could hardly keep eye contact with him, and he hadn't made it easy. Every time I looked up from my canvas, he'd be staring with that stupid crooked grin of his, toned arms crossed over his broad chest. I had to remind myself not to drool and to keep my head down.

But I hadn't been successful in trying to act normal since Ellie kept glancing at me out of the corner of her eye. I could tell she was suspicious considering how much attention he'd given me the past six weeks and especially since she made a few comments about us hooking up a while ago. I can't say I blame her, though—the way he looks at me would make a blind man suspicious.

However, I know we have to act normally when people are around. As hard as it sounds, it's also hot. It's like this little secret that only he and I know...a secret everyone would die to hear about.

By Saturday morning, I'm antsy as hell.

Ms. Jones has been blowing my phone up all morning, double- and triple-checking everything. I'm scheduled to help assist guests and talk them into buying. There'll be several of us walking around to help interpret the paintings for anyone who asks, but Ms. Jones knows I've done this the most out of all the other girls.

On top of all that, I have to fit into a gown, do my hair and makeup, and find shoes that match. I'm normally on top of it all, but lately my brain has been preoccupied with other things.

Things like Professor Hampton.

And his hands.

And his eyes.

And his perfect lips.

And anything to do with him, which has made me unable to function at anything else since he kissed me Wednesday night.

And speaking of that kiss, I can't get the taste and feel of his mouth out of my mind. I replay it over in my head so I won't forget it. I've kissed numerous guys in the past, but his kiss was different.

I hear knocking on my door and yell for them to come in. I know it's Kendall. We're supposed to head to the gallery, and I know she's going to ream my ass for not being ready yet.

"Aspen!"

"In here!" I call from my bathroom. I hear her walk down the hall and see her as soon as she comes through the door. "What in the hell?" I break out in laughter. "Why aren't you dressed?"

"That's because I can't get the damn dress over my ass." She scowls. "It fit me a few weeks ago."

"Maybe you're bloated?" I spin her around and pull up the dress. "Okay, suck in." I pull it tighter, but the zipper doesn't reach. "When I count to three, inhale as deep as you can and hold it." She does as I say, and I yank up the zipper, just barely getting it to latch. "There."

She turns around with a frown. "I can't even breathe."

"Do you have another one?"

"If I had another one, I wouldn't be trying to squeeze into this!"

"Let me unzip it, and you can wear one of my dresses."

"Are you kidding? Your stuff is even tighter than mine."

"Not all of them!" I counter. "Come on." I drag her into my room and open the closet doors. "There has to be something in here that'll work."

Finally, we find something that won't have her passing out from lack of oxygen.

"I look like a stripper," Kendall complains less than an hour later, staring at herself in the mirror.

"Silver is in," I say unconvincingly. "You look fine."

"I'm not an idiot, Aspen. I make one wrong move and it'll rip in half, giving everyone a free show."

"At least it'd help sell lots of paintings," I tease, laughing at her dramatics. "But just to be safe, don't bend over."

"That's it. No more Taco Bell runs." She rubs a hand over her waistline as if she were pregnant. "Mama needs to get rid of this food baby."

I can hardly keep it together to slide my shoes on. "Come on, Little Mama. Hair time."

"Maybe if I dye it pink and puff it up like an eighties hairstyle gone bad, it'll direct everyone away from the fact that this dress is two sizes too small."

"I don't see what you're fussing about. It accents your ass and chest."

"The only time I actually have a chest and it'll be while I'm at work," she whines, flailing her arms against her sides.

"As a newly single girl, you can use this opportunity to network with potential dates."

The glare she shoots me tells me she's not amused. "Just finish your hair."

My mouth tilts up in a knowing smirk at her silly remark. I decide to leave my hair half down and pin the rest up with a red-and-silver clip. I complete the look by curling the ends and spraying it. I apply my makeup as usual—smoky eyes and red lips.

"Ready?" she asks, leaning up against the wall. I try to hide the smile that's forming on my face at the fact that she can't sit. She's been standing there waiting for me for at least a half hour.

"All ready."

"Finally. I was about to pass out."

"Are you sure you want to wear that?"

She checks the time on her phone. "Even if I did want to change, there's no time. We have to be there in five minutes."

I grab my clutch off the table and follow her out. The event is from six to ten, but Ms. Jones wants us there an hour early.

"It'll be a miracle if I last all night in these heels." She sighs, cautiously stepping down the staircase.

"You get used to them."

"Oh, I'm sure people who have long, toned legs and petite feet struggle with wearing heels."

I groan at her bad attitude and remark. "That's it…we're hitting the open bar first."

"Now we're talking."

I know Professor Hampton is going to be at the event, but nothing could've prepared me for how I'd feel the moment I first saw him in his sleek, black tuxedo, crisp white shirt, and smooth black tie. He looks flawless. I want to run my hands down his chest.

Butterflies build in my stomach as I clench my thighs at the thought of his lips on mine again. His hair is combed back, the sides trimmed short. He looks like he came straight out of a GQ magazine, and I want to subscribe to every issue.

I pretend I'm not looking at him or memorizing every inch of his solid body. I keep my gaze low enough to keep him in my peripheral vision. He's talking with one of the bartenders, laughing and already holding a drink in his hand.

A drink. That's exactly what I need.

"Aspen!"

Or not.

I turn and see Ms. Jones speed-walking with her arms flailing right toward me, Christine chasing after her with a frazzled look on her face. "Hi!" I smile at the pair. Ms. Jones is a walking, talking bundle of nerves, and poor Christine looks like she's trying to hold on for dear life.

"Thank goodness you're here."

"Everything okay?"

She's panting, and I can tell she's about to have a nervous breakdown. "No. Yes. Well. I'm freaking out a little."

Christine stares pointedly and mouths, *a little*? It takes everything I have not to giggle. Tamping down the humor, I give Ms. Jones my undivided attention.

"Okay, what can I do to help?"

"I need you two to make sure everyone is doing what they're supposed to be doing."

"Of course we will."

"We have some important people from the community coming and everything needs to be perfect."

Placing my hands on her shoulders, I look her straight in the eyes. "It will be, okay? Everything is planned to the last detail. Christine and I have it under control. This is *your* event. Enjoy it."

She takes a deep breath and exhales slowly. "Right. Okay, thank you."

I release her shoulders and smile. "Anytime." I wink before she walks off, Christine trailing behind her, my words going right over her head.

Kendall walks over with two drinks in her hand and a sly smirk on her lips.

"What's that look?" I ask.

She hands me a glass of champagne. "Nothing." She takes a sip, and I know she's full of shit.

Glancing behind her, I notice the other bartender that's setting up is staring right at her ass. "Nothing...*right*," I drawl with an over-exaggerated tone. "So are you ready to schmooze for the next four hours?"

She sighs. "As long as there's a drink in my hand at all times."

I frown, finally realizing the issue. "You miss him," I say softly.

She shrugs, avoiding eye contact with me. It's been two weeks since Kellan broke up with her, and I've been so busy with my own drama that I haven't even been paying attention to the pain she was feeling from it.

"Tonight, we drink away our inhibitions." I clink my glass with hers. "Tomorrow, we pay for it." I smile when I finally get a laugh out of her.

"Deal."

After finishing my glass, I set it back down. The doors are going to open soon, and I need to get my head into the game. I'll be the attendant in the America in the Thirties Exhibit. Each one has an attendant available to help push sales and be ready to answer questions about the paintings.

Kendall isn't as familiar with them, so she's placed by the front doors, welcoming everyone to the event and directing them to the silent auction, bar, and food.

I decide to use the restroom quickly before the doors open. My heart races as I walk down the hall, and I know if I don't take a few minutes to breathe it out, I'll only feel worse as the night goes on. I usually live for these events. I love talking to other people about art and hearing their interpretations of the pieces. It's these events that make juggling school and work worth it. But having Professor Hampton here is making me more nervous than usual.

"Aspen…" I hear his deep, hoarse voice before I see him. I spin around and face him as he walks toward me.

"Hi, Professor Hampton." I grin. "You look great. Black suits you."

He flashes a shy smile as he brushes his fingers over the stubble covering his jawline. He steps closer. "What did I say about calling me that outside of the classroom?" When his gaze travels from my eyes to my mouth, my body shivers in anticipation of his hands on me again.

"Oh, right." I swallow. "Sorry…I'm…you make me a little nervous," I admit and wish I could stop rambling.

His hand reaches out and caresses my cheek. I press my face into his palm and my eyes flutter closed. His other hand wraps around my waist and closes the gap between us.

My eyes open as I feel his breath against me. "You make me more than nervous, Aspen Evans." He leans down and softly brushes his lips against mine. "You look breathtaking, by the way. It's going to be impossible to keep my eyes off you all night."

"Then don't." I close the gap between us, craving a taste. I know we're alone in the hallway, but a part of me still feels anxious at the thought of getting caught.

Although it makes kissing my professor that much more exciting.

He takes a step forward, making me step back. He takes another and another and soon my back is pressed firmly against the wall. His mouth moves more aggressively, pulling my lower lip in between his and sucking it lightly before pressing his tongue against mine. I wrap my arms around him, feeling his taut muscles against my fingers.

As soon as I moan, his hips grind against me and pin me to the wall in a blistering hot kiss.

"Morgan…" I say on a soft whimper.

"Say it again," he demands.

"Morgan," I whisper. He grabs my wrists and lifts my arms over my head against the wall.

He moves his mouth down my jaw and lands on my neck. His arousal presses against my lower stomach and my body shivers, both in excitement and nerves. When he slides up, he pulls my earlobe in between his lips with a sharp inhale.

"If you kiss my neck and suck on my ear, your pants are coming off." The words blurt out of me without a second thought, but the moment they release from my lips, he nips my neck.

"*Jesus Christ*…" he growls, pressing one last kiss against the flesh of my neck. "Just when I was trying to talk myself out of taking advantage of you, I'm reminded that you may be the one taking advantage of me."

"No one said willpower was easy." I wink and he lets out a soft laugh.

"Screw willpower." He kisses me once more before the voices from the front get louder. "Shit."

"I think we have to get back to civilization."

"Unfortunately." He frowns. He takes a couple of steps back, giving me room to adjust myself. I comb my fingers through my hair and fix my lipstick, sure someone is going to notice how swollen my lips are.

I decide I should walk back first to avoid any suspicions. My heart is nearly beating out of my chest, but not because of the reasons before. This reason is a much better excuse. I look over my shoulder and see his gaze fixed on me as I walk away. "Find me later, *Professor*." I wink and confidently walk away.

The only thought in my mind as I walk back to the front is how much I want to kiss him again…and again and again, and how I want to do much more than kiss.

Screw rules and consequences. I don't want meaningless one-night stands anymore.

I want someone who understands me on a deeper level. Someone who's passionate about what I'm passionate about. Someone who could grasp the pain and emotional baggage I carry around.

I want that someone to be him—Morgan Hampton.

Chapter Twenty-One
Morgan

I don't know what came over me, but the moment my lips touched hers again, I was helpless to stop. Seeing her in that tight red dress that hugs her curves like a second skin, add the plunging neckline that accentuates her perfect breasts, and I was a goner. On a normal day, I was out of control around her, but this threw me straight over the edge.

I'm drawn to her and refuse to fight it any longer. Knowing she feels the same way has me itching to get her alone again.

Aunt Mel is furiously bouncing around, double- and triple-checking that everything is set to go. I know she's a perfectionist, so I pull her aside. "Where can I help?"

"Oh, Morgan." She sighs. "You're here to enjoy. Don't you worry."

I eye her suspiciously. "Let me help."

"Well, jump in anywhere if you insist." She finally smiles. "Don't forget to have fun, too." She winks and leans in to kiss me on the cheek. I plan to enjoy myself, but not the way she's thinking.

Soon the doors open and people swarm in. I walk in between people, greeting and welcoming them to the event. I keep my eyes out for Aspen, wanting any excuse to look at her. She looks completely flawless, smiling and chatting. I hear a sweet laugh come from her, which completely lights up the room. I wish I could wrap my arm around her and claim her for everyone to see. But I know I can't, and I know I sound ridiculous for even wanting to claim her, but I can't help the way she affects me.

I haven't felt this way in years, and I feel high just thinking about it. There's no doubt that everything about her consumes me. I've been infatuated with her for weeks, and now that I know what her lips and body pressed against me feel like, I only want more. More of *her*.

Everything is going amazing until that douchebag, Shane, walks up to her. She keeps her gaze low, but his hand on her arm doesn't go unnoticed. My blood boils at the sight of him.

I hate that she even gives him the time of day, but I know we can't go public with whatever we are. It's too new to even discuss it at this point. However, that doesn't mean I want to watch another guy draped all over her.

After a few minutes of balling my hands into fists, I decide to interrupt their little chat. I grab two champagne glasses off a tray and walk over to her. "You looked like you could use a drink."

"Thank you," she says, grabbing it and turning her body toward me.

Shane clears his throat and grabs Aspen's attention back. "Oh, Morgan, this is Shane. Shane, this is Morgan, Ms. Jones's nephew."

I don't want to be anywhere near the guy, especially not touch him, but I plaster a fake smile and shake the moron's hand.

"Ah, the nephew. Explains why you're here then."

We release hands, and I furrow my brows. "Excuse me?"

"Oh, nothing." He scans over me and then moves to Aspen, his lips tilting up into a knowing smirk.

What the fuck does that mean?

"You're working at the school, right?" he asks as if to throw it in my face.

"He's my art professor," Aspen interrupts. Although she means to take the focus off me, she ends up only encouraging him.

"You know what they say? Those that can't do, *teach*." He pats me on the shoulder with a tight squeeze and excuses himself.

My eyes narrow as I watch him walk away. If I didn't have an appearance to uphold, I'd punch him until I saw blood.

Pushing the Limits

"Ignore him," Aspen scoffs, annoyance in her tone. "He's an idiot."

"Clearly."

She tilts her head, and a small smile surfaces. "Seriously…he's not even worth being pissed over. He's a decent guy normally, but he's just mad I won't go out with him."

"You won't?" My brow arches. *Does that mean he sees me as a threat, then?*

"Don't act so surprised. I do have standards." She grins.

"Good to know." I take a sip of my champagne and continue staring at her.

"I have to get to my exhibit. People are starting to wander around and Ms. Jones will have a mini heart attack if I don't get a few buyers."

"You'd have a buyer in me, but I can't find what I'm looking for."

"Is that so?" She bites her lip. "You wanted to buy one of *mine*?"

"Of course. I've only been suggesting you put a piece in for the past month." I know those aren't for sale, but I would've asked Aunt Mel to make an exception.

"You could've told me that was why."

I lean in and softly whisper in her ear, "And what fun would that have been?"

I sip back the last of my drink and walk back through the crowd. I know she has a job to do, so I busy myself with the silent auction.

An hour passes since I've felt her body against mine, rather *pinned her against the wall and made love to her lips,* and yet I'm anxious to be near her again. I want to know what she's doing, what she's thinking, and if she's thinking the same thing I am.

Kissing her feels like an addiction—one I don't ever want to recover from. It felt different from before—much more intense and passionate. It's validated everything I've been wondering about.

Walking around with a glass of champagne in my hand, a tap on my shoulder grabs my attention. I spin around and nearly lose my grip on the stem of the glass when I see *her.*

"Hi, stranger." She flashes a small smile, and my jaw ticks at the sweetness of her voice.

"What are you doing here, Jen?" I hiss, keeping my voice low.

"I had a ticket. Small world."

I clench my teeth. "Not that small."

"Your mother told me you'd be here. Aunt Mel put my name on the list."

I swallow back the rest of the champagne before setting it down. "Well, have a good time." I take a step to walk around her, but she grabs me by the arm and pushes me back. "What are you doing?"

"I want to talk."

"There's nothing to talk about."

"After being gone for five years, there's plenty to talk about."

I sigh, irritated she's cornered me, but I don't want to make a scene, so I agree. "You have five minutes."

She flashes a victorious smile, but I ignore it. She follows me out into a quiet hall at the back of the gallery.

"Okay, what is it?" I shove my hands in my front pockets and lean away from her.

"You look good, Morgan."

"Cut the shit, Jen."

"Wow…" She shakes her head. "Even five years later, you still hate me."

"What were you expecting?"

"Maybe some understanding?"

My brows arch. "*Understanding*? You want me to understand why you decided to fuck around on me?"

"You were gone, Morgan! All the time! All you did was work and when you weren't working, you were painting. For hours!"

"*That's* your excuse? Hard work and dedication are your reasons for cheating?" I choke out a pathetic laugh.

"You never made time for me. You never made time for *us*! I tried to tell you. I tried talking to you, but you never wanted to leave the house."

"That's not true. Plus, if I wasn't working, who'd you expect to pay off your student loans?"

"You still could've made time for us. It was as if you gave up." Her features soften, and I know she's about to release the waterworks any minute.

"No," I say sternly. "You're the one who gave up. You're the one who went behind my back and screwed Ryan. You're the one who broke us, *not* me." I don't even know why I'm entertaining this conversation. It's one I'd been trying to avoid this whole time.

I start to walk away, but she pleads for me to stay. "Don't go! I'm sorry, okay?"

"Yeah, sorry. A lot of good that does me."

"Your mother's been able to forgive me. Why can't you?"

I spin around and face her. "Because I'm not that dense," I say harshly.

"I'm not here for me, I swear."

I look down and notice the impressive diamond on her left hand. I imagined for years what it'd feel like to run into her again after all this time, but one thing I wasn't counting on was having an audience nearby. But now it didn't matter. I can look at her and not feel a single thing for her. Those feelings I once had for her are long gone, which have been replaced with resentment and anger.

My eyes narrow. "Then why are you here?"

"I'm here for you. For Ryan."

"That's bullshit."

"Morgan, we were together for six years. Because I haven't seen you for five, doesn't mean I don't still know you. I know you better than you think."

"Is that so?" I mock, rubbing the stubble along my jaw.

"You're beating yourself up over his death. You're living with the guilt and it's eating you."

My throat burns at the way she reads me. "I don't need your psycho-babble shit. I'm handling it as well as I can. Don't think you can just come back into my life and fix me. It doesn't work that way."

"I'm not trying to fix anything, you stubborn ass. I'm trying to give you closure."

Just being near her is making my blood boil. I can't have this conversation with her—especially here. She's the reason I left, abandoned my family, and stopped believing in love.

"I need to go," I say, walking away.

"Morgan, please!" I hear her pathetic pleas.

She's completely ruined everything. I'm seething and the only thing I can think of is getting the hell out of here.

I find Aunt Mel and quickly whisper in her ear that I have to get going. I make up an excuse that Natalia needs me and kiss her goodbye on the cheek. I don't see Aspen on my way out, and I don't look for her either.

Chapter Twenty-Two
Aspen

Everything about tonight is going perfectly, and I never want this euphoric feeling to end. Minus the part where Shane and his pride showed up. But not even he can ruin my good mood.

I haven't stopped smiling since Morgan kissed me. My body shivers every time I think about him, which has been all night long.

The evening comes to an end, and I scan around the exhibits looking for him, but I can't find him anywhere. My stomach somersaults at the thought of not seeing him again tonight.

"Hey, Ms. Jones!" I smile as I find her drinking in the corner with Christine. "This was fantastic!" I give her a hug, and she enthusiastically returns the gesture. I can tell she's had a bit too much champagne.

Not that I blame her. She ordered the high-priced stuff, so she should enjoy it too.

"It was! I can't thank you enough for being here. Oh, Aspen, you're my favorite." She leans her head on my shoulder and sighs.

"With that, I'm going to head out," Christine says, offering me a friendly smile and a quick hug as she walks by.

I burst laughing, amused at Ms. Jones's theatrics. I call Kendall over and tell her to help me get her to a chair.

"Where's Morgan? I'll tell him to take you home."

"He left a while ago."

Wait, what? Why would he leave without saying something?

"Oh, he did? Why?" I ask, wondering why he'd leave without telling me.

"Natalia called and said she needed him home." Her eyes close, and I panic. My heart speeds up at the mention of him having someone at home waiting for him.

Who the hell is Natalia?

Ms. Jones is out before I get the chance to holler at Kendall for help. I've never seen her like this before, but I'm certain she took anxiety meds before the event started, and I know you shouldn't mix those with alcohol.

Kendall helps me get her into the back of the car. She drives as I search for Ms. Jones's phone. "I'll call Morgan. Someone will need to check up on you," I say to her, although I'm not sure she can understand me.

"I'll be fine," she slurs. "He's with Natalia."

She says her name again, and it's like nails on a chalkboard. "And who's Natalia?" She passes out again before I even finish my question.

"Shit." I look through her phone for his number, but when I call, he doesn't answer. I decide to leave a voicemail, so when he's done *entertaining*, he'll know what's going on.

"That was interesting." Kendall sighs after we get Ms. Jones inside her house and in bed.

"I doubt she'll remember any of that." We get back in the car and buckle up.

"God, I hope not. However, it could finally get me on her favorites list." She smiles as she turns the car on.

I snort. "Don't count on it."

"So I hardly saw you tonight. Everything okay?"

"Me?" I quickly glance over at her. "Yeah, fine. Just tired," I lie.

"Yeah, me too. Ooh…let's stay up, eat junk food, and watch movies until we pass out."

Her serious tone has me cracking up. "I didn't realize we were fourteen again."

"Hey, don't be a Debbie Downer."

I reach for her hand and hold it in mine. "You're a good friend, Kendall."

"I think maybe you misunderstood when I suggested we stay up and watch movies together..." she quips. She flashes a witty smile, and I lean my head on her shoulder, laughing and squeezing her hand.

"I can be a much better friend if I had some booze."

"You're in luck. I happen to know a place."

Kendall and I stop at the bar Zoe works at, and since we didn't change clothes, people stare at us like we have the plague. But we don't let that stop us. I don't tell them why I'm angry-drinking, but they don't notice anyway.

"Alright, ladies. Blowjobs on me!" Zoe shouts over the noise.

"Now we're talking!"

She hands us each a shot with whip cream on top. "No using your hands!"

We smile and accept the challenge, taking the shot glass in our mouths and swallowing it down.

"Oh my God!" I wipe the cream off my face. I look at Kendall and laugh at how much cream is on her nose. "I think you missed your entire mouth."

"Trust me...that's the whole point." She winks, licking the cream off her lips.

"I'd rather have it on my face than in my mouth," Zoe blurts out, making us all burst into a fit of giggles. Clearly, the alcohol has taken over.

I'm not a clingy girl by any means, but when a guy kisses me, gets me all hot and bothered, and then leaves with no explanation, I'm allowed to get pissed. So therefore, I drink.

And drinking usually leads to bringing a guy home with me.

"Dude, that guy has been staring at your ass from the moment you sat down." Zoe directs my attention to a guy standing behind me.

"I'm in a sexy red gown. I'd be worried if guys weren't staring."

"You're so humble," Zoe mocks. "You two better be getting a cab. Give me the keys."

"Yes, boss lady," I say in a condescending voice as Kendall hands

---

them to her. "But maybe I can get lucky and find a different ride home." I wink and finish off the drink Zoe made for me earlier and ungracefully slide off the stool.

"Call me later so I know you're safe!" Kendall hollers, but I adjust my cleavage and walk away, letting the alcohol take over all my pain.

Chapter Twenty-Three
Morgan

I slam the shot glass onto the table as the alcohol burns its way down my throat. I should go to bed, but with the way things ended tonight, it's more than necessary.

Natalia is staying over at my parents' house, so I'm left with my thoughts and a bottle of whiskey, which is never a good combination.

Jennifer. Aspen. Jennifer. Aspen.

How the hell did the evening go from kissing Aspen to walking away from Jen?

I have no fucking clue.

Hence the whiskey.

I want to call her, explain everything, but I know with the condition I'm currently in, that's not a smart idea. This whole situation has my head in such a mess. I don't even want to think about it anymore.

But I can't stop the thoughts from swarming in. Thoughts of Jen bring me to thoughts of Ryan and all the pain they caused me. The guilt of never forgiving him or even talking it out hurts the most. Jen shattered my heart, but Ryan was my brother. I should've at least mended things with him.

I pour another shot and throw my head back. I should've called him. I should've visited. I shouldn't have left. I shouldn't have let the bitterness and anger consume me so much that I neglected my family for five years and waited until it was too late. He died before I could tell him I still loved him and that we could move on from this. But I was a coward.

The only closure I need is that he died a hero. I don't deserve anything more than that.

I wake up sometime between the sun rising and the front door slamming shut. I'm not sure if I'm asleep or waking up from a bad dream.

Within seconds, I hear Natalia and my mother screaming at each other and then I know.

I'm in a real-life nightmare.

Memories of the night before surface quickly as the alcohol left in my system spins the entire room around. I curse, feeling the effects of last night. My head pounds and my body aches.

I dress quickly and head out to the living room to see what all the fuss is about. Natalia runs to her room the moment she sees me.

"What the hell is going on?" I follow my mom to the kitchen. She immediately begins rummaging through my cupboards.

She grabs the bottle of bourbon and a glass. "I'd like to know that, too."

"Mother, it's not even noon. What are you doing?" I jerk my head toward the glass. She drinks casually, but since Ryan's death, she's been drinking more.

"There's a reason God didn't give me a daughter. I can't take all this emotional crap." She pours the bourbon in her glass and takes a sip.

That makes two of us.

"What's the issue? Is she okay?"

"Morgan, I don't know. She was fine at breakfast and then suddenly she copped an attitude with me. Screaming something about her dad, how I'm not the boss of her, and she hates everyone."

I narrow my eyes. She's never talked to me like that before, so I know something serious has to be going on with her.

"I'll talk to her." I grab a glass of orange juice first and suck it down with a couple of Aleve.

"How was your event thing?"

"It was going great until you sent Jennifer," I snap, setting the glass down in the sink. "Thanks for that, by the way."

"Morgan..." she pleads as I start walking away.

"Any chance this has anything to do with Ryan's uniform?" I turn to face her.

"She asked for it a few nights ago, but I couldn't part with it." Her voice is soft, pained.

"She's eleven, Mom. She's lost both parents and feels disconnected from everyone," I try and explain. "She needs something to hang on to. Something that'll help her not feel so alone."

She bows her head, nodding. "I miss him so much."

Stepping close, I wrap my arms around her. "I know, Mom. Me, too."

I walk her to the couch and tell her to sit and wait for me. "I'm going to go talk to her."

I go to Nat's room and find her sitting on top of her bed with a pillow pressed against her chest.

"Hey, Shorty."

"Hi," she mumbles against the pillow.

"Wanna talk about what happened?"

"Does it look like I do?" She presses her face against the fabric.

"Grandma isn't always rational when it comes to stuff like this. She's suffering, too," I remind her. "But I think we can work something out."

"What's the point?" she counters, sniffling. "She'll find a way to make a big fuss about it."

"I have a lot of his boxes here. You can have anything you want." I wrap an arm around her shoulders and hold her close.

She stays silent a moment before speaking up again. "Do you think he and my mom are up there together?" She peeks under her lashes, a small hopeful smile spreading across her face.

I smile in return. "Yeah, absolutely. I also think they're looking down on you. You have two guardian angels, and I think that's pretty special."

Her eyes widen a bit, and her smile grows. "I like that," she approves, nodding.

"Hopefully, one day, this all makes sense. I don't know why bad things happen to good people, but I know he's in a better place now. He's probably up there dancing with your mom..."

She snorts. "Yeah, he's probably teaching her his bad dance moves, too."

"Your mom was a beautiful dancer. Hopefully, she rubs off on him." I wink at her, squeezing her tighter. Lena was a fabulous dancer all through her high school and college days. She danced professionally for a while before having Natalia, but when she was born, Lena devoted all her time to being a mom.

"I hope I get to see her again one day. I hardly remember her. Sometimes I think I do, but I don't know if it's just from something my dad told me about her, or if I do remember."

"Maybe it's both, but the important thing for you to know is you never have to stop talking about them. I'll always be here, Shorty."

"Thank you." She curls into my side, and I hold her tighter.

I place a kiss on top of her head and whisper, "I love you, Natalia."

After I'm sure she's okay, I walk into the living room where my mom sits on the couch, swirling the ice that's left in her glass. Her head is bowed, and I know something's eating at her.

"We need to talk," I say.

"I know I'm not handling this right." She frowns. "She reminds me so much of him."

"There's no right or wrong way to handle losing a son, Mom. But I do want to know what you were thinking by telling Jennifer where I'd be. I can't believe you even talk to her." I sigh, brushing a hand through my hair as I think about the grudge I still hold in my heart.

"I'm not a huge fan of her either, Morgan. But she made you happy. She once made your brother happy, and as much as that sounds wrong, I'm glad you had each other."

"She's also the reason I left," I remind her, my teeth clenching.

"I know, sweetie. I know." She pats my knee in only a way a grieving mother can. "I thought she could help give you some closure, a little clarity."

"What do you mean? Why would she have anything to offer me?" *Besides pain, that is.*

She narrows her eyes as she shifts on the couch. "Do you know why Ryan made you Natalia's guardian?"

"I assumed it was because I was her godfather."

"Right. But when you left?"

"I assumed he'd pick someone else," I respond honestly, as much as it hurts to say it. I still remember the day he asked me to be her godfather. I was beyond honored, but more than that, it bonded us in a much different way.

"A couple of years after you left, I told him he needed to adjust his will. Make it more updated." She pauses a moment, and I can see the pain in her features as she talks about this. "He refused."

"What do you mean?"

She shrugs, lowering her gaze. "I told him I was worried about him not keeping his paperwork updated in the event something happened. I wanted to make sure he protected himself, considering he had a risky job. He wouldn't do it."

My jaw tightens at the thought of them having this conversation, my mother always so worried about him when he worked. "Why not?"

"He said no matter what your relationship was, and even if you never spoke again, he trusted you more than anyone in the world. He knew you'd be the best person for Natalia and so he didn't change it."

I bow my head, tightening my eyes as I let the guilt eat me alive.

"He was right," she finally says, putting her hand on top of mine. "You are the best person for her."

"I love her," I say, my throat tightening as I think about what would have happened to her if I hadn't returned.

"I know." She flashes a genuine smile. "You two are good for each other. Both grieving over the same person. Both struggling with change."

A few hours after my mother leaves, Nat finally comes out of her room wrapped in one of her blankets.

"Feeling better?"

"Yeah, I'm fine." She plops on the couch with the remote and starts flipping channels.

"What do you want for dinner tonight?" I ask, hoping to get a reaction out of her.

"I don't care."

"We could go out."

"No, thanks."

I wrap a hand around the back of my neck and squeeze. All her answers are short and robotic. I decide against pushing her and leave her alone for a while.

But the more I'm left to my thoughts, the more they go to Aspen and her fucking amazing lips.

I'm torn between calling her and waiting until class on Tuesday to talk to her in person.

Before I have time to decide, I hear Nat call my name.

"Coming!" I shout and head into the living room where she hasn't moved. "Yeah?"

"Can you make spaghetti?"

Her question catches me off guard at first, but the moment I remember the meaning behind it, I smile wide and reply, "Of course, Shorty."

She flashes a satisfied grin, and a moment later, her gaze flies to the TV screen. I head into the kitchen and dig around my cupboards, doing a mental checklist to see if I even have all the ingredients.

"Don't forget meatballs!" she hollers from the couch. "And cheese!"

"I won't!" I shout with a knowing smile. Ryan's wife was Italian and from a large family of amazing cooks. When they first started dating, he tried to win her parents over by cooking his infamous spaghetti and meatballs.

It ended up being a complete disaster, and they never let him live it down, but it ended up being Natalia's favorite. He continued to make it even though, compared to his wife's cooking, he was awful. Tonight was the first night she's requested it since he died.

I manage to make it exactly how she likes it, meatballs and all. After cleaning up the kitchen, I grab a beer from the fridge and go check up on Natalia, who's been reading in her room since dinner.

"Bed in fifteen," I say, popping my head through the doorway.

She doesn't move. Or speak.

"Nat? Did you hear me?" I ask louder.

Nothing.

I walk next to her and grab the book out of her hands.

"Hey!" she screeches and leans up to reach for it, but I pull it up even higher. "Have you gone mad?" She hisses.

"Have you gone deaf?" I arch a brow.

She makes a face and reaches for it again.

"Fifteen minutes," I say firmly, handing the book over.

"I was reading that." She scowls. I repeat my words again as I walk toward the door. "Yes, I heard you. Bed in fifty."

"Fifteen!" I call over my shoulder with a smile and walk out.

Natalia has another therapy appointment this next week, and even though she's been going for months, there's not been much progress. I know she's going through a lot, even more so at her age, but I wish I could wrap my arms around her and promise that everything will get better someday.

But I won't make that promise.

I can only promise that I'll be here with her as we work through it.

I walk down the hallway to my office and sit behind my desk as I focus on the boxes piled up in the corner. They aren't mine, but they represent a part of my childhood. After Ryan's funeral, Mom asked me to take them for her. She said she couldn't go through them or even look at them right now. She held on to a few of his personal belongings, but his childhood memories were too much to bear. Hell, I can barely look at them without feeling anger and resentment pile up inside me, but Natalia will want his things one day. Until then, they'll continue to taunt me.

I can remember the day Ryan moved out of the family house fresh out of high school. Boxes and boxes of his childhood all packed up as we moved them into his own apartment. Excitement ran high for him that day, but I was one part sad he was leaving and one part ready to have the house to myself. I hadn't even entered high school yet, so maybe another part of me was a little jealous.

Whenever he had friends over, they'd goof around and talk about all the parties they planned on going to. Although he was strict with his studies, he knew how to have a good time.

We piled his boxes into the back of a friend's pickup truck and hauled them to his tiny new apartment. It was a dump—old, ragged carpet and dents on the walls with a bad paint job—but he was so excited. Mom and Dad didn't have the heart to burst his bubble, so they shared in the excitement with him.

Once everything was unloaded into his new apartment, we set up his futon sofa where he told me he planned on having a lot of *sleepovers* and needed the bed in the living room. I might've been thirteen, but I wasn't a moron. I knew what he meant.

Then I helped him put together his new coffee table and TV stand that our parents bought him as a housewarming gift. They were the only two pieces in the whole place that looked decent, but I gave it six months before parties and dancing girls broke those in.

The tattered boxes of old trophies and school art projects are all Natalia has left of him. He should've been the one to show her all his memories. Be the one to tell her all about how he won the basketball championships, about his disastrous date to prom his freshman year, and the picture that perfectly captured the moment his date puked down his tux during Senior Homecoming. So many memories that were his to share.

I was surprised when my mom didn't want to take these back, but even though I hate the thought of them, I'm glad Nat will have them close by for when she's ready.

I check my watch and head to Natalia's room.

"Alright, Shorty. Lights out."

"Just one more chapter," she whines.

"How many pages is that?"

"Only like...twenty."

"No. Put it down."

She flattens it on her chest and glares. "You're a real buzz kill."

"And you're a real pain in my ass, but it's still time for bed. So c'mon. Get ready."

"You sure swear a lot."

Shit. "Sorry. I forgot."

"It's not like I've never heard my dad swear before."

"Well, adults sometimes swear. But I'll try to remember not to when you're around, okay?"

"Whatever." She places her book on the nightstand and gets up. "I'm going to brush my teeth."

She begins to walk toward the bathroom, and I notice the sadness in her eyes.

"We can talk about it if you want." I know there's a reason she brought up her favorite meal tonight after everything that happened this morning with my mother.

"There's nothing to talk about. He's dead."

I quickly grab her wrist and pull her toward me. "I know, Nat. I know. But we can talk about him sometimes. It might help ease some of the pain." She stares with an unreadable expression. "I feel it, too. I miss him every day."

"Then why weren't you ever around? Why didn't you visit?"

I'm such a fucking asshole.

"I should have." I sigh. "But I was dealing with my own shi—*crap* and avoided it by staying away from here."

"What kind of shi—*crap*?" The corners of her lips curl up a little, and I know she's mocking me.

"Personal crap. When I left, I was in a bad place. I never wanted to come back."

"But you did," she counters.

"I did." I press my mouth into a firm line. "I had to."

"For me?"

"Yeah. But for me, too. It was time."

She nods, and the corner of her lips curls up a little more. "Night."

"Good night."

I finish another beer before heading to bed. Before Ryan died, I'd spend my evenings painting, but that doesn't appeal to me anymore. The idea of painting makes me feel more guilty. Ryan encouraged me to follow my dream once I discovered it, even when Mom and Dad vocalized their disapproval about it as a career path. He was always supportive and encouraging, not that it surprised me. He was always selflessly helping others. If anyone deserved more from this life, it was Ryan. And he can't even watch his daughter grow up.

Life doesn't play fair.

Chapter Twenty-Four
Aspen

Not hearing from Morgan is killing me.

And I hate that I'm acting like *that* girl. The one that pines over a guy who never calls them after a date. The one who gets all emotional and stupid because that guy looks at them with perfect eyes and dimples, and then wants to cry because they haven't talked to you since you gave them the best kiss they've ever had.

Yeah, I'm *that* girl. And I hate it.

Being on the other side of the fence is a real drag. Feeling used and worthless is a new low for me, but I'm determined not to let him know he's lowered me to that level. Once he left me high and dry Saturday night, and not hearing from him since, he can kiss my ass. He owes me one hell of an explanation, especially about this Natalia girl, but I'm not going to go begging for one.

I walk into his classroom right on time, not giving him any extra time to talk to me. If he wants to give me some lame ass excuse, he's going to have to work for it.

"I heard the gala was a huge hit!" Ellie smiles as I sit next to her.

"It was." I smile in return.

"I wish I could've gone."

"You should've told me. I would have reserved you a ticket."

"Nah, that's okay. I'd have no one to go with anyway."

"If I hadn't been working, I would've gone alone, too."

"Oh my God! We should go out this weekend!" Her lips spread into a wide, giddy grin. "Yes. We can grab some dinner, go out for drinks, and maybe dancing?"

That sounds fun, so I easily agree. "I'm in!"

Professor Hampton rounds his desk and connects his gaze with mine. He looks tense and eager, but I don't give him the satisfaction of knowing he's pissed me off. I keep the sly smile on my face as he discusses the week's assignments.

"There's an opportunity for extra credit coming up. Even if you don't need it, it's a great class to participate in. Broadway Street Gallery is hosting a life drawing workshop this weekend. If you attend, all you have to do is show me your work from the event to receive the credit. Even though it's extra credit, I think a lot of you would benefit from the practice."

I'd forgotten about it until now. Ms. Jones hosts special events year-round, but this year she was able to reserve a nude art model for a session.

"Life drawing has many benefits. It teaches you to see, teaches you how to draw what you can see, and enables you to develop your own style. There are only a few places in the area that host these types of classes, so you might want to consider it for the experience alone."

Knowing he'll be there at the same time puts me on edge. He has me so sexually frustrated I'm ready to jump the next guy who looks at me.

However, considering I left the bar the other night with a random guy and had every intention of sticking to my usual one-nighter, and then failing after I shut him down and sent him home, I'd say that's not the best plan.

I'm sexually frustrated because it's *him*. He's confusing and irritating, and I can't help wanting to rip off his clothes. I want to hate him and scream at him for kissing me and then leaving. But I also want him to acknowledge that kissing me meant as much to him as it did to me. It was hot and passionate. I'd never felt that way from a kiss before.

It makes no sense, but I shouldn't let it affect me. I'm the one who doesn't get attached and knows better than to let emotions get in my way, yet I'm the one who's left feeling the ache in my chest.

As we all work on our projects, I avoid any eye contact with him. It's much harder than it sounds, but I study the paper as if it's a map to a million-dollar treasure chest. I won't give him the satisfaction that I'm dying to see if he's looking at me, too.

"Your shading needs work," I hear him say from behind me in a distant tone.

I clench my teeth to keep myself from telling him off. I don't want to make a scene with witnesses around, but the closer he leans in, the more I'm tempted.

"I'll work on it," I reply roughly, keeping my tone low.

Ellie glances over with a concerned look, but I quickly flash a smile in return. She focuses on Professor Hampton as he walks away. I shrug as if I have no idea what his problem is, and she makes a face behind his back. I bite my lip to keep from laughing at her antics, finally putting me in a better mood.

Class comes to an end, and my heart hasn't stopped pounding in my chest. I have no idea what he's thinking, but I'm bailing as soon as possible.

"Aspen, I'd like to speak with you after class, please," he announces as I put my easel and supplies away in my bag. I cringe at the sound of his demanding tone, and if it weren't for twenty pairs of eyes on me, I'd tell him to fuck off.

But instead, I smile and respond, "Sorry, I'm in a huge rush. I have to be somewhere."

His throat tightens as he swallows. He knows he can't argue with me in front of everyone, so he shrugs it off.

"Oh, sure. I'll be here early for class on Thursday. You'll come then."

"I'll do my best to be there," I lie in a condescending tone. He knows I'm putting on a show for everyone eavesdropping.

I walk out with my dignity intact and an extra pep in my step. Ellie rushes up to walk with me and notices the sly smirk on my face.

"What the hell was that?"

"Nothing." I keep walking with my bag over my shoulder.

"Really? If that was nothing, then I'm a reborn virgin."

The corner of my lips turns up in amusement, but I turn my head so she can't see the smile creeping on my face. "I don't know what you're talking about." I turn toward her and keep a straight face. "I'm meeting a friend and couldn't stay."

She studies my features, trying to read me, but I don't let it show on my face.

"Alright, if you say so," she says, but I know she's not buying any of it. "Any plans for spring break?"

I let out a relieved sigh at the change of topic. "I'm supposed to fly home, but I haven't decided if I'm going or not."

Speaking of which, my mother's expecting me in two weeks.

"You?" We walk through the front doors and the warm breeze blows the hair off my shoulders.

"Oh my God! Is that a hickey?" She points to my neck, and I quickly cover my neck.

"What?" I ask in a panic.

She bursts into laughter, nearly choking. "I so got you."

"You're a real bitch."

"You thought you had one, which means there *is* something going on with Professor Hampton."

Fucking hell.

"I assure you there is nothing happening."

She squints, not believing my words. "But there was? Or will be? C'mon, I may be a lot of things, but I'm not an idiot. I can smell the sexual tension between you two. It's so obvious, the rest of us all have bets for when you're going to finally hook up."

My eyes grow so big I'm worried they'll fall right out. I can't tell if she's messing with me or not, so I walk away. "Gotta go!" I call out. "Bye!"

I hear her laughing behind me. My cheeks heat at the thought of other students getting suspicious of the two of us. What happened is never happening again, I've decided, so I don't know why I'm worried, but the last thing I need is the reputation of a student who sleeps with her professors to get good grades.

My work merits my good grades and that's not something I'm

willing to jeopardize. Graduate schools have been contacting me since my sophomore year and considering it's a competitive program, I need all the references I can get in order to be accepted into one of them.

I walk into the gallery Wednesday morning with all the memories of Saturday night still lingering in my mind. That kiss. His lips. Those stupid, sexy dimples and charming baby blues. I hate that he affects me the way he does. Hell, even in my dreams, my body craves him.

But that doesn't justify him kissing me and leaving me behind like a meaningless and forgotten one-night stand. Talk about the pot calling the kettle black, I've done the same thing dozens of times and never felt an ounce of guilt. Being on this side of the situation is foreign and I don't like it. Not one bit.

After stowing my things in my locker, I head to Christine's desk to see what's on the schedule for today. I'm completely shocked when I walk up and she is smiling and humming lightly.

"Wow, this is a nice change of pace to your usual grouchy morning attitude." Her cheeks flush and her attention reverts to the papers in front of her. "So, what's the cause of this early morning Cinderella moment? Should I watch out for singing birds and dancing mice?"

"Oh, shut up, Aspen!" She shuffles her papers, again avoiding eye contact.

"Oh. My. God. You got laid, didn't you?" I tease, inching closer.

Her face turns about ten shades of red and she flips me off. "I did, and you were right. A little D did wonders." Christine's voice has that new relationship dreaminess I've become used to hearing from Kendall whenever she gets a new boyfriend.

I laugh, clapping my hands in praise. "Of course, I was right. I'm always right when it comes to the D. There is nothing like a big D to fix a bad attitude."

"Lord, Aspen, you are terrible." She shakes her head, fighting back a smirk. "Time to get to work, crazy lady. You've got back-to-back tours today. Two buses full of middle-schoolers."

"Guess I better get some more coffee if I'm chasing kids all day." I couldn't have asked for a better distraction from Morgan.

Chapter Twenty-Five
Morgan

After Aspen blew me off Tuesday, I need to talk to her in person and explain everything. Telling a girl that the same night I kissed her, my ex-fiancée just happened to show up isn't something I want to explain in a text or phone call.

I head to my office early before Thursday's class in hopes she comes in like I asked her to, but from her prompt response, I have a feeling she won't.

"Morgan?" I look up and see Claire in the doorway of my office with a bright, eager smile.

I groan. *Can this day get any fucking worse?*

"Yeah, hi," I mutter, not in the mood to humor her. "What can I help you with?"

She steps in and takes a seat across from my desk. "I was wondering if you are attending the life drawing workshop this weekend."

"Yeah, I'll be there. I'm hoping some of my students show up."

"Oh, yeah. Me, too. Although I'm not sure what to expect with first and second-year students. Most of them are only concerned about where to get a fake ID and how to get out of their homework." She snickers.

That makes me grin a little. "Well, at least that prepares me for what to expect from them in the next year or two."

She laughs, way more over-the-top than necessary. "I promise to do my best in taming them before then." She winks, and it makes my skin crawl.

"Are you attending?" I ask only to be polite.

"Yes. I love these types of events. So, since we're both going, I was wondering if you wanted to do dinner or drinks after."

I shift in my chair, uneasy and reluctant about how to answer her. "Um, I'm not sure—"

"Oh, sorry!" I hear Aspen's sweet voice behind Claire. She's standing in the doorway, her cheeks bright red. "Didn't realize you were in a meeting. I'll see you in class," she quickly rambles off before I can stop her.

Fuck. She came.

Silence lingers in the air, as I don't attempt to finish answering her question. "I'll let you go." I stand, encouraging her to do the same. "Class will be starting soon, and I should get ready."

I escort her out the door, and she surprises me by wrapping me in a tight hug. It's more intimate than a colleague-to-colleague hug, and now I'm cursing myself for not setting her in her place earlier.

"Bye, Morgan. See you later." She winks before walking down the hall, and I cringe.

Turning, I see Aspen glaring from down the hall.

Seriously? This would be my fucking luck.

She steps back when I go toward her.

"Are you kidding me?" she whisper-hisses. "You sure get around, *Professor.*"

Her condescending tone fuels the rage inside of what she's accusing me of doing. "You don't know what you're talking about, Aspen."

"Oh, right. I'm the idiot who bought everything you said, all those lines you fed me, all those times I thought you were sincere and understanding—it was all bullshit." She seethes, and my jaw ticks once again.

This couldn't be going any fucking worse. But then she continues.

"Then I find out you have some girl waiting for you at home the night of the gala." She takes a couple steps closer, hurt evident in her features as she narrows her eyes. "Also, the exact same night you kissed me. So forgive me, Professor, but I know exactly what I'm talking about. You're a playboy who gets his kicks by flirting with your students—I can only imagine how many of them fell victim to your smooth ways in Ohio—but let it be known, I'm no longer going to be that student." She takes another step. "I have standards, and I'm glad I found out before it was too late."

"Are you done?" I smirk, crossing my arms over my chest. She's so wrong about me that I find it amusing.

"Yeah, in fact, I'm done with your class as well. I'll take the summer class with another professor who can keep his hands and lips off me," she snaps before turning on her heels and walking in the other direction.

I'm tempted to chase after her, grab her arm, and pin her up against the wall to show her how wrong she is, but I can't risk a student or another professor walking by. Touching a student is strictly off-limits and getting fired for that would follow me and prevent me from getting hired again.

I roughly brush a hand through my hair, frustrated that I have to let her walk away. There are fifteen minutes before class starts, so I grab my stuff and head to the classroom, hoping to God she shows up anyway.

But when she doesn't, I know I've completely blown it.

Now I'm not sure I'll ever get the chance to explain why I bailed Saturday night. It was a spur-of-the-moment decision, and I wish I had stayed, but Jen had me in such a rage, I needed to get out of there.

Now Aspen thinks I'm the asshole who kissed her and left without a word. Not only that, she thinks Natalia is a woman I'm dating who lives with me.

Fuck, this is such a mess.

Chapter Twenty-Six
Aspen

I haven't slept in days and am going crazy.

I've been pacing my apartment since before the sun rose, and I need some fucking coffee, but I broke all my damn coffee cups.

Clearly not my brightest move ever. But being rational isn't exactly on my radar at the moment.

I pound loudly on Kendall and Zoe's door Saturday morning, and I know they're going to be pissed. "Let me in! I know you're home," I shout through the door like a maniac.

"Jesus Christ, Asp—"

I barge through before she can finish her sentence. "Give me something to break," I demand frantically.

She closes the door and faces me. "What?" she asks in a gravelly voice. "What are you talking about?" She brushes the hair off her face.

"Something breakable. China. Glasses. Stupid figurines. Anything will do." I pace in her living room.

"Alright, hold on…" She drags her feet to the kitchen and returns with a glass plate. "Will this do?"

"Yeah, perfect," I say in a rush, grabbing it from her fingers. I raise it above my head and forcefully slam it down on the hardwood floor. The plate shatters into a million little pieces, the sound echoing off the walls with a loud bang.

"What the fuck is going on?" Zoe walks in from her bedroom. She looks at the damage, wide-eyed and speechless.

"I'm breaking shit. Got anything?"

"Have you lost your mind?" She turns and studies me. "Are you okay? You aren't blinking. Have you slept?" She reaches out to feel my forehead.

I bat her hand away and scowl. "I'm fine!" I shout. "I need to break stuff. Why is this a hard concept?"

"For starters, you want to break *our* shit."

"I've broken everything possible in my apartment, which, unfortunately, wasn't much."

"Fine." Zoe exhales. "Only if you tell us what's going on."

"I can't…" I start to break down. "I-I don't know what the hell is happening. My mind and body and heart…I just—"

A tear slides down my cheek before I can wipe it away.

"I've never seen you like this, Aspen," Kendall says softly, stepping closer.

"I know." I wipe my cheeks. "This is why I need to break something. I don't let guys in for a reason. I won't risk the heartache that comes with it. It's too much!"

"Ooh, heartbreak anger!" Zoe's face lights up with a grin. "Why didn't you say so? I'll get the plates. Kendall, you get the wine."

"It's seven in the morning!" she reminds her, but Zoe shoots her a look. Kendall sighs and does it anyway.

I want to burst into tears, but I keep it under control. I have no idea why Morgan is affecting me this way. We've hardly done anything at this point, but it feels like more than just the physical attraction. It's more than the kissing and how he sets my body on fire. We have a connection that's hard to resist. It's the mutual interests, the passion for creating art that mean something to us, and the understanding of what it means to each other. The pain, the guilt, the inner struggle.

I'd never met anyone who's completely understood before.

"Before I give you anything to break, we get to hear the whole story," Zoe demands, and I groan.

"Can't I break a plate without being interrogated?"

Kendall snorts. "Not likely."

Pushing the Limits

"Why didn't I just fuck him and move on like the rest of them? Why'd I have to go and like the stupid jerk?" I ask aloud in a harsh tone. Kendall hands me a plate and watches as I smash it on the floor. "Who kisses a girl—twice—and then leaves? Who the hell does that?" Kendall hands me another, and I add it to the rest of the shattered pieces on the floor. "And why does he have to be my goddamn professor?" I yell out before I have a chance to realize what I'm saying.

Their jaws drop. Silence lingers in the air except for my heavy breathing.

"Holy shit, Aspen," Kendall finally says. "The professor you were talking about before?"

"Yes," I quickly answer and continue, "I need to fuck him out of my system. Fuck him and kick *him* to the curb. It's the only foolproof way I know."

Kendall and Zoe stare, wide-eyed and flashing toothy grins.

"What?" I finally take a breath.

Zoe waggles her brows. "You like this guy."

"More than any other guy you've been with," Kendall agrees.

"I did. Before he pinned me up against the wall and kissed me the way he did…"

"Must've been some kiss," Zoe mocks.

I sigh.

"It was. But it's so much more than that. It's the way I feel when I'm around him. The way he interprets my creations. The way he looks at me as if he's trying to figure me out…and then I find out he has a girlfriend *after* telling me he didn't. So he's like the rest of them."

I grab the last plate and slam it down.

"I should've known. Opening your heart only gives people permission to break it. And once it breaks, it bleeds."

Once I help the girls clean up, we settle in with trashy reality shows and order in Chinese food. As much as I was keeping my feelings to myself about Morgan, I know I can trust them. The more I spend time with them, the closer we get.

It's almost as if they've been filling the void in my heart this whole time, and I hadn't even realized it. Ever since meeting them, I'd kept my walls up, cemented and foolproof. But little by little, they've knocked them down, wall by wall. And the thing is, I didn't even notice it until now.

Ariel and I used to talk about everything. Sometimes we'd even stay up late and talk about what we wanted to be when we grew up or what college was going to be like. Even how we'd get pregnant at the same time so we could experience it together.

I hadn't realized how much I missed having someone to listen to me until Kendall and Zoe came along.

"So, we need to know *exactly* what happened," Zoe starts. "Who made the first move?"

I take a bite of my egg roll and furrow my brows as I contemplate who *did* make the first move.

"Um…I think it was mutual, but I want to say it was him. We'd been getting closer and closer all semester, but it was him who initially crossed the line. He rubbed his hand over my jaw and when he leaned in, I leaned in, too."

"Did your whole body explode? Was your mind having a mini-freak-out?" Kendall asks eagerly.

"No, I'm not twelve. But I have brought Tristan into the shower with me a couple times since then."

"Who?" Zoe's nose wrinkles.

Kendall snorts. "Her partner in crime."

I grab a piece of chicken and pop it into my mouth. "It's creepy you know that."

"Well, then stop leaving him out in the open if you don't want people to see." She reaches over and grabs a box of noodles.

"It was in the shower!" I defend. "Stop being a snoop and you wouldn't know these things."

"Wait a minute…" Zoe interrupts. "We're talking about dildos, right?"

Kendall and I burst out laughing, the noodles spewing out of her mouth as we take in Zoe's confused expression.

Once I'm finished clarifying who Tristan is, we all lounge on the couch in our pajamas with glasses of cheap wine for the rest of the night.

It wasn't glamorous, but it was exactly the night I needed.

I'm better after my night in with the girls. I've never felt that way before—the need to be destructive—but it felt good to release that anger instead of forcing it down. Opening my heart and mind and allowing myself to be vulnerable reopened a lot of the wounds from my past. Several tears and broken dishes later, I almost feel refreshed.

After work, tonight is the life drawing workshop, and I'm tempted to skip it, but I already promised Ms. Jones I'd stay and help clean up.

"You coming tonight?" I ask Kendall over breakfast in her kitchen. "Come see what the fuss is all about."

"If I wanted to see a naked woman posing for an hour, I'd watch porn."

"Classy." I giggle. "But for those with fewer brain cells than the rest of us—" I glare at her with a sly smile. "It's an amazing opportunity for artists. The models pose in these positions that help expand our skills. You aren't looking at a naked person. You're creating life on paper."

"And with that, I'm skipping breakfast." She stands and tosses her plate in the sink.

"You are so narrow-minded!" I grip my coffee cup.

"Perhaps. I'll leave the creative and open mind to you."

"Like you even had a choice."

She walks over with the coffee and refills my cup for me. "I might skip work altogether." She groans, setting down the carafe. "I want to lie in bed and watch Netflix."

I flash her a cheeky grin, sympathizing with her broken heart. "I'm not sure Netflix pays the bills, babe."

She curls her lip in disapproval.

"We could go buy more plates and break them?" I offer, arching a brow.

"Or you could stop breaking my shit and buy me new plates?"

I smile. "Okay, deal."

The gallery is busier than usual for a lazy Sunday, so I'm booked with tours back-to-back. I love it when there's a massive amount of chatter and shoes clicking on the hardwood.

By late afternoon, I'm ready to pass out. Fortunately, it's time to set up for the class, which takes my mind off being exhausted.

"So we have three of the rooms blocked off for tonight. There need to be at least fifty chairs in each with extra easels," Ms. Jones explains to Christine and me how we have a few others helping out too since there is a lot to be done. "At the front of the room needs to be a stool sitting on top of a white sheet."

We nod in understanding and as the groups break away, Christine follows me. I'm busy moving chairs around and can't help but notice the dreamy face Christine has while she's setting up the area where the model will be. There are going to be three models tonight and they will each rotate every forty-five minutes from room to room, offering different poses to each group.

"What's the smile for?" I ask, knowing it must be because of the guy she's been seeing.

"Oh, nothing," she says, playing it off. "Just thinking about my date last night."

I mentally high-five myself for being right again and to remind her that she needs to work on her poker face. "And how is everything going with this new beau of yours?"

She sighs. "It's great."

I chuckle. "See, I knew you needed to get laid. I should be a therapist. If you're sad—*sex*. If you're mad—*angry sex*. If you're anxious —*shower sex*. Everything can be fixed with a little d, but a big D is always better."

She rolls her eyes, laughing. "We better get this done before Ms. Jones comes in here and has a coronary."

By six o'clock, everything is set up and ready. People who purchased a ticket begin arriving and setting their things up. I'm super excited, especially when I start seeing a few classmates from Professor Hampton's class.

"Hey!" I hear Ellie's sweet, Southern voice.

I turn and she charges for me, engulfing me in a large hug. "Hi!"

"Which room are you going to be in?"

"Oh, I don't know. Wherever there's room left over."

"I'll save you a spot!" she calls out, which reminds me I need to grab my supplies from the front desk.

"Oh, perfect. Thanks!" She walks away into one of the rooms as more people enter.

"No slacking on the job," I hear Kendall's teasing tone behind me. I smile wide. "What are you—"

"I came to caffeinate you. Looks like you need it, too," she tells me as I cover a yawn.

She hands me a cup of hot deliciousness. "Thank God. I love you so much."

"I know. As you should."

After grabbing my bag, she follows me into the same room as Ellie. "I'm observing *over here*." Kendall stays in the back with a few of the other workers.

"You're missing out!" I snicker.

Once the seats are filled, Ms. Jones introduces herself and thanks everyone for coming. She explains the details of the night, establishing the rules of no photography or jumping from room to room. I can tell she's a bit nervous, but excited. This event is great exposure for the gallery and helps get people in the doors with the hopes of them returning.

She then announces the model will be out shortly and skips off to the next room to do the same.

"You have an extra charcoal pencil?" Ellie leans over and whispers.

"I think so." I lean over and dig around in my bag when I see Morgan out of the corner of my eye.

Fucking hell.

I'm not sure if he's noticed me or not, but I try to fight the urge to stare at him.

"Here you go." I hand her one of my pencils as the model walks out. She releases the white robe she was draped in and sets her pose. Her long, brown hair is flat against her back except a small chunk in the front that covers one of her breasts.

I decide against using the easel and set my sketchpad upright on my legs as I begin outlining her features. The room is eerily silent as everyone studies the woman in front of us. She's standing at an angle, one leg extended and the other straight. Her right arm is placed over her chest and resting on her left shoulder. Her head is angled to the ground, her eyes low and steady.

I drown out thoughts of Morgan and stay focused. The adrenaline rush from drawing a live nude model sets in, and soon, I forget there's a room filled with other people.

People start to shift in their seats as the first session comes to an end. The woman smiles as she puts her robe on and walks out. We get a fifteen-minute break before the models rotate.

"If that wasn't inspiration to get into the gym, I don't know what is," Ellie blurts out the moment chairs and people begin to move around the room.

I laugh and reassure her she has nothing to complain about.

"Oh, trust me. Where I'm from, fried chicken and Mama's famous gumbo are a regular occurrence in the kitchen. Add in her fried gator, homemade apple pies, and banana pudding, there's no wonder I can't shed weight."

I stare at her, lost in everything she said. "Wait, did you say *fried gator*?" I cringe.

"Oh my God!" she squeals, making me jump. "You need to visit me this summer in Monroe. We'll get tattoos and eat all the Southern food you can stuff in your mouth. You'll never want to leave."

I blink, unmoving.

"Why aren't you blinking?" she asks.

I swallow and blink. "How did losing weight turn into me getting a tattoo and eating alligator?"

She snickers, but I'm not kidding at all.

I'm not eating that.

"I'm good with burgers and fries. I'm a simple Midwestern girl," I say.

Pushing the Limits

"Stop being a wuss." She nudges her shoulder into mine.

"I think I need to get some water," I tease, standing and walking out before she can chase me down and make us blood sisters or something.

I'm careful to avoid looking in the direction of where I saw Morgan sitting. I walk to the vending machine and buy a bottle of water before heading back.

Before I step into the room, Ms. Jones comes flailing with a look of panic on her face. "Aspen! Oh God." She manages to blurt out before coming to a stop in front of me. She's panting and her cheeks are flushed.

"What's wrong? Everything okay?" I twist the cap off my bottle and take a drink.

"No! One of the models is in the bathroom puking her guts out. She says she can't continue to the next rotation. What am I going to do?"

"Okay, um…" I stand there, trying to think of a solution. There are only five minutes left before the next session is to begin. "What if we put half of the chairs in the empty room to each of the other rooms where the other two models are?"

"There's no room for that many chairs! They'll never fit." She paces in front of me, frantically cursing to herself.

"Can you get someone else? Did you have a backup or know of anyone who'd be willing to do it?" I know it's a long shot, but I can't help asking.

"No, I never thought to. And go figure, we completely sold out tonight, so the rooms are all packed. Fifty people are in that room expecting another model, and I have no one!"

"I'll do it!" I blurt out, and she halts in front of me.

"What?" Her brow arches.

"Yeah. I'm not a professional or anything, but I can pose."

"Are you sure?"

No. "Yes."

"Oh my God, Aspen! You're my lifesaver!" She hugs me.

Again with the damn hugs around here.

"I owe you."

I want to say something about how much she's done for me and how she allows me to sell my AR Collection here, but the words don't come. And it's true, I owe her for keeping my secret, but now, I'm second-guessing my offer.

When she pats my arm and thanks me again, all I can do is nod in response.

Reality has set in.

I'm going to be naked in front of fifty strangers.

Fifty pairs of eyes will be staring—studying and drawing every inch of me for the next forty-five minutes.

"Okay, you'll be in the first room. I need you to de-robe and get out there stat."

"Right, sure," I stumble. "Wait, which room is that?" She points to the room I was just sitting in. "Oh, no, no, no. I can't go to that one." Morgan, Ellie, and most of the students from my class are in that one.

And Morgan—my professor—*who I kissed.*

"Yes, the other two models are already set up in the other two rooms. I need you in there, Aspen." Her tone is serious, and I can feel the blood draining from my face.

"Um, alright. I'll do it."

"You'll be fine, darling. You have a great ass. Just get in there and pose." She walks away before I can sputter out another word.

Did she compliment my ass?

I quickly release a breath and head into a room where I undress and wrap the robe around me. I have no idea what I'm doing, but I don't have time to freak out. I tighten my robe and walk out.

Chapter Twenty-Seven
Morgan

S he's barely glanced at me since the moment I walked in, and I know she's seen me. Some of my students are here, so I can't risk one of them seeing us. She should know I want to talk to her, but I'm afraid I've pissed her off to the point of no redemption.

I notice she hasn't returned from the short break and that people are starting to get restless. As soon as I shift in my seat to go find out what the holdup is, the door creaks open and people quiet down.

I adjust my sketchpad and get ready for another session when I see Aspen in front of the group in only a sheer robe.

My brows shoot up to my hairline. *Fucking hell. What is she doing?*

She avoids eye contact with everyone as she releases the robe. I watch it fall to the floor and my jaw drops.

I remind myself how to breathe.

Her golden hair is wrapped up in a messy bun with a few stray pieces that lie against her neck. She adjusts the stool and sits on the edge of it. One leg is propped up while the other leg crosses over it. One arm is bent behind her on the stool, keeping her upright, and the other across her lap, exposing her chest and stomach.

People begin moving their pencils, using their thumbs, and closing one eye to measure out the length of her head, torso, and legs. They're studying the technical parts of her—skin and bone.

I can't stop staring at her long enough to blink. She's gorgeous.

My jaw ticks knowing everyone is seeing her this way. I've felt her lips on mine. Her body against my body. She's more than just skin and bones. She's also smart and passionate and breathtaking in the way she creates art—brave for the way she pushes through the obstacles and strong even when she's weak.

But I see more than what's on the outside—the goose bumps covering her skin, her bottom lip quivering, her right eye twitching as it always does when she's nervous. She knows I can see her and can't do a damn thing about it.

I decide to finally put pencil to paper and draw her the way *I* see her. From the outside, she's brave, flawless, and confident. But I know the truth. She's vulnerable and guarded. She relies on sarcasm to cover up the inner pain she's battling. She only gives people a small part of her, scared that if she gave any more, it would completely break her.

She uses art to cope, and without it, she'd be a ticking time bomb.

My pencil moves across the paper effortlessly as I sketch her features. She's strong in the way she holds herself. Her lips part and eyes lower, but they flutter every few seconds as she struggles to hold still.

The room is eerily silent, all focus and attention on her. I wish I could remove the image of her from their memories and pretend she was never here at all, but for a first-time nude model, she's holding her own well.

As I'm working on the shading, a soft tap on my shoulder gets my attention, and I turn to see Aunt Mel standing behind me. Her face is lit up as she glances around the room, watching people finishing up their drawings.

"Isn't she doing great?" she whispers, leaning down next to my ear.

I swallow, glancing away from my sketchpad. "Yes. What happened to the other model?"

"She got sick but is feeling better. She should be able to do the next rotation."

Oh, thank fucking God.

Pushing the Limits

I was about to have an ulcer at the thought of another group of fifty people watching Aspen.

"How did you rope her into doing it last minute?" I ask casually, hoping she doesn't sense my irritability.

"Oh, I didn't. She volunteered." She smiles and my jaw ticks again. *Of course she did.*

Chapter Twenty-Eight
Aspen

M y heart is thumping so hard in my chest that I have to talk myself down before I have an anxiety attack.

The room is silent except for the scratch of charcoal and lead rubbing against the thick paper. Their gazes are concentrated and focused. Their hands move rapidly as they outline my features and create a piece of me—the *outside* piece.

The strong-willed, fierce, put-together me.

Ellie stares with wide eyes. I can tell the corners of her lips are pulled into a cheeky grin. I hadn't planned for this at all, so I can only imagine what's roaming around in her head. I chance a quick look over at Morgan and notice him staring. He hasn't moved, and I'm not even sure if he's blinked since I sat down. I know he's probably the most shocked of us all.

But then his features soften, and then those deep dimples reappear. His pencil moves across the paper as he looks between the paper and me. He's not just drawing the lines and angles of my body. I can tell from his expression that he sees something more than every other person here. He sees right through me, down to every flaw and insecurity.

His body is angled toward me, more than the other artists in here. His back isn't slouched, and his ankles aren't carelessly crossed. His stance is strong and defensive. He's on guard as if he's trying to control his thoughts and actions and knowing people can't see him react.

He's hardly in control at all.

I can't help the thrill that jolts through me knowing he's watching me, sketching his interpretation of me. He's all I've been able to think about all semester, so after kissing him twice, my body is ready to explode. His lips, his hands, his eyes—they're all magnetic to mine.

I wanted him to see the real me—the person I hide from everyone else. But I don't know that I can. After the small taste of heartache over his deception, I'm not sure I'm capable of ever being that person.

But when I thought I found someone I'd at least want to try with, he goes and takes it away from me.

I exhale a breath of relief as I slip on the robe and tie it around my waist. I silently walk out and head to the back room to get dressed. The other model is in there already, sucking down a bottle of water.

"Thanks for taking my place," she says with a sincere smile. "I forgot to eat, and then the nerves got to me."

"Oh, no worries. I understand. I'd never done *that* before." The adrenaline is still pumping through my body.

"It definitely gives you a high feeling," she admits. "But it looks like you did great."

"Thanks. I'm ready to go and hide. At least a dozen of my classmates are out there." I blush thinking about it. I may put on a brave face when I'm out with friends and flirting with random guys, but that's with alcohol buzzing through me.

I sat naked in front of strangers, completely sober.

I sat naked in front of Morgan.

I swallow and exhale, needing to slow my racing heartbeat.

"You did great. Be proud." She winks and takes off her clothes.

"Oh, you probably need the robe."

Apparently, we're going to undress and redress right here.

I hand her the robe and grab my clothes, quickly putting them on. I've already embarrassed myself enough. I don't need to extend out the process.

"Good luck!" I say as she walks out.

Thank God that's over. I sigh.

The door opens and then closes, and when I turn, I'm face-to-face with Professor Hampton.

"Can I help you?" I cross my arms.

"What the hell do you think you're doing?" he hisses, reaching for my arm and pulling me toward him.

"Oh, are we speaking now? You have to let me know, considering we're always on your terms."

"Cut the shit, Aspen. I'm not playing." He growls.

"Neither am I! One minute you're all over me, the next you're walking away as if nothing happened. I can't keep up, Professor! So tell me what it is you want."

He stares intensely while his jaw tenses and his body presses firmly against the door. His chest moves rapidly as he contemplates his next move.

He pushes off the door, lunging toward me. His gaze is fixed on mine as he wraps a hand behind my neck and pulls us together. His other hand squeezes my hip as we become a heated frenzy of mouths and tongues. I lean into his chest as he pulls my bottom lip between his teeth.

A strangled moan releases from my throat as I try to catch my breath. My arms wrap around him, pulling him as close as possible. His hand grips my neck, tilting my head up toward him more. He takes a few steps until I'm pressed against the other wall. I feel the hard bulge in his pants as he rolls his hips against mine. My body tilts up to greet his, wanting to feed the carnal desire within me. He groans and pushes into me harder, making me clench my thighs at how wet my panties are feeling.

Pushing the Limits

Ms. Jones's voice echoes in my head about Natalia—about him having a girlfriend and leaving after kissing me. The rage builds up inside me, and I push my hands against his chest until his lips are off mine.

We're panting and staring at each other in frustrated breaths. Anger fuels me as I remember the reasons I'm pissed at him.

I grab my purse and walk out the back door, making sure not to disturb the group's last session. Everyone is focused on the model and their drawings. I try my best to silently leave, but I hear his footsteps behind me.

As soon as I push through the front doors, rain pours down on me and soaks through my shirt. *Fucking great.*

"Aspen!" he shouts from behind me, his feet hitting the wet pavement.

"Go away!" I continue walking down the sidewalk.

"Goddammit, would you just stop and listen?"

I spin around quickly, the soft hairs that fall out of my ponytail clinging to my wet face. Before I have time to recover or brush them away, he wraps a hand around my neck again and pulls me toward him. His lips cover mine again and my body reacts to him before my brain has time to catch up.

I push him away again. "You can't just kiss me whenever you want!" I scold, irritation and desire fighting for control.

His dark green shirt sticks to his chest like it's painted on him. The wet strands of his hair drip down over his forehead, and I resist the urge to brush it away.

"Then why did you kiss me back?" he challenges.

"Because I'm an idiot! I don't get involved with men who aren't available. But you led me on. *All damn semester!*"

He steps back, scrubbing a hand along his jaw. "What are you talking about? I told you I don't have a girlfriend. I've found any possible reason just to get a few minutes alone with you, crossing all possible boundaries just to be near you."

"Does the name Natalia ring a bell? Because according to Ms. Jones, you guys are quite the happy couple," I mock, my tone condescending and angry. The rain pours down harder on us, drenching us completely.

He throws his head back and lets out a deep, amused laugh. It fuels my rage even more at the way he's *laughing* at me.

"I'm glad you think this is hilarious. However, I don't have time for guys like you in my life. Especially ones who treat women like pieces of meat."

"Oh, I hadn't realized you met my friend, Kettle. You two have a lot in common."

His features tighten.

"God! What is wrong with you? Have you inhaled so many fumes in your life that you're unable to function or think clearly?"

"Had you given me a second of your time, I would've explained that to you."

"Excuse me for not wanting to listen to your bullshit lies when Professor Van-Horny-Pants was draped all over you."

"That's a one-way fascination. Not mutual. Never was nor will it be. Also, I had to leave the gala because someone unexpectedly showed up that night, and I wanted to avoid any drama."

"You mean your girlfriend showed up? That was the unexpected guest, right?"

His brows pinch, and I know I've got him by the balls.

"Stop acting like you're so innocent in this, Professor. I only kissed you with the assumption that you were single. But after hearing about Natalia, it's clear you're just like the rest of them. I may sleep around, but I don't mess with other women's men."

"For starters, I don't have a girlfriend. I haven't had a girlfriend in the five years since I left. I told you that. As far as Natalia goes, she's my feisty eleven-year-old niece who lives with me. My brother's daughter."

He arches a brow, and the realization hits me smack in the face.

"You're raising your brother's daughter?" My brows lift. "Why haven't you told me?"

"I was going to. I thought until we established what this"—he waves a hand between us—"was that I should wait before telling you something like that."

Pushing the Limits

He takes a step closer and grabs my hand. "I swear, Aspen. I'd never hurt you intentionally. Things between us are going to be complicated while you're my student and I'm your professor. But I'm willing to try because I want to make this work with you." His words sound genuine, almost pleading, but I can't help but want to push him away.

"You hardly know me."

He pulls me against him, our bodies drenched and clothes soaked. "You've let me in more than you realize. I know about your pain, your past, your heartbreak. I know you're guarding your heart in every way possible. I see it in your eyes when you paint. The only time you're unguarded is when you're creating art. Your pieces reflect everything you won't let people in to see."

"I'm more broken than you realize. I've told you I'm a mess. Probably more than you can handle."

His other hand caresses my cheek and wraps around my neck as he leans in and slowly kisses my lips. My body relaxes and leans into him, allowing his kiss to take over.

"If you'll let me in, I promise to give you everything you need."

My eyes stay closed, the rain smacking us from above. "I don't even know what I need," I admit. "I've never done this before."

"Then we'll find out together." His mouth covers mine again as my arms wrap around his body, holding on to him with every possible ounce of strength.

"Come home with me," I say breathlessly, practically begging.

He smirks. "I thought you'd never ask."

I barely pull my keys out of the door before his lips and hands are on me again. He blindly kicks the door shut and wraps his arms around my waist, trailing kisses down my jawline and neck.

"You're shivering," he whispers in my ear. "You should take off these wet clothes."

I smile and nod in agreement.

"And probably take a hot shower," he adds, curling his fingers under my shirt and lifting it up.

"You should, too. Wouldn't want you to get sick or anything," I say, grabbing for his belt and undoing the buckle. "Better yet, we should conserve water and shower together."

He reaches around and undoes my bra. "I like the way you think."

Once I unzip his pants, I pull them down. He kicks them off and presses his body to mine again. His fingers fidget with my jeans, but the dampness makes them stick to my legs. I break away quickly, yank them down, and then toss them to the floor.

He wraps a hand around my waist as I pull him toward the shower. His other hand palms my breast and squeezes. I moan my approval into his mouth and kiss him harder, deeper.

Pushing the bathroom door open, I reach for the light, but before I can, he wraps his arms around me and lifts me up. He sets me down on the counter and pushes us against the mirror, sliding his hands up to my breasts and pinching my nipples between his fingers.

My head falls as I release a loud moan. I love his hands on me and could never get enough. He sucks on my collarbone as his fingers twist my nipples. I almost can't take it and need him to stop, but then he brings a hand between my legs.

"Baby girl, are you wet?" I hear the excitement in his voice.

"Is that a trick question?" I nearly gasp as his fingers rub over my pussy through my panties. His hand moves faster and harder, forcing my hips to roll against him.

My back arches as he whispers over my ear, "Tell me, Aspen. Say it."

"Take off my panties and find out, *Professor*," I taunt, feeling his fingers rubbing even harder.

He pushes them to the side and slides a finger inside.

I gasp and lift my hips.

"Like this?" He pushes a second finger in as his thumb rubs against my clit in a perfect rhythm.

"Yes, *yes*. Just like that!" I scream, wrapping a hand around his arm and holding myself up with the other against the countertop.

His fingers push in deeper as he increases his pace. I can hardly take it anymore as he rubs his thumb faster. I'm so close, about to explode, before he pulls his fingers out and wraps his lips around them, sucking the juices right off his fingertips.

Pushing the Limits

"Mm, you taste incredible." He exaggerates his voice, pushing his tongue in between his two fingers.

"That was cruel," I hiss.

An evil grin spreads across his face and deepens his dimples. "What did I say about calling me professor outside of the classroom?"

"Oh, is that how you want to play? Because I'm the queen of delayed gratification."

"Is that so? Sounds like a challenge."

"Don't forget who you're playing against. I once painted for eleven hours straight without eating or taking a break." I lean toward him as I continue. "*Standing.*"

He leans in and pulls my lower lip in between his teeth, biting gently before releasing. "Now the smell of your arousal is on both of us. How long do you think you can wait before feeling me inside you?"

My body shivers at the thought of his cock deep inside of me. I've dreamed and fantasized about it, wondering how it'd feel. Now I am inches from it.

"You're enjoying this way too much, Professor. Whose rules are you willing to bend?" My body buzzes, anxious for him to give in.

"The only thing I'll be bending is you over this countertop. I plan to rip your panties off, pull your hair, and fuck you hard." His voice is seductive and heavy with promises that I'm begging for him to fulfill. Perhaps I'll let him win this time.

My eyes light up as a smile pulls from my lips. "Show me."

His mouth covers mine in a heated frenzy. I wrap my legs around his waist and pull him between them. His erection presses against my pussy, and I moan. "Tell me what you need first, Aspen."

His hands grip my waist, keeping our bodies locked together. "I want your hands on me. Attack my tits like you own them," I beg. "I like it rough," I admit.

His head bends and leans against my shoulder. "Jesus fucking Christ," he growls. He lifts his head again and sucks along my neck and jaw. His hands slide up my chest, and he cups my breasts, digging his nails into the skin as hard as he can. Already primed from his wicked fingers, I nearly explode at the way he does exactly as I asked.

I clench my thighs, trapping him closer. I want him inside and can't wait any longer.

"Morgan," I whimper. He rocks his hips harder against me, letting me feel exactly what I do to him. When I reach for him, he pulls his hips back where I can't reach. "Morgan!" I squeal. I know he likes it when I say his name, so I scream it over and over until he gives me exactly what I want.

He hooks his fingers in my panties, my arousal nearly dripping down my legs as he slides them down and they drop to the floor. Instead of taking off his boxers, he kneels and spreads my legs wider.

"Keep screaming, sweetheart. Let me know exactly how much you like it."

Before I can protest, his hands wrap around my thighs and pull me closer until his mouth covers my pussy.

I moan as his tongue fucks me better than I've ever experienced before. I always figured he'd be good, but never imagined *this* good. My fingers dig into his shoulders, clawing and scratching his skin as he sucks and licks. He wraps his lips around my clit while pushing a thick finger inside. He finds a perfect rhythm, and soon, I'm screaming and tightening my thighs in a heated frenzy.

"Morgan…" I pant, unsure if I want him to stop or go faster. I can barely take it anymore.

"Give me another, baby. Let me feel how turned on you are."

"I can't," I cry out. "Holy shit." My hips go wild as he adds a second finger and fucks my pussy so good, I nearly rip his hair out. "You have to stop. I can't take it anymore."

"I decide when I stop, baby girl." He sucks my clit again as his fingers continue their steady rhythm.

I lock my legs around his neck and squeeze. It only encourages him to go faster and harder. I explode around him. He licks up my arousal and sucks it off his fingers. My limbs feel numb, and I'm not even sure I can walk.

"Fuck, Aspen. You came so hard, sweetheart." His lips press against my inner thigh. He stands up and cups my face. "You alright?"

"I have mixed feelings."

He snorts. "And what's that?"

"Mixed between wanting to stab you for ignoring my pleas and wanting to ride you so fucking hard, it'll feel like your dick is going to fall off." I grin, knowing neither of those is appealing to him.

"I'd like to see that," he teases. "The second one, that is."

"I'm sure you would."

"But first, we need to shower." He kisses me softly, and I groan before he walks away to turn the shower on.

Steam begins covering the room, and after a few minutes of rest, I'm more anxious than ever to taste him.

He slides his boxer shorts off before opening the door and calling over his shoulder, "You coming?"

He winks while holding the door open for me. "I was hoping this time it'd be you." I lower my gaze to the hand stroking his cock. It's rock-hard and aching for relief.

I slide off the counter and walk to him. He leans down and kisses me, pushing us inside. He closes the door behind him and cups his hands around my face as we settle in under the hot stream of water.

His lips are soft and sensual, which makes them so addicting, but I'm not going to pass up the opportunity to taste him first. I want to see his face as I wrap my mouth around him.

I push against his chest and break away. I kiss down his jaw, neck, and chest until I'm kneeling in front of him. I grasp his cock in my hands and slowly stroke up and down, swirling my tongue around the tip. He groans and rocks his hips toward me, pushing in deeper.

Our eyes lock as I wrap fully around him and take him deep into my mouth. He moans, tangling his fingers through my hair while I squeeze his shaft. I stroke and suck, deep and fast until he chases his own pleasure.

His head falls as he releases, and I swallow down all of him. He groans as I swirl my tongue around his sensitive tip once more.

"Christ, Aspen…" he growls. He reaches down for my hands and helps me to my feet. He tilts my chin forward and brushes his lips against mine, tasting his own arousal. "That was amazing," he whispers. "*You* are amazing."

We stay under the stream of water, kissing, touching, and teasing.

He washes my body, and I wash his. It's sensual and sexy, and I can't believe I finally get to have him this way. It's the most romantic thing I've ever done with a guy. Usually, it's drinking, a quick fuck, and passing out until the next morning when I not so politely kick him out.

But this, with him…is so different from anything I've ever experienced before. The connection we have, the passion we share, and the feelings I have for him make it all worth the struggle to finally get here.

Chapter Twenty-Nine
Morgan

Feeling Aspen shake against my tongue and hearing her deep, throaty moans have me on an adrenaline rush I've never felt before. The way she tastes, the way she shivers from the slightest touch of mine, and the way she takes control makes it impossible to resist wanting more of her.

I attack her mouth as if it's my reason to breathe. I suck on her bottom lip, biting lightly before massaging her tongue with mine. My hands have a mind of their own, rubbing alongside her body, feeling every perfect inch of hers under my skin. I lower them down to her ass and squeeze, pushing her closer until she's pressed against my chest. My dick hardens again as her pussy rubs against me, begging me to touch her and give her the release she's craving. I want to fill her so fucking deep, but I want my time with Aspen to last as long as possible. I don't want this to ever end.

"I think we've warmed up enough," she moans against me.

I smile at what she's implying. If I had no self-control at all, I'd bend her over and fuck her against the shower wall, but I don't want our first time to be in here. I want her on the bed and to memorize every inch of her while I take her slowly. I want my body to sync with hers, letting the intense connection we share take over.

But I'm not without flaws. My willpower can only go so far.

"Where do you want it, sweetheart?"

"Bedroom," is all she says before I turn the water off and kick the door open. Her mouth latches to mine as I wrap my arms around her and pull her up, wrapping her legs around my waist. She directs me down the hall to her bedroom where I set her down on her feet and push her up against the door. "Now where?" I whisper in her ear, brushing my lips against her neck.

"Bend me over the bed," she orders, and I do.

I spread her legs wide as she arches her back. Fuck, she looks amazing like this. Spread out and ready for me. I can't remember the last time I wanted someone this badly. She's all I've been able to think about for weeks, and I'm finally going to feel every intimate part of her.

I ask if she has a condom, and she points to her bedside drawer. I quickly grab one and slide it over me.

"Keep talking, baby. Tell me what you like." I rub a hand up her spine, pushing her chest down farther. Her ass lifts up higher as I position myself against her pussy.

"I told you I like it rough. Deep, hard, *fast*."

I groan at how confident her words come out. Most women are too embarrassed to tell you what they like, but not Aspen. She's vocal, and I love it.

"Fuck. I might not be able to stop with that mouth of yours." I press the tip into her pussy with a slight push, not giving in to her demands.

"Good. That's exactly how I like it."

With a deep growl, I rock my hips and fill her as deep as I can. Her pussy squeezes me, making me groan and flex as I adjust to her tight grip. I never want to stop. Not when she makes me feel this good both physically and emotionally. I haven't had that feeling in years.

She lays her arms flat on the mattress over her head and opens her legs wider for me. I grab her hips, fisting the skin alongside her body and keeping a fast pace. She's panting and moaning in between cursing and demanding it deeper and faster. Fuck, this girl's insatiable.

"Jesus, Aspen," I growl, leaning over her and wrapping an arm around her chest. "I can't get enough." I palm her breast, and she screams. "I love hearing you say my name, sweetheart. Say it again."

"*Morgan*," she whimpers.

"Such a good girl."

Soon, she's chanting my name. I rock harder and faster, feeling her tighten around me as she lets out another jarring breath. "*Oh my God!*" Her body shakes and releases against me, her hands fisting the sheets for support.

Her body goes limp and weak, so I grab her hips and spin her around. I gently lay her back down on the bed and kiss her lips. I slide my hand up and grab her breast, pinching the nipple in between my fingers until I hear that deep, throaty moan of hers. God, I love that sound.

Her hips arch, and she rubs her body against mine. I smile at her eagerness as I thrust back inside her, this time slow and deep. Her head falls as I rock my hips, feeling her body tighten around me once again. I want to release with her, but I also don't ever want to let her go. This feeling—this euphoric high—is something I thought I'd never have again.

"Morgan," she whispers, grabbing hold of my upper arms. "I had no idea it could feel this good," she admits. Even though she's flushed, her cheeks turn a light shade of red. I can tell she doesn't normally engage this way during sex and even though it feels natural between us, it's still new for her.

"Sweetheart, had I known, there's no way I could've waited this long. But I can't say you haven't made the wait worth it."

"You act as if I made you wait, Professor," she mocks.

I pull out slowly but then push back in as deep and hard as possible. She yelps and digs her nails into my skin. "What did I say about calling me that?" I taunt. "I thought I warned you about the consequences."

"The risk was *worth* it."

She flashes a cocky grin, and I know it's a lost cause. She wraps her legs around my waist as I kiss along her jaw and wrap my hand in her hair. She rocks her hips with mine, controlling the pace and showing me exactly how she wants it. I love that she likes to be in control and isn't afraid to take over.

I roll to my back, putting her more in control. Her fingers press into my chest as she rides me as throws her head back, moaning and panting. I squeeze my hands around her hips, keeping up with her pace. Her tits bounce in my face, and I can't take it anymore. I lean up and pull one into my mouth, sucking her nipple and massaging the other one with my free hand. She screams and rotates her hips faster. I move to her other breast and suck that one, too.

I groan, continuing my assault on her breasts with my lips and teeth, moving from one to the other as she continues tightening around me.

"Holy shit," she gasps, feeling the build-up inside her. I know she's close, and it's going to be fucking intense.

"Come on, sweetheart. Let me hear you." I wrap a hand around her and smack her ass cheek twice. "I want those cheeks to burn."

"*Oh God yes…*" she moans all at once, her pussy tightening around my cock as she screams again, pushing her hands down against my chest as she comes. I release inside her seconds later, unable to control it any longer.

"Fuck, my girl likes that."

She falls on me with a smack, her breathing erratic. My arms lie slack against the mattress as we come down from our highs.

"Aspen…" I breathe out her name like a prayer.

"Yes?"

"You are incredible."

Her body shivers in response.

Wrapping an arm around her, I shift our bodies so we're on our sides. Then, I dispose the condom and toss it into the small wastebasket by her nightstand.

Her legs are still intertwined with mine as I cup her jaw and rub the pad of my thumb gently over her cheek. She leans into my palm and smiles.

Leaning in, I softly brush my mouth over hers. She parts her lips and slowly kisses me. Her rapid breathing vibrates my chest as she wraps an arm around my hip and pulls me closer.

Pushing the Limits

Being with her is so much more than I ever imagined. After all this time of thinking about her and feeling this pull between us, it's surreal to finally have her. My emotions are in overdrive, and I'm not sure if I can control them anymore.

She's managed to take my heart and heal it from the inside out. She's helped me see things I've been blind to for far too long. I never thought I'd get this feeling back.

I don't remember falling asleep, but I know she was in my arms when we drifted off. Waking up to an empty bed, I'm worried she's off somewhere freaking out about what happened between us.

The entire apartment is dark, and I realize it's because it's dark outside. I internally start freaking out, searching for my phone and clothes, when I remember my mom is keeping Natalia overnight. She is off from school tomorrow, and my mom wanted to take her clothes shopping in the morning.

Walking out of her room, I head down the hallway and find my boxer shorts and clothes in a pile outside the bathroom. Once I pull on my boxers, I throw the rest on the floor.

Faint music comes from the other room, so I quietly walk to the door and peek inside. Aspen sits on a stool in front of an easel with only a sheet wrapped loosely around her. With a brush in one hand, she strokes over the canvas. She has a large bright light shining down on it, but the rest of the room is covered in darkness.

Music plays from her phone as she hums along with it. I recognize the lyrics, and when the song ends and repeats again, I know it's meaningful to her.

I see another stool near the wall and quietly grab it. She glances over her shoulder and smiles as I set it behind her, then set my legs on each side until she's between them.

"You're sitting," I say more like a question, wrapping my arms around her waist.

"My legs needed to recover."

"Fair enough." I chuckle, kissing her cheek softly before brushing my lips against hers. "What are you making?"

"Recreating the tree my sister and I always used to climb." She continues blending the leaves. A girl is lying on the grass, and another is up in the branches. "We were both competitive. Always challenging each other to see who could go the highest and who could climb the fastest. It was just something we always did."

"Sounds like it was an important part of your childhood."

"It was." She sighs. Her body tenses against mine, and I wonder if she's hesitant to say more. "It's been six years, and I can't get the image out of my head. I paint it over and over. I'm not sure if it's to purge the memory or to torture myself for not saving her. The fall broke her neck, and she was gone before I could even climb down to her."

My body shudders at the image, but the pain in her voice nearly kills me. Not only did she lose someone extremely close to her, but she also witnessed it.

I study the canvas harder and realize the blood isn't where it should be. "Why is the blood down here?" I ask softly, pointing to her sister's wrist.

"She was a cutter," she states directly. "It started a couple years before, and I never understood why. But I always felt the pain when she did it. Something inside me knew."

"Did she get help?"

"The first time. After that, Mom and Dad said it was a cry for attention and stopped doing anything about it. Mom thought it was a phase and she'd grow out of it. Dad thought she was trying too hard to stand out, be different since she was constantly in my shadow. It wasn't until her death that we saw the cuts on the inside of her thighs. She had a drawer of razors and just piles and piles of paper."

I lean down and kiss her shoulder. I can see it hurts to relive the events of her sister's death, but I can't help but feel proud of how open and honest she is about it.

"What was on the pieces of paper? Notes?"

"Drawings."

"She was into art, too?"

"Yeah, but I hadn't known at the time." Her gaze lowers. "She never showed me anything or mentioned it." She shrugs, her eyes meeting mine again.

"It might've been her way of coping or at least trying to. She probably wasn't proud of it and hid it," I offer.

"I think I do that, too. I paint to cope with the pain of losing her. It's the only outlet I've given myself, never grieving or accepting reality until now. It's burdened me for years."

"Did your parents ever acknowledge it after her death? Were they supportive of your art growing up?"

She shakes her head. "Hardly. Even as a hobby, they thought it was a waste of time."

"That's a shame. You have one of the most beautiful styles I've ever seen." I cup her cheek and rub the pad of my thumb over it. "It's their loss."

A small smile appears on her perfect lips. I lean in, softly kissing them.

"You're right."

"Glad to hear you say that." I grin against her mouth, getting distracted by how full and soft they are. Quickly, I swipe a finger into the red paint and smear it across her cheek.

"Oh my God!" she squeals.

She tries to get away, but I grab her wrist and pull her closer, swiping another finger along her arm.

"You're so going to pay for that!" She laughs.

I jump off the chair before she can get even. She chases after me as she tries holding the sheet that's wrapped around her with one hand and dripping paint from the other. She eventually corners me and covers my chest with her handprints.

"Such a little devil." I grin, grabbing her wrists and swinging her around. The sheet drops from around her as I rub my chest against her back.

"Damn you!" She giggles, trying to wiggle out of my hold.

My palms slide up her sides, rubbing them over her skin, and when I cup her breasts, covering them in red as well. I squeeze them in my palms, her body relaxing against mine as I massage them and hum in her ear.

"Fuck, baby…" I moan, distracted by her perky tits. Blood rushes to my groin, pulsating and straining to be inside her.

She takes advantage and swings her elbow into my stomach, just hard enough that my hands release her. She runs for more, but I manage to grab her elbow and pull her back, smearing more all over her neck and chest.

"Nice try. I like you naked and covered in paint." I flash a knowing smirk, wrapping a hand around her waist and securely holding her in place. "Actually, I prefer it."

"That's good to know. I was thinking of making it a regular thing. Start a new fashion trend and all." She wiggles her body against mine.

"You wouldn't dare." My nostrils flare.

"Wouldn't I?" She arches a brow. "Standing naked in front of dozens of strangers was *definitely* a rush. I might consider making it a daily thing."

I lean in, capturing her lower lip in between my teeth. I softly release it and run my tongue along the length of it. "Don't even think about it. The only person who's allowed to see your naked body is me."

"You own my body now?" she taunts, smiling sweetly. I want to say yes. I want to own her body and do whatever I want to it.

"Shall I prove it to you?" I ask hoarsely.

"I'd like to see you try, Professor." Her eyes are hot as they burn into mine.

"What have I been saying about calling me that?" I growl, bowing my head down into the crease of her neck.

"That every time you hear me say it, you want me to ride your face until your tongue goes numb," she says matter-of-factly, making my cock strain against my shorts.

Pushing the Limits

"*Fucking hell*, Aspen," I groan, dragging my teeth along the flesh of her throat. "You're going to make me come before I even get inside you." I inhale her sweet scent, driving me even crazier.

"I can think of many ways to make you come."

Her words elicit another tortured groan from my throat. I pull her closer, taking her mouth in a passionate kiss. My hands drop to massage the curves of her ass, moving my hips against hers, taunting her. Without any warning, I bring my hand up and slap it down on her ass cheek, quick and hard, causing her to squeal. She breaks away as she arches her hips.

"Let's get you cleaned up, my dirty girl," I say above her ear, giving her ass another quick slap.

"Keep doing that and we may never make it to the shower." She lowers her hands down my chest and palms my shaft over my shorts, teasing me until the buildup becomes too much and I yank her hand away.

"That's enough," I hiss, clenching my jaw as I try to control my emotions.

Grabbing her hand, I walk toward the bathroom. Once inside, I pull us into the shower and pin her body against the wall with my hips.

The hot water slices over our bodies as I caress and gently clean her skin.

We become a mass of hands and legs as our bodies fuse, neither wanting to let go.

"Morgan," she moans my name like a prayer and a plea. I know she's hungry for it, her body tightening and begging for a release.

"Turn around, sweetheart."

She does as she's told, completely entranced by my words and the feel of my hands against her. I grab her wrists and pull her arms up over her head, securing her palms against the wall. I look at her in this position, completely mesmerized by this stunning woman, completely taken aback by how strong my feelings for her are.

I drag my hands down her body, kneeling behind her as my fingers burrow into her ass cheeks, spreading her legs open for my assault. Like a man possessed, I slide my tongue up her perfect pink slit.

Spreading her cheeks wider, I expose her bare flesh all the way up to her tight hole. I fuck her with my tongue, deeper and faster, sliding it up and down her smooth skin. Her hips shake as she moans, begging for more.

She's all I can breathe and taste.

Groaning inwardly, I insert a finger inside her as I suck on her hot clit. It's plump and needy, her body rocking with every move my finger makes.

"That's it, baby," I praise as I thrust harder. She's close, but I'm desperate to feel every part of her explode around me.

"Turn around," I order, sitting against the other wall. She does and places her hands flat against the wall, her hungry pussy angled to my face.

Wrapping my hands around her thighs, I suck on her clit. She rocks her hips as my mouth devours every eager drop.

Pushing her legs wider, I slide my hand to her tight little hole. Then, I push a thick finger inside as my lips find her clit again. Her hips rock wildly, moaning and cursing in between heavy breaths.

"Yes, yes. I love that."

Her words encourage me further, fucking her sweet pussy with my tongue as I finger-fuck her ass, both throbbing and tightening with every thrust.

She shudders, her body unraveling more and more with every intense second. Pushing my thumb inside her wet cunt, I suck her clit as my finger thrusts into her tight hole. She screams as she comes, her hips frantic as I taste her release.

The water turns cold as she pants against the wall, trying to catch her breath. I push her body down on mine, wrapping her legs around my waist as I stay seated on the floor. Her chest moves up and down, still breathing heavily, a flush still high on her cheeks and down her neck.

Palming her cheek, I guide her mouth to mine, but there's no teasing and eagerness this time. With my tongue, I nudge her lips apart and slide mine in to claim hers, slow and sweet, ignoring the cold beads cascading down on us.

Her hard, cold nipples are pressed against my chest, the blood rushing to my groin as she clings to me. I want to sink deep inside her and feel her come against my cock, but this sweet, simple moment makes my heart squeeze as I think about how fast I'm falling for her.

My heart also aches at the fact that I have to hide it from the rest of the world.

"You're shivering," I whisper, brushing wet strands off her face. "Let's go warm you up."

"I'm sure you have many ways of warming me up, don't you?"

I chuckle at her amused tone. "There's only one way to find out."

The sun is brutal in the morning and today's no different. Except for the fact that I've had little to no sleep, but I'm not even a little upset about that. The entire night was spent with Aspen—in her bed, her studio, and shower. It's a night I'll never forget.

I finally peel open my eyes and see her cradled peacefully in my arms, exactly where she passed out a few hours ago. I know we have to get up and ready for the day, but I could lie here with her all day.

I smile as I cup her cheek and softly rub my thumb over it. She shifts, moaning as she tries to roll away.

This all feels so natural. It's hard to believe it's the first night we've spent together. It's been so long that I nearly forgot how it felt to wake up with someone I cared about.

"Sorry, sweetheart. But I have to leave and get ready for work."

"Do you have to?" She groans and wiggles closer. "Play hooky." A small smile appears, and I brush my lips against them.

"I wish I could."

"It's not like they need you there anyway. They can work on their projects without you," she taunts.

"Take it back!" I dig my nails into her side, making her jump.

"Stop!" She squirms as I continue tickling her.

"Say it, then," I tell her.

"Okay, okay. I take it back!"

"Are you saying I'm not useful?"

Her eyes finally open and her smile widens. "Oh, Professor, you are *very* useful." She winks and wrinkles her nose. Damn her fucking cuteness. It's going to be impossible to keep my attention and hands off her during class.

I lower my arms down and around her waist until my hands reach her ass cheeks. I give her a quick slap and she squeals. "Oh my God!" She laughs and tries to pull away from my grip, but I smile and roll over her, holding her hostage against the mattress with my hands around her wrists.

"You sure love to break the rules, don't you, Ms. Evans?" I lean over her body and kiss the top of her nose.

"Only the ones that come with benefits."

"I should've known you were a rule breaker. You and Ms. Chatty Pants are always whispering to each other." I smirk, grinding my hips against hers.

Her hips arch, and she groans. "To be fair, we were whispering about you."

My brow lifts with a pleased smile. "In that case…" I lean down and cover her mouth as I spread her legs apart with my knee. "Guess that means I'll have to make you scream until you lose your voice so we don't have that problem anymore."

"You wouldn't dare!" She gasps, trying to push me away.

"You're cute to try and stop me." I wink and begin lowering my body down hers, kissing her neck and chest along the way.

I lick and suck my way down her abdomen, loving the way she squirms underneath me. At the apex of her thighs, I spread her wide so I can claim what's mine.

"So wet for me," I hum, blowing cool air over her heated flesh, causing goose bumps to rise on her skin. I slowly lick the length of her and she shudders. "I need to hear you," I demand.

I begin fucking her with my tongue, my lips, and teeth, eating her as if I need her to breathe. I'd make her come on my face, wouldn't stop until she was screaming my name, losing her voice in the process.

Eager moans issue from her throat as her body arches off the bed, my mouth clamped on her, not willing to release her until I taste her.

"*Fuck…*" she screams. Her hands tangle in my hair, pulling and squeezing as her thighs clench around my neck. I suck harder and look up at the expanse of her body, admiring the flush of her skin as I wrap a hand around her breast. Her nipples are hard, little rosy points, begging to be sucked next.

Her head falls as she fists the sheets.

"You need it, sweetheart?" I growl, meeting her gaze. "Say it."

"Yes! *Pleasepleaseplease…*" Her aching pussy throbs. "I'm so close…"

Her hips buck, grinding her cunt against my mouth, taking what she wants. I suck and lick until she shakes, releasing her sweet juices.

"Mm…" Moaning, I lick my lips.

She tilts her head with an enticing smirk. "That's a satisfied look you've got on your face there, Professor."

My cock jumps at her velvety tone, all sated and smooth.

"I've warned you about calling me that, Ms. Evans." I crawl up her body, wrapping a hand around her wrists and pulling them up over her head.

Aligning my tip with her center, I roll my hips and when the tip rubs against her swollen lips, she lifts her hips.

"No, no, no…" I taunt, pulling away from her.

"I thought you had to leave?" she challenges. "Either fuck me or let me do it myself."

Jesus.

I lean over and grab a condom from her nightstand. I rip it open and hand it to her. "Put it on."

She takes it, keeping her gaze fixed on mine as she rolls it over my length. Her sweet little hands wrap around my length before I can stop her.

"Rub your clit," I demand, aligning myself against her opening. She does as I say, leaning back and rubbing circles around herself. "Now watch me."

Looking down, she positions herself so she can continue as I slide deep inside her, the buildup already intense as she hugs my shaft.

"That's my girl," I hum. "Keep going." Her hand moves faster as I thrust harder, feeling her body shake every time I hit that one deep spot that's sure to keep her screaming.

Moaning, her body shudders, and her thighs shake as I pull her legs up to her chest. She's wide and open for me, my cock pushing deeper with every eager thrust.

"Aspen, baby…" I growl. "Fuck, you feel amazing."

"Don't stop," she pleads, her hand furiously working her sensitive clit.

I lean down against her chest, wrapping her legs around my waist as I cup her ass cheek in one hand. I work against her harder and faster, her body quick to keep up with my movements.

I wrap my mouth around her breast, sucking her nipple and biting lightly. She yelps, begging for more. I squeeze it hard in my palm, giving it a gentle slap before I clamp down on her again.

"*Yesyesyes*…oh my God."

"Christ, I fucking love it when you're loud, baby."

"I need to come…*please, please* let me come."

"How do you want it, sweetheart?" I slow down a bit, her chest pounding rapidly against mine. "Tell me what you want."

"Bend me over," she begs. "Take control."

A heated growl releases deep in my throat at the intensity of her words. I love that she trusts me enough to take care of her, all fear of showing her how my feelings ease as I flip her over.

Once I lay her flat on her stomach, I kneel and slap her ass cheeks. "*God…*" I mutter. Her flesh flushes a rosy pink from my handprints. Palming her cheeks, I spread her as I line up with her entrance and thrust inside with one long stroke.

A sweet moan hums from her lips as I slide a hand up her spine and grab a fistful of her messy hair. I tug lightly, exposing her throat. Then I thrust inside her again, deep and smooth. She's so wet, but I can't get enough. As I slide my other hand under her chest, I palm her breast and fuck her recklessly.

"Mm, Morgan..." her voice is a breathless plea as her fingers dig into the mattress, moaning my name again. "Yes, like that."

"Thatta girl. Let me hear you, sweetheart," I demand.

She clamps down around my cock, screaming my name as she shakes.

"*Jesus*...your cunt's tight when you come." I bury myself deeper, chasing my own release.

I barely catch myself before collapsing on top of her. Once I roll to the side, I quickly dispose of the condom.

Aspen's still trying to catch her breath, all sated with mussed-up hair. The epitome of the just-fucked look. I lean up on my elbow and look down at her smiling face. She's everything I could've asked for but never thought I'd have, and I'm falling hard. Gently, I brush her hair back, tucking the wayward strands behind her ear, and then lightly kiss her lips.

We lie there, catching our breaths, kissing—until her stomach growls, breaking the silence. Her cheeks turn pink, and she hides her face behind her hands, laughter filling the room.

Her embarrassment is adorable.

"Sounds like we need to get some food in you," I tease. "We wouldn't want you to get *hangry*."

"Can we pretend that never happened?" She wrinkles her nose. "And I don't get hangry!"

"It's my experience that all women get hangry when denied food."

Playfully slapping her ass, I grab her hand and then pull her up. I was supposed to leave an hour ago, but she's worth it to be late.

As we walk toward the kitchen, I stop and notice the canvases displayed in the hallway. They're covered with portraits of her sister and some with them together.

I carefully rub a finger along one, tracing the lines of her face. "What was her name?"

"Um..." she stumbles, glancing down. "Ari."

"Sorry, I didn't mean to—"

"It's fine. It's getting easier to talk about her."

I give her a sympathetic smile. "I can't get over how beautiful they are. I notice you use a lot of similar colors in your pieces of her."

"Yeah." She smiles. "Teals and yellows," she explains, her eyes bright and wide. "Each color means something."

"What are hers?" I glance over at her staring hard at it.

"Happiness and laughter. She was the teals and yellows of my life. Always laughing, always smiling. Her happiness made me happy. Before she started cutting, we'd always get into trouble for talking and giggling past our bedtime. She'd make up stories and they always made me laugh at how creative and crazy they were. I'd pull my sheets over my mouth to cover the sound, but our parents' room was down the hall and they always heard us."

My heart squeezes. "I love that. Teals and yellows."

She nods with a small smile. "Yeah. It's how I want to always remember her."

"You can remember her any way you want. She's your memory. Her life might've been short, but it's made a big impact on you." Her gaze lowers as she fidgets, and I'm afraid I've pushed too far. "Aspen?"

She clears her throat. "I'm fine."

I check my watch and groan. "I'm sorry I have to leave so early." I wrap an arm around her and pull her body to mine. "I'll see you later?" I ask, kissing the top of her head.

"Yeah, of course." She returns a forced smile.

"Don't forget to eat something," I remind her as she walks me to the door. Before walking out, I tilt her chin and place a soft kiss on her lips. "Bye, sweetheart."

Chapter Thirty
Aspen

Teals and yellows.

Ariel could make me laugh until I was in tears. Our dinners were spent giggling at the table while our parents scowled in warning. Eventually, they cracked and ended up laughing at her jokes, too.

The way I paint her is how I saw her on the outside—bright, funny, and confident. People look at my abstract pieces and see a girl full of life—a girl who has her whole life ahead of her, can be anything she wants, and the freedom to express herself.

After the first time I found her in the bathroom, someone else surfaced in place of the sister I knew. Ariel wasn't Ariel anymore. She'd changed, and I couldn't figure out why or what had caused it.

I think that's what kills me the most. Perhaps, had I known, I would've known how to help her.

Those painful thoughts and memories are what inspired my Ariel Rose Collection. I think about telling Morgan the truth, but I can't help the fear of it changing how he sees me. They're dark and some are even creepy. They represent her inner struggle that she hid from the rest of the world and the sadness that surrounded her—the part she didn't let anyone else see until it was too late.

When I make art, I release something from deep inside of myself. I welcome the bad thoughts, feeling that same sadness and the memories to fuel that same internal struggle to create something on paper. I give into the depression and express those feelings on the canvas.

I'm not sure how I can explain that to someone, especially him, without scaring him away. Or maybe it's because when I do, it'll mean they're no longer just for me anymore. Our memories are sacred and letting someone else into that part of my life feels more intimate than I'm willing to share.

But the longer I don't tell him, the worse the consequences will be.

I sleep over at Morgan's house Monday night, except neither of us sleeps, but I sneak out before his niece wakes up.

Sadly, I have to go through the whole day of classes and a shift at the gallery before I can go to his night class and see him. It's going to be hard keeping a straight face after I've had my mouth wrapped around his cock less than twenty-four hours before that.

But I'm a professional.

I can do this.

The moment he steps into the classroom, my cheeks heat. I'd hoped chatting with Ellie beforehand would help distract me, but my body shivered the moment I saw him.

Perhaps I can't.

Lowering my head, I bite my lip to keep the stupid grin off my face, but it doesn't work. I can't stop it from spreading across my face when he walks in all teacher-like—briefcase in hand, crisp button-up shirt tucked into his dark dress pants. He barely flinches as he sets his briefcase down on the desk and looks out at us.

"Evening, everyone." They all straighten up in their seats. I avoid eye contact with him but find it hard not to be drawn by his deep voice and bright eyes. The sexual charge between us is strong, I'm almost certain everyone in the room can feel it. But they go on as usual, grabbing their supplies and working on their projects. Next week is spring break, so we have the rest of this week to finish our assignments.

Midway through class, Ellie grabs my attention. "I forgot to ask, how the hell did you end up standing naked for the life drawing workshop? One second you were sitting next to me, *clothed*, and the next, you were in the front, buck naked."

I cringe at how many people saw me naked that night. I hadn't had much time to think it through, but I don't regret it either. Ms. Jones needed me, and I'd do anything for her after how much she's done for me.

"The model got sick after the first set and needed a replacement. My boss needed a fill-in, and I volunteered." I shrug it off as if it's no big deal.

"Was it awkward? All those people staring at you?"

"They weren't *staring*," I correct. "They were drawing me. There's a difference."

She snorts. "Hardly. But if you say so."

She goes back to her painting, but every few minutes, she glances over and furrows her brows.

"What?" I tilt my head, lowering my brush. "You want a second viewing? A personal session maybe?"

She laughs quietly and shakes her head. "Nah, the first show was good enough to last me a while. However, I figured out why you've been acting so weird."

"I have not," I defend.

"You're more timid than usual, and every time Professor Hampton walks around us, you blush and lower your head like a cowering animal."

"I do not."

She smirks. "He saw you naked," she clarifies. "I'm sure he barely remembers the first class," she states, reminding me of Morgan's and my first interaction.

A small smile slips from my lips. "How'd you feel if one of your professors saw you and stared at you for an hour?"

"I thought they weren't staring?" she quips, arching a brow. "Plus, if it's a professor as hot as him, then I'd feel aroused, sweaty like my loins were on fire and he was the only one capable of putting them out."

"Oh God. I just threw up in my mouth." I lower my head even more, embarrassed at how she's talking about him. I know it's not a secret how good-looking he is, but he's so much more than that. He always has been.

I start to notice students nearby are looking at us. I give Ellie a side glance that tells her she needs to keep it down.

"Sorry," she whispers with a devilish smile.

We manage to get through class without any more outbursts of laughter. I purposely pack my things away slowly, waiting for the rest of the students to file out. Ellie stands around waiting for me, but I find an excuse to get rid of her.

"Oh, I have to ask him something quick. I'll catch up with you."

"I don't mind waiting. My ex-boyfriend and roommate finally moved out, giving me the freedom to do nothing at all." She frowns, and I can see she's still struggling with the breakup. She found him in bed with her roommate, Rachel, and he acted as if she was supposed to join their little party. She was devastated and has been covering up her feelings about it since.

I nod instead of arguing. "It's okay. I'll ask him later. It's no big deal."

"Are you sure?"

"Yeah, I'll walk out with you." I pull my bag over my shoulder, and we head out down the hallway.

I ask her about her ex-boyfriend, Chad, and if she wants to talk about it. She rambles on about how she gave him all her best years. She'd been hoping they'd be engaged soon and planning a wedding after graduation.

"You're too young to want to be tied down," I say. "You have plenty of great years ahead of you."

"I'm an art student who spends my nights painting and reading.

Pushing the Limits

When I'm not at work, I'm studying or crying over fictional men who'll never appear in real life."

"What you need is a girls' night," I declare. "I have a couple friends who'd love to go out if you're interested. Maybe this weekend?"

Shrugging, her eyes lower. "Sure, maybe. Can I bring my friends, Kindle and chocolate?"

I shove my shoulder into hers and laugh. "No. You'll have to break the news to them that they have to stay home and keep your bed warm for you instead."

She finally cracks a smile. "Alright, fine. I can manage one night out."

"Trust me. Kendall and Zoe are my sole reason for getting through this past year. You'll love them," I reassure.

As soon as we walk out, I pretend to have left something in the room. I tell her I'll chat with her Thursday about this weekend and say my goodbyes. It's my chance to quickly see Morgan.

The hallway has already cleared out. Most of the students bail as quickly as they can after night classes. I don't expect to see anyone, but as soon as I walk past a dark room, a hand grabs me from behind and covers my mouth, pulling me against their chest and into the empty room.

I'm ready to scream and elbow-punch whoever it is when I hear Morgan's voice in my ear. "It's me."

He releases his hand and spins me around.

"You scared me half to death!" I whisper loudly, slapping a hand to his chest.

A warm smile forms on his face. "Sorry, I needed to kiss those lips. And maybe this neck. And…"

He pulls me closer as I wrap my arms around him and lean into him, soaking up every forbidden second we have before one of us has to leave.

"That was awkward," I say as soon as he releases me.

His brows furrow. "The kiss?"

"No." I laugh. "Being in class with you. Ellie kept asking why I was acting weird, which I hadn't realized I was. Did you think I was?"

"I don't know. I was trying hard not to focus on you." He cracks a smile, and I chuckle again.

"We're so bad at this."

"It's going to be fine," he promises. "We'll have a whole week off for spring break, and then half a semester left to go."

I groan. "That's a long time."

"Trust me, I know. It's how long I've been waiting to feel your mouth against mine..." He smirks. "But it'll fly by. Don't worry. Act normally in class. Participate as usual. Ask questions. Undress me with your eyes if you feel the need."

"Sure, no biggie. Just pretend I didn't have my professor's cock down my throat. No problem."

He covers my face with his hand again and shushes me with a quiet laugh. "And learn to talk *quieter*." He snickers before releasing me.

"No one is even here. Relax."

"You never know. I could have a stalker waiting out there for me."

"For your sake, I hope so. You could use the distraction from constantly staring at my chest."

"Only when you wear shirts like that." His gaze purposely glances down at the low V of my shirt.

"And what about when I wear short skirts and heels?" I prompt.

"You better not," he threatens. "Jeans and turtlenecks are the only things you're allowed to wear in my classroom."

I snort, shaking my head at his exaggerations. "I don't even own a turtleneck."

He groans, throwing his head back. "Lord, you're trying to kill me, aren't you? Punishing me for kissing my student, and now you want to punish me while she sits in my classroom half-naked and untouchable?"

"Good way to test your willpower, *Professor*." I wink, giving him a chaste kiss before heading out of the classroom first. "Feel free to follow me home, though."

Chapter Thirty-One

Morgan

G od, I wish I could.

Though, I wouldn't wait until we were at her place. The elevator, maybe. But it'd be a challenge.

After I pick Natalia up from my mom's, she nearly passes out when I get her in the house. We talk a little before her eyes flutter closed, and I write myself a mental note to ask about her night at breakfast in the morning.

As I walk through the house, making sure doors are locked and lights are turned off, I can't wipe the stupid smile off my face. Aspen's consumed my mind for so long that it's surreal I finally have her.

However, I need to make sure the board doesn't find out. Jeopardizing our futures would be the worst-case scenario.

But I can't *not* have her. Having my heart ripped out again would be the end of me. She fits me so perfectly. We've been two broken puzzle pieces all this time, waiting to find the other piece to connect to, to finally feel whole.

Once I change clothes, I settle into bed with my laptop. I'm behind on updating grades, so I need to enter midterm grades tonight before students leave for spring break.

Thirty minutes later, I hear a soft knock on the front door. I walk down the hallway and inhale sharply when I open the door and see Aspen.

"Hi…" My face lights up. "What are you doing here?"

She starts unbuttoning her long trench coat and slowly walks toward me. "Came to surprise you," she drawls, her voice laced with seduction. "Thought since you couldn't come to me, I'd come to you." She sweeps her tongue across her lower lip.

Tempted to rip that coat off her, I grab her hand and pull her inside. She shuts the door with the back of her heel and molds her body against mine. My cock hardens when she rocks her hips against mine, teasing and taunting me before I can do anything about it.

"I have a feeling you're going to be the death of me," I growl in her ear, grabbing her hand and wrapping it around the noticeable bulge pressing against my pants.

"At least you'd go out in style," she offers with a devilish smile.

"Stay quiet. I'm about to make your body scream." I cover my mouth with hers, pushing until her ass hits the wall. I know she has nothing underneath that thin coat of hers by how her hard nipples press against the material, and I'm about to make her pay for it.

I kneel in between her legs before she can stop me and tear open her coat, exposing every smooth surface of her body. My hands wrap around her thighs, spreading them wider for me. I can smell her arousal instantly, making it nearly impossible to wait any longer.

"What are you doing?" she hisses, struggling to close her legs. "Isn't your niece sleeping?"

"Exactly." I look up and grin. "So you better stay quiet." She rests one hand on the wall and tangles the other in my hair.

I can hardly control myself when I get that first taste of her sweet pussy. She's drenched for me. As my tongue slips inside her and runs along her slit, a sultry moan slips out of her. I nip her inner thigh, and her breath hitches.

"I told you to be quiet," I remind her.

Her eyes gloss over as she sucks her bottom lip between her teeth. I can't help but be amused at this little game. Aspen's no shrinking violet in the bedroom, so I imagine this will be a challenge for my little vixen. With a devilish smirk, I plunge my tongue fully inside her. She's quick to rock her hips as she tries to take control.

I look up her body and then into her sea-blue eyes as my heart leaps in my chest, admiring how perfect she looks. I love that she's watching me pleasure her. My cock pulses at the thought of being inside her and squeezed by her slick walls.

I slide a hand up her stomach and wrap my fingers around her bare breast as my tongue continues its delicious assault. I can tell she's fighting the urge to scream by how hard she's biting her lip, so I decide to palm her breast harder and tease her nipple between two fingers as I flick my tongue faster and deeper inside her.

"That's not fair," she pants, her fingers pulling my hair harder. "At least take me to the bedroom where I can fuck your brains out." Her bluntness nearly makes me choke, but I don't give in to her pleas.

"Nice try, sweetheart," I say, lifting her leg and placing it over my shoulder, granting better access. She's taken off guard and ends up unbalanced on one of those fuck-me heels I'm appreciative of, smacking her head against the wall. Her eyes widen in panic and she glances down the hallway. I can't stop tasting her, so once a moment passes and things remain quiet, she tilts those full lips into a sultry grin.

Mm...fuck, yes.

I suck her clit and flick my tongue over the tight bundle of nerves. She releases an agonizing groan, the strangled sound making my cock throb harder against my zipper. I scrape my teeth against her in response, and she moans deep from within her throat, her leg tightening around my neck.

I love how she abandons all her insecurities in these moments. She knows what she wants and chases it—and right now, she wants my mouth. I'm happy to oblige.

Skimming my hand lightly up her leg from ankle to thigh, I slip my fingers up to her pussy, teasing her when I shallowly insert a finger.

"Yes." She releases a soft and eager moan. "More, please."

I ignore her sweet begging and lightly circle her clit with the tip of my tongue and slowly slip my finger inside with shallow thrusts. She puffs out a breath in frustration and tries to lower her leg off my shoulder, but I quickly grab it. I tightly wrap my free arm around her thigh, dig my nails into her flesh, and hold her open. I'm not letting go of her that easily—not until I've fully fucked her delicious hot cunt.

After harshly putting her where I want her, I decide to put her out of her misery. I suck her clit and push two fingers deep inside her. I rotate my wrist, pushing deeper, and her walls tighten around me with each thrust. Glancing up her body again, I watch as her pants and cheeks flush with pleasure.

God, I want to taste her orgasm. She's close.

"Give me one," I demand and lick up her slit until I tongue her clit. Her head falls back against the wall and her body nearly succumbs to the floor as I increase the pace. "Let go, baby."

"Fuck...*Oh my God*." Her thighs shake.

"That's it. Let me taste it, sweetheart."

She shakes her head, though I know she's desperate to scream.

Once I release her leg, I stand. My fingers continue working her cunt as my thumb rubs along her clit.

My free hand cups her jaw and rubs a soothing finger against her cheek. "Come, Aspen," I demand again.

Though she can barely breathe, I kiss her hard while my fingers work her pussy. She finally gives in and her body shatters, soaking my fingers.

"So fucking good, baby," I whisper. "I know you can give me one more."

"I can't," she chokes out.

I continue my assault on her clit as she teeters on the edge.

"Fuck my fingers." I thrust in deeper.

Her hips rotate, then grind against my palm.

"My good, sweet girl," I murmur. "Take what you need."

As she continues, she wraps a hand around my neck and pulls my mouth to hers. I give her what she needs as she releases another explosive orgasm.

Goose bumps cover her skin as she leans against the wall, sated and panting.

"You're so fucking beautiful." I kiss her gently and she smiles.

Pushing the Limits

"You have magic fingers."

I arch a brow. "Did you think they were only meant for painting?"

"Oh no, I knew they had *many* talents."

Bringing my lips to her neck, I ask, "Want me to show you what else they're capable of doing?"

"Yes, *please*."

"I can arrange that." Lifting her into my arms, she quickly wraps her legs around me.

Her words are low in my ear as I walk us to my bedroom. "I want you inside me. *Now*."

Tangling my fingers in her hair, I pull her head back until our eyes meet. "Patience, sweetheart."

Once we're in the bedroom and I've locked the door, I set her down on the mattress and push off her coat, then toss it aside. She watches with eager eyes as I strip off my clothes and add them to the pile on the floor.

Grabbing a condom from the dresser, I roll it over my length. She leans back as I slowly crawl up her body, pressing soft kisses on her smooth skin. When I reach her breasts, I pull her nipple into my mouth and suck as if my life depends on it. I know she likes it rough.

She groans, digging her nails into my arms, which only feeds my desire more.

Those eager hips of hers rock wildly against me as her heat presses against my cock.

"I need you, Morgan." Her voice is quiet yet demanding. "Now."

Looking up from her chest, I smirk at her sultry tone. "You don't know the definition of patience, do you?"

Her lips part as I grip her thighs and spread them wider. I press my tip against her opening and watch as her eyelids flutter, anticipating my next move.

I lean over her as I slowly push inside, feeling the tightness of her walls enveloping me. Her hips arch up as her head falls back.

She releases a deep, loud moan without warning, and I quickly cover her mouth with mine, taking in her sweet sounds.

After rolling her on top of me, bending her over the bed, and fucking her recklessly, I curl around her body, tangling my legs with hers and holding her close. Aspen quickly falls into a deep, sated sleep. I lie there for a few more moments as I run my fingers over her skin and contemplate how we'll make this work. I'm determined to find a way without either of us having to sacrifice our positions at the college.

Chapter Thirty-Two
Aspen

It's officially spring break and the first time in years that I've happily spent an entire morning in bed. It's only been a week since Morgan and I first hooked up, but it feels much longer. We've been building a relationship for the past seven weeks, so I know a lot about him already, yet there's more to learn about each other.

Waking up in Morgan's arms every morning has been complete bliss—almost unreal. He looks as if I'm the only woman in the entire world, reminds me how beautiful I am and how much he loves my paintings. Guilt soars through me as I think about the secret I have yet to confess. He's told me about his ex-girlfriend and the reason he left five years ago. The betrayal ran deep, and I worry about how he will react when he finds out about the Ariel Rose Collection. He's talked a little more about his brother and how close they were growing up. He's given so much of himself, but I still struggle with opening up.

My mother's called me at least a dozen times in the last couple of weeks. I've ignored them all, knowing exactly what she wants. I don't owe my parents anything, and I'm not going home to amuse her. Being around them is toxic, and it's the last thing I need in my life.

Morgan dropped Natalia off at school early this morning and crawled back into bed with me. It felt so easy, so natural in his arms.

The warmth of his skin and the tenderness of his grip lulls me right to sleep.

"Time to wake up, sleepyhead." He gently shakes my shoulder, but I groan and roll over. "Aspen," he says with amusement. "I made breakfast."

"Stick a feeding tube in me and nourish me that way," I mumble. "Your bed is too comfortable."

He rolls me toward him until I'm on top of him. "You need to eat."

"Stop being so bossy. You can't be all *professorly* in bed." I crack a teasing smile.

"Professorly? Lord." He laughs, then pulls me up with him. He wraps his arms under my body and lifts me. "I'll force-feed you if I have to."

"I'd like to see you try." He flashes me a sly smirk, and I know I'm in trouble.

He carries me into the kitchen and sets me down on the counter, then hands me a glass with something that looks like the Hulk threw up and nods his head at me to drink it.

"Here, drink this."

"What is it?" I frown.

"It's a protein smoothie. Try it."

"It looks disgusting." I smell it and wrinkle my nose. "Smells disgusting, too."

He glares. "It has peanut butter and blueberries in it."

"And?" I prompt, knowing there's something worse.

"Spinach."

I extend my arm and hand it back. "Yup, no, thanks. I'll stick with normal food."

He grabs it. "You aren't even going to try it?"

"Just because you like to eat fruity spinach goo doesn't mean I can't eat eggs and a pound of greasy bacon."

He raises his brows. "You aren't going to be young forever," he chides with a wink. "Having healthy eating habits will help you maintain a healthy diet as you grow older."

"Wow, I didn't know you were a professor by day and a nutritionist by night," I mock.

He shakes his head. "You're on your own then, pretty lady. I haven't bought bacon in years."

"But pizza you're okay with?"

"Only on cheat days."

I jump off the counter and stand in front of him. "So, like every day?"

He wraps an arm around me and playfully slaps my ass. I yelp in surprise and try to wiggle out of his grip. "Don't tempt me to put you over my knee, woman."

I roll my eyes. "Now if you added bacon to that smoothie, we'd have a deal."

"Not a chance."

"You're no fun." I glare, and he frees me from his arm. I walk to his fridge and start digging around. "You have no food in here." I push around the pizza boxes and takeout containers. "What do you guys eat?"

"Natalia says I'm a bad cook."

"Guess we're stopping at the grocery store sometime today." I shut the door and start digging through his nearly empty cupboards. "I'll hop in the shower and then we can go." I turn to him leaning against the counter, holding a cup of coffee, and smirking like something's funny. "What? Did that sound girlfriend-ish? It did. Crap. Can we pretend that never happened? I didn't—"

"Aspen," he interrupts in a low, amused voice. "I want you to sound girlfriend-ish."

"You do?"

He sets his cup down and steps toward me. "Yes. I've been thinking about you for weeks. If I didn't, I wouldn't want you around all the time. I was worried you'd think I was being too clingy."

I crack a smile as warmth fills my heart at his sincerity. "We're bad at this, aren't we?"

"Yeah, too bad this stuff doesn't come with a manual, huh?"

"Oh, I'm sure there are, but none that apply to the *How to Secretly Date your Professor* genre."

"I don't see why we can't start one." He rubs the scruff over his jawline, deep in thought. "Step one: Fall for a student who is beyond

239

brilliant, sexy, and sassy. Step two: Be around her as much as possible without people getting suspicious. Step three: Don't get caught."

I burst out laughing at his lame list and shake my head. "Bestseller right there, baby."

He grins. "Then I could quit my job, and we wouldn't have to keep it secret any longer."

I suck in my lower lip and arch a brow. "But then what fun would that be? If everyone's going to know it defeats the whole purpose."

He slaps a hand on his chest. "Wait, so you're only with me for the thrill?"

"Obviously. You thought it was your good looks and charm?"

He grabs my hips and tickles me. I bend over, laughing, trying to get out of his grip, but he's too strong. "Stop it!"

"Take it back!"

"Never!"

He grabs my legs and throws me over his shoulder.

"What are you doing?" I squeal, smacking his ass with both hands.

"Grocery shopping will have to wait. Looks like you need to be taught a lesson first." He slaps my ass with the palm of his hand, and I know exactly what *lesson* he's talking about.

I've only been to my apartment this week to change clothes and wait for Natalia to go to bed before sneaking over. As much as it feels weird to have slept over here every night, it also feels natural.

Morgan's still sleeping, so I sneak out before his niece wakes up. I want to bring some of my art supplies over as well. I get antsy if I don't paint after a day or two.

Tiptoeing to the kitchen, I pull open the fridge and grab a bottle of water and yogurt to eat before I leave. As soon as I shut the door, his niece stands directly next to it.

"Uh…hi," I stumble. I look like a hot mess of sex hair with last night's makeup still on. *Great first impression.* "You must be Natalia." I extend a hand, but her gaze stays focused on mine. "I've heard a lot about you."

"I know who you are."

My brows furrow as my arm falls to my side. "You do?"

"I also know you've been sneaking in every night for the past week. I may be eleven years old, but I'm not stupid."

I swallow, unsure of what to say. "Oh, well, I don't think Morgan was ready to tell you yet."

Her arms are crossed as she shakes her head in the most dramatic way an eleven-year-old can. "He doesn't get girls at all. Just a heads-up."

Smirking in amusement, I nod. Her spunkiness is adorable. Based on what Morgan's told me, we have a lot in common. She's built up walls to block her feelings and to keep herself at a distance. It's heartbreaking for someone so young to hold in so much grief, especially with the loss of two parents.

"Thank you for the tip." I wink. "Maybe I can make dinner for us tonight. What do you think?"

She shrugs. "Sure. As long as you're a better cook than Uncle Morgan. He's had to change the smoke alarm batteries twice since I've moved in."

I crack a smile at the visual of Morgan burning food in the kitchen so much that the batteries have died.

"What's your favorite food?" I ask, hoping to soften her up.

"Hm…I don't know. I've been living on cold pizza and Grandma's leftovers, so…anything." She finally smiles.

"I know." I smile in return. "I'll make famous Chicago-style hot dogs."

Her brow arches. "Hot dogs?"

"Not just any hot dogs," I defend. "All-beef hot dog on a poppy seed bun topped with mustard, relish, chopped onion, tomato slices, pickle spear, sport peppers, and celery salt. It's delicious. It's the custom Chicago dog." It's nostalgic thinking about home and how, as a family, we'd always get them from the hot dog stands on the corner.

Her eyes widen, and I fear I've scared her off. But then she blinks and smiles. "Sure, sounds great."

That night, I bring over all the ingredients and make her and Morgan a traditional Chicago-style hot dog meal complete with cheese fries. They loved it.

It feels like sharing a meal with the three of us has sealed the deal. The acts of an *actual* relationship.

"Please tell me we can keep her?" Natalia looks over at Morgan with wide doe eyes. I laugh, embarrassed, but filled with a sense of pride.

"As long as you supply the groceries, I'm happy to cook," I speak up before Morgan can respond. "Except spinach." Morgan shoots me a knowing glare. "Sorry, honey." He winks.

Chapter Thirty-Three
Morgan

Everything in my life feels like it's coming together for the first time in years. Natalia and Aspen have hit it off, and I can't imagine spending each night with anyone else. I lie in bed wide awake as Aspen sleeps cradled in my arms. She looks flawless. Her golden hair is wrapped up in a messy bun. She's in a tank top and shorts, so simple, yet so breathtaking. The confidence radiates off her whether she realizes it or not. She's a beautiful person inside and out, and sometimes I wonder why she'd be interested in a guy like me.

Ryan is always on my mind, but tonight, he's more than usual. I can hardly remember the days when we weren't at each other's throats but growing up was always an adventure. He was always into athletics, but I didn't get into lifting weights until college. We were so opposite, it's not a surprise we would always butt heads, but as we grew older, we grew closer.

I still feel an ache in my chest at how I left things with him. Though I can't do anything about it now, I can devote my life to raising Natalia the way he would've expected. I see him in her so much. His bright eyes. His laugh and smile.

I kiss the top of Aspen's head and carefully sneak out of bed without waking her up. I walk to my office where his boxes are stored. I start unstacking them, ripping them open. I stop once I reach the picture albums. I sit against the wall as I hold them in my hand, staring at the cover that's labeled *1980 to 1990* on it.

Slowly, I open it and see his baby pictures right away. He was my parents' firstborn, which means he has an abundance of baby pictures. By the time I was born, he was five years old. I stare at one of our first pictures. He's holding me on our old couch. He held me in his lap as he smiled for the camera.

A soft smile forms on my lips as I continue flipping through. So many pictures of us growing up, playing and wrestling around in the grass. We took a family vacation every year and even some of those are in here. The one time we drove up to the Grand Canyon and I lost my first tooth along the way. When we first went to Disneyland and took pictures with Mickey and Goofy while we wore those ridiculous Mickey ears on our heads.

I flip another few pages and come across the ones from our first days of school. Mom took a picture of us in front of the same tree every year from my kindergarten year up until his senior year of high school. He'd always wrap his arm around me and stand tall, making sure he looked bigger than I did.

I lift my head as I hear the door creak open. Aspen's silhouette peers through, and I hate that she's going to see me this way.

"Are you okay?" She drops to her knees and touches my face. "What are you doing in here?"

I look down at the photo album and then up at her. "I couldn't sleep."

"What are these?" She rubs a finger over the album.

"Family photos. They were Ryan's."

"Can I see?" she asks sweetly, and I can tell she's trying to be sensitive about it.

"Of course." I pat my hand on the floor and she shifts next to me. She loops her arm through mine and rests her head on my shoulder as I close the album and start over from the beginning.

For the next two hours, we sit there, sifting through albums and pictures. The memories make me sad and happy at the same time. I'm glad I have them but sad we won't have any more to make.

"You were a stud growing up," she taunts. "You two looked a lot alike." Her face softens.

"Yeah, we look a lot like our dad. The Hampton gene."

"What happened to Ryan?"

The kindness in her voice has me fighting the huge wave of grief. I've held onto it so tightly, but her genuine interest in this part of my life could break that dam. I flip to the end of the book where there are a couple of pictures taken on the day he graduated from the police academy. His smile was wide and proud. His then-fiancée, Lena, stood beside him as she wore her new engagement ring.

Ryan's life had only begun. When he and Lena got married, they got pregnant with Natalia. He was all set to have his happily ever after and the career he busted his ass for, but unfortunately, things didn't play out that way for him.

I take a deep breath and start explaining.

"He'd worked for the Berkeley PD for about thirteen years at that point, but he wasn't on duty the day he died. He had a weird addiction to gas station coffee and always went and refilled his cup before picking Natalia up from school. Some young punk walks in and starts waving a gun at the cashier, demanding he clean out the register. Ryan, being who he was, tried to talk the kid down. He waved a few other customers who were inside to hide as he stayed up front with the cashier.

"According to the cashier, he was using police tactics to get him to surrender his weapon, so they could all leave unharmed. He didn't carry his gun while he was off duty, but it was tucked away in his car. Once he calmed the kid down and got him to lower his gun off the cashier, he tried getting him to drop it and kick it over to him. From the security tapes, it shows Ryan motioning to the cashier to get out. The cashier tripped and the kid got startled and ended up pulling the trigger."

I've not looked up from his picture as I've talked, but I glance at Aspen, needing her reassurance to continue. There are fresh tears along her cheeks and a small hand over her mouth as if she's trying to hold back a sob. I lean over and brush a gentle kiss on her cheek, tasting the saltiness of her tears.

She curls into me, wrapping her arms around me as best as she can in this position. "Then what?" Her voice is soft and encouraging.

I inhale another deep breath and continue. "He hit Ryan in the side, missing everything vital. Had that been the only shot, he would've survived. After the cashier had run out the door, Ryan tried to apply pressure and stall the bleeding. From the security tapes, you can see how the kid was getting agitated and pacing as Ryan struggled to get a hold on the gunshot wound. The responding officer arrived quickly, but the sirens spooked him even more. He locked the front doors and continued waving his gun around. Ryan continued to talk to him, reassuring him that they could walk out of this, but the moment more cop cars arrived, he freaked out and pulled the trigger again. That time, it killed him."

Aspen's shoulders shake, and I can tell she's trying to be strong for me. Honestly, I need her strength because reliving it all is painful, but I know I need to deal with the reality of it before I can move forward. I need to find a way to let myself grieve without the guilt taking over.

"The kid didn't get far once he ran out the back. They caught him only a few blocks away. He was only fifteen years old. Only a few years older than Natalia. A kid ruined not only his own life but stole away Nat's whole world and my brother's life, too. But I fully believe he died a hero that day, and I'm proud of him for sacrificing his own life to save another's." My voice cracks with sadness, but I remain strong. "I'm so angry at myself for not fixing things with him. Stubborn pride and stupidity kept me away for five years, and I'll never get that time back."

Aspen pulls the big book off my lap and replaces it with her body. Her slight weight and comforting arms are everything I need at this moment. I bury my face in her strawberry scented hair and release the burden of it all for the first time since I last saw him at his funeral. She grips me tighter, her voice soft and full of affection when she tells me how sorry she is.

She doesn't fill the silence with a bunch of nonsense chatter or try to fix things like other people do. She gives me her acceptance and quiet strength as if she can sense that it's exactly what I need.

A soft creak from the hallway makes our heads jerk up. Natalia peeks in slowly, a blanket wrapped securely around her. She frowns, and I can tell she's heard us.

"Come here." I nod.

Aspen moves over, making room. Natalia shuffles in between us, grabs the blanket, and unravels it. She lays it across our laps as we sit next to each other.

I grab the photo album and place it gently on her lap. She looks down, tracing her finger over the lines of the photos. Warmth fills my heart even though grief is consuming the rest of me.

I glance over at Aspen, her lips pulled into a soft smile as she looks at me. She wraps an arm around Nat and lies her head on top of hers, placing a quick kiss on her temple.

After several moments of Natalia turning the pages, I rub my hand on Aspen's neck, getting her attention and mouthing a quick 'thank you.'

I'm so lucky to have someone like Aspen holding me up. I'm supposed to be doing that for her, but it's as if she knew I needed her this time. It's as if she knew we could be each other's strength.

It's at this moment I realize how hard I'm falling for her. Not a crush or someone to fill a void, but genuine, head-over-heels, can't-get-enough-of-her kind of feelings.

It should scare the shit out of me, but all I can do is smile and hope she feels the same way, too.

Chapter Thirty-Four
Aspen

I'm dreading the fact that classes are starting up in two days. Spending every day with Morgan other than work has made this one of the best weeks I've ever had. I can't remember ever feeling like this with someone before—mainly because I never allowed myself to. But he's made me want to open up and let him in, and I don't ever want that feeling to go away.

"Do you have to go to work today?" he groans, pulling me into his arms as we lie in his bed. I have a long shift today, but all I want to do is stay in bed with him.

"Unfortunately, yes," I mutter with a sigh. "You can come visit me," I offer. "Bring Natalia. I'm sure Ms. Jones wouldn't mind."

"No, except she cannot know about us."

"But Natalia knows."

"Yeah," he says with a frustrated grunt. "I'll talk to her first."

I hate that he has to ask his niece to keep our secret, but it's the only way. Ms. Jones is on the school board at CSLA, and she would be ethically bound to tell the school. I don't want to put her in that situation, so it has to remain between the three of us only.

He squeezes me tighter and presses a chaste kiss on my lips. "I'll start the coffee."

I quickly shower and change. I dry my hair and pull half of it up.

Pushing the Limits

Morgan comes in with my cup of coffee, filled with my favorite mocha creamer and topped with whipped cream. He's mastered it well.

"Thank you." I smile and finish applying my eyeliner. "I have to leave in ten minutes, though. No distracting me," I tease, knowing that he'll try.

"Oh, what fun is that?" he mocks with a knowing grin.

"Ms. Jones may be your aunt, but she's still my boss. I need her reference to hopefully get into a graduate school. Can't be pissing her off."

"She's a real softy at heart. She may look and sound all tough but put a puppy in her hands and she melts like butter."

I snort at the visual. "Unless you have a puppy handy, I better get my ass to work."

Once I clean up my mess, I finish my cup of coffee before kissing him goodbye. Then I give a quick wave to Natalia before backing out of the driveway.

She's warmed up to me so much in a short amount of time. It's hard to believe she's only eleven. Losing parents will do that to you, though. You're forced to grow up faster than you should.

I arrive to work with two minutes to spare. After I place my belongings in my locker, I put on my vest and nametag. As soon as I slam it shut, Shane walks in with a crooked grin on his face.

"What are you smiling about?" I inquire. I hadn't spoken to him much since his rude attitude at the gala, but I'm in an unusually happy mood and decide to look past it.

"You'd only be lucky to know. Too bad you're screwing Ms. J's uppity-two-shoes nephew." He cracks a smile and all the blood drains from my face as he grabs a soda from the vending machine.

My breaths are shallow, and I can't think of a comeback quick enough before he continues.

He shakes his head with a knowing grin. "Don't worry. Your secret's safe with me." He cracks open his Coke can and walks out, then winks over his shoulder.

"Wait!" I finally manage to take a breath. The features on his face soften. "How'd you know?"

He takes a sip of his soda and shrugs. "Lucky guess."

I playfully punch him in the shoulder, earning an exaggerated groan as he rubs his hand over the wound. "You've got a good arm."

"Shane."

"Alright, alright. Keep your panties on."

I flash him a warning look.

"He couldn't keep his gaze off you. I watched him all night. It wasn't a look of getting in your pants, either. It was as if he couldn't breathe without being around you."

His confession shocks me, sending my heart into overdrive with a noticeable thud. Shane has never shown this side before but turns out, he's more than abs and ass.

Lowering my head, I think about that night. He'd kissed me so passionately in such a raw moment of weakness that I was almost taken off guard.

"I hope it works out. He seems okay." The corners of his lips perk up in a taunting smile.

"Please don't say anything," I plead, my eyes desperate.

"Trust me, Aspen. I have no desire to be known as the work gossip." His quip tone instantly puts me at ease.

"Thanks, Shane."

"But if he hurts you, I get first dibs on punching the guy out."

I chuckle, appreciating his playful banter. "You've got it."

We walk out, separating as I head down the stairs for my first tour.

I grab a quick drink once the tour is over and head up to Christine's office for the rest of the day's tour schedule.

She's on the phone, so I quietly grab it from her desk and look it over. As soon as I start walking out, she stops me. "Aspen, wait a sec."

I turn to her finger up in the air as she quickly finishes her conversation before hanging up.

"Sorry." She groans. "A couple packages came for you."

"Here?" I step in front of her desk.

"Yeah…" She turns around and grabs a box, placing it on the desk with a loud thump. "From Illinois?"

I turn it around and rub a finger along the box with my mother's handwriting. "My mom." I groan.

"Well, there's another one. Why would she send them here?"

"Because she lives to ruin my life."

Her forehead wrinkles. "What?"

"I blocked her address from sending me stuff. Birthday cards, Christmas packages, letters. They always get returned, and apparently, she finally got smart and stopped shipping to my address." I sigh, hating that she found a way to get them to me. "I'll take them down to the post office and return them."

She gives me a curious look, and I know she wants an explanation.

"We don't get along well."

"I figured that."

"She used to send me stuff all the time when I first moved away. I left and didn't look back. I hated being home and surrounded by the things that reminded me of my sister. I wanted to detach from that part of my life, but she was hell-bent on reining me in."

"So you blocked her from mailing you things?"

I shrug. "I know it's harsh, but it was the only way. She wouldn't stop. I'd return them and tell her to stop sending me cards and money. My resentment was too heavy to accept anything else from them."

"Maybe it was her way of asking for forgiveness?" she offers. I know she doesn't know the whole story, no one does, but she has a close-knit family, so it's hard for her to understand not wanting to be involved in each other's lives.

"I wasn't ready to forgive her," I admit. "It's a little complicated."

"Sounds like it." She frowns. "I'm sorry either way. I wish I knew how to help."

"Don't be sorry. I've accepted that my parents and I have an odd relationship." *If you even want to call it that.*

"You aren't even a little curious to know what's inside? Two large packages. I'd be dying to know!" Her face lights up, the anticipation evident in her features.

"Fine." I sigh. "Only because you're making me!" I playfully scowl.

Her lips widen in an over-enthusiastic grin. "Yay!"

I shake my head at her. "It's probably all my old stuffed animals chopped into tiny little pieces."

She wrinkles her nose and stands across from me, cutting the tape off the sides. "You're so morbid."

I open the sides as she cuts them loose. Then, I notice the familiar handwriting on the notebooks packed inside.

"Are these your journals?"

I shake my head, grabbing the first one on top and tracing the lettering of her name written out. "My sister's."

"Are they all notebooks?" She peeks inside again. There are stacks of them, all different colors, but all with the same lettering written on top. *Ariel Rose.*

"Her journals," I respond.

"Have you seen them before?"

"No. I'd only seen her sketchpads. I had no idea she had these." My voice is somber, shock and fear taking over my head.

"Why would your mom send you these?" she asks the same question I'm wondering myself. "Do you think the sketchbooks are in the other package?"

My eyes lift to hers, mind spinning at the realization. "Let's open it," I say hurriedly.

She lifts the other box on top, ripping the tape off as fast as she can, not even bothering with the scissors this time. Once the sides are lifted open, I see them. On top is one of the sketchbooks I looked at after her funeral, but underneath is a stack of books I'd never seen before.

"Oh my God…" I breathe out.

I grab one, thinking how much smaller it feels in my hands than six years ago. "I hadn't seen these."

I flip through it, remembering the way I felt when I first saw them. *Sadness. Heartache. Pain.*

The heavy shading in each one guts me. I feel sick but swallow it down. She drew these for a reason…inspired by some inner demon.

"The talent runs in the family," Christine says softly and sincerely. Besides Ms. Jones, Christine is the only person here who knows about the AR Collection. She's in charge of the financial books, so there was no way around it. But I trust her and Ms. Jones over anyone else.

"I hadn't even known she was drawing until she passed. She never shared them with me."

Pushing the Limits

"Really?" I hear the shock in her voice. I was too.

"Yeah, I'm not sure why. Perhaps she was afraid to show me them."

There have to be dozens of notebooks and sketchbooks, which means she'd probably been hiding them for years.

"Do you know what they mean?" She leans over and looks at them as I flip through the pages. "They look sophisticated for her age."

"I know," I agree. "She'd spend hours wandering the fields, always falling asleep in the grass on warm summer days, or so she'd say. I always assumed she spaced out and got lost, but thinking about it, she always did carry a small backpack with her."

"She wanted privacy," Christine suggests. "Maybe it was therapeutic for her." She gives me a sympathetic look, seeing how hard this is for me.

She knows about Ariel falling from a tree, but she doesn't know about the depression and cutting. These drawings are a window right into her mind of what she was suffering through.

"She suffered from depression," I explain, the words continuing without restraint. "My parents didn't believe her, brushed it off as her wanting attention. They were ignorant to believe that one of their precious children wasn't perfect. Either that or they didn't want to spend the time helping her. Ariel kept it all inside. You couldn't tell because she acted like a normal kid, always cracking jokes and smiling. But once my parents found out she was cutting, they turned their heads and pretended it wasn't happening."

"That's awful." She covers my hand with hers when I realize tears are falling down my cheeks.

"I'm sorry. I'm acting like such a baby." I'm quick to wipe the tears away and close the sketchbook. I hate that my walls are crumbling down right in front of her. I can feel them tumbling down one by one.

"Don't be sorry, Aspen."

"I think maybe I should take them home."

"That's a good idea. I'll let Ms. Jones know, and we'll figure out the rest." I choke back a sob and thank her, placing the folds of the box. "I'll tell Shane to come help you put them in your car if you want."

I nod and keep my eyes low.

Shane notices the dramatic shift in my mood the moment he helps me carry them to my car. He looks at me as if he's thinking twice about asking me what's wrong.

"Thank you," I say softly, shutting the door to my car.

"I'll follow you home," he says. When I look up at him, his expression softens. "Help you carry them inside."

"Okay." I turn toward the car and then get inside.

I thank him again once he sets the boxes inside my apartment. I offered to carry one, but he batted my hands away.

"Feel better, Aspen. I'll let Christine know you made it home safely." He winks, a friendly smile spreading over his face.

"Thank you, Shane."

"Anytime."

Chapter Thirty-Five
Morgan

Having Aspen to myself for most of the week has been incredible. Waking up next to her, eating breakfast, spending the day in bed watching Netflix, and laughing with each other.

I'm like a lovesick teen all over again.

The worst part is her having to go into work, but since it's Saturday, Natalia and I get to spend some quality time. We're going to *drop by* the gallery for a bit, go out for lunch, and do whatever else she wants.

"Are you ready?" I call out as I lean against the front door. "I thought you were putting some shoes on?"

"I'm looking for my purse! Gimme a minute." She shuffles around some things on her desk.

"A purse?" I question. "You're eleven. You don't need a purse."

She finally walks out with a bag in her hand. "I'm a girl. I have stuff."

My brows furrow with an amused smile. "What stuff could you possibly have? Pantyhose? Lipstick? Diary?" I tease.

She rolls her eyes as she walks past me and out the door. "You have so much to learn, Uncle Morgan."

She says it so dramatically I can't help snickering. "Trust me, Shorty. I know."

We arrive and Natalia nearly jumps out of the car before I even put the gear into park. I practically chase her all the way in, hollering at her to slow down, but she's so excited and doesn't even hear me.

I told Aunt Mel we'd be coming, so she's already waiting for us at the front entrance. She adores Natalia and is stoked to show her around.

"Good morning!" I hear her cheerful voice as she wraps her arms around Nat.

"Morning!" I come up behind them and wrap an arm around her shoulder with a squeeze. "She's extremely excited in case you haven't noticed."

"I have!" She smiles wide. "I'm so glad you brought her. We're going to have a blast!" She winks down at Natalia and grabs her hand.

This is my chance to go find Aspen, so I casually excuse myself for a moment. "I'll catch up with you two in a bit. I'm going to use the restroom."

"Okay, find us when you're done," Aunt Mel calls over her shoulder. They've walking toward one of the exhibits as I scan the room for Aspen.

I continue looking around but can't find her anywhere. I want to ask where she is without sounding suspicious, but I'm not sure that's possible.

I grab my phone out of my pocket and text her.

MORGAN

Hey, Nat and I came to visit. Where are you?

I'm not sure if she'll have her phone on her or not, but it's worth a try. I catch up with Aunt Mel and Natalia as they're walking through the Forty under Forty exhibit. It must be one of their new ones because I haven't seen these before.

"How are things going?" I stuff my hands in my pockets.

"Good!" Natalia spins around, her face glowing with excitement. "It's so beautiful here. Makes me want to draw something myself."

"Good eye for art must run in the family," Aunt Mel says with a wink. I haven't told anyone other than Aspen that I haven't painted in months, so everyone assumes I'm still doing it.

"I could get you your own supplies, Shorty," I offer. "I also have a bunch in the basement that you can use."

"Really? I'd love that!" She wraps her arms around my waist. I've never seen her this excited before.

We continue walking around, and I casually look around for Aspen. I find Christine, but still no Aspen. She walks up to Aunt Mel and flashes a small smile.

"Shane followed her home. I think she'll be okay."

"Oh, thank you, darling. I feel awful." She presses a hand over her chest.

My interest is piqued as I try to read between the lines of their conversation. "What happened?"

"Aspen received a couple packages from her mom that were upsetting, something about journals, so she went home for the day."

My blood pressure rises the moment she says her name and mentions her mother. I don't know exactly what happened, but I know their relationship is rocky at best.

"Aunt Mel, can Natalia stay here with you? I have to run somewhere quick. I'm sorry." I kiss Natalia on the head and not so subtly run out before she can bombard me with questions.

I fly out the front doors and call her cell, but it goes straight to voicemail. I try again as soon as I'm in the car and drive out of the parking lot.

Voicemail. *Fuck.*

I speed to Aspen's apartment, unable to focus on anything other than her. I've seen her break down on a number of occasions, her anxiety triggered from far less than situations like this.

Once I'm inside, I jog up the stairs two at a time. I'm panting as I arrive at her door, ready to knock it down as I hear blasting music coming from the inside. I knock on the door but turn the knob anyway. There's no way she can hear me over the music.

Stepping inside, I immediately scan around for her. "Aspen!" I shout. "You here?"

I walk through the kitchen, to her bedroom, and out to the living

257

room before I check her studio where I finally find her, notebooks spread wildly all around her. Her knees are to her chest with her arms wrapped around them.

"Sweetheart, what happened?" Rushing to her, she looks up—her eyes red and swollen, her makeup smeared down her cheeks. She lowers her face, tears streaming down her cheeks as she shakes her head.

Leaning over her, I grab her phone that's connected to the speakers and shut off the music. "Baby…" I plead. "Talk to me. Please." My voice cracks as I beg for her to say something.

When I tilt her chin up, more tears run down. Her breathing is unsteady as she counts softly.

"Aspen." My heart pounds in my chest as I watch her crumble in front of me.

"She let go," she finally chokes out, taking a deep breath. "She didn't fall." More tears run down her cheeks as I try to comprehend what she's talking about. "She. Let. Go," she says one final time.

Wiping her cheeks, she finally looks up with a numb expression.

"Tell me what happened." I keep my voice calm without showing how I'm dying inside seeing her like this, feeling completely helpless.

"I can't get my heart rate to slow down," she finally tells me. "I've never had an attack this badly before."

"What can I do?" I rush out in a panic. "What do you need, baby?"

"Just hold me. I have to ride it out."

I pull her into my lap and hold her, soothing her the best that I can. Rubbing my hand up and down her arm, she fists my shirt and cries into my chest. My heart shatters as her body shakes with every hiccupping sob. Pressing my lips to her forehead, I place a soft kiss and tighten my arms around her.

We stay like that until her breathing steadies and the sounds of her crying dissipate. I want to comfort her and ask what's triggered such a bad one, but what could I possibly say that would have any value at this point?

"Morgan…" she whispers.

"Yeah, baby?" I brush the hair off her face.

"I feel like the part of me that I had left from before she passed has officially been ripped away from me. It's been shattered, leaving me broken pieces of the person I used to be."

"I'm so sorry, sweetheart." I close my eyes and take a steady breath. "Tell me what happened. Aunt Mel said your mom sent you something?"

"She packaged up my sister's old journals and sketchbooks and sent them to me."

"Did you know she kept them all this time?"

"I didn't even know they existed." She shudders against me.

"Why would your mom send them?"

She shrugs. "I don't know if she read them and wanted me to read them too or if she was cleaning stuff out and thought I'd want them. She didn't send a note or even tell me she was sending them. She gave me no warning at all."

"So you've been going through them since you left?"

She nods.

"That triggered your attack?"

"I read them." Lifting her head, she sniffs and wipes her cheeks off. "They're awful."

Rubbing the pad of my thumb under her eye, I brush away the mascara that's smeared. "Tell me."

She shakes her head.

"Baby, please." I rub a hand along her throat and jaw. "You don't have to suffer in pain alone anymore. Let me take some of that burden." I rest my forehead against hers, feeling her hot tears against my cheeks.

Slowly, she leans forward and grabs one of the open notebooks on the floor next to us. "This was from a month before she died." She clears her throat as she begins to read.

I had the same dream again last night. Each time, it becomes scarier and darker. The dark shadows close in on me, making me claustrophobic. My throat tightens, and I choke out for air, but I can't breathe. I always wake up right before I pass out, but I feel the darkness surround me as I try to fall asleep.

She swallows and turns the page. "This is a few days later." She begins reading again.

The dreams are getting worse, and I can't sleep. It feels as if there's this demon living inside me, torturing me in my mind every time I close my eyes. It dampens my mood immediately, and I feel nothing but fear. During the day, I'm back to normal, but as soon as the sun sets, I'm scared again. I'm scared because I know what's coming.

She turns another page. "This was a couple weeks before she passed."

Aspen is so excited about our birthday that's coming up. I keep thinking of ideas on what to make her, but I can't think straight anymore. Even in school, my eyelids feel so heavy that I almost fall asleep and my teachers constantly ask if I'm okay. It's embarrassing when all the kids look at me like I'm a circus freak. I wish the dreams would go away. They're getting darker and more detailed, making it harder for me to wake up from them. A few nights ago, voices echoed in my dreams, saying awful things and telling me to do those awful things.

I'm more alone than ever. I'm afraid to tell Aspen. I don't know how to explain it to where it'll make sense. The anxiety makes me want to cut more and deeper. I cut until I bleed and nearly pass out. Sometimes it helps centralize the pain and focus on that instead of the sadness. Other times, it helps me forget, even if it's temporary.

Mom and Dad think it's all an act, so I pretend everything's okay when they're around. I pretend I'm their happy, adventure-seeking girl. Aspen sees the scars but always looks away. I think she's afraid to talk about it, and I'm afraid she'll start seeing how weak and tortured I am. I wish I knew how to explain it so they would understand, but when I try to sleep, it feels as if the life is being sucked out of me more and more each night.

I'm not sure how much more I can take.

"This is a week before." She flips the page again.

I cut deeper than I ever have before last night. My wrists have all scarred over, but my legs are like fresh canvases, waiting for my marks on them. The sight of fresh blood surfaces a new wave of emotions—one part relief, one part grief.

My thighs ache with the dull pain that the razor left behind. I focus on the pain, focus on the blood gushing down my legs and over my knees and ankles. I feel as if I'm floating and the world can't catch me. The feeling is only temporary, but for those few moments, the pain vanishes and I'm no longer that girl.

But then reality crashes back in, and I'm that girl again. The dreams, the dark thoughts, the sadness—it consumes me. It's getting harder to pretend that everything's okay. Smiling *is a chore and acting like everything is fine is a constant reminder that it's not.*

I just have to wait until our birthday.

One more birthday with Aspen.

Because I love her.

Tears fall from my cheeks with agony written all over her face. I want to reach inside and take all her pain away, but I know this has been haunting her for too long to ever fully be pain-free.

"You don't have to read anymore."

She sniffs, wiping her cheeks. "No, I want to."

She flips the page and starts again.

I died in my dream last night. I've had similar dreams before of floating up to the sky and watching from above as my body lies motionless. It doesn't even hurt. There's no pain, no remorse. All I feel is relief. I'm lighter, and for the first time, I smile genuinely.

When I wake in the morning, I know I shouldn't be feeling those things, but I can't help it. I want to feel those things—the happiness, the relief of no longer being in pain—but I never will if I'm here, suffering.

Our fourteenth birthday is tomorrow and Mom is already preparing everything. Aspen is glowing as usual, talking about how in a couple of years, we'll be getting our driver's licenses. Then she goes on about how much fun it's going to be, going to proms and homecomings, dates at the movies, football games on Friday nights. I always agree and smile, but inside, I'm dying. I want to puke anytime I think about those things. How long am I supposed to pretend? I'm hanging on by a thread and the only thing getting me through it is knowing Aspen and I will share our special day one more time.

I love her with my whole heart. I cry in my bed at night when I know she's sound asleep, thinking about how much I'm going to miss her. How much I'm going to miss. But this weight on my chest feels so heavy that I can barely breathe anymore. I hate that I can't be like her, talk about what the future holds, and all the stuff she gets excited over. But as I look at the scars on my body, I know the pain is overbearing. Aaron barely pays attention to us anymore as it is, with his part-time job and new girlfriend, but lately, he's had this look in his eye as if he knows something's different. I smile to put his worries at ease, because...what else can I do?

Aspen's voice is somber and gravelly, but she wipes her face again and turns the page.

"This is her last entry." Her throat swells up as she chokes out a sob. I grip her tighter as if she'll float away at any given time.

I love you, Aspen.

Her hand releases the journal as she bows her head down and cries. I shift her body into mine as the journal falls to the floor. I hold her with everything I have. She clings to me like I'm her life support, her body shaking and convulsing. She releases the energy she has left and shatters around me.

Chapter Thirty-Six
Aspen

M y body feels wrecked as I wake up and feel warmth around me.

I've no idea how long I've been asleep or what time it is. I reach for my phone, but it's not in my usual spot on the nightstand.

I shift, trying to feel around for it on the floor, but an arm pulls me back, and as I inhale his scent, I know Morgan is lying with me here.

"What are you looking for?" he asks, his voice deep and hoarse.

"My phone. What time is it?"

"It's the middle of the night. You fell asleep in my lap."

My breathing staggers as I remember everything from last night. "I'm sorry," I whisper. "I'm such a mess."

"Aspen…" He grabs my jaw and tilts it upward. "I don't ever want to hear you say that again, you understand? If anything, I'm sorry. I'm sorry you're going through this. I don't know what I'm supposed to be doing, but I'll do anything to help you."

I close my eyes as tears begin to fill up. "You're doing it. You here is all I need."

Feeling my chest tighten, I press my body against his and inhale. His strong arms capture me in a tight grip and mold our bodies.

We lie there until my breathing steadies, but I still don't feel right.

"I think I'm going to take a shower."

Pushing the Limits

"Are you sure? I'll hold you all night if you need." He looks down as the corner of his lips tilts up.

"Yeah, I think it'll help me feel better."

He presses a soft kiss on my forehead. "Holler if you need me, okay?"

"I will. I won't be long." I shift and throw the covers off. Then I grab a change of clothes before walking out of the room.

Needing to soothe my dry throat, I walk to the kitchen for a glass of water. It feels as if I've been crying for hours and that my body is drained of every ounce of energy possible. Setting the glass down in the sink, I walk out and glance at where my studio is. Notebooks are spread out on the floor, my easel and canvas are still out, paint tubes scattered alongside.

I take a step and shiver as memories of reading over her journals smack me right between the eyes. The words she wrote, the pain she felt, the secret she took to her grave—all these things that'll haunt me for the rest of my life.

Feeling my throat burn with acid, I cover my mouth and run to the bathroom as the water comes up. As I lean over the toilet, dry heaving and crying, I can't focus on anything but the emptiness inside.

Anticipating another attack, I brace myself for what's to come.

That's the one thing people never tell you about anxiety—people like me *know* it's an irrational state of mind, but we can't stop it from happening. Everything in my logical brain screams that it's going to be okay, I'm fine, that this is ridiculous, but that other piece of me can't see that logic and refuses to listen. The dichotomy of it all is overwhelming and completely frustrating.

Splashing cold water on my face, I look down into the sink, watching the water swirl down the drain while my mind shatters my walls and leaves me helpless. I don't know how long I stare into the water, but my eyes burn with tears and my chest aches heavily with guilt.

Pushing off the vanity, I start the shower and undress, needing to cleanse my body. Thoughts of her consume my mind, images of that day take over, and soon, I'm curled up into a ball as the water streams over me.

I hear Morgan's muffled voice above me as he grabs me and pulls me up. "Aspen!" My body goes limp as the emotional exhaustion cripples me, pressed against his chest as he holds me tight and walks me out.

"Sweetheart, open up. Please." I hear the desperation in his tone as he places me down on the bed.

I try, but they close the second I get them to open.

"Can you hear me?"

I nod.

"What happened?"

"I don't know. I'm so tired," I manage to say.

"I'm going to get you dressed, okay?"

I nod again, lying helplessly as he dries me off with a towel and dresses me like I'm a two-year-old. It's mortifying, but my body is so drained, moving is impossible.

"I know what I need to do," I finally say as he tucks me in.

"Shh, baby. You need rest." He soothes me with his hand over my head and pushes my hair away. "Let's talk when you're feeling better."

With no energy to argue, I allow sleep to take over.

Chapter Thirty-Seven

Morgan

I don't sleep the entire time I lie with Aspen. I watch.

    I watch and make sure she's breathing. I watch her chest move up and down in a steady rhythm. I watch her body calmly sleep as I tuck her inside my arm.

I wish I knew what to say or even do for her. I know when I first returned home and I'd run into friends or friends of my parents, they'd give me that look. The look of pity. They'd tell me how sorry they were and offer to help if I needed anything.

But there's never a right thing to say to anyone who loses a sister or brother. Even with the circumstances, the emptiness still exists. But she's been fighting this battle for six years. Six long years with no answers or closure, and it's all coming to the surface.

I can't blame her for handling it the way she is. I wish I knew how to help her through it.

"Aspen, sweetheart," I whisper as I kneel next to the bed. She's still in a deep sleep, but I don't want her to think I left her. "Baby, I have to pick up Natalia from my mom's and take her to school. I'll be right back, okay?" I set a glass of water down on the nightstand. "I brought you some water."

She shifts, moaning as I rub a hand alongside her arm. I kiss her temple and stand.

After dropping Natalia off at school, I make a quick coffee run before heading to Aspen's apartment. I expected her to still be sleeping or at least be in her bed, drinking the water and relaxing.

But that's not the scene I walk into at all. Hardly.

When I walk in with our cups of coffee, I hear music blaring from her studio again, and I immediately panic that she's right where she was last night. I set the coffees down on the kitchen counter and go to the studio, anticipating the same scene as I walked into the night before.

There's paint everywhere, her brushes strewn on the floor haphazardly, and she's standing there in the middle of a mini-tornado.

"Aspen?" I call out slowly, walking up behind her in hopes I don't scare her. "Sweetheart?" She's standing in front of her easel, making harsh, aggressive strokes. I can feel her anger seething from the back of her head, smoke blowing out of her ears.

I watch as she furiously attacks the canvas with her brush, making stroke after stroke, no real concept of what she's creating. I notice the finger marks along her jeans where she's wiped the paint from her fingers. Her beautiful golden hair is in a tangled mess on top of her head.

I stand next to her and see the tight lines on her face as she stays focused. I call her name again, but she doesn't budge.

Walking over to the speaker dock, I turn off the music. The silence is deafening. The moment the sound ceases, Aspen turns, and her arms collapse at her sides. Then, the brush falls to the floor. I've never seen someone look more devastated than she looks at this moment. Her normally bright eyes are swollen and bloodshot. Her lips are puffy, but not in the sexy way after she's been thoroughly kissed. It's the kind when someone's been crying. And by the looks of it, she has a lot.

"Aspen…" My voice is rough with emotion.

Her face crumples and fresh tears fall down her cheeks. Her voice cracks on my name, her body sways, and I close the distance between us, wrapping her in my arms before she can fall. She buries her face into my chest and fists my shirt in her hands.

"Sweetheart, what happened?"

After a beat, she steadies herself and speaks. "I called my mom."

"C'mon, let's sit," I offer, but she shakes her head.

"I asked why she sent me them. I asked if she's read them or if she had any idea she was feeling that way."

"What'd she say?"

She wipes her cheeks with the back of her hand. Her gaze is fixed on the wall. "She denied everything. Said she was going through old things, cleaning up the room, when she found a bunch of her stuff. She was going to give them to me when I came home, but since I never did, she mailed them instead."

"You don't believe she didn't read them?"

She shakes her head. "No, she sent them knowing what was inside them."

"Why would she do that?"

"Because she's punishing me."

I place my hands on top of her shoulders, and she finally looks up. "Why would you say that?"

"Because you don't know my mother. Something changed the day Ari died. The mom I knew died along with her. When I didn't come home, she sent them, knowing they'd hurt me. She's awful like that."

A fresh wave of tears falls down her cheeks, but this time, she doesn't wipe them away. I see the pain in each tear that slips down to the floor.

"I'm so sorry," I say, pulling her to my chest. I don't know what to say, or even if there is anything I can say, so I hold her for as long as she needs it.

"As much as I hate her, I'm glad she sent them."

"You are?"

She steps back and nods. "It gave me what I needed. It gave me answers. Knowing the truth is more painful, but at least I'm not left with what-ifs." She blinks. "I hate that she suffered. I hate that she didn't tell me, and I hate that I didn't know."

"I know, baby." I rub a hand up and down her arm, feeling the goose bumps against my palm. "It can't be easy to digest."

I help her clean up, her mood shifting from bitterness to sadness. I know this can't be easy for her, but I don't push her to talk about it. I know her life's been shifted upside down.

"Thanks for helping me clean all that up," she says softly as we lie on the couch.

"Of course," I say soothingly. "I'm not going anywhere," I remind her.

She wraps an arm around my waist and nuzzles herself under the crook of my arm. "I know."

Chapter Thirty-Eight
Aspen

Hearing my mom's pathetic excuses over the phone makes me want to vomit.

She's managed to ruin half of my life, and I can't stand the thought of giving her any more to control. She's a puppet master, manipulating people into thinking she's one person but is a horrible woman inside. Ari's death wrecked her, as it did me, but instead of leaning on each other to heal, she poured more hurt and added to the pain.

Now that I've officially told my mother off and let go of whatever relationship we had left, I'm finally content. It wasn't much, but she managed to place a hold on me that I finally released.

No more.

I only wish it mended the ache in my heart. The fact that Ariel let go of my hand on purpose is killing me instead, but I don't want to go back to that girl—the girl whose friends all give pity looks and bow their heads anytime I'm around. I dealt with enough of that during high school.

Morgan's been incredible. He only mentions it if I bring it up and is sincere in listening. He watches me work and it no longer makes me nervous. Rather, I find it soothing, comforting in the way he interprets the pieces.

271

Natalia and I watch movies when Morgan's in his office. I notice a lot of her in me—shutting down and building walls up. Grief isn't an easy thing to deal with as a child especially, but protecting your heart is the only control you feel you have when the pain takes over.

"What's your favorite subject?" I ask one night when we're alone.

"Reading," she responds, avoiding eye contact.

"What's your favorite book?"

"The Hunger Games."

"Oh, I haven't read that one yet."

"It's way better than the movies," she confirms.

"Aren't they always?" I crack a smile.

"Yeah, usually."

"What's your favorite sport?" I push for any excuse to get her to talk.

"Football."

"Really?" My face lights up. "Mine, too!"

"It's hard to resist hunky men in tight pants."

I burst out laughing, but her face barely moves. "That was funny."

"You don't have to do this." She sighs, keeping her gaze glued to the TV.

"Do what?" I furrow my brows.

"Pretend to be nice to me."

"Who says I'm pretending?"

"It's a classic rookie move."

My nose wrinkles, confused. "Excuse me?"

She finally turns toward me, a serious expression on her face. "My dad dated a lot. Not girlfriends, but they'd come in and out for a while, always smiling and pretending to tolerate me for his sake. I knew it was all fake."

She's smarter than I realize.

"Well, I'm not faking, just so you know."

She shifts her eyes to the screen. "Doesn't matter either way."

"How come?"

"You think you and my uncle are going to be one of those long-lasting types?"

Pushing the Limits

I purse my lips, a crease forming on my forehead. She's eleven but talks like she's thirty. "Honestly, I don't know."

"Exactly."

"I went through the same phase as you when I was younger."

"What phase?"

"Pushing people away, not wanting to make friends with anyone, not wanting people to take pity on you, or think you're fragile and weak. You build up these inner walls that prevent you from hurting any more than you already are. I get that because I've been doing it for over six years. But you know what?"

She faces me, frowning. "What?"

"It gets lonely. And tiring. Always pushing people away."

She studies my features for a moment before speaking. "So, why did you?"

I shrug. "It's all I knew how to do in order to deal with what I was going through. I didn't have a support system until recently, and it was how I dealt with the anger inside, but holding it in for so long becomes more of a burden than a release."

Her lashes lower and I know I've hit a sore spot.

"I'm sorry," I whisper, hoping I haven't upset her. "I just want to help."

"It's fine."

"You can talk to me about it anytime you want. I lost my sister when I was a little older than you, and so I know a thing or two about being angry." I flash a small, sincere smile, and she returns it, the first time I've seen a genuine one on her face.

Morgan and I spend every free moment with each other in between classes and work. I know he's worried about me from the way he's always asking if I'm doing okay. He's concerned about my anxiety and one more thing putting me over the edge to have a complete panic attack. I can't say I blame him, considering the circumstances, but if I keep myself busy enough, I don't have time to think about it. I can process Ari's notebooks on my own without dragging everyone else with me since the only one who needs to work through it is me.

Being around Natalia is a nice and welcome distraction. We chat every time I come over, and I'm starting to feel her get closer to me, which both terrifies and excites me. She's already gone through so much heartbreak, and I don't want to cause any more if something happens between Morgan and me.

But I don't let myself think about any of that because being with Morgan feels right. We're even getting better in class, pretending that nothing is happening between us, and Ellie hasn't mentioned anything since, so I think it's working.

I've been tempted to go to his office and surprise him in nothing but a bra and panties, but I know we have to be smart about this, so we keep it strictly student and teacher on campus.

But the moment we go to his or my house, all bets are off. The heat and passion haven't sizzled one bit. It's the first time I've ever felt this way, the need to constantly *want* more of someone. It drives me insane —in the best way possible.

A week passes and things are still as smooth as ever. I keep Ari's journals in my room, not wanting to be too far from them. Even though she wanted to take her secret to the grave, I like having a part of her with me.

By the following Monday, I nearly skip around campus like a little girl who found out she's going to Disneyland. I'm dying to tell someone, maybe Ellie, but I know I should at least wait until this semester is over, so she doesn't taunt me every chance she gets.

After my first morning class, I go through the commons area to the small café when Professor Van Bergen walks directly toward me.

"Hey," I say politely, waiting for her to walk past me, but her feet stay planted on the ground.

"Aspen…" she drawls out my name and my body shivers. "I've been meaning to speak with you."

My brows furrow. "Oh? What about?"

"I think you know exactly what."

My heart starts beating faster, and I'm certain she can see the sweat forming on my forehead.

"Sorry, I have no idea. Is it school related?"

A sly smirk spreads wickedly across her face. "You could say that."

I swallow. "What is it?"

"I'm going to need you to end your little relationship with Professor Hampton."

My heart stops.

At least, I think it does because I can't breathe.

"Yes, I know. Don't look so shocked."

I blink and keep my composure the best I can. "I've no idea what you're talking about."

"No?" She fishes for her phone and grabs it out of her purse pocket. "Do these pictures not imply something going on between you two?"

They're pictures of us talking after class. One is of us outside even, his hand briefly brushing mine, but he doesn't hold it.

"It proves nothing," I say confidently. "It's my word against yours."

She tucks her phone in her purse and leans in closer to my face until our gazes lock. "And whose word do you think the board will believe?"

"Why would you want to get him fired?"

"I don't, but I wouldn't mind seeing your scholarship and graduate school references disappear."

My jaw ticks at her implication, and I want to claw my fingers into those stupid, deceiving eyes. "I have one year left," I defend. "What is it you want from me?"

"I want the little love birds to break up. *For good*. None of this pretending you've broken up stuff because, honey, I'll know."

My back stiffens, and I resist the urge to wipe that devilish grin off her stupid face. "And how would you know? You plan on following

275

me? Putting a GPS locator on my car? Why should I even believe you?" I cross my arms, ready for a fight.

"I'm a smart woman, Aspen. Do you want to risk it? One indication that you've told him is all I need. With one press of a button, the email regarding your little, forbidden affair will be sent directly to the board and dean, pictures included."

"So you're willing to get him fired and throw away my chances at getting into grad school for what…to prove a point?"

"It doesn't matter why. But if you must know, I saw him first. We were hitting it off until you shook your twenty-something ass and grabbed his attention away from me. So if you want to remain on the track to grad school without getting a single parent fired, you'll gladly do exactly what I ask."

Shit. She knows about Natalia.

"You're an evil bitch," I hiss.

Her lips tilt up into a pleased, victorious smile. "Glad we're on the same page." She steps around me and shimmies her ass, stomping on my heart with every click of her heel.

I want to cry. And scream. But mostly cry.

This man has managed to mend my aching heart, and now, I'm forced to break his.

I turn and head straight for my car with my head down.

At least, I wait until I'm inside to release the tears.

Chapter Thirty-Nine
Morgan

I know Aspen isn't okay.

I wish she'd open up and let me in. But I can't blame her entirely.

I'm good at shutting people out as well.

But I had hoped we were past that. She's made me want to tear down my walls, even when it hurt to admit that pain aloud.

Monday, she sends me a weird text saying that she won't be able to come over after work, and I know in my gut something's wrong. But instead of interrogating her, I give her the space she needs.

Tuesday comes and goes, and Wednesday's the same.

By Wednesday night, I can't take it anymore. I go to her apartment and knock on her door, knowing she won't be expecting me but needing to speak to her.

She hardly acts affected by me standing in her doorway. I want to grab her, tangle my hands in her hair, and kiss her. But she steps back and allows me to come inside.

"What are you doing here?"

"That's all you have to say? What the hell is going on, Aspen?"

"I've been busy."

"So you can't return a text?" I challenge. Her gaze lowers to her feet as she shrugs. "Jesus, Aspen." I brush a frustrated hand through my hair and start pacing.

"Sorry."

"What's going on? Are you avoiding me because you don't want this? Or is something else going on that I don't know about? Is it about your sister? Or Mom? Aspen, please. Talk to me."

She finally looks at me, and I see the pain in her eyes.

I blow out a breath. "I'll take that as a yes."

"I'm sorry, Morgan. I never meant to hurt you."

"Really?" I choke out a mock laugh. "That's bullshit."

"I'm going through a lot and need to get my shit together before I can fully be with someone." Her voice is shaky and unconfident, but I don't call her on it.

"I opened up to you, Aspen. About everything. I trusted you. Apparently, it was only one-sided."

"I told you a lot more than I tell anyone. It's not easy for me…" she defends, and I see the truth in her features. "But you're right, it is a good thing. It proves this isn't meant to work."

And the piece of my heart that I still had left *shatters*.

"I can't believe you're fucking doing this." I brush a hand through my hair, squeezing and pulling in frustration. "What happened? What's happened from the last few days of everything being great to you wanting to break up?"

"Nothing," she reassures me. "I can't keep pretending anymore."

"*Pretending*? Pretending what?"

"I'm not who you think I am. I have a lot more issues I don't feel right burdening anyone with—especially you."

"Wait, what? Whatever it is, we can work through it. I promise, Aspen. I'm not scared because of your past. I want to fight it *with* you. Why won't you let me?"

She swallows as she fights against the tears falling down her cheeks. Seeing her struggle makes me want to desperately touch her.

She bows her head and curses before looking up, her eyes red. "My sister…" she begins, wrapping a hand around her throat and stumbling. "Her name was Ariel Rose."

I freeze, letting her words sink in. "Wait, *what*?"

Pushing the Limits

"I told you. I'm not who you think I am." Tears free fall down her cheeks, and her voice trembles when she continues. "I've been lying, pretending to be someone I'm not. And I can't do it anymore. I *do* care about you and wanted to spare your feelings."

Grunting, I pace. "Too fucking late." Then, I walk out the door, ignoring the burning pain in my chest and resisting the urge to run back to her the second I leave.

Speeding the whole way home, I ignore every aching desire to turn around and call her on her bullshit.

She's Ariel Rose?

How can that be?

She's told me on numerous occasions that her pieces are personal, she doesn't like sharing them, or—

Of fucking course.

Ariel Rose is her freedom to be whoever she wants without any consequences of people putting a face to a name.

But why didn't she tell me? I could see her not wanting to tell me right away, but what about once we were *together*? We were with each other all the time. Before class, after class, and sometimes in between. Every day we were growing closer, and I thought the feelings were mutual.

Hell, I know they were mutual.

But perhaps her demons were worse than I thought? Or maybe I was a distraction until she worked through them?

The unanswered questions scream at me, making me question everything I thought I knew about us.

Chapter Forty
Aspen

I haven't slept in days, and I'm certain all my tears have dried up because I can't even get one stupid tear to drop. Or maybe I'm too weak to make any more.

The way he looked at me is forever burned into my brain. Betrayal, hurt, anger. The moment he left, I sank to my knees and cried. I hurt the one person who meant more to me than anything. The one person who saw me for me—more than what is on the surface.

He saw through me.

But what hurts even more is how he walked out…

But I deserve it.

Every minute of pain since then, I deserve it.

I've skipped his Thursday night class because I couldn't bear seeing him. I know it's the coward's way out, but what can I do? My heart is completely shattered. Seeing him would only bring me over the edge.

After sulking alone on the couch all Friday night, I grab a bottle of wine from my fridge that I've had sitting in there for weeks. I decide I want to read more of Ariel's entries, but if I'm going to go in self-torture mode, I need some liquid courage.

Walking out of the kitchen, I hear banging on my front door. It's Kendall and she looks like a hot mess.

Pushing the Limits

"Here to join the party?" I hold up the bottle of wine in my hand and give her a sympathetic look.

"Can I, please?"

I extend my arm and motion for her to come in, shutting the door behind us. "Self-pity, party of two."

She walks to the kitchen, dragging a chair behind her, and grabs two wine glasses from the top shelf. "Surprised you even had any glasses left."

"They were smart and knew to hide up high in the cabinet where I couldn't reach them."

She snorts. "Wine me." She puts her glass out in front of me and waits for me to pour some.

"So are you going to tell me what's going on?" We walk to the living room and sit on opposite ends of the couch.

"No. Are you going to tell me why you've been moping around your apartment all week?"

"No."

We sit and drink our wine. After two glasses, I turn on the TV and ask what she wants to watch.

"Anything that isn't romance, romantic comedy, or has even a smidge of kissing."

She doesn't have to continue for me to know what's bothering her. *Men.*

I click through Netflix and scroll through the thrillers. I finally stop on *Silence of the Lambs* and when she doesn't object, I press play.

For the next two hours, I block everything out and stare at the screen, grabbing another bottle of wine in between. We don't talk. We sit in silence and drink.

It's a relief.

"Now that I've gotten you drunk and scared to sleep alone, are you going to tell me what's going on?"

She wrinkles her nose and giggles. Oh yeah, she's a goner.

"I had sex with someone."

"And it was so bad you had to come over here for a wine fest?" I raise a brow.

"No, it was good. *Really* good." Her cheeks redden.

"Then what's the matter?"

She shrugs, blinking. "I kept thinking about Kellan the whole time. Comparing and wondering if it was going to be as good, or if I was going to be good for him, and then his name slipped from my lips."

My brows lift. "Did he get mad?"

"No, I don't think he heard me."

"So?"

"So…I *shouldn't* be having sex with other men while thinking of my ex. Don't you think that's weird?"

"No," I tell her honestly.

She chokes out a laugh. "I do. I'm not used to meaningless sex. It was great, but I felt so cheap afterward."

"Yeah, you eventually become numb to that."

"I don't want to be numb, though. I want a relationship."

"It's not all it's cracked up to be."

"How would you know?" she teases, but I don't smile.

I can't.

So I opt for the truth.

"Being in a relationship is scary. Opening yourself up to be vulnerable, showing your flaws and insecurities. It's terrifying," I admit.

"Yeah." She closes her eyes and leans against the couch. "Why can't this shit be simple? Man meets woman. Woman falls for man. Man and woman get married and live happily ever after."

"Because you grew up believing Cinderella's fairy tale."

She sits up and opens her eyes, gulping the last of her wine. "Is that too much to ask? A handsome prince being all sweet and kind to his princess? No cheating, lies, and crushing hearts."

"Sounds like a Taylor Swift song." I snort.

"Don't be a love hater." She scowls.

I giggle into my wine and contemplate telling her the truth. The rational side of me says, *no, the wound is still too fresh,* but the drunken side of me says, *tell her!* Plus, it'd be great to finally get it off my chest and tell someone.

"I'm not," I say honestly. "If you must know, I fell for someone."

"*What?*" She screeches so loud, I'm sure the old guy who lives next to me and always forgets to turn his hearing aid on heard. "How's that even possible?"

"Even the flawed and damaged are capable of love," I singsong.

"Alright. You better spill. *Everything...*" she slurs, grabbing the neck of the wine bottle that's been empty for over a half hour. "After we get more wine from my place." She sets it down, and I chuckle.

"Okay, fine. But you have to promise not to get all sappy on me." I point a finger at her as we walk out the door, wine glasses in hand, and down to her apartment.

"No promises." She opens her door and nearly trips over herself in the process. "Especially since I'm starting to see double."

Laughing, I shut the door behind us. When we enter her apartment, Zoe's sitting on the couch in her rubber duck footie pajamas, stuffing her face with popcorn.

"I'm too drunk to even make fun of you." I plop my ass next to her. "Pass the popcorn."

She shifts the bowl into my lap and sighs. "There is no reason why three hot girls should be wallowing with wine and popcorn on a Friday night," she states. "What is wrong with the universe?"

"Rather, what's wrong with us?" I offer.

"Aspen has a secret." Kendall giggles, sitting on the love seat. "But I'm not supposed to tell. So shush." She covers a finger over her lips and Zoe giggles.

"Apparently, you've forgotten what the meaning of a secret is!" I say, shoving another handful of popcorn into my mouth.

"God, did you save any wine for me?" Zoe wrinkles her nose.

"Why do you think we came over here? We needed to stock up."

"Okay, grabbing the wine..." Zoe stands up and walks toward the kitchen, calling over her shoulder. "Don't you dare start without me!"

"Jesus Christ," I mutter. "I'm going to need a lot more wine for this."

Zoe walks in, waving a bottle of wine in each hand and an extra glass for her. "Good thing Kendall's a wino. We're always packing over here."

She pours us each a healthy amount and sits next to me. "Alright, so spill. What's this secret?"

I bring the glass to my lips and swallow half of it. I choke it down and wipe my mouth. "Okay, ready?" I exhale and they nod. "Remember when I mentioned I kissed my professor?"

"Morgan," Kendall clarifies with a satisfied grin.

"We started secretly dating and sleeping together," I begin, trying to keep my emotions in check. "And I fell hard for him. Like full out making the walls rattle, can't get enough, butterflies in my stomach every time I'm around him kind of falling."

"Holy shit!" Zoe gasps, and Kendall's eyes widen in shock.

My cheeks redden. "Yes."

"Oh my God! This is so much better than the *Housewives of Orange County*." Zoe grabs the remote and shuts the TV off. She shifts her body and faces me. I flash her a playful scowl and she smirks.

"I've let him in closer than I've ever let a guy before. It felt foreign, weird, and I was scared. But after finding out the horrible news about my sister and dealing with my mom, he still never left. He kept reminding me how much he was here for me and it was so much different than I was used to. No one's ever been there for me like that before."

"He sounds like a keeper," Kendall confirms.

"Wait," Zoe interrupts. "So what's the matter? Are you scared to let him in all the way?"

"Well, it wasn't easy at first, but he managed to break down my walls and little by little, I was letting him in. Everything was going perfectly."

"Then what?" Kendall asks, taking a sip and locking her gaze on mine.

I lower mine, trying to keep it under control, but it's a struggle. "Then I broke up with him."

Kendall spews her wine all over her lap as I blink the tears away that threaten to burn my eyes.

"Jesus, Kendall," Zoe complains, shifting away and laughing.

"What the hell, Aspen? I thought this was a happy story." She knits her brows, wiping off the wine from her clothes.

Pushing the Limits

I point to my wine glass. "Would I be drowning myself in bottle after bottle of wine if it were?"

"Tell me what happened."

"Someone caught us," I finally admit. "She said she'd go to the board and get my scholarship and grad school references stripped if I didn't break it off with him."

"What a jealous bitch," Zoe blurts out. "Why didn't you tell her to fuck a duck or something?"

I snort, shaking my head. "Because I need to get my degree and graduate, or I'll be stuck here, living next to you guys."

"Well, besides that."

I shrug. "I don't know. Maybe because a part of me is scared to let him in all the way. Hurting him and breaking it off was easier than waiting for the inevitable."

The truth in my words feels like a knife twisting in my heart.

"So you're going to let some desperate housewife, who's clearly not getting laid, dictate your future?" Kendall challenges.

"What choice do I have? He's raising his niece all by himself. He could get fired and then what?"

"I don't think you should run away because of her or because you're scared of what will happen. That doesn't seem right at all," Zoe insists, the wine making her a bit too loose.

"It's not," I agree. "But it's a lot to risk. And then what if I risk it for nothing?"

Kendall sets her glass down and sits up.

"Sometimes it's letting them in that helps you feel whole again. Even if you feel like a mess yourself. Maybe it's not meant to last, but maybe it is. You'll never know if all you do is run away."

"Even knowing how it ends up?" I inquire.

The corner of her lips tilts up. "Yeah. Being in love is one of the greatest feelings in the world. You risk your heart, but it has to be better than going through life without it at all."

"All's fair in love and war," Zoe says.

"Love is a battlefield," Kendall adds with a giggle.

"Okay, okay, I get it. No more clichés needed." I laugh into my wine glass, finishing up the last sip.

I think about everything they said while we sit and watch movies. I wish it were only my own insecurities to work through, but knowing that someone has the potential to destroy us—I can't do that to him.

Chapter Forty-One
Morgan

Nothing makes sense.

Not without her anyway.

Seeing her, pretending my heart isn't shattering every time I look at her, is getting harder and harder.

But I do what I do best in times like these. I distract myself, drowning myself in work, hang out with Natalia and sleep.

Mostly sleep.

I'm trying to understand it all, but I can't. I fight back the tears, but eventually, I give up and surrender to them. I don't care anymore.

As I'm making dinner for Nat and me—she's glued to the TV, watching some game show—the doorbell rings. And then it rings again. Nat barely even flinches.

"Don't worry, I'll get it," I over-exaggerate. But the moment I open the door, I wish I hadn't.

"Fuck..." The word comes out before I can stop myself.

"Guess I deserve that." Jennifer stands across from me, pursing her lips in a *please don't slam the door on me* look. I won't lie, it sounds tempting since the sight of her makes my blood boil, but trying to be the better man, I don't.

I shake my head. "Sorry, I didn't mean to say that."

"It's fine."

We stand there, silent and awkward.

"So what are you doing here?"

"I was hoping we could talk," she says sincerely. "I promise I won't stay long."

"Did my mother put you up to this?"

"No, I swear she didn't." She sounds genuine, so I push the burning hatred in my heart aside.

After a beat, I open the door wider and let her in.

"Smells good. Have you learned to cook since you left California?" she asks, taking off her coat.

"I've been practicing."

Natalia comes strolling in and snickers. "He lies."

"Nat, go to your room. I'll call you when dinner's ready."

"What?" She gasps. "Why do I have to leave?"

"Because I have a guest, and I don't need you eavesdropping on our conversation."

She smirks and shakes a finger. "Getting smarter, Uncle Morgan."

Jennifer furrows her brows as she watches Nat walk down the hall to her room.

"What was that all about?"

I shake my head and walk toward the kitchen, her following behind. "She thinks I don't get women."

"Well…"

"Trust me, I know. Apparently, I know nothing at all." My chest tightens as I think about Aspen. I busy myself by the stove and direct all attention to her. "So, tell me why you're here."

She sits at the breakfast bar and lowers her eyes. "I want to tell you what happened," she begins, but I'm quick to cut her off.

"Jen, don't. It's been five years. I'm trying to move on."

"I know. And I want you to. That's why you need to hear this."

I inhale, sighing. I'm not prepared to have this conversation. "If I let you talk, no more uninvited visits."

"Deal."

"Alright. Dinner will be ready in ten minutes. So make it quick."

"I don't know if you ever knew, but Ryan and I didn't stay together once you left. We stayed friends, but that was it. I know you don't want to know anything about us, which I don't blame you at all, but I think you need to know that Ryan beat himself up every day about what he did to you. He knew it was the ultimate betrayal and he hated himself for it."

My throat tightens, unable to say anything.

"Up until then, he was in a bad place. When you left, he went and got himself help. He went to therapy and wanted to be the best dad he could be for Natalia. He wanted to be a better person. He loved you so much, Morgan. Even though he was older, he looked up to you and valued your opinions so much. After a few years, you hadn't come back. He lost himself again, but Natalia helped him stay on track. When your mom mentioned the will to him, he refused to change it. He knew you were the best person for her and you are. You're everything and more to that little girl."

I tilt my head up to the ceiling, not wanting to release the tears, but her words are so genuine and soft, they burn right through me.

"Why are you telling me this?"

"Because I know you, Morgan. You're dwelling on how you didn't get home in time. The guilt is so obvious on your face, and it keeps you from moving forward."

"How would you know any of this, Jen? You haven't been in my life or know anything about it." I can't stop the defensive tone in my voice, but I hate being told how I'm feeling.

"You know I'm right."

I shake my head, not wanting to give her the satisfaction that she *is* right.

"You can't move on when you never confront your feelings. You bury them, and I know that's what you've been doing since he passed away."

"Yeah, well…who else should I blame?"

"Blame whoever you want but don't push it away as if it didn't happen." She sighs, choking back her own tears. "Your mom told me you don't paint anymore."

I shake my head and choke in a laugh. "Of course she did. That's what I get for telling my mom."

"That's a shame. You're talented."

"I haven't exactly been inspired."

She stands and pushes her chair in, wrapping her jacket around her arm. "Find what inspires you and hang on to it. But don't let the guilt keep you from living your own life. Not only for you but for that precious little girl, too. She needs you more than anything."

She walks away without a glance. As much as the anger builds up inside me at what she did, I know her words are true.

I've been beating myself up and probably always will if I don't let the feelings surface and learn to deal with them properly.

Being with Aspen, I thought I was and that I could get past it or at least learn to move forward. I hoped we could fight our battles together and come out stronger.

I'm lost without her.

Chapter Forty-Two
Aspen

I can't remember the last time I've slept. My sleeping pills make me tired enough to get a few solid hours in, but I still wake up numb.

It feels like months, but it's only been a couple weeks. If I'm not at work or school, I'm in bed, *not* sleeping. I listen to my favorite songs on repeat until I cry myself to sleep, which actually only ends up being a couple hours at a time until a memory of him—us—wakes me up.

He doesn't look at me during class. I can't blame him, but it's killing me. I can't even blame him for being upset about that, but he hardly even fought for me. The moment I told him the truth about the Ariel Rose Collection, he let me go. He walked out, ripping my heart in two on the way.

I've been trying to distract myself as best as I can with working a couple extra shifts at the gallery and chatting with Ellie—anything to avoid the urge to look at Morgan.

The semester ends in about a month, and then I won't have to see his tense, expressionless face twice a week anymore. I can see he's putting on a front, smiling and cracking jokes with the other students —except me, of course.

Ellie notices a change in my behavior and pushes me for answers. I play it off as having a stressful couple of weeks. With finals approaching, I've been staying up late studying and coming to school overtired. It's not farfetched considering my zombie-like look, so she buys it.

I should've known I couldn't avoid them for long. After last weekend's wine fest, I've avoided hanging out with them so I could wallow alone.

"What are you doing here?" I ask casually, not trying to sound rude, but today's a day I'd rather suffer alone in silence.

Kendall and Zoe stand at my door with their arms firmly crossed and a sly smile on their faces. "You're not spending your birthday alone in pink kitten pajamas and fuzzy socks."

I look down and scowl. "What's wrong with fuzzy socks?"

Kendall snorts and Zoe pushes her way inside. "We come bearing gifts, birthday girl. Come on."

I groan, shutting the door behind them as they walk in and aim right for the couch. "These gifts better get me drunk."

"Would we get you anything else?"

We settle in with our glasses of wine, and I lie against the arm of the couch before Kendall eyes me up and down.

"You look like death."

"Thanks."

"I take it you didn't karate chop Ms. Bitch's face off?" Zoe arches her brow, sitting on the other end of the couch.

"Nope."

"I bet the three of us could take her," Kendall offers, getting a small smile out of me.

"It's not that," I assure them, even though it's part of it. "I'm not a fan of celebrating my birthday." It's the truth, but after six birthdays, I've gotten good at being numb to it.

"Alright, up. We're going out to do something fun for your birthday. You need a distraction." Kendall stands up.

"I have a distraction. Her name is Chardonnay." I hold up my almost empty wine glass and grin.

"You can't drink yourself to death." Zoe grabs my hand and pulls me up. "You drink *while* doing something fun. That way it looks recreational." She winks, and I resist the urge to laugh.

I don't have the energy to argue, so I do as they say.

An hour later, I'm showered, dressed, and looking semi-decent. Kendall insists on driving, so I can't escape early. Not that I'd even try at this point. Anything is probably better than wallowing in my apartment alone.

"Where are we going?" I ask from the back seat.

Yeah, she wouldn't even let me sit in the front.

"You'll see. Be there soon," she calls from the driver's seat.

"Don't you think turning on the childproof locks is a bit extreme?" I pout. She meets my eyes in the rearview mirror, and I can tell she's scowling. "Fine," I mutter.

We pull up to a small Ma and Pop shop with large white windows and a chandelier in the foyer. Above the door reads, *The Art Shoppe.*

"What are we doing here?"

"Come and see," Zoe says, opening the door and getting out.

Kendall opens the door for me with a wide smirk.

"Come on," I groan. "Why are we here?"

"It's called a Sip 'n Paint and, Aspen Danielle Evans, you are going to enjoy it. Do you hear me?" she orders in a motherly tone.

"Fine," I groan and follow her. "As long as I can Sip *A lot* 'n Paint."

She snickers, leading us through the entrance.

By the end of our party, I feel much better—probably because I've managed to have six glasses of wine—but nevertheless, it ended up being more fun than sitting in my apartment alone. Kendall only drank half a glass since she was driving, so I took the liberty of drinking hers for her.

That's what friends are for.

Once I'm home and the alcohol burns off, I'm alone again—alone in my apartment, reminiscing about everything I've managed to lose in my life. I only have one year left of college before graduate school. I could go anywhere. Move. Travel. But even with all my options and potential experience, I'd choose to be here with Morgan. I'd leave it all behind if it meant we could be together.

Ms. Jones has been so wrapped up in the gallery, she hasn't

noticed anything at all. Or at least, she's pretending not to. During my weekend shift, I overhear her phone conversation.

"Oh my God!" Her high-pitched tone grabs my attention. "Is she alright? Are they doing an X-ray?" She pauses. "Let me know when you find anything out. Tell her Aunt Melly loves her, okay? If you need anything, call me. I'll leave here right away." Her voice is serious, and I can't help eavesdropping to hear the whole story. "Are you sure? I can come to the hospital if you need me to." My breathing quickens as I think about who she's talking about. "Okay, call me later, dear. Bye-bye."

She rounds the corner, nearly bumping into me, before I can walk away and pretend I wasn't listening in. Startled, she drops her phone in her hand and it lands on the floor with a crash.

"I'm so sorry!" I quickly reach down to grab it the same time she does and we bump heads. *Jesus.*

"Oh, are you okay?"

"Yes, I'm sorry. Again. Geez. I hadn't meant to run into you."

"Oh, it's not your fault. I was distracted and not paying attention." I raise my brow, shocked that she's taking the blame when it was clearly my own fault.

"Oh? Is everything okay?" I ask, hoping she'll tell me what the phone call was all about.

"Natalia fell from the monkey bars at school and they think she broke her ankle. They're at the hospital waiting on the X-rays."

"Oh no," I shriek. "If you need to leave, I can stay late."

"No, it's okay, dear, but thank you. Morgan's going to call me as soon as he knows."

"She must be so scared," I mutter. And he must be freaking out.

She pats me on the shoulder, her eyes soft and genuine. "She'll be okay."

I nod.

"Your shift's over?"

"Yeah, I was going to clock out."

"Well, have a great night." I watch as she walks away.

As I'm driving home, I can't get Natalia out of my head. She's a lot like me, and I think that's why we bonded so well. She's felt loss and has had trouble grieving, expressing her feelings through anger instead of processing it.

And if I'm honest, I miss her.

I've missed Morgan every single day, but I hadn't realized how much of *us* I missed. Hanging out at his place, eating, and watching movies. Natalia was a little stiff at first, but she easily came around. She accepted me, and I hadn't realized how attached I got in such a short amount of time.

I drive past my apartment building and head to the hospital instead. Morgan may be off-limits but checking up on Natalia isn't. I want to see her even if he hates my guts. I'm sure she doesn't understand why I stopped coming around.

Once I walk through the emergency room entrance, I stop at the registration desk to ask about her. They tell me she's in a room and waiting on X-rays still.

"Can I see her?"

"Are you a relative?"

"Yeah, I'm her aunt."

"Oh, okay. Her uncle's in there already with her. She's in bed seven." She points me in the direction. "Right down that hallway."

"Thank you," I say in a rush, already walking down the hallway before she figures out I'm lying.

My heart races as I think about seeing Morgan face-to-face. He's avoided eye contact with me as much as possible, but this time would be unavoidable.

As I stand in front of her door, I inhale deeply and then knock.

"Come in," his rough voice demands.

When I push the door and walk in, I see his soft eyes change as soon as he realizes it's me.

"Aspen!" Natalia's voice directs me to her where she's lying on the hospital bed, her leg covered in blankets and ice packs as she chews on an orange popsicle.

"Hi," I say hesitantly. "I hope it's okay I came." I direct my attention to Morgan, but he stares silently. "I heard what happened and wanted to make sure she was okay."

"Hell yes, it's okay you're here," Natalia answers for him, and he scolds her for her language.

"Dude, they have Xbox here!" she shouts enthusiastically, and when Morgan gives me his nod of approval, I step to the side of her bed.

"That's exciting." I flash her a sympathetic look. "How are you feeling?"

"I'm fine, but the school called Morgan and he rushed me here like an overbearing mama lion."

"You're not fine," Morgan interrupts with a firm tone. "Your ankle swelled up to the size of a watermelon."

My body shudders at the image. "Are you in a lot of pain?"

"I was until they gave me some meds."

"Ahh…" I smile. "Explains why you aren't feeling anything."

She shrugs and cracks an unapologetic smile, finishing up her popsicle that's turned her lips orange.

A nurse comes in and instructs us that she's taking Natalia to get an X-ray. Morgan kisses her forehead, and I squeeze her hand. "Good luck." I wink at her and she smiles.

The nurse rolls her bed out of the room, leaving the two of us behind in awkward silence. We haven't spoken since the breakup and now there were no students or easels to buffer between us.

"How are—"

"You look—"

We blurt out at the same time, nerves fluttering through my body. We laugh, mine more awkward because he's staring. I can barely take my gaze off the floor, but at the sound of his amusement, I peek up at him.

God, he looks good.

He always looks good. But there's pain in his features.

"Thanks for not kicking me out. I wanted to see Natalia."

"She's been asking about you. I knew she'd be happy to see you."

"I should get going. I hope everything turns out okay." I lower my head and walk toward the door until he stops me.

"Aspen, wait." His words come out frantic. I stop but don't turn around. He pauses shortly before speaking. "Thanks for coming," he finally says, and I hear the agony in his voice as it cracks. It nearly cripples me.

Painfully, I silently nod and continue walking out of the room. Every step I take is another wound to my heart that I'm not sure will ever heal.

Chapter Forty-Three
Morgan

Natalia was sent home in a cast and restricted to using crutches four weeks ago and has another four weeks left. Thank God, because her mood swings are driving me insane.

She's not happy about it at all since school is ending for her soon and she'll have to spend part of her summer on the couch, but when I bribed her with her own Amazon account to buy books and magazines, she perked right up.

I've seen Aspen in class twice a week for the past month and it's been the worst few weeks of my life. Nothing compares to seeing her at the hospital after that first week, only inches away from me, and not being able to touch her. I so desperately wanted to wrap my arms around her, kiss her lips, and beg her to say we can work this out.

On top of that, Claire's been glued to my hip more than usual. Always 'popping' into my office to say hello or invite me out to lunch or coffee. I've turned her down every time, saying I was too busy with grades or was bowing out early to run errands. She smiles and says "Okay, maybe next time" and I always agree, but I have no intention of ever being alone with that woman again if I can help it.

Once my brief and pathetic lunch break is over, I head into my office and notice a note left on top of my desk. For a split second, I anticipate seeing Aspen's handwriting but know she'd either call or text me if she had something to say.

Flipping it open, I sigh when I see it's from Claire. Another invite I have to decline.

Why can't this woman get the damn point?

Instead of calling and rejecting her, I head down to her office to put an end to this once and for all.

Her office is down the hall from mine, but when I reach it, I hear her voice on the other side of the door speaking loudly on the phone.

I can't hear what the person on the line is saying, but her voice is so nasally, it echoes through the door with each loud syllable.

"Oh yeah, she bought it. Stupid undergraduate twit." She starts laughing as the other person speaks. "No, not yet. But he's coming around. We'll be hooking up by summer because well, look at me. He won't be able to resist for much longer. He'll be over that Aspen girl the moment I get him alone."

My blood boils at the sound of her name. She's talking about Aspen and me...and something she did.

Before I can stop myself, I push open the door and stand firmly in the doorframe. Her jaw drops the moment she sees me and begins stuttering to her friend that she has to go before clicking the receiver button.

"Morgan, hi." Her face lights up to act as if nothing is wrong. "Did you get my note?"

I step inside and slam the door closed behind me. I walk in front of her, leaning my palms flat on top of her desk. "What the fuck did you do?"

She leans back. "What do you mean?"

"I heard your conversation, Claire, so quit the shit. What did you say to her?"

"What's it to you?" She leans toward me in her chair, crossing her arms in defiance. "Student-teacher relations are against the school's policy. You know that," she says in a condescending tone.

"That's none of your fucking concern. Now tell me what you said to her. You did something to scare her away, and I'm not leaving until you tell me."

"Or what?"

"I'll file a sexual harassment suit against you. I saved every single note and email you've sent me. I've also declined your offers seven times in the past semester. One complaint and you can kiss that promotion goodbye."

Her brows furrow.

"Yeah, I know about that. You're applying for the art advisor position. How do you think a sexual harassment complaint will look on your record?" I challenge, her body slouching in defeat.

She sighs, gritting her teeth as my words soak in. She has no choice.

"I told her to break up with you," she finally confesses.

"Why?" I demand.

"Because I wanted you for myself. Hasn't that been obvious?"

"I've never given you any reason to think I was into you. Haven't *I* been obvious?"

"I thought you were playing hard to get."

"You thought wrong. What did you threaten her with?" I lean in closer. "What could you possibly have to hold against her?"

"Her scholarship and grad school references. Your career." She flashes a sly grin. "You two made it too easy. So much at risk. And for what? An easy lay?"

My hands ball into fists, her indifferent tone feeding my anger. "You've no idea what you're talking about."

She scoffs. "Is she worth your career? You have a child to take care of now. Don't throw it all away and ruin your lives for a meaningless hookup."

I snort, rubbing the scruff on my chin as I step back. "It's unfortunate."

Her upper lip curls in confusion. "What is?"

"That you don't have a compassionate bone in your body. Just because you can't possibly understand how it feels to be with someone who makes you feel good and someone who can change your life for the better, doesn't mean the rest of us can't."

I don't bother waiting for a response. I walk out and lock up my office, then run to my car.

Pushing the Limits

I head straight for the gallery. I know Aspen doesn't work on Wednesday afternoons, but Aunt Mel does.

And she's who I need to speak to.

Aunt Mel and I chat in her office for at least an hour. I tell her everything, from falling for Aspen to the Ariel Rose Collection, and Jennifer. Though I expect a harsh lecture in return, she only smiles while I talk.

"Why are you grinning?"

"You young'uns always think you're so much smarter than us old folks. I had my suspicions. Ever since I asked her to take you around for the tour, I saw the look in your eyes. Then I'd see you visiting, finding any reason to go look for her. The night of the workshop..." She flashes a mischievous smile. "Your jaw tensed the moment you saw her up there. I watched you draw her, seeing something that everyone else was missing."

I lift my brows, not wanting to admit or deny anything.

"You think I'm too old to see when two people have chemistry, Morgan?"

I laugh because what else can I do? "I can't believe you never said anything."

"I may be losing my mind, but when Jennifer broke your heart, I never thought you'd move on. I wasn't sure if you'd even come home, but you did. And now you deserve your happiness, too." She smiles. "Even if she is your student," she finishes with a sly grin.

"Yeah, that's the problem."

"Aside from that. What did you do to screw it up?" She raises a brow when I give her a puzzling look. "That's why you're here, isn't it? To confess the truth and find a way to make it up to her?"

"It's not what I did…it's what I *didn't do*." I should've known better. I could see how much it was hurting her to say those words, so why didn't I fight harder? Why didn't I tell her I'd do anything to show her we belong together? Instead, I walked away, allowing her to think she didn't matter to me. She sacrificed her feelings for my career, sacrificed our relationship to make sure no one else found out. Now, I need to prove myself to her—prove that I'll always fight for us.

"If you want my advice, which trust me you do, you need to do something big—romantic gesture big!" Her hands expand in front of her. "*Big*!"

"You're right. That's exactly what I'm going to do." I smile and round her desk, wrapping my arms around her. "I had no idea being home would feel this good. I would've been home a lot sooner."

"Better late than never." She smiles sincerely. "Now get going. You have a lot of work to do."

I shake my head with a laugh as I head out the door. "Yes, ma'am."

Chapter Forty-Four
Aspen

"Cheers to our last final!" I say way too loud, but Kendall and Ellie raise their glasses and clink theirs with mine.

We all throw our heads back and down the shot. I cough as the alcohol burns my throat, but I can't even find the means to care. Today was the last day of finals, which means a whole summer to start fresh. Seeing Morgan in class twice a week has been torture, but I got through it. My heart may have been wrecked, my mind a clusterfuck, and my body weak from sleepless nights, but I made it through.

I've introduced Ellie to Kendall and Zoe, knowing she'd make a great addition to our single ladies' group. It's a nice way of saying how sad and pathetic we all feel. But Jack Daniel's never fails to please us.

"Philosophy was a fucking bitch," Kendall exclaims.

"I told you showing up would earn you at least a B. How hard can that be?" I sip on my Jack and Diet Coke.

"Because, apparently, showing up is one thing, but snoring during class is a huge no-no."

Ellie snorts, nearly spewing alcohol out of her nose. Laughter fills the air between us and soon, Zoe walks over, telling us she's cutting us off.

"Ugh, you can't do that!" I whine. "This is a celebration!"

"I think you've celebrated enough," she deadpans. "I'll call you ladies a cab."

"Don't be a stick in the mud!" Kendall pouts, clinging to Zoe's arm. "I'll find a cute guy and bring him home for you. You've been low on the D for a while."

"Oh, that usually cheers me right up," Ellie adds, making us all giggle at Zoe again.

"I need a new job," Zoe groans, ringing up our tab and telling us to wrap it up so she can call a cab for us.

"Speaking of jobs," Ellie slurs. "Any chance they're hiring where you two work?"

"I can ask Ms. J. What kind of job are you looking for?"

"One that pays." She giggles.

"I'll see what I can do," I offer with a smile.

Once we pay our tabs, I take one last drink before grabbing my clutch and heading out. Our cab is already waiting for us, and since tomorrow's the first official day of summer, I offer to let Ellie crash at my place, which is a true testament to how far I've come these last few weeks. After reading Ari's old notebooks and my time with Morgan—as short-lived as it was—I've been through a spin cycle of devastation and recovery. Using the information about Ari's past has given me a sense of closure, as devastating as it was to read.

Morgan's helped me more in these past few months than years of counseling did. I never thought I was capable of giving part of me to another person, but he's proof that I can.

"Jesus, Aspen. It's like a museum in here." Ellie walks down the hall, studying all the pieces I have hanging on the walls.

"Oh, I have a lot more. I hung up my favorite ones." I grab an extra blanket and pillow from my room and bring them out to the couch for her. "Sorry I don't have an extra bed. The couch is comfortable, though."

"Oh, it's fine," she says, spinning around and walking toward the living room. "Thanks for letting me stay."

"Anytime." I smile internally at how easy that comes out. A few months ago, having someone stay here, in my personal space and surrounded by all my personal artwork, would've given me an anxiety attack. However, the thought of people seeing and asking about them doesn't freak me out as much anymore.

"Wanna stay up with me for a while?"

I can barely keep my eyes open, but I say yes anyway. I grab my comforter and pillow and sit on the chair across from her.

"Can I ask you something?"

"Sure."

"Have you ever been in love?"

I swallow. I hadn't expected *that* question. "I'm not sure. Sometimes it feels like it was going in that direction. As quick as it happened was as quick as it was ripped away. I'm almost positive, had it worked out, I would easily have fallen in love with him." The corner of her lip curls up in a genuine smile. "What about you?"

"Yeah, I had that intense *can't-stop-thinking-about-you* kind of love. It was life-changing. My body lit up any time we were together and when it was over, I was lost."

"I know that feeling," I say.

"It's the absolute worst."

I nod.

"But if I had to go through it all over again, I would to feel that again."

"Yeah, me too," I agree. "I want to believe that everything happens for a reason, but some days are harder than others."

"Destiny has an evil way of teaching us the life lessons we're meant to experience."

"So you want to tell me about him?" I prompt.

She smiles and lays her head against the pillow. "Maybe at breakfast."

"Deal." I smile in return, rest my head, and drift off. The memory of him and his touch is so fresh in my mind. Sometimes I dream about him and wake up feeling him next to me. Then I peel my eyes open and realize he isn't.

Those are the worst kind of mornings.

I wake up Sunday morning feeling refreshed from having yesterday off. Finals ended Friday, but after drinking all night, I needed that extra day to recover.

However, this is the official first week of summer, and I'm going to slap a positive attitude on and smile happily.

After slipping in the shower, burning my breakfast and nearly my apartment down, and my car running out of gas on the way to work, I'm ready to crawl into bed and scream.

Why can't fresh starts ever be on my damn side for once?

I finally make it to work, frustration and annoyance radiating from me as I walk inside. I called to let Ms. Jones know I was running late. She was surprisingly understanding and even complimented me on how nice I looked when I finally arrived.

Once I assured her I was fine to come in, she told me I'm needed for filing paperwork.

Every possible thing that could go wrong today has gone wrong and it's only ten in the morning, and now I'm being sent to the back?

Someone up above is getting a real kick out of torturing me today.

Four hours later, I'm dying from boredom. I decide to take a break and head to the employees' lounge to grab a snack.

Ms. Jones paces around the hallway three times before I finally get suspicious enough to stand and find out what's wrong with her.

"Okay, spill it."

"Huh, what?" She spins around, biting her nails. "Oh, nothing, dear. I'm supposed to do inventory tonight, but I promised Natalia I'd go to her play."

"Oh." My face softens.

"But maybe I can come in late and do them then…" she starts thinking aloud to herself. "No, security will be gone by then. Shit."

There are stress wrinkles around her eyes as she thinks of a plan.

"I'd be happy to do it for you. I mean, I have nothing planned anyway," I offer.

"Really? Are you sure?"

"Yeah, I'd hate for you to miss her play." Morgan has mentioned how close Natalia and her have gotten since she moved in with him.

"Darling, you're a gem! Thank you!" She wraps me in a tight hug, and I'm taken aback by how grateful she is. "Shane will still be here, so you don't have to worry about being alone."

"Alright."

"Come when the gallery closes. Everything's in the office. Help yourself to any snacks you may find in there."

A nervous giggle passes her lips.

"Okay then. Guess I'll be back tonight then."

"Sounds good."

She starts walking down the hallway before she stops and turns. "Oh, and wear something nice. 'Kay, bye." She sprints off before I can ask what she means.

I've never been to the gallery after hours before, but I rejoice in the fact that I'll be alone for a while. I might even walk around and blast some music. Hell, I might even dance around in my underwear.

Using the key Ms. Jones gave me, I enter through the back. It's dark except for a few security lights to guide my way. It's eerily silent, but it feels safe. Being here instantly brightens my mood.

I walk through a few of the exhibits before making my way up to Ms. Jones's office. The closer I get, the more I hear faint music playing. I stop and strain to hear where it's coming from.

Perhaps someone left it on in their office?

Then, I notice the spotlights are still on. I know we turn them off at night, so I round the corner to go turn them off. The music grows louder and soon I figure out where it's all coming from.

"Oh my God!" I shriek, nearly jumping out of my own skin. "You scared the hell out of me. What are you doing here?"

"I'm here for you." His warm smile and bright eyes captivate me. I can't believe he's here.

"Morgan…" I whisper, unable to believe it for myself although he's standing right in front of me. Stepping closer, I realize what the lights are shining on. "Holy…" It's a large abstract piece behind him. He moves to the side so I can fully see it. It's stunning, unlike anything I've ever seen.

Underneath is a plaque with the words *A Thousand Years* written on it.

My favorite song to work to.

I blink at the memory of him finding me in my studio listening to it on repeat. "Is that *me*?"

My feet are frozen to the floor, but he comes toward me until we're face-to-face. "Yes." His hot breath skims against my skin.

"Why? Why are you here?" I'm too stunned to ask him anything else.

"I told you. *I'm here for you.*"

"You made that?"

"Yes."

"But you haven't painted in almost a year."

He grabs my hand and rests it on his chest. "I was finally inspired."

Tears start blurring my vision, and I resist the urge to wipe them away. "I don't understand."

"You're the teals and yellows of my life, Aspen. Happiness and laughter. I've had a lot of tough lessons in my life, but one thing is for sure—I'm not letting that go."

"But I broke your heart…" I say, hot tears falling down my cheeks. "I lied to you."

His jaw tenses as he wraps his other hand around my hip and pushes us closer. "I know about Claire. I know she blackmailed you and that you had no choice. I know you only said those things because she threatened you."

My eyes widen in surprise, feeling terrified that she's for sure going to go to the board. "I couldn't let you lose your job over me," I start to explain, but my throat closes up.

"Aspen, stop." He wipes the tears from my cheeks. "I've been falling for you since the moment I laid eyes on you. When I first saw your pieces, I knew I needed to know who that girl was." He brushes

308

his finger across my cheek, and I shiver. "But more importantly, I knew you were going to change my life."

I pull in a deep breath.

He continues, "I should've fought for you. I should've known better, but I let my own insecurities make me think less of you. I thought by letting you go that easily, I'd be sparing my own feelings. But it didn't. It only made me realize what an ass I was because I should've been more confident in our relationship. I knew you better than that and for that, I'm sorry. God, Aspen. I'm so damn sorry."

My chest squeezes at his words, and I'm unable to speak.

"I'll fight. I'll fight for you. For us. And this time, I won't let you walk away from me. When I saw you at the hospital, I shouldn't have let you walk away. You deserved for me to fight harder even if you were the one ripping my heart out."

The corners of his lips tilt up in a sly grin.

"I've waited for someone like you to come into my life, and I'm not going to let you get away. I admit I was scared. But with you, all that doubt and uncertainty vanish. Every day without you has felt empty and pointless."

And just like that, the world around us fades away, because here at this moment, it's only him and me. No one else matters.

"How can I love when I'm afraid to fall…" I repeat the words of the song that he titled the piece from as the tears continue falling down my cheeks. I know my eyes are bloodshot and my makeup is smeared, but I don't care.

"But watching you stand alone, all my doubt goes away," he continues the song, his gaze fixed on mine. He brushes a finger, wiping my cheeks.

"I'm sorry I had to hurt you. The impact of not having you in my life opened my eyes to what heartbreak was, and now that I know, I never want to feel that way again."

"I promise you, Aspen. You'll never have to. Because this is it. I want you, and I don't care who all knows."

"But how?" I choke out. "How can we be together?"

His deep dimples reappear, giving me the reassurance I need. "I'm not working at the college anymore. I won't be your professor, and we won't be breaking any rules."

I shake my head. "I can't let you quit your job for me. Not when you have Natalia to take care of. I can't be that selfish."

He pulls me closer, his lips brushing softly against mine. "It's too late. I took another job offer. A much better one."

My brows rise. "You did? Where?"

"You're looking at it."

"Here?" I gasp.

"Aunt Mel is retiring next year, and Mr. Cross asked who she'd recommend taking over her position. She mentioned me before I even told her about you. Once I did, she made it official. I'll do a year of training, working under Aunt Mel until she officially retires."

"Oh my God!" I squeal, tightly hugging him. "You're going to work here?"

"That's right, Ms. Evans."

"Great, you went from being my professor to being my boss." I snort. "I'm certain there's a work policy on dating employees."

"I won't officially be your boss until next year, which means we have the whole year until we have to start breaking the rules."

I chuckle, wrapping my arms around him. "You sure do love pushing the limits, Professor Hampton." I press my mouth to his, pulling his lower lip in between my teeth and sliding my tongue inside.

"And you sure love the consequences."

"Only when they double as benefits." I wink.

He laughs, tightening his hold on me. His features turn serious as he grips my chin with his fingers. "Falling in love with you has been the best experience of my life. I hope you know that. I wouldn't change it for anything in the world. I love you, Aspen."

The smile drops from my face as I soak in his words. My heart rate speeds up as the tears surface, my body humming at how those words affect me.

"Falling in love with you has been the hardest experience of my life, but it was worth every moment to hear you say those words."

He flashes a satisfied smile, his dimples appearing just enough so you can see the creases in his cheeks. He brushes a thumb over my chin and pulls me to him for a slow, soft kiss.

My body takes over, eager to taste and feel him again.

And it's everything and more.

"I love you, Morgan," I whisper. "More than I ever thought was possible to love someone else."

Chapter Forty-Five
Aspen

For six years, my life has revolved around one thing—pain. I've let it take over my life, fueling the guilt and anxiety for everything I lost. Although I will always love my sister and the years we shared, I can't let it control my life any longer.

Letting go will be a constant struggle, but with Morgan by my side, I have no doubt I'll be able to better control my anxiety. The strength I get from his support gives me confidence that I can overcome the things I've struggled with for so long.

I'm not sure if it was finally knowing the truth of what happened and why, or if it's because of meeting Morgan—perhaps it's the combination—but my life is full of hope instead of constant guilt. Finally, the weight has lifted, and I'm seeing a future full of possibilities and happiness. He's peeled back layers I never even knew existed. He's managed to dig his way right into my heart, the very thing I'd sworn off years ago.

Natalia and I began painting together. I bought her an easel and her own supplies so she can work whenever she wants. Morgan signed her up for some workshops for kids her age at The Art Shoppe. When she isn't busying herself with that, she has her face stuck in a book. She tells me about each one she creates and even lets Ms. Jones put a couple of them up in the gallery after several rounds of pleading.

My favorite ones are the ones of her mother. She can't remember much about her, but she draws what she can. She tells me stories about her and her dad, the fun things he'd take her to, and all the pictures he'd take of them.

I can see a lot of Ryan in Morgan and think about how much it must hurt Natalia to see the resemblance. But for her age, she's handling it well and starting to act like a typical eleven-year-old. She's laughing more and slowly opening up. We've been able to bond over teasing Morgan about his lack of cooking skills. I've been trying to teach him and show him some of my techniques. He's getting better—in that the smoke detector goes through fewer batteries than before.

Morgan and I take turns sleeping over at each other's places. If Natalia spends the night at a friend's or Morgan's parents' house, he stays with me. Otherwise, I stay over there and make sure they stay fed.

Music plays softly as I work in my studio. Different shades of purple-and-red paint cover my fingers and jeans. The blend of warm and cool colors is the perfect mix for the abstract I'm currently working on.

The brush strokes effortlessly along his jawline and cheekbones. His eyes are bright in the mix, showing his softer and gentler side. Light purple and deep red cover the rest of him, representing the meaning of this whole piece.

I hear him walk up behind me. My body shivers as he gently wraps his arms around my waist and nuzzles his nose in the nape of my neck.

"Mm…you smell good."

"That's the smell of oils and working for hours, or what normal people call *sweat*," I tease.

"Strawberry," he murmurs. "You smell like strawberries…and cream." He nips on my earlobe, pulling it in between his teeth and sucking lightly.

"Don't get any ideas," I threaten. "The last time you mentioned strawberries and whipped cream, it took three hours to wash it out of my hair."

"That's only because you kept distracting me in the shower." He kisses down my neck, sending goose bumps over my skin. "But at least you were *thoroughly* cleaned." He flashes an amused grin.

"Can you at least wait until I'm finished? It's almost complete."

"You have five minutes," he growls in my ear and then slaps my ass.

Thirty-seven minutes later, I step back and examine the canvas. "It's finished," I call out. I smile as I study it. I can't wait to frame this one.

"What's this one called?" He rests his hands on my hips and pulls me against his chest.

"The Professor," I answer with a smile.

"He's very...brightly colored."

I lightly elbow him in the stomach. "It's you."

He presses his lips against my neck. "What's it mean?"

"The colors represent healing and love." I face him, wrapping my arms around his shoulders. "You're the purples and reds of my life."

He leans down and presses his mouth to mine. "You're the purples and reds of *my* life," he repeats my words. "Many, many, many reds." He brushes his tongue along my lower lip before pulling it in between his teeth and sucking it lightly, then releasing it. "I love you, Aspen Evans." He kisses me. "I love how passionate you are. I love how much you love Natalia and me. But I think the thing I love most is how adorable you look covered in paint."

"If you think that's adorable"—I take the brush covered in purple and wipe it across his forehead, leaving a nice bright streak over his skin—"you should see how adorable I am when I kick your ass at paint wars."

He pulls my body against him, making me gasp. He grabs the brush from my hand and wipes it all over my cheeks and nose. "It's *super* adorable how you always think you can beat me. Too bad that's not going to happen!"

I manage to push out of his grip long enough to grab another tube.

Pushing the Limits

"You're so dead!" I scream, smearing it on my hands and covering it over his arms and neck.

We continue chasing each other around the room, giggling and eventually surrendering to each other. I drop everything, wrap my hands around him, and then hold him close to my chest.

"I love you, Morgan Hampton. Thank you for bringing happiness back into my life." I arch my neck and smile up at him, his warm eyes making me fall harder and harder for him every single day.

"Thank you for letting me in so I could." He kisses the top of my nose and squeezes me tighter against him. "Now…about that shower?"

I burst into laughter and lead the way.

Chapter Forty-Six
Morgan

Running my hands along her neck and arms, I rinse the soap and paint off her body. She watches me, our gazes locked.

I lower my arms and her hands cover my chest, rinsing the soap off. I study her features, still in shock at how flawless she looks. She's naturally gorgeous, but her confidence and strength radiate off her. She's beautiful on the inside and outside.

Wrapping a hand around her body, I cup her neck and pull her to me. The water streams over us as I kiss her in wanton desire, heated with passion and need. Her arms move up my chest and wrap around my neck as we devour each other. Slowly, she pulls away, tugging my bottom lip in between her teeth, playful desire dancing in her bright blue eyes.

Once she releases me, her tongue glides across it, soothing the sting. She travels down my throat, marking the skin as hers. She licks a trail up to my ear and gently pulls the earlobe in between her teeth, eliciting a groan from deep in my chest.

Tangling my fingers into her wet hair, I pull her lips to mine and kiss her deeply. Her wet chest rubs against mine, those hard little nipples begging for my attention. Running my hand from her waist up to her breast, I palm it roughly before I pinch her nipple between my thumb and forefinger, rolling and tugging it.

Pushing the Limits

"Mm...*yes*," she moans into my mouth as she rubs her lower body against me, searching for friction. "*Please, please, please...*" Her voice cuts off when I pinch her other nipple. I fucking love that my girl likes it rough.

"I know what you need, sweetheart."

Aspen glides her hand down between our bodies, wrapping her fingers around my length, squeezing tightly before moving her hand in a quick, hard motion. I tweak her nipple hard in warning. I know she's trying to get me to lose control, but that's not in the cards tonight. Pulling away from her, I turn off the water before stepping out of the shower. Without warning, I lift her over my shoulder and slap her ass with a firm hand, the sound ringing through the room, and echoing off the walls.

She yelps in surprise, a satisfied grin on my face as I tighten my hold around her thigh. "Behave yourself," I warn as I walk into her bedroom.

I lay her on the mattress and don't waste any time before climbing on top of her. After parting her silky legs, I spread them wide and attack her cunt like a starved man. I suck her clit, lashing it with my tongue. Her thighs clench, threatening to close around me. I push her legs farther apart, holding her how I want to—keeping her at my mercy.

She's breathless as she makes incoherent noises and fists the sheets.

Throwing one of her legs over my shoulder, I plunge two fingers deep into her tight little pussy, thrusting harder and faster. She pushes her body closer to my mouth, begging for more.

"Let me hear you," I demand as I curl my fingers, hitting her G-spot with every deep thrust. "Fuck my fingers, baby. Take what's yours." Her whole body seizes as her orgasm explodes, covering my fingers in her release. Leaning back onto my knees, I make eye contact —her eyes full of passion and love. Her chest heaves with every breath she takes.

Slowly, I lay my body on top of hers, covering her completely. She reaches up to kiss me, but I pull away, instead rubbing my fingers across her lips. "Taste yourself. So sweet, so *mine*."

317

Her tongue slowly licks across them, and I groan at how hot her following my orders is.

"Mm..." She makes little moaning noises, my cock pulsating harder against her at how much she enjoys tasting herself. "But you taste better."

She pushes against my chest, and I give in to her silent demand. Rolling over, I pull her with me.

Aspen scoots down the bed, coming to her knees beside my body. Grabbing the base of my cock, she sucks the head into her hot mouth. Without conscious effort, my hips thrust up into her, making her take another inch. I tangle a hand in her hair, pulling gently, but enough to get her attention.

She smirks around my cock, a devious, playful look in her eyes. Slowly, she takes me again, inch by inch, as she keeps eye contact until she finds the bottom of my shaft and that hot little tongue of hers rubs against the sensitive underside of my length.

"Jesus Christ," I groan, squeezing my hand tighter between her locks. "So goddamn hot watching my cock disappear into your mouth, baby." She slides her tongue up my shaft before pushing me deeper down her throat. "*Fuck*," I hiss, my head falling against the mattress as she breathes hot air against my throbbing cock.

Shit, I'm going to explode if she keeps this up, which is the exact opposite of what I want to do.

Cradling her face between my hands, I lift her away from my cock, much to its disappointment. I can almost hear it cursing me for stopping her.

She pouts. "I was enjoying that."

"I'm not coming in that sexy mouth tonight."

Before she can protest further, I roll off the bed. She flips in defeat, watching me curiously. Quickly grabbing a condom, I rip it open with my teeth and hand it to her.

"Roll it on, baby," I demand, my voice thick with desire to be inside her.

She sits up, taking the condom from my hand. She looks up at me through those perfect eyelashes. She puts the thin rubber over my tip and slowly rolls it down my shaft.

Pushing the Limits

"Now, lie back," I command. "And close your eyes."

I walk to the end of the bed and latch my fists around her ankles. I easily pull her to the edge of the bed and spread her legs.

"Morgan!" she squeals.

Lifting one of her legs over my shoulder, I thrust inside, filling her with my full length. Her laugh is abruptly cut off. My name falls from her lips full of unbridled passion.

"You're so fucking tight."

Her head is thrashing against the bed sheets, making her hair stick up every which way. As she moans, I thrust harder and deeper, digging my fingers into her hips. She'll have bruises in the morning, but she loves it.

"Touch yourself," I demand in a raspy voice. "Let me hear how good it feels."

One hand lowers down her stomach and lands on her clit, rubbing aggressively in sync with my thrusts. Her other hand palms her breast as she continues rubbing against herself. She moans louder, rubs faster. I dig my nails into her hips, pounding rougher and dying to feel her come apart.

My hand slides up her stomach and cups her other breast. I give it a little slap, and her body shivers in response. I hum, leaning over her more.

"More," she groans.

"You like that, baby?" I palm her breast harder, rolling the nipple tightly between my fingers. "You love the things I do to you, don't you?"

"I love it," she hums. "Attack my fucking tits like you own them."

"Goddamn," I growl, rolling my hips into her deeper.

Grabbing her wrists, I pin them to the mattress. My hands cover her breasts, squeezing, pinching, slapping. The rougher I am, the louder she moans. She nearly flies off the bed as she screams my name.

"Fuck, Aspen." I'm close but need to feel her tighten around me first. I release her and crawl down her body. "Turn around."

She's quick to obey and rolls over to her stomach, pushing her plump ass straight out in the air—waiting for me.

I cup her pussy as I slide a hand around my length, feeling how wet and ready she is for me. I decide I need more of her pussy first and crawl under her legs.

"What are you—"

"Ride my face." I align my mouth, wrapping my hands around her legs and cupping her ass cheeks.

She rolls her hips as I part her lips and slip my tongue inside. She rocks harder as I twirl my tongue.

"That's it, sweet girl. Fuck my face hard and fast."

She whimpers as I bring her over the edge.

I slow my pace as she rides out the high, her body humming with pleasure.

"I can't get enough of how good you taste." I press one last kiss before shifting my body and sliding out from under her. "Don't move yet." I grab her body and align her hips with mine.

I press the tip of my cock along her swollen lips, coating it with her juices. "Are you ready, sweetheart?"

"Not there…" Her voice is barely a whisper. "Fuck my ass. I want it rough. Don't hold back."

"*Aspen…*" I hiss in warning.

"I want it," she pleads, shaking her hips.

She's dripping against my cock, greedy and hungry.

Coating my length before sliding it up her ass, I press the tip inside. She arches lower, opening herself even more. I slap her ass and dig my nails into her hips. Rolling my hips, I push in, and her moans grow louder.

"Fuck," I growl. "It's so tight. You sure you're okay?"

"Yes. Keep going."

"Not without lube, baby." I step away to grab some from the nightstand. She'll be sore tomorrow as it is, I'm not about to go in raw.

Once I'm covered, I pour some down her crack and lather it over her tight hole.

"Morgan," she whines, wiggling her ass.

"Sorry, I'm capturing this image in my head for my spank bank later."

"*Morgan!*"

I chuckle at her eagerness, tossing the bottle and aligning behind her once more.

"Never any patience," I tease.

Once I slide in, her breath hitches, and I wait for her to adjust before burying deeper.

"Rub your clit, sweetheart. I won't be able to last long with how tight you are," I tell her.

She puts a hand between her thighs and rubs fast. I slide in another inch until neither of us can take anymore. Moving with her, we form a quick rhythm.

"So goddamn tight, baby. I'm gonna come."

"I'm almost there, don't stop."

Reaching up, I yank her hair and thrust faster. "Be a good girl and make that pussy come."

As soon as she does, I follow behind, bottoming out as I fill her up.

Her moans and screams are nearly inaudible as we fall off the ledge together. Before she collapses, I dip my fingers in her cunt and coat them with her release so I can steal a taste.

"Goddamn," I mutter. "Open up."

She falls to the bed and rolls over, opening her mouth for me. I insert two fingers and she licks them clean.

Once I've disposed of the condom, I wrap her in my arms and tangle my legs between hers.

Cupping her face, I feather kisses across her cheeks. Settling in against her lips, I press a soft kiss.

"I love you, Aspen. With everything that I am and will be, I love you so much."

Her breath catches, and a tear slips down her temple. I kiss the dampness from her face. "No need for tears, beautiful."

"They're happy ones," she reassures. "I love you, too, Morgan. More than I ever thought possible. You've made me feel whole after feeling empty for so long. You took a damaged person with a broken soul and showed me how to take my life back."

"You're the one who's given me a reason to live at all."

Epilogue

Aspen

FIFTEEN MONTHS LATER

"I can't believe it's already time for you to leave." I pout, tightening my grip on her.

"It's only for a semester," Kendall reminds me. "Maybe two if the eye candy is *really* sweet."

I release her and force her to look at me. "Listen, under no circumstances are you allowed to return pregnant, married, or both. And for the love of God, do not fall for a professor while you're over there."

"And what fun would that be?" She flashes a crooked smile.

"Kendall Jane Mueller, I mean it!" I scowl with a serious tone but laugh when she wrinkles her nose.

"It worked for you," she mocks, throwing her bag over her shoulder.

"Only because we live in the same zip code." I roll my eyes. "Should I remind you of all the heartache we went through first?"

She pulls me in for another hug and kisses my cheek. "Stop worrying. I will be fully engrossed in my books and watercolors. Promise."

Pushing the Limits

"Good, and if you happen to find a handsome lad, you could maybe hang out or something."

"Considering they have English accents, I don't anticipate having a hard time finding any male companions." She waggles her brows.

I snort and shake my head. "I'm going to miss you."

"We'll text and email, okay?"

"Yes, you better!" I steal one more hug. "Okay, you better go before you miss your flight."

She smiles and heads toward the security line. "Love you!" she calls out one last time with a wave.

I wave and watch as she makes her way through the line. "She'll be okay," Morgan says from behind, giving my shoulders a gentle squeeze.

Sighing, I frown. "I know, but I've seen her almost every day for the past three years. It's going to feel so quiet and lonely."

He grabs my hand as we walk out to the parking garage. "I'm happy to fill the void for you," he taunts with amusement. "Pillow fights in our underwear, gossiping about celebrities, and who wore it best."

I playfully punch his shoulder. "Very funny."

"I thought so."

"Don't forget the wine. Drunken pillow fights are way better."

"Damn, I was going to the wrong parties when I was in college."

I roll my eyes and sigh. "You're ridiculous."

He takes a quick step in front of me and pushes me through a door that's marked *employees only* before I can stop him. The hallway is empty, but there are closed doors all down the hall, which means anyone could come out at any time.

I feel the arousal through his jeans as he arches his hips against me. "What are you doing?" I hiss quietly.

"What? Never engaged in public sex before?" He lifts a brow.

"Don't even think about it," I warn, but he presses his mouth to that spot on my neck that instantly paralyzes my thinking. "Stop it." I laugh, pushing my palms against him, but it's no use. His body feels like cement against mine. "Don't make me scream," I threaten. "Because I will."

323

He wraps his hands around my wrists and pins them against the wall above my head. "I plan to make you scream nice and loud, baby. No worries there."

His lips trail along my neck, switching between sucking and kissing on my earlobe and jawline. I curse that he knows all my sensitive spots that get my body buzzing. He knows it's impossible for me to resist him when he does that.

"Can you at least hold off until we get in the car?" I ask. "There's cameras everywhere."

One of his hands lowers down my body and slides in between my legs, rubbing against the fabric of my jeans. "Not until I have you shaking and screaming my name."

"No," I whisper loudly. I try to push against his chest with mine but it only drives him to move his hand harder.

"Be my good fiancée and let me give you one."

"Damn you," I groan because he knows I love it when he calls me that.

The hallway we're in is dimmed, not as bright as the main walkway, so I finally give in and relax into his hold.

He unbuttons my jeans and lowers the zipper. He slips a hand inside my panties and continues his delicious torture. "Now let me hear you."

I bite my lip to keep from moaning, but the faster he goes, the harder it is to stay quiet. He notices my struggle and crashes his mouth over mine.

The pleasure crashes into me like a ten-foot wave and I can't hold back any longer.

"Fuck," I curse, squeezing my thighs together.

He removes his hand and slowly licks his fingers covered in my arousal.

"That was evil," I whisper-hiss.

With a smirk, he winks. "You enjoyed it."

He buttons my jeans, leaving me soaked and wanting more. "Now let's get you home before I fuck you right here against this wall."

"God, yes. Lead the way." I grab his hand, nearly skipping to the car.

Bonus Epilogue
Morgan

A unt Mel's retirement party was a blast. It lasted all night long and into the early hours of the next morning. After a day of rest, I officially begin my new job as the gallery manager.

"You look so cute," Aspen gushes, straightening my tie.

I frown. "I wasn't going for cute. *Dead sexy* maybe…"

She shoots me a scowl, then rolls the collar over and slides her hands down my new button-up dress shirt.

"Professional?"

"Besides that." She roams her down my body. "You look extremely *handsome*."

"Thank you." I give her a quick kiss.

"And cute," she blurts out.

Wrapping my arm around her, I give her a quick smack on the ass. She yelps and laughs, batting my grabby hands away.

"I'll miss you." I kiss her forehead gently. Aspen moved in a few months after I proposed, and we've spent every day together since. She and Natalia grew closer. We took advantage of the summer to explore San Francisco, doing all the touristy stuff that locals take for granted, and even set up a studio in my basement big enough for all three of us to paint in.

But this was a good and exciting change. We'll continue working together, and soon Aspen will start her first semester for her master's degree at the University of San Francisco in Museum Studies.

Everything's fitting together perfectly. I understand Natalia most of the time thanks to Aspen for deciphering her *girl code* or whatever the hell that is.

"Well, Mr. Hampton," she says, handing me the new briefcase she bought me as a new job gift. "You ready for your first day as gallery manager?" She wraps her arms around my waist and tilts her head so I can kiss those full, cherry lips of hers.

"I sure am, Future *Mrs. Hampton*." I kiss them as if they're my lifelines. "I love you."

"I love you, too."

Once she releases me, I walk toward the door, then call out over my shoulder, "No sending me naughty pics."

She flashes her infamous smolder she knows I find irresistible.

"Save that for tonight!" I blow her a quick kiss before opening the door.

"I expect you to rip off my little red panties with your teeth in celebration tonight," she quips.

"And I expect you to be a good girl and come on my face."

Her cheeks redden as she squeezes her thighs. "You're going to pay for that!"

I waggle my brows. "Challenge accepted!"

Author's Note

Thank you so much for reading to *Pushing the Limits*! I hope you enjoyed Morgan and Aspen's story as much as I enjoyed writing it in 2015. Since then, I've revised and re-edited their story to my modern-day writing style.

When I first started this book, I ended up scraping 40,000 words, or half of the book at the time, because I struggled to get it right. The way I envisioned their story wasn't playing out on paper and it wasn't until I added my own personal struggles to Aspen's character did it really start to hit and flow how I wanted it.

I've struggled with anxiety most of my life in a way that most people around me couldn't understand and though my grief wasn't the same as Aspen's, it was a level of grief for a loss of a life I thought I'd have.

I started painting in high school and though I didn't keep up with it, my creative outlet turned into writing. It became therapeutic, and I found myself wanting to do it each day, similarly to Aspen, who needed to paint to deal with her emotions in a healthy way. I know many people who suffer from anxiety can't always find that level of passion to help them cope and if that's you, I hope you find your outlet in reading. From one anxious person to another, we got this!

If you enjoyed this forbidden and emotional romance, then you'll love SHOULDN'T WANT YOU

I shouldn't want him—my older fiancé's *son*.
He's arrogant, unapologetic, and annoying as hell.

Keeping my distance is easier than it sounds, especially now that he's moved in with us. He's constantly in my space, invading my boundaries, and taunting me with his good looks and devilish charm.

I want to hate him. To push him away.
To confess our secret and forget what happened.

But then the rug gets ripped out from underneath me and my life gets turned around.
Except this time, there's no going back.

If you enjoyed this forbidden and emotional romance, then you'll love THE INTERN TRILOGY

She's sexy, fierce, and a loud-mouthed know-it-all... and she's completely *off limits.*

Cecilia isn't your typical college student. Hell, she isn't a college student at all, but that doesn't stop her from applying for one of the biggest and prestigious enterprises in the Midwest.

She wants it. She takes it.
She doesn't let anything get in her way when it comes to finding out the truth.

When Bentley Leighton, soon-to-be CEO of Leighton Enterprises, meets "Ceci," he's instantly impressed. He doesn't have time to train a new intern. However, when he sees her that first day, his intentions begin to change.

He's the boss. She's the intern.
Nothing can happen. It's against the company rules.

Then again, rules were made to be broken.

What starts as innocent flirting becomes raveled up into so much more—*secrets, lies, deceit.*

From small town romance author, Brooke Montgomery, comes a Southern family saga series based in the fictional town of Sugarland Creek set in the mountains of East Tennessee.

Book #1, Here With Me

I shouldn't want him.

Fisher's the new farrier on my family's horse ranch.
He's twice my age and workplace relationships are off-limits.
He also happens to be my ex-boyfriend's dad.

As a show horse trainer, I put my life on the line each time I saddle up.
When a trick gone wrong nearly ends my career, he's the one who helps me in my recovery.

We're complete opposites.
He's quiet and reserved.
I'm loud and a thrill-seeker.

Regardless, the bond we build is undeniable, but it's not so simple.
He's a broken man trying to mend his relationship with his son.
Getting involved would destroy everything.

To avoid that, we instate a no-touching rule.
No side glances or flirty texts.
Definitely no sneaking around in the tack room.

But one moment changes everything.
And we break them all.

About the Author

Brooke Cumberland is a *USA Today* Bestselling author who wears many hats on any given day. She co-wrote under the *USA Today* Bestselling duo, Kennedy Fox for six years before going back to solo writing small town romance as **Brooke Montgomery**. She lives in the frozen tundra of Packer Nation with her husband, wild teenager, and four dogs. When she's not writing, you can find her reading, watching ASMR and reading vlogs on YouTube, or binge-watching a TV show she's most likely behind on. Brooke's addicted to iced coffee, leggings, and naps. She found her passion for telling stories during winter break one year in grad school—and she hasn't stopped since.

Find her at www.brookewritesromance.com
and follow her on social media:

facebook.com/brookewritesromance
instagram.com/brookewritesromance
amazon.com/author/brookecumberland
tiktok.com/@brookewritesromance
goodreads.com/brookecumberland

Written under Brooke Cumberland:

The Intern Trilogy

Pushing the Limits

Shouldn't Want You

Someone Like You

Written under Kennedy Fox:

Checkmate Duet series

Roommate Duet series

Lawton Ridge Duet series

Only One series

Bishop Brothers series

Circle B Ranch series

Bishop Family Origin series

Love in Isolation series

Make Me series

Written under Brooke Montgomery:

Sugarland Creek series

Made in the USA
Monee, IL
16 August 2023

41105092R00203